THE VAULT OF MALREMA

K K Sutton

Inscribe Publishing, Guildford, England

The Vault of Malrema

First paperback edition printed 2014 in the United Kingdom.

A CIP catalogue record for this book is available from the British Library

ISBN 978-1-909369-01-6

Published by Inscribe Publishing, Suite 232, Chremma House, 14 London Road, Guildford, Surrey GU1 2AG, England.
Cover Design and typesetting by Inscribe Publishing.
Printed and bound in Great Britain by IJgraphics, Guildford, GU4 7WA

THE VAULT OF MALREMA

BOOK II

IN

THE RESTORATION

OF

THE CROWN OF LIFE

BY

K K Sutton

Dedication

To Gill my wife, Benedict, Genevieve and Francesca, my children, without whose love, practical help and encouragement, this second book in the trilogy would never have been written.

BOOK II

A COLLECTION OF WRITINGS

The Story So Far

Kyros and Lenyé are Royal Krêonor cousins secretly pledged to be married. The Families are torn apart by their usurping Uncle Morthrir amidst rumours that their parents are dead. The youngsters are surrounded by Morthrir's warriors: Kyros swims to an island named after Hoffengrégor, the ancient Prophet; Lenyé escapes; Beth, Quinn and the other siblings are seized.

Morthrir, in seeking to become Ruler of the Waking World, overthrows his brother, Dareth; tries to destroy Kyros; and wants Lenyé as his bride. He calls a Grand Convocation on Mount Malkamet to confer total spiritual power on himself.

Kyros descends to the Realm of Travail, meets the True King, from the Realm of the Blessèd Throne, and learns to use his name against Vashtani, a leader of the Dé-monos – spiritual beings opposed to the True King. He destroys their fortress, rescues his companion and recovers the writings of Hoffengrégor.

Lenyé is aided by the Prophetess, Yanantha, who helps her to seek the Lost Blade of Zerigor. She finds it at Mount Nastâri, and uses the Nastrim, a race of giants descended from the Dé-monos and Krêonor women, to crush one of her Uncle's armies.

Rafé was Dareth's adviser. He now appears to serve Morthrir, but uses the power of the Convocation against his new Master.

Beth and Quinn escape, discover their parents are imprisoned in Uncle Morthrir's castle, and try to rescue them. They travel with Rafé but Beth is overcome by a release of spiritual power. They go to Ishi-mi-réjá, an old woman with a miraculous stone, and Beth is cured. They use her stone to try and stop the power of the Grand Convocation summoned by their Uncle.

Lenyé

Yanantha says, '...*behind your Uncle Morthrir there sits a far greater power than any mortal can ever challenge unaided. That power is what you have to bring down and vanquish. But it is beyond mere human wisdom and strength to ever master. Without the lost Blade, even Kyros' return will avail little.*'

Yanantha bestows on Lenyé the language of all creatures and sends three friends to help her: Chuah-te-mok, the eagle; Ariella, a lioness; and Mamma Uza-Mâté, a she-bear.

Ariella sees Lenyé's distress at being separated from Kyros and helps Lenyé express her love for him: '*But until your Father gives his consent, it can never become a proper engagement, can it?*'

'*How can he if he's dead?...Maybe we have to make up new rules for a situation like this. But I know one thing that won't change: Kyros will never break his word to me, or me to him.*'

Ra-Na-Jiri, a cobra, is planted in Lenyé's group by Rafé to watch her, so he can control what Morthrir knows about her.

They head for Mount Nastâri where Ra-Na-Jiri and Lenyé are welcomed as the Nastrim snake-god and his consort. Lenyé sees that Acwellan, the Executioner, bears two swords: the one she is seeking; and an exact copy to fool others, with a nick in the hilt guard so he can identify it. She learns that Vashtani is Acwellan's Father; and Acwellan expects Vashtani and the Dé-monos to re-enter the Waking World very soon: '*All it needs is a word of power from a human being with the right authority in this world... Then the Breaking-in will begin.*'

Her Uncle's warriors reach the mountain and Acwellan is suspicious, '*I have challenged your...Krêonor army to fight for you... If they win, they take you. If I win, I keep you for my Father...you will be a bride either for Morthrir or Vashtani, whether you like it or not.*' But Lenyé despatches Acwellan to the *Death of the Undying* in the Realm of the Departed where the Nastrim go when slain by ordinary weapons in the Waking World, and seizes the Sword.

She leads the Nastrim against her Uncle's first army, but is confused about how to use the Sword: at a critical point in the battle, it stuck in the scabbard and she only just had time to grab Acwellan's other sword instead. *What was it Yanantha said? "It is not a weapon of war, but an instrument of justice and peace. If you are truly the one, then once you find the Blade, it is down to you and you alone to use it for its rightful purpose". I'm not sure I understand what that means. Mamma Uza-Mâté had said much the same thing: "That was Zerigor's fatal error: using the Sword as a weapon of war". Who is there to help me work it out if Yanantha didn't know?*

Lenyé is victorious against her Uncle's army and chooses to use the Sword of Justice to rally the Nastrim in a final confrontation with her Uncle.

Kyros

Kyros eludes his Uncle's warriors on the island and wrestles with the True King at the entrance to the forbidden Spiral that leads down to the Realm of Travail. Kyros prevails and enters, but must pass seven tests to prove he is worthy of Kingship.

His first test is to trust the inner guiding of the True King rather than his own ability. At the bottom of the Spiral he meets Hoffengrégor, the ancient Prophet, who confirms that by saving Harbona, an enemy, Kyros has passed the second test: to value someone's life above his own freedom. He instructs Kyros in the third test which is learning to speak the name of the True King against his spiritual enemies when all other weapons fail: *'His name, uttered by someone from the Waking World who knows him and walks in his ways, creates a bridge directly to the True King himself. It's as though he is right there with you in that situation and allows the En-luchés, the Guardians of Light, to break through any opposition you encounter and come to your aid...You have the choice: either to use that power or rely on your own abilities. In fact, that is your third test. And it's the best advice I can give you in so short a time.'*

Hoffengrégor gives him two scrolls of ancient writings: one can be opened immediately, the other only at the appointed time.

But they are stolen from him. Kyros is taken by Vashtani and a cohort of Dé-monos who fool him by clothing themselves in light and posing as En-Luchés. Kyros calls out in the name of the True King, and the real En-luchés rescue him; but the Dé-monos escape to their fortress with Harbona and the scrolls.

Stellatus, leader of the En-luchés, instructs Kyros in his fourth test: to use the name of the True King to destroy Malvi-Quîdda, the fortress of the Dé-monos. Kyros seeks the Sacred Pilgrims of Lohr in the Realm of the Departed to help him, but has to cross the River Lammista-ké, whose waters can strip a person of the contents of his mind. He meets Decatur, a Nastâr despatched to the *Death of the Undying*, and learns that Acwellan, is seeking to release all the dead Nastrim back into the Waking World. They fight over recovering the Sword of Justice and Kyros is thrown into the River. He calls out to the True King to save him and has a vision of himself with the True King laughing together, *'You asked me my name when you were not ready to receive it.'* The True King's eyes narrowed as he became serious, *'Now you are ready.'* He lowered his voice and whispered, *'My name is Luchianó-bé, Lord of Light. I entrust you to carry my name with you. You have my authority to use my name in any Realm, but especially when you return to the Waking World. You must gather my people and speak my name to them, for they have largely forgotten it or scoff at it.'*

When Kyros and the Sacred Pilgrims destroy the fortress, he rescues Harbona, recovers the scrolls and is instructed by Stellatus to pronounce judgment over the Dé-monos.

'Very well.' Kyros felt a new surge of power run through him. *'Bind them and cast them into the everlasting fire reserved for them in the Realm of Consumption.'*

A terrible cry went up from Vashtani. 'You cannot do that! Not ahead of the appointed hour.'

With a clarity of insight Kyros spoke out and his voice rang with a new authority. 'This is the appointed hour! Now the judgement of Luchianó-bé, Lord of Light, has come upon you.'

Morthrir

Morthrir, realising he has lost the impetus of surprise in capturing Kyros and Lenyé, calls a secret convocation presided over by the ten Priests of the Hidden Power to locate Kyros and Lenyé and renew his spiritual power. But the convocation ends in failure: Kyros is protected by a far higher power; Lenyé is surrounded by rocks so that the Priests cannot locate her; and the spiritual power Morthrir requested is diverted away from him.

Morthrir is furious and agrees to a Grand Convocation that will call up the Lord Abbérron, initiator of the Hidden Power. In a dream he enters into a pact with Abbérron: his life in exchange for complete power. He is shocked when a written contract is handed to him the next day to confirm the agreement. He sets out for Mount Malkamet to attend the Grand Convocation, thinking he can alter the outcome of the contract and have supreme power, but still retain control over his own life. On the way he receives a message that the first army sent to fight the Nastrim and seize Lenyé has been destroyed. He has one more army, but expects that the outcome of the Grand Convocation will make it unnecessary to use his warriors as he will have tremendous spiritual power at his disposal. He is at a point of no return: he must have this supreme spiritual power to destroy his enemies and render himself unassailable, whatever the cost!

Rafé

Rafé, former adviser to King Dareth, masterminds the coup for Morthrir to be crowned. Morthrir sends Rafé to his own castle at Onadestra to arrange a fatal accident for his barren wife, Faria, so that Morthrir is free to marry Lenyé. But Rafé is pushing Morthrir to overplay his hand and bring him to ruin. He joins the Priests of the Hidden Power and uses the convocation to divert power away from Morthrir and place a cobra near Lenyé to spy on her movements. He persuades Beth and Quinn to travel with him to Onadestra where their parents are imprisoned.

Rafé meets with Eawen, the Chief Priest of the Hidden Power. During their discussion, Eawen whispers, *'There is tremendous spiritual potential locked up in everyone, but at certain key moments, particular individuals are prepared and called forth to reclaim their spiritual power and control the destinies of others. I believe Morthrir is such a person and his time is fast approaching. He will stand and speak a word of power that will echo through the Waking World and call into being a new spiritual order to direct the future course of our existence.'*

'When do you think this will happen?'

'I believe it is imminent. There is a Grand Convocation called for the Summer Solstice on Mount Malkamet. That is where it will happen. I'm certain of it. Now you are officially part of the Priesthood, make sure you're there.'

When Rafé arrives at the castle in Onadestra, he deceives Beth and Quinn into going on further to the Royal Hunting Lodge, to find their parents. With them out of the way, he prepares for the Grand Convocation on Mount Malkamet.

Beth and Quinn

Beth and Quinn escape from their Uncle Morthrir, but overhear a conversation proving their parents are still alive and held prisoner at Onadestra, their Uncle's own castle.

They are stopped by Rafé, whom they think is a traitor, and decide to team up with him for the long trek to Onadestra to rescue their parents. They suspect Rafé has his own agenda, despite what he said, and follow him to a secret meeting in the woods. They witness their Uncle attending a convocation to try and discover the whereabouts of Kyros and Lenyé. The spiritual power generated by the Priests affects Beth, and she is thrown into a trance. Rafé and Quinn take her to Ishi-mi-réjá, an old woman whose name means *Miraculous Stone*. The old woman cures Beth and tells her, *'The stone of Ishi-mi-réjá never lies. This is between you and me and no-one else, except your cousin.'* She leaned

over and whispered in Beth's ear, 'You are going to uncover the secret
behind your Uncle's rise to power.'

When they reach Onadestra, they accept Rafé's instructions and head off towards the Royal Hunting Lodge, but Quinn isn't convinced. He persuades Beth to go back to Onadestra and find out what is going on. They are surprised by a company of soldiers who chase them towards Mount Malkamet, but hide amongst an outcrop of rock as they see a mule-train, led by Uncle Morthrir, coming up a steep pass ahead. Their Uncle commandeers a soldier's horse and orders the other five to ride with him across the grassy plateau to the mountain. Beth and Quinn see a shadowy figure, which had been tailing the soldiers, follow their Uncle some distance behind. Beth catches a glimpse of his face in the moonlight and recognises Rafé.

They chase after Rafé, but are surprised to find Ishi-mi-réjá waiting for them amongst some boulders. She leads them to the edge of a ravine at the top of Mount Malkamet. In the ravine below are gathered various robed figures in preparation for the Grand Convocation. Beth holds up the Miraculous Stone in both hands, while Ishi-mi-réjá and Quinn support her, one on each side. Quinn is able to see over the edge of the ravine. For as long as Beth holds up the stone, the wind howls around the figures below him and disrupts their power. But as soon as Beth's arms droop, he can see a pocket of stillness surround the figures, the flames of the torches burn without flickering and the power of the Convocation is released.

Conclusion of Book I
Lenyé is poised to march South with the Nastrim soldiers, destroy her Uncle's remaining army and rescue Beth and the others.

Kyros knows his victory against the Dé-monos in the Realm of Travail has triggered the recovery of the Sword of Justice in the Waking World, and must warn the new keeper to use it immediately to rid the Waking World of the Nastrim. He is set to return to the Waking World with Harbona using the power of the name of the True King.

Beth and Quinn, together with Ishi-mi-réjá, resist the Grand Convocation to prevent their Uncle gaining the spiritual power he seeks. But the Convocation is too strong for them, the Miraculous Stone disintegrates in Beth's hands and she and Quinn fall to the ground. Ishi-mi-réjá vanishes.

Rafé finds out about Lenyé's victory over Morthrir's army through his connection with the cobra, and passes Morthrir a note with the intention of forcing Morthrir into taking the irrevocable step which he thinks will bring the man down.

Morthrir, knowing he is about to lose everything, makes a final gamble to receive spiritual power on Mount Malkamet, but is forever haunted by Abbérron's mocking voice, '*All I needed was for you to believe in your deepest being that I can give you whatever you ask of me, and, in return, you can give me what I demand of you. And you have sealed it by oath. Nothing can break that.*'

As the image of Abbérron began to fade and with the four Summoners and ten Priests regrouped in front of him, Morthrir faces West, takes the final step, and passes the point of no return: *Then he spoke aloud using unfamiliar words and names that came to him as if some other being was using his voice, and the mountain reverberated to his command. 'Let the Guardians of the Spiral be thrust aside and the seals broken. Let the spiral itself be opened from the Realm of Travail. Let the Dé-monos be released again into the Waking World.'*

Morthrir's voice rose to a final crescendo, and, without any hesitation or stumbling over the name, he cried out: 'Let the Hidden Power of My Lord Abbérron come to me!'

PART I

THE BREAKING-IN

Chapter One

'Let there be confusion and conflict between Lenyé and Kyros,' Morthrir's voice cut through the raging storm like the crack of a whip; 'so they become estranged and cannot unite against me!'

He stood on the flattened peak of Mount Malkamet with arms upraised, 'Let all weapons and power that either of them relies on be stripped away. Let Kyros be destroyed,' he continued, 'and Lenyé fall in love with me and willingly become my bride.'

With the disappearance of the Lord Abbérron's image, the wind surged around him, tearing at his waterlogged cloak, while the rain lashed at his upturned face. 'Let the Dé-monos appear before me.' Morthrir knew his words would prevail so that his conquest of the Waking World could begin. 'And let this accursèd rain cease and this infernal wind die away!'

The four Summoners knelt directly in front of him, with the ten Priests in a horseshoe shape around them. As they bowed with their faces to the ground, the rain slackened to a light drizzle and dried up altogether. The wind lifted and blew the heavy clouds away before dying down; the rising sun silhouetting Morthrir's outline from behind.

Morthrir was amused at the expression of the Summoner in white robes as the man raised his head and muttered, 'How can he command the elements, when we failed?' The man bowed his head again and cried out in awe, 'My Lord Morthrir!' The other Summoners and the Priests took up the chant as they raised and lowered their heads: 'Lord Morthrir. We bow before you!'

'From now on,' Morthrir addressed the prostrate figures,

'Abbérron will no longer appear to you at any Convocation, for his power has been transferred to me. As far as you are concerned, I am Abbérron. And you will do exactly as I say, or face the consequences.'

Morthrir lowered his arms and approached the Summoner in white robes. He caught hold of the prostrate figure and lifted him to his feet, reaching out his other hand to pull back the hood.

He gasped in surprise. 'We've met before. You were amongst the leaders of the Tsé-shâmé when they visited some years ago.'

'Correct, Sire. We have been preparing in secret for many years till the appointed time.'

'We?' Morthrir grabbed the Summoner dressed in black and, without raising him to his feet, ripped back the hood. 'You also I recognise.' He continued with the red- and grey-robed figures, pulling off their hoods as well. 'What is the meaning of this? All four of you were with that Tsé-shâmé delegation. When I searched for you afterwards, you had disappeared.'

The figure in white spoke for them all, 'We came to see for ourselves whether you were prepared for the next step or not. When I spoke to you, it was to confirm your readiness, and to warn you that "*the time of fulfilment was drawing near*".'

'Who are you?'

'I am Jumar-jé, leader of the Summoners. We are Krêonor who sided with the Tsé-shâmé against Zerigor and fought in the war that destroyed the first civilisation. Zerigor was not fit to be King, but we knew another man would arise with power to rule the Waking World. Only we could make it happen, and escaped from the wreck of the Island of Bara-mâla at the Beginning.'

'Impossible. You must have been alive for a thousand years!'

'We have lived under the Hidden Power of the Lord Abbérron, preparing for this day. You can become like us, for the Hidden Power is with you in great measure.'

'I thought the Summoners were from another Realm; and you turn out to be mere men, even if you have lived for so long.'

'We clothe our deeds in myths to confuse the inquisitive and protect our identities. But now, nothing can be hidden from you.'

Morthrir turned to the Priests. 'Since this is a time of uncovering, let us see who these are.' He stepped towards the prostrate figures and pulled back the hood of the first one. Again he gasped. 'I know you as well. You're Eawen the Henosite, who gave me my name and rescued me from the River Rubichinó.'

'I am privileged to have witnessed your empowerment, Sire.'

Morthrir grunted and continued on down the line pulling back hoods to reveal the identities of all the Priests, but didn't recognise anyone else till he came to the last one. 'Rafé!' He hauled the man to his feet. 'What are you doing here?'

Eawen interrupted. 'I valued him so highly for his sensitivity to the Hidden Power, that I was able to welcome him to the Priesthood quite recently.'

'Hmph!' Morthrir frowned. 'You may be a Priest, Rafé, but you are also my foremost counsellor. Now that the Convocation is over, I want you back at Onadestra to carry out my orders.'

When Rafé didn't answer, Morthrir snapped, 'What are you waiting for? Make sure you're there before me!'

Rafé turned and scrambled down into the ravine towards the group of horses near the bottom of the slope, where they were picketed under an overhang of rock.

'Who's for breakfast?' Morthrir raised an eyebrow at the remaining Priests and the Four Summoners.

Already the early morning sunrise was beginning to steal into the sky and touch the underside of the last few remaining clouds with fingers of soft pink. A gentle breeze wafted the scent of alpine flowers to the summit where they stood.

He frowned as the Summoner in white began to protest: 'Sire, we always separate immediately after a Convocation and break our fast away from this hallowed place.'

'Nonsense. We must celebrate while we are all together. I insist you share this moment with me. I will not have such a unique opportunity wasted.'

'But we do not have any food with us, Sire.'

'That's no problem.' Morthrir cupped his hands to his mouth and shouted after Rafé's retreating figure. 'You won't need your horse, Rafé. I want it for something else.'

Rafé turned and called back, 'But Sire. I must have my horse if I am to carry out your orders.'

'You'll have to use your own legs instead.'

'It will take days to walk to Onadestra.'

'If you hurry, you might catch those horsemen your soldiers chased last night.' He broke off, laughing. 'Ask one of them to let you have his horse.'

'They could be anywhere by now, Sire. Why would they have come as far Mount Malkamet?'

'Never leave things to chance. If you don't find them, I will.'

Rafé turned away, skirted the group of horses, and headed on down the steep slope.

Morthrir shouted to the soldiers where they sprawled on the grass near their camp in the ravine. 'Sergeant. Slaughter Rafé's horse for breakfast.' He was amused to see the look of shock on the man's face, even from that distance.

He turned to the remaining Priests and Summoners, saw their stunned faces, and revelled in the enormity of the power that flowed through him, before laughing: the sound echoing round the ravine and rising to one long hysterical crescendo.

When Morthrir had recovered his breath he cried out in triumph, 'This will go down in history as the First Breakfast of the New Order in the Waking World that will last for a thousand years; with me as the Supreme Ruler!'

Chapter Two

Lenyé sat on a rock outside the main entrance to the Nastrim fortress at Mount Nastâri with Captain Turvil, and watched the army prepare to move out. Her mind was in a whirl: Beth's life was at stake and she needed Kyros with her. Where was he?

Yanantha said to her, *"Do not be afraid for Kyros. He will return to you somehow. But in a way unlooked for and to fulfil a destiny that is still hidden from me"*. If he did return, where was she supposed to find him? Lenyé sighed. The only thing she could do was head for their special beech tree at the Pool of Alesco and check if he'd been there or left some kind of sign as to his whereabouts.

The more she thought about the battle that wiped out her Uncle's warriors and the Field Commander's taunt of executing her sister if Lenyé didn't return to the palace, the more her resolve hardened. She would never submit to her Uncle, but use the Nastrim to destroy his final army and rescue Beth! She glanced at Ariella and Mamma-Uza-Mâté sprawled on the coarse sand of the plain; then at Chuah-te-mok higher up the mountainside. Ra-Na-Jiri was to ride in her saddle bags with part of his body across the horse's back. But there was no sign of him.

As the Chief Crafter approached, she held out the copy of the Sword of Justice and pointed to the nick in the hilt guard. 'I'd like this repaired, please. I don't want to catch myself on it.'

'Very good, Your Highness. When I've finished there will be nothing left to feel.' He took the sword back into the mountain.

Lenyé knew Acwellan used the nick to identify the Sword of Justice. She could tell it by the weight, but obviously he couldn't.

'You're very quiet,' Lenyé turned to Captain Turvil.

'I miss Decatur's leadership. He saw things so clearly. We struggle with the legacy of the Dé-monos as our Fathers, wanting to conquer and rule the Waking World; while our Mothers, as daughters of the Krêonor, bequeathed us this maddening urge to birth children. But we can never have any progeny, so are a dying race. And we dare not start a war that might destroy us and doom us to the *Death of the Undying*. Without offspring, there is no hope for the future. You see our dilemma? We are a wretched race with no one to deliver us: until you arrived.'

'Yet you will march with me at the risk of your lives.'

'Because if you hold up the Sword of Justice and we walk under it, we will be despatched to Elasis, our final place of rest.'

'Is that all it takes? I could do this for you now.'

'No. We hold you in too high esteem to go back on our word. We will help defeat your Uncle. But then you must fulfil your word and release us from the Waking World.'

'Of course.'

'All the Nastrim must march out with the soldiers, including the King, his retinue and our females. We are so confident of winning through your leadership that we all want to be in place to pass under the Sword together. None of us is to be left behind.'

If this was their final demand Lenyé realised she would have to accept it. 'Very well. Let them come. But they mustn't hinder your soldiers in battle.'

As they talked, Lenyé watched the final preparations for the two companies: the main army of soldiers and a few archers to follow Captain Turvil across the plain, with wagons and equipment for mounting a siege; and her company of archers with a few soldiers to march through the forest.

She was amazed at how adaptable the Nastrim were. They had taken the shoulder harness which ordinary Nastârs wore to pull their wagons, and converted them to horse collars. Now each wagon would be hauled by a team of six captured horses, freeing up a large number of soldiers to be ready for battle.

Lenyé looked up as the Chief Crafter returned, and studied the hilt guard as he explained what he'd done.

'I certainly can't see it.' Lenyé took the Sword from him and rubbed her thumb all round the hilt guard. 'Or feel it. You've done an excellent job.'

'Thank you, Your Highness.'

She smiled. Now that Acwellan's mark had been removed, only she could tell the swords apart by the difference in weight.

Lenyé swapped the two swords round a few times, secured them on her back and stood up. 'It's time to move out.' Ariella and Mamma-Uza-Mâté followed as she and Captain Turvil walked down to the waiting companies. Chuah-te-mok hovered overhead in anticipation. But there was still no sign of Ra-Na-Jiri.

As she mounted her horse, Lenyé recalled the words she spoke into the darkness on the night of the raging storm she saw far away in the South-East when she couldn't sleep: "*Uncle Morthrir... half your army is wiped out, we have a strategy to destroy the rest of your warriors and seize Terrazarema, and I hold the Blade of Zerigor that will motivate the Nastrim against you. If you harm so much as a hair on Beth's head you will regret it. You're not as invincible as you think*".

She thumped the pommel of her saddle in anger: Kyros might never come back; or worse, return too late. Lenyé couldn't wait any longer. If she didn't find any trace of him at the special beech tree, she would have to bring down her Uncle alone!

7

Chapter Three

Kyros felt power surge through him as he and Stellatus surveyed the debris of Malvi-Quîdda, the ruined stronghold of the Dé-monos in the Realm of Travail. He watched the En-luchés drag Vashtani and his cohort away to the Realm of Consumption; the chains of light binding the Dé-monos appearing to tighten as they struggled.

Stellatus turned to him, 'I fear Abbérron's counter stroke even more now that Vashtani has been bound. It will affect you when you return to the Waking World. You must find out what it is and learn how to counter it. I think your fifth and sixth tests will be involved here and are closely linked together.

Kyros nodded and scratched his chin, realising the beard that had been growing since he first fled with his siblings and cousins from Uncle Morthrir's troops, was now quite long and matted and covered the lower part of his face and upper lip. He raised his hand to his head and found his hair was also long and thick.

He turned and almost tripped over Harbona who was lying prostrate behind him. 'What is the meaning of this?'

'My Lord,' the man cried out. 'I plead mercy for attempting to lay hold of your Royal person.'

'And if I grant you mercy?'

'I will forever be your grateful servant.'

'How do I know you will be true to your word?'

Harbona knelt before Kyros, pulled out the medallion with its inscription for service to Morthrir, tore it from his neck and hurled it away. 'I renounce all allegiance to Morthrir. You risked your life to save me when I was your enemy. I was deluded by Morthrir, but now I swear allegiance to you, My Lord.'

Kyros weighed Hoffengrégor's words when they discussed Harbona at the base of the Spiral: *"Do not judge too quickly. A man may be forced to serve the wrong master through ignorance or circumstance or folly. Only when he is obliged to choose between him and a genuine alternative can the man truly be judged"*.

'Very well.' Kyros raised his right hand and indicated for Harbona to do the same. 'Repeat after me: "By the authority vested in Prince Kyros to act for the Crown, I hereby receive my freedom from servitude to Morthrir. I swear on oath to serve Prince Kyros, being faithful in all things, even to the laying down of my life in the Waking World. So let it be!".'

Kyros pulled Harbona to his feet and embraced him. 'Welcome to the Royal Household. I appoint you as bodyguard to protect me and all those I hold dear.'

Harbona bowed. 'Thank you, my Lord. I will serve you, not just out of duty, but with love and respect as well.'

'I'm glad,' Kyros held the man's gaze. 'Service freely offered is more precious than anything I could force from you.' He chuckled. 'I see your hair and beard have grown like mine.'

'It must be something in the atmosphere of this place. I'll trim them as soon as possible, for I always carry a razor.'

'You have done well, Kyros,' Stellatus interjected. 'By swearing this man into your service, you now have the True King's authority to release him back into the Waking World. You may take him with you when you go.'

Kyros nodded his thanks and then saw Osâcah, leader of the Pilgrims of Lohr, behind Harbona, and beckoned. 'You helped destroy Malvi-Quîdda, which will release spiritual power in the Waking World.' Kyros embraced him, 'Farewell, my friend. Return to the *Place of Rest.*'

'We will help again, if the True King permits,' Osâcah replied.

The rest of the Pilgrims shouted in agreement. Then they

marched past Kyros to follow the En-luchés and the prisoners, as the way back to the *Place of Rest* lay in the same direction.

Kyros rejoiced at the many friends who served the True King. He felt on the brink of great deeds and his experiences here were a training ground for future victories. He raised his hand in farewell as they passed and watched until they were a blur in the midst of the dust they kicked up far out across the plain.

He turned as Stellatus interrupted his thoughts. 'When you spoke the name of the True King here it had immediate effect. In the Waking World, Abbérron will try to rob you of this power. Remember, the name of the True King is a place of refuge for those who love and follow him. Hide in his strength when the storms of opposition rage around you.'

'I don't understand.'

'If things are not so clear to you in the Waking World, do not despair, but hold on to what I have just said.'

Kyros was about to turn away when his knees sagged, 'What was that?' He clutched at Stellatus' shoulder. 'There it is again.' Kyros' legs buckled and he slumped to the ground. He felt Harbona grab him under the armpits and lift him up, but his companion cried out as though in pain.

'Look out, My Lord.'

'What are you both on about?' There was a note of alarm in Stellatus' voice.

'Something is pulling me forwards!' Kyros swayed as though about to fall over.

Stellatus shielded his eyes with his hand. 'The Guardians of the Spiral!' he cried in dismay. 'They are being overwhelmed. I have to leave you to fend for yourselves.' He pointed to their left, 'Head for the entrance of the Spiral as quickly as you can.' With that the En-luchés was gone: no song; no attempt to take Kyros or Harbona with him; he simply vanished.

Kyros staggered and felt Harbona's arm about his shoulders to steady him. 'We'll have to run across this plain. Stellatus needs all the help he can get.' He broke into a trot and started sprinting, much as he'd done when he led the Sacred Pilgrims of Lohr to surround Malvi-Quîdda.

Again he felt that tugging sensation. With a cry of surprise he was yanked off his feet as though being sucked forwards, and he was hurtling through the air in the direction of the Spiral. He tumbled over and over in his flight, aware of Harbona moving with him. He saw Osâcah and the Pilgrims, followed by the Dé-monos, writhing and thrashing in their chains of light, and finally the En-luchés, all moving in the same direction.

A screeching, whistling, shrieking turbulence enveloped him, as if being sucked into a vacuum, hurling him towards the entrance of the Spiral. The blinding light of the Guardians was gone. Instead, Kyros saw Stellatus with his robe billowing out, as the En-luchés was tugged into the entrance. With a resounding cry, Stellatus disappeared. The force sucked Kyros in as well and dragged him up the void in the middle of the winding spiral of rock that he had so feared on his downward journey. He heard the shouts and cries of those who came after him. Suddenly he shot out of the Eye of Hoffengrégor and looked down on the charred wreckage of the island, before hurtling over the top of the Dangst Rock and the trees of the forest.

He saw Harbona and the Pilgrims following him. The En-luchés scattered in every direction. But the Dé-monos held together in a tightly packed body of darkness, interspersed with glints of light from their bonds, as they disappeared in an Easterly direction.

Kyros crashed through the canopy of the forest hitting several branches, and was aware of numerous twigs whipping across his face in his descent. He thudded onto the ground, felt the wind knocked out of him, and knew no more.

Chapter Four

Once Rafé walked round the bluff of rock at the bottom of the ravine and was out of sight, he looked for a place to climb up the edge of the ravine itself. He wanted to search the place where the resistance came from last night and found a break in the rocks. As he scrambled up, he was distracted by shouts and movements and the neighing of a single horse from the bottom of the ravine, sensing a collective fear as the other horses joined in.

He carried on climbing, and was surprised by the terrified neighing of horses immediately above him. He paused, unsure of what to do: the sound of horses ringing in his ears; Morthrir's mocking laugh rising above the mayhem and the man's harsh voice declaring himself Supreme Ruler. He started climbing faster as the rocks gave way to a grassy stretch, oblivious of his scratched hands and grazed knees, but still the terrified neighing of horses punctuated the air, until one final shrill, almost scream, came from below. Instantly he smelled death, like a dark pall rising up to engulf him.

He skirted a huge rock and came upon two tethered horses bucking and pulling at their pickets and neighing in fright. They swung round to face him as he approached, but he called to them in a soft voice and walked slowly towards them with one hand out, till they let him touch them and gentle their muzzles. He patted their cheeks, stroked their manes and spoke to them as he examined the tethers and made sure they hadn't pulled away.

Rafé spotted the saddles under a lee of rock, and noted the soaked patches where the overhang had failed to keep all the rain off. When the horses had settled and were no longer jumpy at his presence, he left them and explored a wider expanse of ground. He gasped in surprise at some bundles of clothes not far away. As he approached, he realised they were bodies: one face down with its left arm outstretched; the other on its side with the knees drawn up almost in a foetal position. It was Quinn. He raced across and turned the other body over: Beth. He checked their pulses. They were both alive, but their breathing was shallow, and they made no response as he shook them.

He squatted back on his haunches to examine the ground around them. How had they got here? What were they doing? And, more importantly, how had they been able to resist the Convocation for so long last night?

Someone else must have been with them. That would explain the power to resist. But whoever it was must have walked here as there were only two horses. Unless the youngsters doubled up on one horse and the stranger used the other. Perhaps it was Ishi-mi-réjá. But where was she now? She couldn't have just disappeared, unless she was overcome by the thunder and lightning and the presence of Abbérron. Surely she wouldn't have left them like this?

He leaned forwards and prised open the clenched fingers of Beth's left hand. Fine grey dust trickled out and seeped away into the tufty grass. He took a pinch of the fragments left on her palm and sniffed at it, but there was no smell.

He must get them away: Morthrir was bound to send those warriors to search up here. But where could he take them? Not Onadestra: that was too dangerous. And Ishi-mi-réjá's cottage was too far. Wherever he took them it would be slow leading the horses with the children strapped to them. What about that shepherd's cot he noticed last night as he skirted wide of Morthrir's company to approach the mountain unnoticed? Unless you knew where to look it was well hidden until you were close to it. He hoped it wasn't occupied. He hadn't seen any sheep near the mountain so maybe the shepherds had moved on to other pastures. He would have to risk it.

He saddled the horses and laid Quinn face down so that he slumped across one, and tied the boy's wrists to his ankles, passing the rope under the horse's belly. Then he sat Beth in the other saddle, leaving her legs to dangle down while he tied her wrists to the reins. Then he walked between the horses, making sure Beth didn't slip out of her saddle and doing his best to stop them getting too close together and bumping Quinn.

The final slope down to the cot was too steep and narrow for both horses. He tethered Quinn's and led Beth's horse down, tied its reins to the door post, carried her into the tiny room and laid her on a pile of sheepskins; then went back for Quinn.

He left the first horse tied up, and unsaddled the other before leading it a little way off to picket it to a peg in the ground with grass round about for it to graze. He sat outside the cot, fondling the other horse's muzzle as it nudged at him, and reviewed the events of last night.

Originally he thought Morthrir was out of his depth and didn't understand what was going on. But there was something unnerving in the way he unmasked everyone; and that killing of the horse for breakfast was utterly brutal. The look of shock on everyone's faces when Rafé had glanced back, especially Eawen the Henosite, confirmed the others felt the same way: even the Summoners. He was horrified at the change in the man!

All his scheming to force Morthrir's hand, and push him beyond the point of no return and so bring the man down, had come to nothing. Instead, he had helped to create a monster. The man had received some kind of power that Rafé had never dreamed existed. How could he ever stop that?

He must get back to Onadestra and protect Morthrir's brothers and their wives from any harm. If the man could kill a horse for breakfast, he might go ahead with his threat to execute them. There was no telling what Morthrir would do now that he had received this power. But what about Beth and Quinn? He couldn't just abandon them.

He sat wrestling with the problem, the warm sunlight and his exhaustion from last night making his eyelids droop.

Suddenly he saw a picture of the cobra slithering towards a lone mountain, and through a series of passages. Rafé felt the snake winding around memories and seeking out something familiar that filled its mind with light and warmth and peace; enticing it away from present reality to a reassuring dream. Then he realised the snake was coiling around something that gave off a golden light, creating a desire in it to keep returning and finding comfort. And, strangely, the cobra wanted him to see it as well, as if trying to send him a message.

Rafé shook his head and blinked. What was it that kept attracting the snake? It had to be more than peaceful feelings. He was about to probe further when the snake moved again. He lost concentration and the connection was broken.

Rafé started at the feel of soft lips on his face and the snort of a horse in his ear. Then he was fully awake. The sun was higher in the sky: he must have dozed and dreamed for some time.

He checked Beth and Quinn were breathing, covered them with sheepskins and left them food and drink from his saddle bags. Then he untied the horse's reins from the door post, led it back up the steep slope to the beginnings of the grassy plateau, mounted, and cantered away: he couldn't delay any longer if he was to get back to Onadestra before Morthrir.

As he rode Rafé heard again that mocking laugh in his mind, echoing up from the ravine, and glanced back at the shepherd's cot. It was already hidden in a fold of rocks. At least Beth and Quinn were off the mountain and couldn't be directly linked to that point of resistance. He hoped they would recover quickly and get away before those warriors found them.

Chapter Five

Kyros opened his eyes and puzzled over the black dots that spun and blurred against a hazy backdrop of green. His eyes cleared and he saw the spreading limbs of a huge tree and the great leaf canopy overhead. He groaned as the sting of numerous scratches to his face, and the dull ache from various bruises, surfaced in his consciousness; and he momentarily re-lived the shock of crashing through the tree-tops before hitting the ground. He reached up and felt the puffiness around his eyes and winced at the rawness of some of the scratches. As he removed his hands he noticed they were covered in blood.

He wiped away the blood on the dead leaves around him and tried to move, but groaned again as something hard pressed into his back. Kyros sat up and found his belt and the bottom of his jerkin had swivelled round. He adjusted the belt and was reassured by the dagger in its rightful place again, but his scabbard on the other side was empty. Where was his sword? Of course; the blade had dissolved before his very eyes when he challenged Vashtani in the Realm of Travail. So, apart from his dagger, he was completely weaponless! Kyros hauled his jerkin back so it was straight and found the offending lump: something was bulging in his pocket. He thrust in his hand and pulled out a roll of cloth: it was the two scrolls Hoffengrégor gave him, which he'd saved from the fire in Malvi-Quîdda. Now, at last, he had time to read them.

Kyros started at a sudden rustle of dead leaves on the other side of the tree trunk. He shoved the roll back in his pocket,

16

crouched forwards onto his hands and knees, crept towards the tree and cautiously peered round the trunk, only to find a blackbird foraging for grubs. Even as he squatted back on his haunches, the blackbird flew off shrieking its warning call and settled on the branch of a neighbouring tree.

He looked around to get his bearings and gave a low whistle of surprise. He knew exactly where he was: the Pool of Alesco; and this was the special beech tree. He went and knelt at the pool and bathed his face; the cold water stinging the open wounds. Then he stood by the tree, reached out and touched the smooth grey bark. It felt alive with memories.

Kyros grinned to himself, recalling afresh the many hours he spent here when he was younger playing with his brother and sisters and cousins. This tree had served as camp and look out place, and the two lower branches that swept away over the pool formed their ship which they used as adventurers to sail to where the island of Bara-mâla may have been. Then they paddled their canoes over the imaginary sunken island and dived to recover chests full of gold coins and diamonds and other treasure. He always led the expeditions and told the others where to go and what to look for: especially he sought the Krêon of Tulá-kâhju, the Crown of Life that Zerigor wore in the Beginning, which was swept from him by the deluge. For this, above all things, was the confirmation of Zerigor's power and the demonstration of unity amongst the Peoples. Even now Kyros dreamed of trawling over the real sunken island with nets to recover the dazzling Krêon and bear it in triumph to the mainland.

Lenyé wanted to dig up the clay pots full of parchments with the writings of the Peoples, but Kyros wasn't so interested. He remembered arguing with her. She wanted to know about the Ancient Wisdom and how to use it in their game, but Kyros told her not to be so stupid: if that wisdom caused the break up of the civilisation in the first place, it wasn't worth having. She didn't speak to him for the rest of the day.

Later that evening he was in a clearing in the forest away from the camp, practising a particular sword stroke on his own, but hastily sheathed his sword as he saw her approach.

'Kyros,' Lenyé's voice sounded husky with emotion. 'I'm sorry for the way I treated you today.'

'How do you mean?'

'I refused to speak to you and avoided you all afternoon.'

'Oh, that?' Kyros waved his hand as though it was only a slight incident as far as he was concerned. 'I thought you wanted a break from being adventurers and went off with Beth to do something else.'

'No, Kyros. That's typical of you.'

'What is?'

'You deliberately upset me today. You never listen to me; or use any of my ideas. You just take me for granted. All the time!'

'No, I don't.'

'You're so stubborn and pig-headed. You have to lead in everything we do. It's always you, you, you. And if you don't get your own way you storm off and sulk!'

There was an uncomfortable silence. Finally Kyros said in a rather quiet voice. 'I knew something was wrong, but I didn't know what.' He slumped down on a nearby fallen tree trunk. 'Has this been going on for a long time?'

Lenyé didn't reply straight away, obviously struggling with her feelings. At last she blurted out, 'Yes.'

'I had no idea I was like that.'

'Well, you are.'

The uneasy silence returned, dragging out the distance between them: he still sitting on the tree trunk, and she standing awkwardly in the middle of the clearing twisting her fingers together. His eyes riveted on them: the tension in her hands wringing the last drops of his own self-importance out of him.

Kyros couldn't bear it any longer. He darted towards her, grabbed her hands and held them tight, not knowing whether he was trying to still his hammering heart or stop that infuriating twisting of the fingers.

Kyros watched with horror as the bright tears beaded in the corners of her eyes, and ran down her cheeks. Then he felt tears in his own eyes, and it was his turn to blurt out his feelings. 'I'm sorry for the way I've treated you. And I did miss you this afternoon. I missed your fun and your laughter, but most of all, I missed being together. I have no right to ask this, but will you forgive me, and be prepared to put this incident behind us?'

'Oh, Kyros.' Lenyé pulled her hands out of his, flung her arms around his neck and kissed him on the cheek. 'Of course I forgive you.'

He slipped his arms around her waist and let her cling there till he no longer felt her tears dripping onto his face.

She pulled away, wiped her eyes roughly on her sleeve and turned to go, pausing at the edge of the clearing to look back at him. 'Thank you, Kyros.'

After she'd gone, he sank onto the tree trunk, feeling dazed. It should have been him thanking her, not the other way round. For the first time in his life someone had shattered his sense of self-importance. He vowed he would never be like that again.

From then on he noticed a marked change in other people's reactions to him, not just Lenyé and the rest of his family and close relatives, but also the courtiers. Instead of dominating as he had done before, thinking it was the only way to interact with others, he found a greater ease in being himself and letting others take a lead when necessary.

It was definitely him thanking her, for Lenyé had taught him a life-changing lesson, and he loved her all the more for it.

At the reminder of Lenyé and the clay pots full of the writings of the Peoples that had sparked the row between them, Kyros realised that now he had a gift for her that would surpass her wildest dreams. No parchment from the sunken island, but the lost writings of the Ancient Prophet himself.

He checked for sounds of anyone who might disturb him, slipped round the trunk of the great tree and swung himself up onto one of the branches that curved out over the pool. He edged along to the spot where his weight set the branch swaying and settled into his favourite curve, that fitted his back and made a perfect spot for lazing the day away. He recalled the times when all eight of them would swarm over these two branches and the platform they'd lashed between for the deck of their ship, and set the whole thing swaying as violently as they could, pretending to be caught in a terrible storm at sea.

Kyros pulled the roll from his pocket, untied the bindings and eased out the contents. There was a sealed parchment which appeared to be wrapped around something else. He put his hand over one of the open ends of the scroll and shook it gently only to find a metallic disk press into his palm. He continued shaking and moving his hand away slightly on each shake until he could pull out a metal cylinder.

The cylinder had no obvious break or mark in it to indicate where it opened; only a small keyhole in one end. He tried shaking it, but nothing rattled. He peered through the scroll of parchment expecting to see a key strapped inside, but nothing. Then he examined the cloth roll and bindings, looking to see if there was a pocket with the key in it. Again nothing. How was he supposed to open it?

Kyros thought back to Hoffengrégor's words when the Old Prophet gave him the roll in the first place: *"Take this; it will help you understand your journey. It contains two scrolls from the Book of Beginnings, which were lost to the Waking World when I fell down the Spiral. After all, if you do not know your origins, how can you discern the right path for what lies ahead? One is sealed and can only be opened by the right person at the appointed hour. The seal on the other one can be broken at will. Do not try to read them now for there is no time, but keep them safe till you return to the Waking World"*. Clearly the one in the cylinder could only be opened by the right person at the appointed hour. Who that was and when it would happen he had no idea. He carefully replaced the cylinder in the cloth, tied up the bindings and returned it to his pocket.

But the other one.

Kyros held it in one hand as he drew his dagger and prepared to break the seal. Even as he did so he felt a tingling in the tips of his fingers, as if the contents of this parchment were going to raise a bigger storm in the Waking World than the wildest shaking of their branches had ever achieved when they were playing adventurers at sea.

Chapter Six

'Sergeant,' Morthrir stared at the man, and then glanced at the other four warriors. They had rigged some javelins into a tripod on the shady side of the ravine and were making fast the ropes to hold the weight of the horse carcass as it dangled down over the edge of a rock. 'How long will the steaks take to prepare?'

'I would leave the carcass to hang for several days.'

'I don't have that kind of time. We need to eat soon, and then move off this mountain.' He placed his hands on the back of the horse and muttered words over it to speed the process. 'Have your men get the fires ready and cook the steaks immediately.'

'Yes, Sire.'

'In the meantime, empty the water skins into your helmets and bring them up to me by the stone altar.'

'Yes, Sire.'

'After you've done that and the meat has cooked, take your men to search at the head of the ravine,' he turned and pointed to where the resistance was coming from last night. 'Whoever you find, hold them at Onadestra until I come. And take the horse I used last night. I won't need it again.'

'How will you get to Onadestra? It will take days on foot.'

'That's none of your business.' Morthrir turned and strode up the ravine, removing his sodden cloak as he went.

As he reached the others he flung the cloak over the end of the altar and ordered them to do the same. 'The breeze and sun will dry everything. Breakfast will be ready shortly.'

Even as he spoke, the Sergeant and his warriors approached

holding their upturned helmets. 'Here is the water you asked for, Sire. There's not very much to go round so many people.'

Morthrir pointed at Jumar-jé, the Summoner from the North. 'Find me the chalice from last night.'

When Jumar-jé returned, Morthrir commanded him to hold it steady while the Sergeant poured some water in. Morthrir took the chalice, muttered words of increase in the name of Abbérron, and poured an equal amount back into each helmet. He was amused at everyone's reaction as the liquid crept up the sides till the helmets were brimming over. Morthrir took one from the Sergeant, raised it to his lips, and indicated the Summoners to do the same. 'Drink, my friends, and quench your thirst.'

'My head's spinning,' Jumar-jé spluttered at his first sip. He tried again. 'Why is it so strong? This isn't water, it's fire-juice!'

'Correct. Pass the helmets to the Priests.'

Morthrir ordered the warriors to bring the food and made the others pass the helmets round again, aware of their separate reactions: the Priests became quite vociferous; while the Summoners remained gloomily silent. Their responses amused him as his own senses were sharpened by the fire-juice and he could think more clearly than normal and see ahead to what must yet be done to establish absolute rule.

When the steaks arrived, the feast began in earnest. Morthrir checked each man had plenty of food; and plied them with draughts of fire-juice till they became merry, and had passed beyond the point of self-control that bound men together in the mysterious level of comradeship that Morthrir was aiming for. Except himself, of course; for he was too high above them and too filled with power to demean himself in such behaviour. But he was pleased with the results, all the same.

He made sure he was the focus of attention in speech and joking and laughter, and these bonds drew them closer to him.

'A toast,' he cried. 'Let this be the mark of our association: that we stand together, bring down all that resist us and set up a

New Order in the Waking World.'

Morthrir glanced at the sky, noting the position of the sun, and watched the warriors ride off down the ravine and skirt the rock at the bottom. He smiled grimly: whoever was causing that resistance last night wasn't going to escape if he could help it.

The feast was coming to a natural end, and he was looking for the right moment to draw things to a close and send them on their way, when something fell out of the sky and landed at his feet. 'Who are you?' Morthrir jumped up, shocked; for he could make out the shape like a huge man, enveloped in darkness and bound hand and foot with chains that pulsated with a bright light. Then more such creatures fell around him.

The figure at his feet looked up at him. 'I am Vashtani, a Lord of the Dé-monos.'

'Why are you bound like that?' Morthrir frowned.

'The En-luchés in the Realm of Travail were dragging us away until your words broke open the Spiral and jerked us into the Waking World.' Vashtani paused. 'We have been brought here to await your will.'

Chapter Seven

Quinn awoke to the early morning sun streaming in through a window and shining right in his eyes. He grunted and turned over trying to shut out the sun, but couldn't: he was too wide awake. He sat up, a sheepskin slipping off, and felt the sudden chill.

Where was he?

He looked around the single room of what must be a shepherd's cot. He'd been lying on a pile of sheepskins, and covered by at least two. Then he saw Beth's head and face poking out from another pile of sheepskins.

'Beth,' he was over to her in an instant, but she was sound asleep.

Someone must have brought them here, but who?

Slowly his mind pieced together the events of last night: Mount Malkamet and the ravine and the figures circling what looked like an altar made of stones, and his Uncle lying on it. Then the flashes of lightning and cracks of thunder right overhead; and that awful crushing sensation in his chest, then Beth's scream, and…and, he couldn't remember any more.

But was it last night? How long had they been here?

Quinn opened the door and looked out. There was the massive bulk of Mount Malkamet not far away. They were in a hidden dip and it looked as if there was a small animal trail sloping up to the Grassy Plateau that led back to Onadestra. He could see a horse tethered to a picket and cropping grass below him and walked down to stroke it. He was so hungry. Maybe it wasn't last night after all, but several nights ago. He was feeling all right, just a bit shaky on his legs.

He scrambled back up to the cot and found some saddle bags containing food and water skins. Beth was still fast asleep, so he settled down outside the cot, basking in the warmth of the sun, and ate some breakfast. Was Uncle Morthrir still in the ravine or had he gone? And what about those other figures? It all depended on how long he'd been asleep, and he had no way of telling. There could be all sorts of people moving away from that meeting. Was it safe to stay here for a while and hide, or should they be moving on somewhere else? If so, where? And it all depended on how much longer Beth would sleep. He cocked his head to one side: he could hear running water and it came from the dip of ground on the other side of the horse.

Once he'd finished his meal, he went back into the cot, gathered up the saddle bags, the saddle itself and the reins and walked down to the horse. He pulled the picket peg out of the ground, shoved it in a saddle bag, grabbed the rope halter and led the horse through a little gully till the cot was out of sight. He continued winding his way carefully amongst the scattered rocks and boulders and clumps of heather till he found a small stream tumbling over a rocky break.

He let the horse drink, while he shoved his head under the little waterfall and rubbed his hair and face. Then he emptied the saddle bags, wiped round inside them with his wet hands and refilled the two water-skins, before leaving the saddle bags to dry in the sun. He wiped down the saddle and harness, and turned to the horse to groom him as best he could.

Quinn spread out his cloak to dry, lay back in the sun and wondered how long he should leave Beth to sleep. He awoke with a start and shook his head. He must have dozed off because the sun was much higher in the sky now: late-morning at least.

The horse had wandered away and was cropping the grass beyond the heather below him. Quinn felt the saddle bags and found they were quite dry inside, so repacked the food and water skins. He skirted the heather, caught hold of the rope halter, led the horse back up to the stream and saddled him, replacing the halter with the harness. Then he slung the saddle bags in place and walked the horse back up towards the dip below the cot.

Quinn reached the ridge that shielded the cot from view and heard the shouts of men. He ducked down and kept the horse hidden behind the ridge while he scrambled up to get a better view through a break in the rocks.

He counted three warriors and six horses. A pang of guilt shot through his mind: he should have woken Beth earlier and made good their escape, instead of falling asleep himself! Then two men emerged from the doorway, one of them dragging Beth by the hands while the other banged the door closed behind them. Beth was wide awake and struggling to get free. Quinn stifled the shout of warning he intended for her. The men obviously had no idea there was another person involved. Just as well he'd taken the harness and food and the horse when he did. He had to stay free and try and rescue her.

The man hoisted Beth onto the saddle of a horse, while another tied her wrists to the reins. Then the men led the horses up the path to the Grassy Plateau, mounted, and cantered away.

Quinn waited a few minutes, then walked the horse up the path and ducked his head as he reached the top. He could just make out the horsemen galloping fast over the Grassy Plateau. He must keep them in sight but not get spotted himself. Somehow, he had to rescue Beth.

Chapter Eight

Kyros re-read the parchment but found nothing to identify the writer except in the final paragraph, which looked like a later addition to the original text: *...as I pen these last words, I, Hoffengrégor, command whomsoever shall open this remnant of parchment and read these words, to not only recover the Sword of Justice but also despatch the Nastrim from the Waking World, otherwise all is lost and the Krêonor will be no more.*

Stellatus was right: the Nastrim had to be dealt with.

The writing described the original Breaking-in: *In his wrath the True King sliced off the peak of Mount Malkamet with his sword, crying out, 'Never again shall any creature enter the Waking World by this route!' He cast it far away where it lodged on the brink of the cliffs overshadowing the Plain of Sanchéso, and called it the Dangst Rock, or Place-of-Chaining. For there he commanded the spirit of air, fire, rock and water to appear; and Abbérron came trembling before him. And he called for the Dé-monos and they cowered in his presence and the light they radiated when they first appeared vanished completely, and they were cloaked in darkness. The True King ordered his En-luchés to round them up and bind them to the Dangst Rock.*

The Rock's origin shocked him. He proposed to Lenyé on it, thinking its association with the Ancient Prophet created a bond with the past to guide them in the future. Did its history affect the words they had spoken? The fact he had been unable to ask Uncle Alkram's permission for her hand troubled him for the first time, almost rendering those words of no effect in his mind.

He was horrified at the massacre of the Pilgrims of Lohr: *The Nastrim were so enraged that they butchered the Pilgrims while their rebel Krêonor and Tsé-shâmé allies looked on and applauded the deed. For the Pilgrims raised no weapons of defence, save that they trusted only in the name of the True King to preserve their lives beyond the grave.*

Any sympathy he felt for the Nastrim after he met Decatur in the Realm of the Departed had completely gone. How could any Krêonor in the Waking World have a relationship with them!

He glanced back to the part that held his attention the most; the True King's judgement on Abbérron and the Dé-monos: *Then he pronounced his verdict upon them: Abbérron and the Dé-monos were forbidden to ever again re-appear in the Waking World. If, by any chance, they did, the final judgement would befall them. The True King's eyes flashed like fire and at the word of his command the ground shook once more, and Abbérron and the Dé-monos were blown back through the fissure in Mount Malkamet...*

Suddenly he knew what Abbérron's counter stroke was: another Breaking-in had occurred. Kyros saw the Dé-monos hurled away to the East as he and the Pilgrims headed North. Had Abbérron come as well? Maybe that was his fifth test: to stop the Breaking-in from gaining ground in the Waking World.

He was so engrossed in his thoughts that he failed to notice the warning cry of the blackbird. Only when it flew off with a loud shrill did he realise the approach of danger. Someone was coming.

Kyros rolled up the parchment with the cylinder in its cloth, stuffed it in his pocket, climbed back along the branch, dropped onto the exposed tree roots and ducked behind the massive trunk. He cried out to the True King on how to deal with this new threat, and how to use the knowledge from the parchment. Instead of the familiar reply, there was silence.

Chapter Nine

Lenyé chatted with Ra-Na-Jiri as he travelled in the saddle bags, his head swaying by her elbow with the movement of the horse. 'Why were you so long getting ready at Mount Nastâri?'

'I was saying goodbye to my favourite recess deep in the mountain. I want to return and make it my nest.'

'Really,' Lenyé tried to hide the irritation in her voice. 'We very nearly left without you.'

She was pleased they'd reached the forest. The company on the plain had made good speed and disappeared from view several hours ago as the trees closed in around her archers.

'How long till we get to Terrazarema?' Ra-Na-Jiri asked.

'The main company isn't going to the capital. They'll lure my Uncle's army out to fight on the plains. Our company should arrive in about a week at the rate we're going.'

'I see.' The cobra rose up and whispered in her ear as he started to complain about how the others treated him, especially not keeping up on a journey, and then riding with her instead. 'They're jealous, that's all,' the cobra hissed. 'As for that eagle. He's so cold and aloof and superior.'

They paused in the afternoon for refreshment and Lenyé left Ra-Na-Jiri dozing in the saddle bags: she didn't have time for petty squabbles. She sat with Ariella, Mamma Uza-Mâté and Chuah-te-mok, but felt restless and stood up, saying she wanted to be alone for a while to think. In reality, she wanted to find the special beech tree and look for traces of Kyros.

'Before you go,' Mamma Uza-Mâté rose up on her haunches.

'There's something we want to discuss with you.'

'Oh? What is it?'

'Your present course of action,' Chuah-te-mok bobbed his head and raised his wings as he leaned forwards.

'You don't approve, do you?' She eyed them all.

'Lenyé. You've grown as a person in such a short time,' Mamma Uza-Mâté's eyes were filled with concern. 'You're a formidable leader in battle now.'

'So?' Lenyé looked from one to the other. 'Chuah-te-mok's words to me were: *Let your courage match your virtue, with great strength now be endowed*. Haven't I done that?'

'More than you can imagine,' Ariella growled.

'And I've *seized the Sword*, as you advised me, Mamma Uza-Mâté; or have you forgotten.'

'No. Of course I haven't,' the she-bear spoke softly. 'But you cannot use the Nastrim to fight your battles.'

'We've had this argument before. What am I supposed to do? Confront Uncle Morthrir and wave a fancy Sword in his face?'

'But the Lay of Hoffengrégor says: *Not by might or human strength shall the final victory be won…*' Chuah-te-mok raised his wings slightly. 'You cannot ignore that forever.'

'Nor can you keep on using the Sword as a weapon of war,' Ariella took a pace towards her.

'That's right,' Mamma Uza-Mâté held up her front paws. 'You have to find out how to use this Sword properly.'

'I haven't used it as a weapon. Each time I tried drawing it in battle, the Blade refused to come out of its scabbard. It's as though the Sword itself is teaching me.'

'That still doesn't mean using the Nastrim,' Chuah-te-mok bobbed his head at her. 'You cannot keep ignoring our advice.'

'I can't wait until Kyros re-appears; if he ever does. I have to rescue my sister, and this is the only opportunity I have!' She stood up and walked away a few paces, before turning back. 'I need to be on my own with some peace to think!'

Chapter Ten

Quinn trailed the warriors to Onadestra, annoyed that he was unable to rescue Beth: the land was too flat and open. Apart from a few outcrops of rock, especially where they watched Uncle Morthrir come up the pass from the ford, there was no where. Besides, he had to fall back a long way to avoid being seen.

He dropped down into the woods as they approached the castle, hid close to the main gates and watched in despair as Beth's horse was led under the arch. He could see them all dismounting and the horses passed to stable boys and Beth was taken through another archway into the castle itself.

How was he going to get her out of there?

He was about to turn away when he froze at the sound of a long drawn out whistle behind him. He whipped round and saw a figure crouching in front of a tree, but it was too dark under the boughs to see who it was. The figure beckoned. Quinn stood up and led his horse towards the tree.

'Rafé,' he gasped. 'What are you doing here?'

'Shh. Come with me.'

Rafé led him deeper into the woods, before turning to speak. 'I can't stay long. Beth's just been brought in and I need to go and question those warriors.'

'What are they going to do to her?'

'It's more a question of what I say. I propose sending her to Terrazarema before your Uncle arrives. It will be easier for you to rescue her once she's out on the road, rather than while she's in the castle. The river's much higher than when we came through, so the ford's impassable. The escort will have to take her over the bridge. I suggest you waylay them where the road curves round close to these woods this side of the river. Here, you'd better take this.' Rafé held out a leather satchel full of food and fresh water skins.

'Thank you.'

'And you could probably make good use of this.' Rafé passed him a spool of fine twine. 'Tie it across the road. It might help you spook the horses and rescue Beth in the confusion.'

Quinn slipped the spool in his pocket. 'How will I know when the escort leaves?'

'It'll probably be some time tomorrow or the next day. You'll have to keep an eye on the main gates.'

Quinn watched as Rafé slipped out of the fringe of the woods and walked towards the castle. Then a sudden thought occurred to him. 'Rafé,' he hissed, but the man was already well out of earshot. Quinn banged his fist on the ground in frustration. He'd been so concerned about freeing Beth that he forgot to ask if his parents were still here. But then he hadn't believed Rafé's story of them being taken to Fantrios. How was he going to find out now?

Chapter Eleven

'I see,' Morthrir recovered from his surprise and studied the figure in front of him. 'What use are bound Dé-monos to me?'

'I can persuade the Nastrim to join forces with you through my son, Acwellan,' Vashtani replied.

'Acwellan? I've heard of him quite recently.'

'He's their Executioner and the real Nastrim leader.'

Morthrir's mind was racing. He could order Vashtani to make the Nastrim hand Lenyé over.

'There is one problem,' Vashtani continued. 'Acwellan swore vengeance against the Krêonor for their slaughter of many of his comrades in the wars at the Beginning.'

'That was a long time ago. Convince him he can deal with me as ruler of the Krêonor on a new basis,' Morthrir smiled at him.

'I have to find him first. For that, I need my freedom. None of us has the power to break these En-luchés bonds.'

Morthrir stooped down and caught hold of the chains of light. 'When you find him, have him hand over a certain Lenyé to me.'

'Lenyé?' Vashtani started in surprise. 'Acwellan promised a girl of that name to welcome me back to the Waking World.'

Morthrir jerked his hands away. 'That young woman is mine. Touch her, and I will destroy you.'

'A thousand pardons, My Lord. I had no idea. Neither did Acwellan. I can always choose another woman.'

Morthrir made Vashtani renounce all claims on Lenyé. Then he grasped the chains again, 'By the Hidden Power, be free!'

The chains parted easily and Vashtani stood up. 'Thank you,

My Lord, Morthrir. I beg you to free my followers.'

As he did so, more Dé-monos, this time unbound, fell amongst them. There were five other leaders apart from Vashtani, making six companies of Dé-monos in total.

Morthrir invited the Dé-monos leaders to join him in council. 'In your opinion,' he indicated the circle of Priests, Summoners and Dé-monos leaders around him, 'what is the most important goal to accomplish?'

Vashtani spoke up. 'The fear of the True King and the Sword of Justice hangs over the Dé-monos. The Sword is kept by Acwellan, but if our enemies capture it, they could defeat us. Also, it has power over My Lord Abbérron himself.'

'Eawen,' Morthrir glanced at the Henosite. 'I thought you said Abbérron was more powerful than the True King?'

'That is correct, Sire.'

Morthrir studied the closed and sunken eyes in the man's face before turning back to Vashtani. 'What about the En-luchés that were dragging you away? Have they come through the Spiral?'

Vashtani grimaced, 'All those who chained us, My Lord.'

'Did any more come?' Morthrir looked at the other Dé-monos leaders, but they shook their heads.

'Could the ones that did get through mount an attack on Acwellan and seize the Sword?'

'That would be quite possible, My Lord.'

'So if this Sword fell into their hands it could affect my rule in the Waking World?'

'Yes, My Lord.'

'I see.' Morthrir paused. 'In that case, Vashtani, go and convince Acwellan to serve me.' He indicated one Dé-monos leader and ordered his division to be available to carry out Morthrir's specific commands. 'The rest of you find the En-luchés and ensure they cannot oppose me.'

'Yes, My Lord,' Vashtani and the other Dé-monos leaders bowed in acknowledgement.

'Jumar-jé,' Morthrir pointed at him and the other Summoners. 'Go to the Tsé-shâmé and the Harmoth. Persuade the respective leaders to put aside their ancient hatred and unite with the Krêonor so that we may be one people, as of old. Tell them to send delegates to Terrazarema and enjoy my hospitality as they wait for the coming coronation.'

'Yes, Sire,' Jumar-jé spoke for the others.

'You Priests,' Morthrir turned to them. 'Send out your thoughts to instil harmony and peace in the minds of all people and unite them to become one again. Start in Terrazarema, then all the other cities, towns and villages of the Krêonor and then spread out to the rest of the Waking World.'

'Yes, Sire,' Eawen replied on behalf of the Priests.

'What about your armies, My Lord?' Vashtani queried.

'My remaining army is held in reserve for a specific mission.'

'Very good, My Lord,' Vashtani bowed.

The whole assembly stood: the Dé-monos, Summoners, and Priests and cried out, 'The Lord Morthrir is great. The Lord Morthrir wields the Hidden Power. The Lord Morthrir is Supreme. We hear and obey!'

The Dé-monos vanished in a dark mist while the Summoners and Priests walked down the ravine to the bluff of rock at the bottom.

Once they had disappeared, Morthrir lay on the altar and covered himself with his cloak. The warriors hadn't returned, so they must have found whoever was causing that resistance and were on their way to Onadestra. Good. He was completely alone. He felt exhausted from the events of the previous night and the high level of energy expended. He was thinking about how to retain the power released on this mountain and where to locate it back in Terrazarema.

A plan was forming in his mind. He would use the deepest cellar at the palace and call it the *Vault of Malrema*: "*Mal*", from

Maliché, Queen of the stars, representing *"wisdom"*; and *"rema"*, from Terrazarema, meaning *"word of power"*. Then he could invoke Wisdom, and speak words of power to establish himself as ruler of the Waking World. But he needed the most potent symbol of Abbérron's power on this mountain: the altar.

The Lord Abbérron had given him the Hidden Power. He felt elated now that he was his own master: no more uncertainties and everyone subject to his command. Even the ravine held no terrors for him. He would stay for the rest of today and most of tomorrow and sleep to recover his strength for the next great step: transferring the altar to Terrazarema.

Morthrir woke at noon the next day, and scanned the ravine. There was no movement. He stretched and yawned, luxuriating in the best sleep he'd had for a long time; feeling refreshed and alive and full of energy. He approached the horse carcass where it dangled from the makeshift tripod and cut the rope, intoning over it, 'Let this lie here for the carrion creatures that feast on the death of others.'

He stood on the altar with his arms folded, gazed towards Onadestra, closed his eyes and pictured the castle and the woods outside. He spoke a word of command to the Dé-monos division retained for his personal use, then let his mind wrap cords about the altar stones beneath his feet. He felt himself lifted up…

When he opened his eyes, he was standing on the altar stones, hidden in the woods with the castle in front of him. Perfect. He could move the altar quite easily. And no more tedious journeys either. He could be anywhere he wanted instantly, and surprise people. 'They will never know when or where I will appear next,' he muttered to himself.

He stepped down, emerged from the woods and picked his way through the jostling crowd to the gates of the castle.

Chapter Twelve

Kyros glanced up from behind the special beech tree as he felt something above him. He saw a black mist approaching fast and discerned figures which he recognised instantly: 'Vashtani,' he cried in dismay. 'His bonds are loosed, and the rest of the Dé-monos are also free. How has this happened?' He scrambled to his feet and raised his right hand. 'I call upon the En-luchés who came through the Spiral with me to regroup and seize these Dé-monos and drag them away to their rightful judgement as I have already commanded.'

He remained standing and watching with his hand raised, but nothing happened. The Dé-monos sped on overhead as though his words were completely impotent, the black mist closed in around them and they disappeared to the North-West in a huge arc that would bring them down somewhere in the Plains of Lohr near the mountains.

He was so shocked at the failure of his words to have any effect that he failed to respond to the fresh warnings of the blackbird until it was too late.

'Kyros?'

The voice startled him, but sounded familiar.

'Why hide behind that tree-trunk when I can see you clearly?'

Kyros suddenly recalled where he had last heard that voice. 'Osâcah!' Kyros emerged from behind the tree and watched his friend thrust through the dense foliage of a holly bush to stand in front of him. None of the branches or leaves sprang back into position; it was as if Osâcah had appeared like an apparition without moving anything. He saw Osâcah start in surprise.

'It is you, Kyros, isn't it? Your face is such a mess I hardly recognise you.'

'Of course it's me.' He took a step towards his friend. 'How did you see me behind the tree-trunk from there? Are you a ghost in this world?'

'Certainly not.' Osâcah approached and they embraced. 'But I am not as I once was; for I can walk through objects which appear solid to you and I can see through them as well. You will never be able to hide from me in this world.'

'Where are your companions?'

'They were scattered in that fall, but we have regrouped and taken counsel together. Some are questioning your assertion that the Guardians of the Spiral would prevent anyone passing back into the Waking World, and therefore doubt the rest of your words. But most of us realise the disappearance of the Guardians was through no fault of yours.'

'So what do you intend to do?'

'Go back to the Plains of Lohr. We saw them as we hurtled through the air and they are no longer the fertile pastures we left. We must till the ground and make it fruitful again.'

'But Osâcah. Surely there are more urgent things to do? Vashtani and his Dé-monos are on the loose in the Waking World, and my word no longer has any effect over them.'

'That's why I came to find you. We felt a great weight pressing down on us as we left the Spiral. Our cries are smothered before they can come to the True King's ears.'

'What has that got to do with me?'

'This is the work of Abbérron against us, and will affect you too, for we felt the same weight at the Beginning when the Dé-monos invaded the Waking World and Fathered the Nastrim. That is what Zerigor battled against, but failed to overcome. You must hold on to what you know of the True King and remain faithful to him.'

'I know. Stellatus warned me about that.'

'Above all,' Osâcah continued, 'guard your heart, especially in your relationships with others in the Waking World. After your victory over Malvi-Quîdda, you are a marked man. Abbérron will use every means he can to undermine you and destroy you, for you are a terrible threat to him.'

'What is to be done?'

'You must understand that only Stellatus and his followers came through the Spiral with you. Many more Dé-monos than Vashtani's division have broken into the Waking World behind them. The forces of the True King are greatly outnumbered and will be hard pressed to achieve any kind of victory.'

'So what will you do about it?'

'We must obey the True King's calling and return to our former pastures. We can only set our hands to what we do best.'

'Which is?'

'Not only must we replant the land, but also stand between the Waking World and the Realm of the Blessèd Throne and cry to the True King on behalf of all those we hold dear that his power may be released over them. That includes you. You must recover your position of authority with the True King in order to fulfil his purposes in the Waking World.'

'But Osâcah. Are you deserting me?'

'Only for a season. We will meet again.'

Kyros watched as Osâcah turned on his heel and was gone, vanishing through the holly bush where he first saw his friend.

Despite Osâcah's warning he still couldn't accept that his relationship with the True King was so difficult all of a sudden? He thought of that unnerving silence when he cried out under the special beech tree just now. Then he recalled his time in the Spiral when he first entered and could no longer hear the True King's voice. Maybe it wasn't his relationship that was the problem so much as the location. Perhaps the True King's voice was harder to hear in the Waking World.

Chapter Thirteen

Rafé sat on the floor of his room in the castle at Onadestra, focused his mind on the snake, and made instant contact. He forced the cobra to reveal what had happened in the recent past.

He saw an image of Lenyé riding on horseback, with two swords strapped across her back and a longbow on her shoulder.

Two swords! He'd been troubled by only one before.

These were not warrior swords, judging by the rich gems of the scabbards. The Nastrim must have given them to her. But why swords that size? Why two? And why identical?

The snake showed him that Lenyé was surrounded by a large company of Nastrim equipped with huge longbows. And they were in a forest. Was she planning to attack Terrazarema?

Then he noticed a lioness and a she-bear sitting with her, and an eagle perched on a rock. Lenyé was speaking but he couldn't hear what was said. Then she stood up and stormed off.

The cobra drew away from the scenario and entered the same mountain as before. He saw a glow approaching, and, as the cobra turned a corner, the light blazed from a golden globe lying in a small rock chamber. So that's what it was. The snake wound around the globe, and Rafé felt a sense of peace and tranquillity: his breathing slowed and his mind cleared. What was this globe?

The snake broke the connection, and Rafé shook his head.

Two swords and a globe giving off soothing light. And Lenyé on the march with Nastrim archers. How much should he tell Morthrir, and how much should he keep to himself?

Chapter Fourteen

Beth sat huddled on the wooden bench in one of the cellars in the castle. It was freezing and she was glad of Rafé's fur-lined hood and cloak, even though it was still a bit damp.

She sighed in despair. Where was Quinn now? Was he all right? And Ishi-mi-réjá: what had happened to her?

Beth re-lived the thrill of using the *ishi-mi-réjá* stone. As she held it up, nothing could happen on the mountain top. It was an incredible feeling of power. But her arms were like lead weights, even when Ishi-mi-réjá and Quinn helped her. It felt as though she was holding the whole Waking World, trying to protect it from what was happening in the ravine below. The lightning was so bright, and the final crack of thunder, right overhead, was so loud, she couldn't bear it. The stone disintegrated in her hands and trickled out through her fingers like fine dust. Suddenly all her power was gone.

She didn't know anything more till those warriors hauled her out of that shepherd's cot and tied her to a horse.

How did she get there, and who laid the sheepskins over her?

Maybe it was Ishi-mi-réjá, but why had she deserted her? And where was Quinn? She kept coming back to that question. She would be heartbroken if anything had happened to him.

She stood up from the bench, stretched her arms and began pacing about the cellar, partly to keep warm, but mainly to break the gloom of sitting there with her thoughts. She counted ten paces across the room past the bed and ten paces from the wall with the door and its tiny iron-barred grill to the outer wall with the air vents at the top. There was still a little daylight coming in, but it was quickly fading and she dreaded being plunged into complete darkness.

She'd counted twenty stone steps down from the main level of the castle, when they brought her here, so the room wasn't too deep underground. Could she climb up to those air vents and get out? She dragged the heavy wooden bench across, turned it over, stood it on one end and propped it against the wall under one of the vents. Then she stood on the lower legs, rested her weight against the top end of the bench, gripped the upper set of legs with her hands and eased herself up so the bench wouldn't slip. She thrust one foot on an upper leg, pushed down, and slid her hands up the wall, arching her back so that she pressed her body against the wall. She brought her other foot up and reached above her head. But all she felt was cold stone. She peered up and saw that her hand was still three or four feet below the bars.

She started at the rattle of keys from the top of the steps.

Beth leaped off sideways, flexed her knees as she landed, and dragged the bench back across the room, turned it over and sat on it, gathering her cloak about her.

A flickering light came through the grill on the door and she saw a warrior carrying two flares, accompanied by one of the kitchen staff. She smelled food and realised how hungry she was.

She watched the warrior thrust the flares into brackets on the wall outside. There was a clashing of a key in the lock and the maid entered, placed a tray on the bench and left. Beth was ravenous, and had the covers off the dishes, but was surprised as the warrior walked in and stood watching her.

'You eat, while I talk.'

Beth looked up startled.

'Don't remember me, do you?'

'No, I don't. Wait a minute. Yes. You look so familiar.'

'High Feast Day. Five years ago. Axe throwing and…'

'Of course. You gave me the stump of beeswax. I've still got it hidden in one of my drawers.'

'You never used it?' he winked. 'Waste of good beeswax.'

'No it wasn't. Sometimes memories are more precious because they link people to each other long after they've gone their separate ways. You never did tell me your name.'

'That's nothing special. I'm called Paco. Where's your sister?' He smiled, 'She must be a young woman by now.'

'I don't know. I haven't seen her for weeks.'

'That's true of the rest of your family. We had some special guests on the top floor before Morthrir rode off to Terrazarema with the army.' Paco sat on the bed and watched her eat.

'My parents?'

'It's more than my life's worth to say. Food is left outside the doors and the empties come back. No one's supposed to know for certain. But everyone's guess is the same. I reckon they put you down here to prevent you finding out for yourself.'

'But how can I reach them?'

'Try the old game larder where they hang the venison and pheasants after a kill. The air vents come out beyond the castle walls so they can lower the carcasses in without having to haul them into the castle. There are no bars on those vents.'

'Where is it?' Beth was up from the bench, suddenly alert.

'Come over here,' he walked to the door and pointed through the grill. 'See that passage at the far end away from the steps. It's along there. You can get up to the kitchens by the steps right outside it, and there isn't a locked door on those steps, either. The larder's empty at this time of year before the autumn hunting season starts. So no one goes down there now. I can make sure the door into the larder is left unlocked.'

'How do I get upstairs?'

'Left takes you to the kitchens. But if you turn right at the top of the steps, you come to the door leading to the main part of the castle. Immediately left is the back staircase. Up three floors, then I'm not sure which rooms. I've never been up there.'

'Why are you telling me all this?'

'Like you said,' Paco smiled. 'Memories link people together.' He paused. 'I'd best be going now. The flares'll burn for a couple of hours. Then I suggest you get some sleep.'

'But how am I going to get out if this door is always locked.'

'I'll have to think of something.' He paused at the door, 'By the way, we've heard rumours of your sister's activities. She's raised a huge company of soldiers and destroyed an entire army of our warriors. That leaves your Uncle with only one army based at Terrazarema. There are many families back home grieving already, waiting for an official announcement.'

Beth heard the click of the lock, and Paco was gone. She was elated at the news, despite her sympathies for the families. Maybe Lenyé would use the soldiers to attack their Uncle. She had to escape and rescue her parents and join up with her sister.

She waited for a while, then hauled the bed across the floor till it was under both vents. She carried the bench so that it didn't scrape on the floor and make a noise, stood it on its end on the bed and climbed up again. This time she could reach the bars and swung herself up. But the gaps in between were too close for her to wriggle through, and the bars too tight in the stonework for her to loosen and pull out. She tried the other vent, but it was no different. Beth smacked the wall with her hand in frustration: she would have to use Paco's game larder after all.

Beth dragged the bed back to its original position, replaced the bench and sat down to drink some more water.

As the flares began to sputter she crossed the room pulled back the covers and settled herself in the bed. The flares finally went out and plunged her into darkness. She lay there thinking for a while. So near. So close to her parents. Just a few flights of steps. All she wanted was to hear her Mother's voice and be held by her. If only Paco could think of a way to leave her door unlocked without arousing any suspicion.

Chapter Fifteen

Morthrir strode down the main corridor of the castle with Rafé trailing after him. 'You say those warriors discovered Beth in a shepherd's cot?'

'Yes, Sire.'

'And Quinn?'

'No, Sire. There was no trace of anyone else in the vicinity.'

'You're sure?'

'Yes, Sire. The warriors made a thorough search.'

'I cannot accept that Beth put up so much resistance on her own. Someone else must have been there. How did you get back to the castle?'

'I found a horse on the Grassy Plateau, Sire.'

Morthrir stopped and spun round, 'Only one. Did you search the area on the mountain yourself?'

Rafé managed to avoid colliding into Morthrir. 'No, Sire.'

'So how did the warriors bring the girl in?'

'They had a spare horse, Sire. I understand it was the one you were using.'

'Yes. Well. Never mind about that. Where is Beth now?'

'In one of the cellars. I thought it best to keep her out of view.'

'Quite right. Does she know about my brothers?'

'I don't think so. I was going to send her to Terrazarema before you arrived to stop any whispers reaching her. I presume she can go with you now, Sire?'

As Morthrir approached the public Settlements Chamber the two guards flung open the double doors. Once in the room

Morthrir faced Rafé. 'Certainly not. Send her by armed escort. I'll make my own way.'

'As you wish, Sire.'

'The sooner, the better; in case she has found out about her parents.' He paused. 'I'm going to move my brothers to the Royal Hunting Lodge at Fantrios. They've been here long enough to arouse interest from the locals. If news gets out, we're in trouble.' Morthrir opened the door and yelled for the Captain.

When the Captain arrived, Morthrir gave the order: 'Have the girl taken to Terrazarema under armed escort. And transfer our guests in the top of the castle to Fantrios once she's gone.'

'Yes, Sire. Will that be all?'

'No. Include my wife in that party for her protection.'

When the Captain had left, Morthrir rounded on Rafé. 'I still think it would be simpler if they were poisoned.'

'Sire. You must keep your options open as long as possible.'

Morthrir sighed. 'Very well. I want you back in Terrazarema once all this is done. Are there enough pigeons to communicate with the palace?'

'A fresh basket arrived this morning from Terrazarema. The ones we sent to the palace should be there by now.'

'Good.'

Morthrir dismissed Rafé, hurried back to the main gates and walked across the road to the woods. He checked no one was watching and slipped in amongst the trees, located the altar and climbed up onto the stones. He faced Terrazarema and closed his eyes, visualising the door into the largest of the cellars, deep in the basement of the palace. When he opened his eyes he and the altar were in exactly the right position outside the door.

Morthrir chuckled: this was too easy!

PART II

THE CONFUSION

Chapter Sixteen

Kyros felt relieved that Osâcah confirmed another Breaking-in had occurred; but what was he supposed to do about it? He walked round the pool to where a burst of sunlight penetrated the leaf canopy and lit up the rocks and tree stumps at the edge, in a golden glow. He checked his pocket for the parchment and cylinder; then stooped with cupped hands for a drink of water.

He scooped again and looked at his hands, as if seeing them for the first time. His skin normally tanned well, but the backs of his hands had never been that dark before. He leaned out over the pool and studied his reflection. His face was a similar colour; or what little of his face remained between the scratches and bruises, the mop of wild unkempt hair and the full beard that had grown. The fierce sun in the Realm of Travail would account for his darkened skin; but Harbona was right: something in the atmosphere must have made his hair and beard grow so much.

He grinned at the reflection of himself in the water; then glanced at his clothes: his breeches and boots were coated in clay from the storm as he circled Malvi-Quîdda. He looked so dishevelled. Who would recognise him now?

He pulled off his boots, scraped away as much clay as possible with a stick, then wiped them with pieces of moss and tufts of grass. He unbuckled his belt, removed his dagger and empty scabbard and slid the belt out of its loops. Then he took off his breeches, draped the legs in the water and rubbed them together trying to remove the stains. He hung the breeches over a branch to dry and laid his scabbard and dagger out on the bank before settling back to study the parchment afresh.

But he couldn't concentrate. His mind kept returning to Lenyé. Where was she? Had she managed to stay free, or had she been captured? How was he going to find her? Maybe he shouldn't show her the parchment after all. It might open up the old wound of that argument they had from years ago. Had she really forgiven him? Perhaps she was just trying to make him feel better about himself. He couldn't help the way he was. Why should he care about what she thought?

The important thing was to get her help in dealing with the Dé-monos. Despite the shock of his words not having any effect earlier, he was confident that the power of the True King's name would work for him here as before. Maybe he was too far away from them, or they needed to be able to hear his voice. Surely Vashtani and his cohort were still under his word of judgement spoken in the Realm of Travail. All he had to do was re-instate that at another time, which would lead to the final judgement Hoffengrégor wrote of in the parchment.

And if his victory over Malvi-Quîdda had triggered the finding of Zerigor's Blade, then he would have to seek out the new keeper and warn him to despatch the Nastrim.

But what nagged the most in Kyros' mind was the strange silence of the True King. It was worse than when he went down the Spiral before he met Hoffengrégor. Was this the work of Abbérron that Osâcah mentioned? What was going on?

Kyros started at a sudden cough, grabbed his dagger and looked up, feeling the adrenaline surge through him. He breathed a sigh of relief: it was Harbona. This would be a test of the man's oath, now that they were back in the Waking World.

'Is that you, My Lord? Your face is hardly recognisable.'

'Of course it is.' Kyros dropped his dagger and stood up. 'I am not fully dressed, Harbona, for I'm trying to remove the clay from my boots and breeches.'

'Have mine, My Lord. I cannot let you suffer this indignity.'

'That was kindly spoken, but I think your breeches would be too short and your boots too small.'

'I hardly know you with your face so badly scratched and bruised. I only recognise you by your hair and beard from our time at Malvi-Quîdda, My Lord.'

'I see you've shaved and trimmed your hair already.'

'Yes, My Lord. Would you like to borrow my razor?'

'There's no time, now.'

'You bear an empty scabbard, My Lord. Have my sword, at least.'

'It would not do for my bodyguard to be weaponless. Otherwise, how will you protect me? You keep it, but thank you for the offer.'

'Then what are your orders, My Lord. Surely we need to find out what has happened to those monsters that captured me?'

Before Kyros could reply, they both ducked down instinctively at the sound of a twig snapping some way off followed by the noise of startled pigeons.

Chapter Seventeen

Lenyé walked through the forest towards the Pool of Alesco and the special beech tree. She hoped to find some clue about Kyros, but was still upset by her friends, and yearned for the peace she always found there by herself, following the little stream as it cut through the rocks and steep, fern-covered banks.

She trod carefully feeling the reassuring tension of the bowstring across her shoulder, and winced whenever the longbow hanging down her back caught in the undergrowth.

Where had Kyros gone? He'd disappeared completely. She recalled the message which Ariella brought from Yanantha: "*She found traces of him on the island and signs of a struggle in the cave mouth..., he must have gone down the spiral*".

Those marks at the cave didn't prove it was Kyros. It could have been the warriors. But why set fire to the island? They obviously thought it was him. That spiral led down to the Realm of the Departed. Was he dead?

She emerged into a small clearing and ducked as a couple of crows flew overhead.

And what was the special destiny that Yanantha mentioned? How could she be so sure he would return?

She was too engrossed in her thoughts to scan the path ahead properly. Her foot caught awkwardly, and a large dry twig snapped as she stumbled on it with her full weight.

Lenyé froze as a flock of roosting pigeons exploded out of a nearby tree and flew off with a loud flapping of their wings.

Chapter Eighteen

Quinn stood amongst the trees at the edge of the woods below the castle and shaded his eyes against the sun. He stared down the valley at the long loops in the road winding down to the flat of the plain and the bridge over the river. The water was almost up to the top of the arches: no wonder Rafé warned him about not using the ford.

Somehow he had to rescue Beth and get her away from any pursuit. It was all very well for Rafé to talk about spooking the escort's horses, but that was easier said than done. He mentally noted where the bends in the road came closest to the woods and picked the second one down, not far below the distinct line in the woods between the dark conifers that rose up to the castle itself, and the broadleaf trees that covered the gentler slopes down to the river and beyond.

He slipped back amongst the trees to his horse, mounted and walked it gently down the slope to the place he'd chosen. He dismounted, tied the reins to a branch and crept out to the road on hands and knees making sure he was concealed by the low lying bushes and scrubby vegetation. This was the perfect spot where the road narrowed into the bend and suddenly became quite steep on one side. The escort would naturally head across to the longer side of the curve.

He assumed Beth's horse would be some way back in the party. If he could get the lead horses to shy, then maybe hers would bolt in response. But would it carry on down the bend in the road or veer off along the little path that ran straight into the woods under the arching branches of the first few trees? If there were bucking horses on the road in front, it was likely to panic and try to get away from them. So he was fairly certain it would take the path. If it didn't, he would have to think again and try something further down near the bridge.

Quinn was going to have his work cut out. He decided to tether his horse deep in the woods, lie in wait at the main gates of the castle watching for the escort to leave, race through the woods and tie his twine in place and then climb into those trees to grab Beth as her horse bolted underneath him.

He checked one length of twine across the road. It was so fine that it would snap as the first horse went through it and probably not notice. If he tied several lengths to those loose boulders on the banks either side of the road: that would be about chest-high on a horse. Several of them, well spaced out and woven together like a huge cobweb, should make the horse react with the shock of the feel and the noise of falling stones as the whole thing pulled away.

He hoped the lead warrior wouldn't see his web of twine till it was too late.

Chapter Nineteen

Lenyé slipped the longbow off her shoulder, squatted down, notched an arrow and drew the bowstring to her ear. She heard a movement to her left and saw a man, clothed as a warrior, dart towards a tree. She followed him with the tip of her arrow, then loosed, hearing the thud as it stuck in the trunk.

She circled to her right, notching another arrow. What was he doing; and was he alone? She peered through a mass of overgrown saplings, and stiffened as she saw another man with his back towards her. He was doing up his belt with one hand, and trying to pull on his boots with the other.

His clothes reminded her of Kyros, and her heart began to beat a little faster in anticipation. But what a mess they were in: his breeches were damp and clung to his legs; and the fashionable slash down the back of his jerkin was scorched and badly re-laced, while the white shirt was also blackened as if it had been on fire.

'Is that you, Kyros?'

The man whipped round and Lenyé stifled a scream, the longbow and arrow wavering for an instant in her hands. The man's great mop of hair and long, matted beard; and the state of his face: she'd never seen anything like it.

'Don't move!' Lenyé remained in her tangled cover, and drew the bowstring. 'Raise your hands slowly.'

The man ignored her command and pulled up his right boot, stamping his foot into the heel. 'I don't talk to hidden voices.'

'You sound like Kyros,' Lenyé eyed the man's dark skin and

the mass of scratches and bruises on his face. She desperately wanted to believe it was Kyros, yet something was niggling at her mind. 'But you don't look like him.'

'If it wasn't for the creepers that hide you, I would say you sound like Princess Lenyé. And I really am Kyros.'

She paused, torn between her desire to run and fling her arms around him and the suspicion that this was some kind of trick. It couldn't be Kyros. After the build up of her hopes, she felt totally devastated. The more she tried to work out if he was telling the truth or not, the more her misgivings deepened. 'Kyros may have been growing a beard when I last saw him, but he's only twenty: there's no way he could grow one like that.'

Lenyé was so intent on the conversation that she was startled by someone crashing through the creepers behind her. Two powerful arms wrapped around her, enabling the hands to grab her wrists, forcing the longbow downwards, and pulling her other hand away so that the arrow slipped from her fingers.

'Let me go!' Lenyé lashed out with one foot, but her captor was too quick, trapping her leg with his and pulling so that she slumped forwards onto one knee with the weight of the man's chest pressing down across her shoulder blades. The man let go of one wrist, prised the fingers open on her other hand and shook till the longbow fell from her grip.

She spun round, pivoting on the wrist he held and punched the man, but he caught her other wrist and jerked both his hands upwards and outwards, so that her arms were stretched apart. She aimed a kick at him, but he blocked it with the side of his thigh, wound his leg around hers and toppled her backwards. She sat down awkwardly in a tangle of creepers, still with her arms stretched far apart.

'Let me go!'

She heard the rustle of dead leaves as the other man approached, then whipped her head round at his laugh.

'I was right. It is Princess Lenyé. But dressed like a page boy. I would have walked past you had I not heard your voice. Surely you know me.'

Lenyé's mind was racing: that was twice the man referred to her as "Princess" Lenyé; but Kyros would never have called her that. What was it Chuah-te-mok said: *"You don't need wings on your arms, but in your spirit: you must learn to rise up and see in the spirit realm, and then all things on the ground will fall into place"*. If ever there was a time she needed the discernment he was referring to, it was now. This man was trying to impersonate Kyros and fool her. 'You're not the Kyros I knew.' Lenyé glared at him, 'Make him let go. He's hurting my arms.'

'Tell her who I am, Harbona.'

'This is Prince Kyros. I chased him down the spiral, but he rescued me from some evil beings and now I'm his bodyguard.'

'Prince Kyros' bodyguard?' Lenyé struggled in the man's grip, but still couldn't free her wrists. 'You're one of Uncle Morthrir's most valued officers. I saw you at Onadestra. This is all a trick. I don't believe you!'

'What would you have me do, My Lord,' Lenyé watched Harbona glance at the other man. 'She loosed an arrow at me.'

'Why wouldn't I try to kill one of Youdlh's warriors?' Lenyé glared at her captor. 'You've been after me for weeks.'

'Let her go, Harbona. Thank you for coming to my rescue.'

'A privilege, My Lord.' Harbona helped Lenyé to her feet.

Lenyé held out her hand, 'Longbow please. And the arrow.' She saw the man nod, and Harbona handed the weapons to her.

'Thank you.' Lenyé stepped away, notched the arrow, drew back the bowstring, aimed the arrow at waist height and kept moving it between the two men. She noticed the empty scabbard dangling from the imposter's left hip: apart from a dagger, he wasn't armed. But he could have removed his sword for cleaning, so it might be close at hand. And the man he called Harbona was fully armed. As long as she stayed alert she could bring down one man and notch a second arrow before the other responded. 'You'd better come up with some answers...' Lenyé was even more suspicious than ever. 'I don't believe you are Kyros for one minute. Have you come to help me attack Uncle Morthrir and free my sister and the others?'

'I had an army, and we overcame our enemies. But they've returned to farm the Plains of Lohr.'

'Farmers! I need soldiers or warriors. What use are farmers?'

She heard the man sigh. 'There's a lot I need to explain.'

'I've no time for explanations. If I don't get to Terrazarema with a big enough force to destroy Uncle Morthrir once and for all, Beth is going to be executed. Then the others, one a day, starting with Quinn, then the next youngest and so on. And you've brought absolutely no help at all!'

'I have Harbona.'

'One man, who may turn traitor and serve Uncle Morthrir again. How do you know he'll be true to you?'

'I've sworn on oath, My Lady,' Harbona interjected. 'I promised to lay down my life for him and all those he loves.'

'Really. Well I hope we won't have to put it to the test. One man. Is that the best you can do? I don't think the real Kyros would be that stupid!'

Chapter Twenty

Beth sat in the saddle while the escort was assembled. Her hands weren't tied to the reins, as there was a long leash from her horse's harness to the nearest warrior; but he held the end in his hand, rather than tying it to the pommel of his saddle.

She was annoyed at not escaping to find her parents last night: there was no sign of Paco even coming to unlock the door. Another guard came with the maid who brought the breakfast things. The maid also brought her a bowl of water and a towel for a wash. But her hair was the worst problem. It was so tangled that her scalp was all itchy and practically driving her crazy.

She was startled by a shout of command and the escort trotted out of the gates and cantered on the flat. She glanced at the castle wall. How was she ever going to rescue her parents?

Two warriors led, two came behind and she was in the middle with her guard. They cantered and walked as the road changed from straight to long looping bends and back again.

Beth eased from a canter to a trot at the second bend by the woods, but the curve was tighter than expected as the road plunged down steeply. The leaders slowed abruptly and the rest bunched up behind. The two lead horses reared at the sound of crashing stones on either side: one threw its rider. Her horse snorted and shied as the two behind hurtled past, upsetting her guard's horse, and making it stumble and cannon into hers. She felt her horse jump sideways and then it was off, tearing the leash out of the man's hand and bolting up a path into the woods. She loosened the reins hoping it would calm down, and ducked over the horse's neck as it plunged in amongst the trees. She glimpsed a figure hanging upside down from the branches ahead, realised it was Quinn, yanked her feet out of the stirrups, let go of the reins and held her arms for him to grasp her by the wrists and lift her from the saddle as the horse galloped away.

She gripped his wrists in response, climbed up him, grabbed the branch he was hanging from, and hauled herself onto the branch. Quinn swung himself up to join her and they both scrambled along the branch and ducked down the other side of the trunk as the first warrior thundered underneath. They climbed down the tree and hid in the undergrowth as they heard two more horses approaching, and then whipped round in alarm at the sound of the first horse coming back towards their tree.

'I've just spotted her horse,' they heard the first warrior shout to his comrades. 'And the girl's not on it. She's either fallen off somewhere or managed to get into this tree. Hold his head still, while I climb up and take a look.'

They watched one of his comrades grab the horse by the harness as the warrior stood on the saddle and hauled himself up into the tree. They froze, fearing he might be able to spot them in the undergrowth from his vantage point, but the man only scanned the branches and tree canopy above him.

Finally he dropped down onto his horse. 'No one there.'

'Hardly likely,' another commented. 'You had to stand on your saddle. The girl couldn't have reached up with her horse bolting like that. She must have fallen off further ahead.'

'One of you catch her horse,' the first warrior ordered, as the last two cantered up the path to join them. 'The rest of you check the area carefully. She must be lying in the undergrowth. I'm going back down to see what spooked the horses.'

When they'd gone, Beth hugged Quinn, 'Thank goodness you're safe. I was so worried about you!'

'Quick,' Quinn smiled at her. 'We need to get back to my horse and decide what to do.'

Chapter Twenty One

'If you really are Kyros,' Lenyé gripped her longbow tighter, 'why are your hands and face so dark?'

'I've been in the Realm of Travail, at the bottom of the Spiral, where the sun is much fiercer and the atmosphere made my hair and beard grow like this.'

'You expect me to believe that?'

'I wrestled with a stranger and met Hoffengrégor.'

'The Ancient Prophet?' Lenyé frowned. 'But he's dead.'

'He may have passed from our world, but he still lives. The stranger I prevailed against was the True King himself.'

Lenyé was shocked: the Ancient Writings said no one could see the True King and live. And she was really puzzled: so he had been down the Spiral. But he must be making the rest of it up. 'That Spiral leads to the Realm of the Departed. If the True King was there, it means he can only reign over the dead.'

'The True King doesn't reign over the dead, but the living; for they have come to him through death.'

'What about Zerigor, then? Did you see him?'

'No.'

'And our parents? They're dead. Did you look for them?'

'No. Of course not. Lenyé, there wasn't...'

'You only saw Hoffengrégor,' she cut him off. 'So you're not certain all the dead are gathered there, are you?'

'The dead don't gather there. They go straight to the Realm of the Departed. That's where I found the Sacred Pilgrims of Lohr: my army of farmers.'

'All this only convinces me how deluded you are.'

'I am not deluded. I've seen it with my own eyes.'

Lenyé's mind was racing. Maybe there was a way to prove his identity after all. 'You're just the same as when we argued over using my ideas in our games when we were younger. I tried to say I was sorry, but you wouldn't change and we all had to pretend how much better a person the great Kyros had become!'

'I thought we'd both been genuine when you apologised that evening. Those were real tears.' Kyros turned away and kicked at a clump of mushrooms before sinking down onto an old tree stump. 'How can you say that now?'

Lenyé followed him with the tip of her arrow. 'Because it's one of the few incidents in my life that would show me you're Kyros.' She was almost convinced at the genuineness of his response, but this man might have talked to the real Kyros and picked up those details. She hesitated before continuing. 'I'm not convinced you are Kyros.'

Kyros sat with eyes downcast, brooding for some time: if this was the girl he knew and loved and was desperate to get back to in the Waking World; how could she treat him like this? Finally he muttered, 'It might help if you told me what you've been up to. You look extremely well armed with that longbow and those two swords.'

'One of them is the lost Blade of Zerigor. I recovered it from the Nastrim.'

'Is that so?' he jerked his head up and stared at her. 'I presume you've executed the judgement over them and despatched them to Elasis, their place of rest?'

'The Nastrim are my friends. I used their soldiers to destroy one of Uncle Morthrir's armies and now we're marching on Terrazarema to finish off the rest of his warriors and rescue Beth and the others. After that, I've agreed to despatch them to Elasis.'

'You mustn't wait that long. You have to do it now! If you use the Sword as a weapon of war, you will be brought down and the Krêonor destroyed. That was Zerigor's fatal error. If you won't do it, then you'd better give it to me.'

Lenyé glared at him. 'The Lay of Hoffengrégor says: "...*not by the hand of any man shall the ancient blade be regained...*". If a man like Zerigor made such a mistake all those centuries ago, then a woman had to rise up in his place and put it right. Sometimes men have to let go of the great deeds that shape the present and put away their pride so that our future may be established.'

Kyros felt his anger rising. 'If you're accusing me of pride, let me point out to you that the words may say *"regained"*, but they don't necessarily mean *"use"* and *"wield"*.'

'Don't be ridiculous.'

'Maybe you need to recognise the limit of your involvement. Give me the Sword. It's time for a man to use it again properly.'

'Who do you think you are, ordering me to do this and that? I will not give it to you.'

'Listen, Lenyé. Stellatus sent me with a warning...'

'It's down to me to use it for its rightful purpose,' Lenyé drew back the bowstring. 'Yanantha sent me to find the Blade and...'

'Do you know what the Nastrim did?' Kyros was on his feet.

'No.'

'They butchered the Pilgrims of Lohr, who barred their way when they were attacking the Krêonor in Zerigor's day.'

'You mean your precious farmers?'

Kyros ignored the interruption, his anger boiling over in sudden rage. 'If you're adamant in using the Nastrim as your allies, then I can have nothing more to do with you, whatever has been promised between us in the past.'

'Really?' Lenyé flared up in an instant: how dare he accuse her like that! 'Well I'm glad to understand your mind at last. Do you know what the Nastrim have endured over the centuries?'

'No.'

'Can you imagine what it is like to be in this world with no hope for a future?' Lenyé felt her eyes blazing with fury; she

65

wasn't going to let him get away with this.

'What's hope got to do with it?' Kyros took a pace towards her.

Lenyé threatened him with the arrow pointing directly at his chest. 'They cannot have children, so they're a dwindling race,' she paused for breath. 'And they are not what they were in Zerigor's day. They came to my aid to defeat one of Uncle Morthrir's armies. If those warriors weren't destroyed, I would have been carried off and forced to become my Uncle's wife!'

'I don't believe you.'

'Would you have waved this precious Sword about and got rid of the Nastrim and let me be carried off against my will? Is that what you would have done if you'd been here?'

'No, of course not. I would have defended you.'

'One man against an army of warriors: they're deadly in battle!' Lenyé glared at him, 'The Nastrim are the only means I have to defeat Uncle Morthrir and rescue Beth.'

'There is more at stake than rescuing your sister. The Nastrim have to be dealt with immediately.'

'If you really are Kyros, where were you all this time when I needed you most? Messing about in some delusional world that no one else has ever seen and can't prove it even exists.'

'It does exist,' Kyros smacked his fist into his palm.

'It's a good job you never had the chance of asking my Father's permission for my hand in marriage, because now I can consider the words that passed between us as null and void. If you're deserting me over the Nastrim, then I am thankful, because now I can go to my friends unhindered by any sentimental ties elsewhere. I don't care if you are Kyros or not, we're through with each other!'

Before he could move, she loosed the arrow and it stuck quivering in the tree stump he had been sitting on. Then she turned on her heel and stormed out of the clearing.

Chapter Twenty Two

Rafé sat astride his horse in the castle courtyard and clipped the pigeon pouch in place on his saddle. He checked the air holes weren't blocked, pulled his horse's head round and walked him out of the gate before gently cantering down the road to the first big bend.

He was still puzzling over how Morthrir had arrived at the castle. One of the sentries saw him walking out of the woods opposite the main gates. When Rafé slipped out to investigate, he found a pile of stones, in a clearing, which looked exactly the same as the altar on Mount Malkamet. But how could that be possible? He watched through a window when Morthrir departed and saw him walk through the castle gates and disappear into the woods. He waited a while and then went to investigate, but the stones had gone. Did that mean he had power to move from location to location without the need for transport? And have the ability to take things with him? Heavy things, like stones! And was it instantaneous, or did it take time? He couldn't answer the last question, but Morthrir had arrived not long after he had himself. Therefore the man could travel as fast as a swift horse. But then the warriors had a spare horse for Beth. That must have been Morthrir's, which meant he didn't use a horse. So the power he had was instantaneous.

Rafé was stunned. If that was the case, Morthrir could show up anywhere he wanted and catch people by surprise. He shook his head. If he was right, he would have to be even more vigilant now in case Morthrir caught him acting against the man's best interests.

No wonder Morthrir didn't want Beth and her guards to ride with him: he wasn't going to ride at all. He must be in Terrazarema by now. Just as well Rafé had brought some pigeons with him. If the ford was impassable, he would have to go by road and that would take several days. Anything might happen in that time.

He was some way down the long looping road to the bridge across the River Rubichinó when he saw a lone rider coming up towards him. He slowed his horse and waited for the man to reach him.

'Something panicked the horses, Sir. The girl's horse bolted up a path into the woods. When it emerged the other side, the girl had vanished. We searched thoroughly, but couldn't find any sign of her. The others are still looking and the lieutenant sent me back to the castle to make a report.'

Rafé's mind was racing. He didn't want any more warriors assigned to the search, but he had to make it look as if he was doing everything possible to find Beth. 'You'd better carry on.'

'Shall I tell the Captain to send a message to Terrazarema?'

'No. I'll take care of that.'

Rafé dismounted and sat on a boulder watching the man till he was out of sight. Then he pulled out his writing kit, prepared a note for Morthrir, secured it in a message cylinder and sent it with one of his pigeons.

He sat watching the pigeon as it circled overhead before flying off towards Terrazarema. He glanced at the sun. Morthrir would get it by evening. If he knew Beth had disappeared, it might push him into doing something rash.

Chapter Twenty Three

Morthrir stood in the underground cellar, his eyes taking in the arched brickwork of the ceiling, the exposed bricks of the walls and the flagstones of the floor. He shivered slightly in the chill atmosphere and turned to the Master Crafter. 'I want the whole room cleared of all this lumber. Put black blinds on the air vents and have everything painted black: walls, floor and ceiling.'

'Yes, Sire.'

'Use white paint for a moon on the ceiling, and stars on the ceiling and walls down as far as the bottom of the arches.' He looked up from the diagram he was studying. 'Get the Royal Astronomer to draw the stars and phase of the moon for the night of 20th to 21st of June this year. Understood?'

'Yes, Sire.'

'Paint these lines on the floor in white. Make the circle as big as possible but leave enough space for three abreast to walk round the outside edge.' He passed the man the diagram before continuing. 'Use reflective paint for all the lines, stars and moon; and matt black for the background.' He paused as he surveyed the room. 'Then have those stones brought in here and rebuilt exactly as they are in the marked space pointing North to South.'

'And how are we to align these marks, Sire?'

'I would have thought that was obvious,' Morthrir pointed to the diagram. 'N is North, S is South, E is East and W is West. Use a compass and make sure you locate those points as accurately as possible.'

'Very good, Sire.'

'Change the lock and make one key each for myself and the Master of the Keys. And have a sign outside the doors inscribed with "*The Vault of Malrema*". Finish it by midnight tomorrow.'

'But the paint won't dry in time, Sire.'

'I have spoken a word of command and it will dry quickly.' He stared at the man. 'I want a bronze sculpture of me standing on a copy of those stones to be erected in the Central Square.'

'Yes, Sire. I will have one of the Royal Artisans come to make some initial sketches of yourself. When will that be convenient?'

'Now. I want the sculpture in place within two days.'

'About the setting time for the bronze…'

'Again, I have spoken.'

'Very good, Sire.'

After the man had gone, Morthrir rubbed his hands together in anticipation: he couldn't wait to release power through the *Vault of Malrema*, and see his sculpture in place in the Square.

He went upstairs to find Youdlh outside the private council chamber. Morthrir led the way in, thrusting between the guards and marching over to the desk before turning to face Youdlh.

'Good news, Sire.'

Morthrir frowned. How dare the man speak first! 'What?'

'I've had word back from our army. They saw the Nastrim force in the Plains of Lohr, but Lenyé was not with them. Shall I go and direct the operation and try and find her?'

'No. Send a company of one hundred horsemen to cover the ground between here and the forest. She may be using their army as a decoy.'

'All the same, Sire. I think I should be with my warriors.'

'I need you here for two things,' Morthrir kept his voice low as he spoke, drawing Youdlh closer to him and whispering in the man's ear. 'Firstly, Beth and Quinn are for ever eluding me. I have a note here from Rafé to say Beth has escaped from her escort. I want this nonsense put to an end once and for all. Go and find two children who look exactly the same, bring them here and have them killed and put into coffins. I want them ready for a state funeral in two days time. Is that clear?'

'But Sire...'

'Make sure they are from different towns or villages well away from Terrazarema. I don't want anyone linking their disappearances together.'

'Yes, Sire.' Youdlh glanced at Morthrir. 'And the other thing?'

'That body your two surviving warriors buried in the forest after they torched the island; who did they think it was?'

'One of their comrades who accompanied Harbona to try and capture Kyros.'

'Not Harbona himself, then.'

'No, Sire. Harbona always wore that medal of honour you presented to him on a chain round his neck. Even if he was badly burned, the medal would still be in place.'

'Any other clues to the man's identity?'

'Harbona was shorter and broader in the shoulders and deeper in the chest. This man was tall. There was only one of my warriors it could have been.'

'What about Kyros?'

'Possibly, Sire. But why would he have fought his way past six of my men, only to let himself be burned to death?'

'That is what we need to find out. Take Dr Nostrea and those two warriors and dig up the body. Let Dr Nostrea examine it. If anyone can identify Kyros: he can. Then bring it back here under cover of dark, and bury it in the Royal Cemetery.'

'Yes, Sire.'

'Oh, and Youdlh.'

'Yes, Sire.'

'Has anyone else seen the body?'

'No, Sire.'

'Then you may need to dispose of those two warriors afterwards. Understood?'

'Yes, Sire.'

Chapter Twenty Four

Kyros slumped onto the tree-stump, wrenched the arrow out from between his knees and sat twiddling it in his hands. He felt as though he had been kicked in the stomach by a horse. All his eagerness and expectations about being back in the Waking World and finding Lenyé and being united with her were gone.

Her words had pierced him like deadly arrows. He felt the wounds would never heal; especially about when they'd been reconciled in the past and yet she still held those awful thoughts about him. And she couldn't even decide whether she recognised him or not. Surely he hadn't changed that much!

He smacked the arrow shaft into his hand. How could she be so emphatic about using the Nastrim and that Sword against their Uncle? Why wouldn't she listen to him?

Then thoughts came surging into his mind. He tried to think when he had them before: they certainly resonated with him. He remembered thinking Lenyé no longer cared for him as he'd been gone so long, and she'd found someone else.

She may not have found another; in fact she was obviously trying to fight off Uncle Morthrir's intentions. But she had rejected him. That's what mattered! It wasn't so much that he had turned away from her: there were higher things to consider. He couldn't disobey Stellatus' last words or the urgent command in Hoffengrégor's writings. Maybe he should have shown her that, but the whole argument had been going in another direction altogether. It was too late now. And how could he face Osâcah again if his bride-to-be was allied to the Nastrim and refusing to use the Sword over them because of her own plans.

That's when he had those crazy ideas: circling Malvi-Quîdda with Osâcah and the Pilgrims. It was the Voices. He'd denied them at the time, rejecting the taunts as they were opposed to all his desires. He recalled the gruelling repetition, redressing their reasoning in more and more of an attractive light, beating down his resistance and weakening his will to the point of utter exhaustion. He remembered the True King whispering, *"You have to resist these Voices. Evil crouches at the door of your heart. But you are able to master it"*. That stirred him to shake it off and rouse his companions and their ensuing shout made the ground tremble.

But the words were insistent in his mind now. Without Lenyé, he would *"be free to chose another woman for his wife"*, as the Voices so clearly put it, *"rather than endure the naïve tenderness he experienced from her"*. Surely there was an element of truth in that: he was mistaking youthful infatuation for real love. He needed the mature love of a woman to sustain a relationship for the rest of his life. He no longer thought Lenyé could do that for him.

She had changed so much. Why was she so hostile when he was the only one to rescue her from their Uncle?

He studied the arrow in his hand. It was the last physical link he had with Lenyé. But she'd loosed it almost straight at him. What did she mean by that? He shrugged his shoulders: maybe he would never know. As if coming to a sudden decision he snapped the arrow over his knee and tossed it away.

'What are your plans now, My Lord?'

Kyros was startled out of his reverie by Harbona. He was so engrossed with his thoughts he'd forgotten the man was there.

'I'm not sure.'

'Perhaps I can be of assistance, My Lord. The young Lady…'

'It must have been obvious just now, Harbona.'

'You love Lenyé and she loves you.'

'Not any more.'

'But it was only one argument, My Lord. Surely...?'

Kyros sighed. 'In the Realm of Travail I could sprint across a plain, speak in the name of the True King, destroy a stronghold of the Dé-monos and rescue you from their clutches.'

'No mean feat, My Lord. And one for which I am grateful.'

'But not in the Waking World. I feel as if all that is now a mere dream, and everything I once trusted in has deserted me. I may have conquered Malvi-Quîdda, but I'm at a total loss as to what's happened to Lenyé. It's all over between us.'

'I see,' Harbona hesitated. 'But to repeat my earlier question, what are your plans, My Lord.'

'I'm still thinking things through.'

'In that case, My Lord. I have a little skill in making traps, and I've noticed a few rabbits. What about something to eat?'

'Why not? Now you mention it, I'm starving hungry.'

He watched Harbona disappear through the trees and felt the silence of the forest descend on him as he began to wrestle with his thoughts again and decide what to do.

Clearly Lenyé had made up her mind, and he was well rid of her. But he had no idea how to stop Abbérron's counter stroke.

He glanced up suddenly feeling he was not alone, despite the intense silence of the forest. But there was nothing there. He stood up and walked towards the saplings where Lenyé had first appeared, and pushed his way in amongst the creepers.

He stopped and gasped.

There, standing before him was a woman clad in white. Her dark hair shimmered as though a light fell about her, and the soft violet sheen of her eyes mirrored her welcoming smile.

'Well met, Prince Kyros.' Her voice had such a beautiful lilt to it: almost musical. 'You need rest and the wounds to your face require tending. Not by chance is this meeting between the future King of the Krêonor and his Prophetess. Come with me.'

Chapter Twenty Five

Morthrir clattered down the steps to *The Vault of Malrema* with the Royal Artisan trailing respectfully in his wake. The man was babbling about converting his sketches to a wax model and scaling it up to full size before making the mould.

'Will you be seated on a horse, Sire? That would have the dramatic effect you were describing.'

'Certainly not,' Morthrir rounded on the man. 'Didn't the Master Crafter tell you?'

'No, Sire.'

'I refuse to share my glory with a mere animal.' They were outside the Vault. 'This is why I have brought you here.' He pointed to the altar. 'I'm going to be standing on a copy of that.'

'Of course, Sire. A very suitable choice, if I may say so.'

Morthrir climbed onto the altar. 'You're the artisan. How do you suggest I stand?'

'That depends on the final effect you want to create. I understand you want the sculpture to make you look imposing, yet be approachable by the ordinary people.'

'Correct. I want to look benign, like a generous Monarch.'

'Very good, Sire,' the Royal Artisan was scribbling away with a stick of charcoal on one of his parchments.

'And wise. That's important.'

'Very good, Sire.'

'And scholarly. Give me an air of intelligence.'

'Perhaps if you held a scroll; that would help to convey what you want.' He passed Morthrir a blank rolled up parchment.

'Good idea. This hand?'

Morthrir watched as the artisan narrowed his eyes and studied him.

'No. Left hand, Sire. And up, onto the chest, as if you were casually grasping the edge of your robe. That's much better.'

'Make me look like a great Statesman, yet humble enough to win the hearts of the people.'

'In that case, I suggest the right hand down by your side and not in a big sweeping gesture like that.'

'Why? This would show I wanted to embrace all people.'

'The right hand is a symbol of power. There's a very thin dividing line between achieving what you suggest and making a threatening gesture that would frighten anyone. Understatement communicates far more powerfully.'

'Like this, then.'

'Yes. That's good. Curl your fingers into your palm, rather than straight like you're doing…a little less. You don't want a clenched fist that also threatens. Much better. Now turn your head slightly as though you were looking away from the strength of your knowledge towards the power of your right hand. Just an indication, that's all. Excellent. You look relaxed, in control, knowing that others are waiting on your every word.'

'Finally,' Morthrir held the man's eyes with his own. 'Make it so that anyone passing the sculpture cannot help a second glance, a pause as though totally arrested by what they see, and then come back to stare in awe.'

Morthrir watched as the artisan scribbled on the parchment again, and then held his position while the man made several sketches from various angles on different parchments.

'Very good, Sire.' The artisan placed blank parchments in between to stop the charcoal smudging and rolled them all up together. 'I think that's all I need from you at the present.'

'Above all,' Morthrir fixed the man with a cold stare. 'Make me great!'

Chapter Twenty Six

Lenyé stumbled through the forest, her eyes a blur of tears. That nonsense of being in another Realm; seeing people and creatures she'd never even heard of. If it was Kyros, he must have gone mad. There was no other explanation. But if he really was Kyros, how could he treat her like that? She thought he loved her. That proved to her, more than anything, it wasn't Kyros.

She had to rescue Beth. If Uncle Morthrir carried out his threat she'd never forgive herself. She couldn't just demand he hand Beth over. She needed to defeat his remaining army, and surprise him with her archers. Why couldn't the man see that?

Lenyé was now within earshot of the Nastrim company and stopped to wash her face in a little stream, hoping no one would notice she'd been crying. She had to get them going again without any time wasted on explanations. She suppressed her feelings and mastered herself for the next leg of their journey.

She emerged into the clearing to find Mamma Uza-Mâté and Ariella arguing with Chuah-te-mok. Even Ra-Na-Jiri was with them. 'What's going on?'

They all whipped round in surprise.

'There you are,' Mamma Uza-Mâté was the first to recover. 'Chuah-te-mok has some urgent news for you.'

'Really?'

Chuah-te-mok told her about the warrior army. He took off to survey the plain, only to discover a dust cloud in the distance in front of the Nastrim forces. When he flew closer, he saw a detachment of warriors rounding up several herds of wild buffalo and driving them towards the entrance of a gorge.

'Why is that so urgent?' Lenyé interrupted.

'Because the Nastrim soldiers are marching towards the other end. It's the quickest route to Terrazarema.'

'I still don't understand what all the fuss is about.'

'The rest of the warriors are circling behind them.'

'What? I thought all the warriors would be between the Nastrim and the route to Terrazarema to guard it.'

'Exactly. It appears the warriors will trap the Nastrim in the gorge and start a stampede from the other end to destroy them.'

'We must tell Captain Turvil to turn his soldiers back.'

'Even if I fly to him he wouldn't understand what I'm saying.'

Lenyé stood there glancing between the four of them, all memories of her grief over Kyros thrust aside as she wrestled with her thoughts: the desire to press on and rescue Beth kept burning in her heart, but the possibility of losing the entire main force of the Nastrim and still having Uncle Morthrir's remaining army to contend with was too awful to contemplate. If the warriors raced back to Terrazarema they could be there ahead of her, or worse, come behind and trap her archers against the city walls. Finally she blurted out, 'I'll have to go.'

Once her mind was made up, she pulled out the writing things, cut off a piece of parchment and scribbled a note:

To Captain Turvil,
Greetings from Lenyé.
The warriors are luring you into a trap in the gorge. Do not enter it. Await my arrival.

Lenyé

She rolled it up, tied it with a bit of cord and gave it to Chuah-te-mok. Then she called the various officers of the archers and soldiers to her and explained the danger to the main force.

She bundled the cobra back into the saddle bags and led the way. Ariella and Mamma Uza-Mâté ran alongside her as she cantered through the forest, with the archers and soldiers running behind.

Lenyé quickly out-paced her Nastrim company, reached an escarpment at the edge of the forest and looked down into the plains below.

'What's going on?' She pointed at the tail end of Captain Turvil's army where it was halted between two spurs of a rocky outcrop that formed a perfect funnel leading towards the gorge.

'I don't know.' Ra-Na-Jiri reared up so that his head was level with hers. 'I can't see that far?'

'There's King Ogandés and his guard. Those must be the cooks, with the female Nastrim around a number of wagons.'

'What does it mean?' Ra-Na-Jiri hissed.

'All the soldiers must be well into the gorge.'

The plain was full of hillocks: but no dust haze of the warriors Chuah-te-mok saw earlier. Clumps of tumbleweed, like great coils of stiffened whipcord bristling with razor-sharp thorns, littered the broken ground in a huge semi-circle around the opening to the gorge, with a wide gash of bare sand down the centre. The Nastrim must have marched right through it.

Lenyé waited for her archers to catch up and ordered them to descend into the plain. They were to scale the rocky outcrop on this side of the gorge and take up positions to defend Captain Turvil's army as it turned and marched out to safety. Her own soldiers she sent to reinforce King Ogandés' guard. She turned to her friends and asked Ariella and Mamma Uza-Mâté to race to the other end of the gorge and raise the alarm if the buffalo were released to stampede through. 'I'll send Chuah-te-mok to pass on messages when he gets back.'

All she needed to know now was the whereabouts of those circling warriors and work out how to get Captain Turvil's soldiers out in time.

Chapter Twenty Seven

Morthrir stared at the Apothecary as he sat at his desk in the private council chamber. He didn't like Doctor Nostrea anyway, but the man's obstinacy wasn't helping the situation.

'I cannot sign this Death Certificate, Sire.'

'Why not?'

'Medically speaking, I am not convinced the corpse is Kyros.'

'Then let us look at the circumstantial evidence,' Morthrir controlled his anger. 'Kyros was seen swimming to the island.'

'I can at least agree to that. There are plenty of warriors who witnessed his actions on the night in question.'

'My men rowed out to rescue him. They found marks on the beech to indicate someone had crawled ashore. A fire began. The warriors thought someone's sword must have struck a rock and set off the undergrowth.'

The Apothecary sighed. 'I know. I did question the warriors myself. The blaze was started by accident. It drove Kyros up the hill to a cave at the top. He tried to protect himself from the flames, but the fire was so intense he couldn't escape and was burned to death.'

'Exactly. That's what I've been saying all this time.'

'But we still have no proof it was Kyros.'

'Who else could it have been?' Morthrir fumed.

'Why was the corpse dressed in warrior's attire?'

'He overpowered a warrior, swapped clothes and tried to fool the others so he could escape.'

'Whoever the man was, his left thigh was broken and his

right arm broken in two places. He couldn't have changed clothes. There were severe fractures in the ribs of his back. The man must have fallen a long way to sustain injuries like that.'

'Maybe the flames drove Kyros into the cave and he fell down a chasm. No one really knows where that cave goes to.'

'If he did fall all that way,' the Apothecary replied, 'he must have been in absolute agony to crawl out again. There is no way he could have overpowered a fit warrior and swapped clothes.'

'He could have changed clothes before he fell. But we have to fill out the Death Certificate with someone's name on it. He was too tall for most of my warriors. It has to be Kyros.'

'The Apothecary sighed again. 'We could always fill it out as an unknown person. That is the most reasonable solution.'

'How will the rest of the Royal Family react? They need to mourn his loss properly, and you are standing in their way.'

'They would be more shocked if the real Kyros shows up!'

'He won't,' Morthrir banged the desk. 'The man's dead!'

'All these deaths are bringing you closer to the throne.'

'What are you implying?'

'The way you are pressurising me to sign makes me suspect that one more heir out of the way is to your advantage.'

'How dare you accuse me of trying to seize the throne! I am as distressed as anyone else,' Morthrir glared at the man. 'At least my brother Alkram's boys are still alive. That proves I'm trying to gather the Royal Family together for their protection.'

'I have a duty to record facts for those under my care. I've known Kyros since he was a baby. I will not do this misdeed.'

'Doctor Nostrea. The Tsé-shâmé are ready to invade. Lenyé is still missing and I am searching for her. She will be distraught if you refuse to let us give him a Royal burial.'

Morthrir picked up a quill, dipped its nib in the ink pot and thrust it into the Apothecary's hand. He slid the certificate across the desk. 'Just here,' he thumped the line with his finger. 'If you fail me in this, do not expect to see your family again!'

Chapter Twenty Eight

Beth and Quinn camped for the night in a natural dell on the far side of the woods leading towards the secret path down to the ford. They'd spent some time running and hiding and outwitting the warriors; the sounds of the bolting horse ringing in their ears till it was caught. Then the doubling back and hiding their trail and wading through streams to cover their scent. They'd found Quinn's horse and ridden through the woods for the rest of the day. Quinn was certain they'd escaped, and the warriors were still searching on the side of the woods nearest the road.

They were exhausted and ravenously hungry and eating cold meats and fruit from the provisions Rafé had given Quinn.

They discussed the events since the night on Mount Malkamet but were still no nearer deciding what power Uncle Morthrir had received; or who had taken them to the shepherd's cot. Beth was convinced it was Ishi-mi-réjá.

'But why didn't she stay?' Quinn had his mouth full of cold meat, but carried on talking anyway. 'I think it was more likely to be Rafé. He certainly seemed to be expecting me when I arrived at the castle.'

Beth was silent for a while, thinking it over.

'And another thing,' Quinn took a swig from the water-skin. 'I was watching the castle gates from the woods, and suddenly Uncle Morthrir was in a clearing a few trees away from me.'

'Don't be ridiculous, Quinn. He couldn't have appeared out of thin air.'

'He did, I tell you. He was standing on a pile of stones, and they weren't there before he arrived, either.'

'You must have been dreaming,' Beth stared at Quinn.

'When he walked off to the castle, I had a good look at them. I'm sure they were the stones of the altar from Mount Malkamet. They were blackened by fire and arranged in the same shape.'

'That's impossible.'

'The following day I saw him climb onto the pile of stones and vanish. And the stones disappeared with him. It must be something to do with the power he was seeking on Mount Malkamet.'

'What are we supposed to do about it?'

'I don't know. Maybe we should head for Terrazarema and try to stop him. I assume that's where he went.'

'I think Lenyé can do that better than we can.' She told him Paco's news about her sister's army and rumours of the special guests on the third floor. 'You were right; Rafé was lying to us before. Our parents are definitely there. We must rescue them first and then try to join up with Lenyé.'

'But we'll never get into the castle.'

'Yes we can,' and she explained about the game larder. 'We couldn't put Paco's plan into action before I was taken out to the escort. But he would still have unlocked the door, though.'

Quinn wasn't very enthusiastic, saying it was one thing to climb into the basement of the castle, but quite another to sneak up to the top floor and rescue four people with all those guards.

Beth was adamant. 'Listen, Quinn. It'll be the last thing those warriors will expect us to do, and completely throw them off our trail. We've come all this way and been through some rough times. I'm not going anywhere else till we've done it.' She glared at her cousin. 'Or, at least, tried!'

Chapter Twenty Nine

The woman took Kyros by the hand and led him out through the back of the saplings deeper into the forest.

Kyros followed without protest, so overcome was he with her beauty and sense of presence. 'Where are we going, My Lady?'

'To my humble dwelling.'

'What about my companion? He won't know where I am.'

'We shan't be long,' and she carried on leading the way.

A sense of peace and unresisting pleasure engulfed him like a heady perfume, and he surrendered himself to her guiding.

Presently they reached a dense barrier of trees and bushes. She led him towards it, but at the last minute turned to the left, and they passed through a narrow entrance that was completely hidden when viewed from the front. They entered a beautiful garden, and Kyros gasped in surprise at a charming house set back amongst well-stocked flower beds.

Kyros shook his head. 'My Lady, I have explored this forest since I was a boy, yet never have I seen this place before.'

'Welcome to the House of Consolation. Only at my bidding can anyone find it. How can I hide it from my future King?'

'You call me the future King, but my mind is full of doubt.'

'You struggle with things too great for you to resolve on your own. Come inside that I may refresh you and heal your wounds.'

She led him inside, took him to his room and fetched hot water for his bath. 'I have prepared this.' She passed him a tray with a full goblet, and a platter with a poultice laid across it. 'Drink my cordial to strengthen you,' she smiled at him. 'And apply the poultice to your face. The honey will ease the cuts and scratches and the Calendula oil will heal the bruising.'

Once he'd bathed and dried himself, he removed the poultice and glanced at his face in the mirror. He was astonished to find the puffiness round his eyes had gone and there were only a few faint scratch marks showing. As he put on the fresh clothes left out for him, he heard the clattering of pans from downstairs. When he descended he found her in the dinning area with the table laid and serving food onto two plates, the wholesome aroma making Kyros' realise how hungry he was.

She was about to sit, but he caught her by the hand and drew her towards him. 'Fair Lady,' Kyros stooped as he lifted the back of her hand to his lips. 'You have the advantage over me. Will you not tell me your name?'

'A thousand pardons, My Lord. I am Yanantha, of the line of those-who-see-the-end-from-the-beginning.'

He hesitated, recognising the name from the argument with Lenyé earlier. This woman must have counselled Lenyé to… He started awkwardly, realising he stood poised a fraction too long with her hand in his. 'So you really are a Prophetess.'

She looked at him as if divining his thoughts. 'Yes, My Lord.'

Kyros helped her be seated before taking the chair opposite.

As she passed his plate, she held his gaze momentarily. 'You are bathed and refreshed, My Lord, and your face is healing well. But I left a razor for your hair and beard, so that you may be close-cropped and clean-shaven like most Krêonor men.'

Kyros laughed. 'No soap can wash away the colour of my face and hands, so I will use it as a disguise in case I meet any more of my Uncle's warriors.'

'If I can help you decide what to do, you only have to say.'

'My Lady, please can you have my breeches washed and dried, my shirt and jerkin repaired and my boots cleaned.'

'Of course, My Lord.'

They continued talking over their food and wine. Once the

meal was finished and the shadows lengthened, Yanantha lit candles and they moved to the log fire in the sitting area.

Kyros listened to the sounds of the fire: the hissing of hot sap and the occasional crackle and burst of sparks as a log burned through and collapsed. His eyes explored the flames of the candles and watched in fascination at the slow build up of molten bees-wax as it ran down the candle stem before hardening, or dripping off a knot of wax into the bowl.

They sat and enjoyed each other's company in the stillness.

Kyros turned to Yanantha, 'Tell me, My Lady. Why do the Nastrim carry a curse in this world?'

Yanantha stirred, as if she had been locked in time, allowing the silence to fill her mind. 'Why do you ask such a question?'

'I need to fully understand the ancient legends about them.'

'They come from a union between the Dé-monos who took wives for themselves from amongst the Krêonor women. So they have inherited characteristics from both parents.'

Kyros sat thinking about his conversation with Decatur in the boat on the River Lammista-ké and the hope the Nastrim had for offspring which they could never fulfil. Lenyé said the same.

'No matter how strong the virtue of their Mothers,' Yanantha continued, as if reading his thoughts. 'It is the taint of their Fathers, the Dé-monos, that still prevails: for the Dé-monos have always taken what is not rightfully theirs.'

'What will happen if the Nastrim are despatched to their Place of Rest?'

'I am not sure. The Dé-monos brought a curse with them that poisoned the Waking World, and ignited the war between the First Peoples and left an atmosphere that continues to affect all people, even now. My belief is the passing of the Nastrim will lift this atmosphere and begin the Restoration.'

'I see. So the sooner that is done, the better for us all.'

'Correct. Why do you ask?'

'I need to focus on this before I do anything else.'

'Then I will help you all I can.'

Kyros was beginning to form a plan in his mind, and the prospect of the Prophetess' aid was very appealing. He had a sudden pang of conscience over Lenyé, but dismissed it. He'd already rejected her because she refused to use the Sword of Justice properly. In any case he felt a strong inner compulsion to seek another who could more than replace Lenyé.

He sat gazing at Yanantha's face, utterly enthralled. In the flickering light of the fire, and the more constant glow from the candles, he studied the smooth white skin and the sheen of her eyes whenever she glanced at him. She was so captivating: exuding a beauty that was more than physical, as though she reflected an agelessness he could almost feel, and the depths of her eyes hid centuries of wisdom. It was as if she had been expecting him. All he had to do was reach out to her and she would be his. But not straight away: it would be no ordinary courting. He would approach this from her point of strength, which must be, he thought, an overwhelming desire to grow in wisdom; and he knew he had something that she would find irresistible. He was prepared to wait till the time was right.

'Tell me, My Lady. What has caused this fresh Breaking-in?'

She started and looked at him in alarm. 'A fresh Breaking-in?'

'That is how I returned to the Waking World. For you must know I was chased down the Spiral by my Uncle's warriors.'

'So I guessed from the charred island and the lack of any evidence showing you to be still in this world.'

'I was forced in against my will and propelled out again by a power that flung many Dé-monos through the mouth of the cave on the island and into the Waking World.'

'I knew something had happened. I felt a release of evil three days ago, but couldn't work it out. Where did the Dé-monos go?'

'I have no idea. They were bound in chains of light by the En-luchés, but the force wrenched them from the En-luchés' guard and hurled them up through the Spiral with me slightly ahead of them. I was propelled North, but they veered off East.'

'And were they still bound?'

'No. I've seen them since and they were free of their chains.'

'Kyros. This is serious.'

'Yes, but what triggered a new Breaking-in?' Kyros persisted.

'Your Uncle is deeply involved with the Hidden Power. He…"*has met with that power and received his life back from the grave to do terrible deeds in the future*". I believe the Hidden Power is seeking to rule the entire Waking World through your Uncle.'

'Ah,' Kyros paused, deep in thought. 'Now I understand. The most terrible deed of all. My Uncle has spoken words of release by the power of Abbérron himself.'

'Please explain.'

'In the Beginning, certain Krêonor renegades sought the Hidden Power of the Lord Abbérron, who commanded them to speak and release the original Breaking-in.'

'How do you know all this?'

'I have a parchment given to me by Hoffengrégor that recounts what happened.'

'From the Ancient Prophet! Do you have it here?'

He saw the eagerness in her face and heard the expectancy in her voice. 'Yes I do.'

'Show me.'

'I think, given the late hour, we should wait till morning.'

'Of course. You need to be refreshed by a good night's sleep.' She rose covered the fire with a guard, snuffed out all but two of the candles, handed him one to light the way to his room and bade him good night. 'Until tomorrow, then.'

Kyros smiled to himself as he climbed the staircase. He was right. She had swallowed the bait completely.

PART III

THE HEXACLE

Chapter Thirty

Lenyé shaded her eyes as she sat on her horse at the top of the escarpment, by the edge of the forest, and watched a dust cloud approaching the other end of the gorge. 'That could be the buffalo,' she muttered to Ra-Na-Jiri. 'I can't tell from this distance. If only Mamma Uza-Mâté and Ariella can get there in time and send me a message.'

'Is Chuah-te-mok still in the gorge?' the cobra moved his head slightly.

'I haven't seen him come out yet.'

She tried to block out her frustration at Captain Turvil's army in the gorge and focused on the semi-circle of tumbleweed. It was several hundred yards deep, and the ground itself was dark compared to the coarse sand and sparse grass of the gash through it. So why were those huge, thorny spheres trapped amongst the hillocks? Normally they blew around on the flatter desert plains. But they were hardly moving in the breeze that stirred the rest of the grasses. That's what bothered her the most.

'You'd better duck your head, Ra-Na-Jiri. We're going down a very steep slope in a minute.' She dismounted and led her horse down the escarpment. When she reached the plain she mounted and set the horse cantering towards the entrance of the gorge.

'Hey,' Ra-Na-Jiri had his head up. 'I'm enjoying this.'

But she wasn't listening. There had to be an explanation about that tumbleweed but it didn't seem important. Lenyé dismissed it from her mind to concentrate on other things. She glanced back to see the archers and soldiers scramble down and race towards the rocky outcrop and King Ogandés. She was half way to the wagons when Chuah-te-mok soared up out of the gorge and flew towards her.

'Captain Turvil is deep in the gorge. I gave him your note.'

Lenyé glanced at the eagle. 'Maybe he doesn't understand his peril. The buffalo were being herded when I came down.'

'Not any more. The warriors released them into the gorge.'

'We must get the Nastrim out.' Lenyé saw her archers at the top of the rocky outcrop. 'Chuah-te-mok. Find those warriors.'

The eagle soared up as Lenyé galloped to the gorge.

'Get your head down, Ra-Na-Jiri. It'll be rough for a while.'

'I'm probably in the safest place riding with you.'

Lenyé smiled at him, but before she reached the Nastrim, Chuah-te-mok dropped down. 'The warriors are some way off.'

'Fly down to the other end and check on those buffalo. Tell Ariella and Mamma Uza-Mâté to get back as fast as possible.'

Lenyé reached the gorge and ordered the wagon drivers to make a semi-circle for defence around the entrance. 'You soldiers and guards line the ring on the inside.'

As she entered the gorge the situation was far worse than she feared. Wagons were everywhere, preventing the Nastrim from moving. She jumped on the back of one, yelling at the drivers, 'Turn those horses round. And the wagons.' She scrambled to the next, yelling for her message to be passed on. 'Get the wagons out and let the soldiers through!'

Chuah-te-mok dropped out of the sky with a shrill cry to hover overhead again. 'I've found more warriors.'

'Where?'

'Hidden in all that tumbleweed. Get out. It's a complete trap.'

Lenyé glanced at her archers and pointed to Chuah-te-mok. 'Show them the range.' Then she scrambled over the wagons and leapt onto her horse to find the warriors. She couldn't believe she'd missed seeing them if they were amongst the tumbleweed.

As she cleared the gorge, she was horrified to see the warriors throwing off coverings of loose grass and springing up amongst the tumbleweed and, even worse, horses scrambling up where they had lain hidden. Within a few minutes they were racing into place to form a huge horseshoe shape around the end of the gorge. There were hundreds of them. Lenyé looked back up towards her archers and indicated the warriors, then pointed up to Chuah-te-mok again.

'Get your head right down, Ra-Na-Jiri.'

She ducked instinctively as the first wave of arrows swept overhead and fell amongst the warriors: horses and riders going down in a flurry of arms and legs. But even as she looked up to check the next volley she was shocked to see warriors bursting in amongst her archers from behind and hurling them down into the gorge, while warrior longbowmen appeared on the rocky outcrops on the other side of the gorge and started bringing down her archers with their own well-timed volleys.

Then the warrior longbowmen were loosing their arrows into the gorge, even as the Nastrim soldiers were trying to turn and get out past the wagons.

The cries of the Nastrim, the shrill neighing of trapped horses and the methodical whizz of hundreds of arrows being loosed were completely drowned out by the thunder of hooves as the horseshoe of warriors outside the gorge broke into their first charge.

Chapter Thirty One

The following morning Kyros started to unroll the parchment but Yanantha stopped him and gave him a pair of linen gloves.

'Wear these, My Lord; the parchment is bound to be brittle.'

'I don't think so,' Kyros continued unrolling it on the table.

'Then he must have written it recently,' Yanantha rubbed a corner between her thumb and forefinger. 'It's practically new.'

'Hoffengrégor said it was lost to the Waking World when he fell down the Spiral. So it's at least a thousand years old.'

'But why hasn't it aged like the ones I keep?'

'You have other parchments of his? I'm sure this one was cut from a complete scroll. Look at the uneven top.'

She felt the edge. 'I know where this has come from.'

Yanantha darted out of the room and came back carrying a clay cylinder. She put on a pair of gloves, pulled the cork top off, eased out a linen roll, and laid it on the table. She opened out the cloth while Kyros placed the container on the floor out of the way and dropped the cork lid next to it.

'Look,' Yanantha partly unrolled the parchment and held the end of it flat on the table. 'Place the top of your piece against it.'

Kyros gasped. 'It's an exact fit.'

'Unless I am much mistaken,' Yanantha glanced up at Kyros. 'The knowledge contained in your parchment is critical to releasing the Lost Blade of Zerigor for its proper purpose.'

She held out her hand to him, 'May I study it for a while.'

'Of course. Let me read the one you have.'

She made room for him as he unrolled her parchment.

Kyros ensured their heads came together across the table. He slipped his hand over the back of hers, but Yanantha was so absorbed she appeared not to notice. He glanced at her. This was better than he expected: she was captivated by the document.

Then the import of what Kyros was reading gripped him and he became totally oblivious to everything else, removing his hand from Yanantha's without realising as he slid the parchment further up the table. He read the whole parchment, returning to a particular section that fired his imagination: *Then I perceived Zerigor, wearing the Krêon of Tulá-kâhju, the Crown of Life, that blazed around his head, and all the Peoples radiated light from their heads, like a circlet of fire around their brow when seen from one angle, or a flat disc of light above their heads from another: and I saw from afar the Perfection of the Peoples. For the island had no need of light by night, or even on a dull day, for the Light of Life shone about them.*

He glanced up, and met Yanantha's eyes. They both started speaking, then broke off. Kyros laughed. 'After you.'

'You're my guest, you go first; for you have descended to Realms where I am not permitted, and may have fresh insight on words that have become familiar to me over the years.'

Kyros read aloud about the Krêon of Tulá-kâhju, feeling again the excitement of his boyhood dream to find it.

'By the tone of your voice,' Yanantha smiled at him. 'I can tell these words have some special meaning for you.'

'All my life I have dreamed of recovering this Crown.'

Yanantha gasped. 'Then you are…' she hesitated.

'What is it?'

'I cannot say, for I am unsure. But to have such a dream, you must be marked out for a very special role.'

Kyros recalled the words of the True King to him, "*Even if a boy like you achieves his dream, it is only a shadow of what it could have been if he would only give his dream back to me. But you have held on to your dream, and it has become the driving force in your life. Now* that you have given it back to me, it has become my dream. Did I not say, 'You were born to be King of your people, but I will make you an even greater King.' Because you have surrendered your dream unreservedly to me, we will prevail together to fulfil it. Any dream that becomes my dream must come to pass in the Waking World".

He stopped short of mentioning this to Yanantha. Instead he carried on reading the parchment: *But alas, as I looked and beheld I observed over a period of some time that the light about their heads flickered and went out, one by one, and the blaze from the Krêon of Tulá-kâhju was diminished and there arose a terrible conflict between the Peoples. As I cried out to the True King for understanding, it was revealed to me that the Tsé-shâmé had sought after a secret knowledge to give them power to overcome Zerigor and place their own ruler in his stead. Many were cast down and breathed no more.*

Kyros banged his fist on the table. 'Why did the light of the Crown and the lights around their heads have to die?'

'Those lights are a sign of living in an unbroken relationship with the True King. The Crown itself had no light of its own; rather, it magnified the light that blazed from Zerigor's head.'

'Why do we not have any light around our heads now?'

'Because men listened to the Voices and tried to kill Zerigor,' Yanantha paused. 'That opened a way for the Dé-monos to enter the Waking World and the curse they brought and the ongoing taint in this world from the Nastrim.'

Kyros frowned, 'If they were removed from our world, would the lights come back?'

'Only if the Peoples of this world are prepared to return to an unbroken relationship with the True King.'

'In that case, the sooner we deal with the Dé-monos and Nastrim, the better.'

'That is the obvious conclusion, but we need to understand how to do it,' Yanantha gazed at Kyros. 'The key to that, I think, is in the parchment you brought back with you.'

Chapter Thirty Two

Lenyé dug her heels in and galloped across the semi-circle to the Nastrim soldiers crouched behind the wagons. 'When I drop my right hand, pull every second wagon inwards and stand in the gap with your javelin-butts jammed under one foot. Point them up at an angle. Hold your ground when they charge, and you should lift the front ranks of warriors out of their saddles.'

She cantered round the rest of the semi-circle repeating her orders, then returned to the centre and raised her hand. She made sure all the wagon-masters were watching her, while she kept an eye on the warriors and counted the timings in her head. 'Now!' she shouted, and swept her hand down.

The wagons were dragged inwards and the Nastrim soldiers filled the gaps with their javelins.

The thunder of hooves was drowned by screams and cries and the shrill neighing of horses as the charge petered out and the warriors retreated.

Lenyé ordered the wagons to be dragged back into place, then whipped round at a shout from behind.

Scores of Nastrim archers from Captain Turvil's army were pouring out of the gorge and racing towards her.

'Form a line behind the soldiers,' Lenyé shouted. 'When I drop my left hand, loose your arrows over the wagons and directly into the charging warriors.'

She took up her position again and watched the next wave of horsemen, and raised her hand in anticipation. When the warriors were practically on the wagons she dropped her hand

and felt the shrill whine of arrows whipping past her they were so close. The devastation this time was astonishing as the whole front rank, several warriors deep, collapsed almost as one, and the riders behind were left floundering. Lenyé raised and dropped her hand again and the second volley of arrows brought down many more warriors as they turned to flee.

The warrior longbowmen from the gorge trained their arrows on Lenyé's ranks, bringing down her own archers from behind.

She ducked as an arrow whistled past her ear.

'That was close,' Ra-Na-Jiri hissed. 'I felt it.'

Lenyé ignored him, her eyes searching for the next threat from the mounted warriors. They'd pulled back and circled to each side of the wagons; then she saw what she'd been dreading for some time: the dust cloud of the remaining warrior army.

She looked back to the gorge and yelled for more troops to come and defend the arc of wagons. Many had scrambled out of the gorge, and were racing towards her, but not enough.

A cry from one of the Nastrim soldiers made Lenyé turn to follow his pointing finger. The warriors bunched at either side of the wagons were racing towards each other at a converging angle to meet right in the centre of the semi-circle. As she tried to work out what they intended she heard the more distant sound of the main army sweeping towards them through the gash in the tumbleweed, the front ranks changing to a *lana din* formation: with both flanks of horsemen accelerating past the central column. As they entered the tumbleweed, an arc of longbowmen sprang up from where they had lain hidden and began loosing arrows over the wagons from their *offset-box formation*.

She faced the charging warriors but whipped round at the sudden thunder of hooves and cries from the Nastrim army in the gorge. She saw a rising pall of dust and jolted with shock in her saddle at a great bang as, presumably, the stampeding buffalo crashed into the Nastrim.

She turned at a shout from in front. The warriors hurtling in from the flanks were passing through each other's line in a spectacular display of horsemanship: a galloping rider from one side cutting across the tail of the one from the other side in such quick succession she thought they must surely collide. Each man twirled a rope above his head with a bolas attached to the end: the weights of the bolas moving so fast they were almost a blur.

As the warriors raced around the ring of defending wagons, they let fly their ropes, the bolas of several warriors wrapping around the rails of each wagon. The warriors anchored the ropes round the pommels of their saddles, and as the slack in the ropes was taken up, the wagons were yanked away, tumbling onto their sides and being dragged off.

The *lana din* formation hit the exposed Nastrim, hurling them down as warrior axes and lances cut into them. The archers behind them were mown down and the arms of the *lana din* formation swept around the King's retinue and the huddled females, and brought them down with their swords and lances.

Lenyé couldn't get the Nastrim army out any faster to counter the appalling devastation, so she galloped at the warriors using her longbow to bring down as many as possible. She refused to think about Uncle Morthrir capturing her: she would rather die in battle than suffer that. A detachment of warriors raced towards her, hemming her in with an ever-moving circle, drawing her further away from the gorge and out towards the ring of tumbleweed. She saw numerous pegs holding the tumbleweed in position and preventing it blowing away. No wonder she'd been fooled. Then she was back to loosing arrows, but various warriors kept galloping across the circle and knocking one end of her longbow askew so she couldn't aim any more. Even as she drew her sword, they would sweep past and try to knock it out of her hand with a lance: she was being deliberately excluded from the battle.

'She was startled by Ra-Na-Jiri's hiss behind her. 'Don't let them chop my head off by mistake. It's you they're after. I'm only a passenger.'

'If you're not careful,' she whispered back in a hoarse voice. 'I might just hurl you at the next warrior!'

Lenyé was startled by a roaring, bellowing, thundering sound and whipped round to see what was going on, her sword almost knocked from her hand as she lost concentration for a split second. A great surge of buffalo and smashed wood from the wagons erupted out of the gorge with Nastrim soldiers being tossed aside like rag dolls. Any Nastrim sprinting ahead of the beasts ran straight into a storm of arrows from the encircling warriors and were brought down only to be trampled under foot by the raging buffalo.

The warrior formations opened up allowing the terrified beasts to escape as they trampled their way through the gash in the tethered tumbleweed, kicking some of it free from its pegs and scattering a whole mass in a flurry of dust and sand.

Lenyé felt frozen in time as the whole rampage surged past her in an endless stream of huge black snorting faces and arching backs as the buffalo tried to jump over each other, and thick stubby legs pumping endlessly as the ever-widening sea of destruction burst out of the gorge and flowed across the plain.

Once they were past, the silence was almost deafening; and Lenyé, herded back by her ring of warriors, was able to look up the gorge at the carnage left in their wake: trampled and bloodied Nastrim bodies with arrows or axes still in them and holding them to this world. The rest of the Nastrim must have slipped through the ground where they died. The bed of the gorge was strewn with weapons and bent swords and snapped longbows and shattered wagons. A few horses were being rounded up by the warriors. Of her original army and archers and the King's retinue and all the female Nastrim, she could see for herself: not one of them was left alive.

'Ra-Na-Jiri,' she sobbed. 'What have I done?'

Chapter Thirty Three

Kyros smiled as Yanantha looked up from her studying.

'I see what you mean about the Breaking-in,' she sounded so excited. 'Listen to this about the renegade Krêonor,' and she started reading from the parchment: *'They were drawn to Mount Malkamet where they put their arts to the test, and invoked the supreme spirit of air, fire, rock and water. And so Abbérron appeared to them and they willingly bowed down before him and worshipped him... Then Abbérron commanded them to speak with one voice and release the Breaking-in.'*

She looked up at Kyros. 'So something similar has happened, and you think it was your Uncle who spoke this time.'

'It has to be.'

'What about this?' Yanantha continued: *'As they did so a huge fissure burst open at the peak of the mountain and Dé-monos from another Realm poured through...'*

'The same thing's happened again,' Kyros frowned. 'Last time the True King expelled them,' he pointed to the parchment. 'There. That bit lower down. How do we stop them this time?'

'I'm not sure.' Yanantha ran her finger down the parchment till she found the right section and started reading, *'Then the True King himself knelt before Zerigor and presented the man with his sword. 'Guard it well, for this is the Sword of Justice. By it, you must rid the Waking World of the Nastrim. For their Fathers, the Dé-monos brought with them a curse of evil, which even now pervades the very atmosphere of the Waking World and touches all things with its taint. Not till the Nastrim are fully purged from your world can this evil be lifted and joy and laughter and unity between all Peoples and creatures be restored.'* She hesitated, 'It only mentions getting rid of the Nastrim with the Sword of Justice.'

Kyros studied her face as she glanced up at him. 'Why did the True King present it to Zerigor? Surely that was a responsibility no man should bear alone.'

'Two reasons, I think. Firstly, it would prove Zerigor was worthy of ruling in the Waking World.'

'And the second,' Kyros prompted

'You cannot impose justice from outside: that would be tyranny. It must arise from within the Waking World. And you're right; it is too much for one person. I believe this will only be fulfilled in a man and a woman so joined in unity that they act as one; and justice and judgement are a natural consequence of their love and fidelity to each other.'

'The writings mention Zerigor. How is a woman involved?'

'As a Prophetess, I can see these things from afar; and the hope of that union has burned within my heart for a long time.'

Kyros lapsed into silence thinking over all that she had said.

Later, at the end of their evening meal, Kyros took her hand in his. 'Yanantha, you said, *"Not by chance is this meeting between the future King of the Krêonor and his Prophetess".'*

'Kyros!' Yanantha tried to snatch her hand away.

'You spoke of *"a man and a woman so joined in unity that they act as one"*. We are part of the unfolding of great events, and have been brought together for a reason.'

Yanantha frowned. 'What are you saying?'

He walked round the edge of the table and raised her to her feet. 'Not just a meeting, but the union of the future King and the Prophetess. For my heart also burns for the release of this *"justice".'* He went down on one knee, still holding her hand and looked into her eyes. 'I'm asking you to be my bride.'

Yanantha started in shock, 'You don't understand what you're saying.'

Kyros stood up and drew her to him, 'After the last few hours of reading together and pondering and talking, I am convinced this is right for both of us.'

She placed her other hand on his chest to push herself away. 'What about Lenyé? She loves you. I'm sure of it.'

'Not any more,' Kyros sighed, let go of Yanantha's hand and paced up and down. 'We met in the forest earlier, and argued over how to use the Sword. She recovered it, but has allied herself with the Nastrim to defeat our Uncle. I warned her of the consequences of not dealing with the Nastrim immediately, but she wouldn't listen. She stormed off saying *"We're through"*.'

'This grieves me greatly. Not just for the two of you, but also because she is appointed to use the Sword for its rightful purpose. We have to trust that she will do it in her own way.'

'Yanantha, I cannot wed a woman who has turned so far away from the path that lies before me. And the Dé-monos still have to be dealt with.'

Yanantha smiled at him, 'I believe it may well be your task.'

'That is why I turn to you,' he took her hand again. 'Together, we can know the unity you talked of and fulfil all that lies before me. Therefore I repeat my proposal. Will you be my bride?'

'I cannot answer you straight away,' Yanantha's voice quavered with emotion; 'for there is much truth in what you say. Give me three days to consider.'

'Yanantha, my desire for you is so great that I will be in anguish of heart and mind until you next speak. Let me roam the forest tomorrow and await your response in three days time.'

'Very well, My Lord. Before you go to your bed, allow me to grant you the gift of understanding and speaking to all creatures. Then I can send you messages by the birds of Sorentina if I reach a decision before then.'

Chapter Thirty Four

Lenyé was distraught. How could she rescue Beth now? The tumbleweed deception was brilliant. The Nastrim must have marched straight through without noticing. And she only saw what the warriors intended. Ariella once said: "*The paw burned in the bush fire teaches the best lesson. You'll be a more wary lioness next time*". But she hadn't learned, and this time the consequences were too awful to contemplate: not just her army wiped out, but the whole Nastrim race. She couldn't even despatch them to Elasis. She'd failed everyone. She wasn't a lioness any more!

And that niggle in her mind as she led her horse down the escarpment: she walked blindly into a trap. They must have been waiting for the right moment. Then the stunning ride to haul the wagons out of the way, and the power of that one *lana din* charge with the whole weight of an entire army behind it. And finally, the buffalo stampede: the bulk and power of those animals magnified as they thundered through the narrow gorge. Nothing else could have wiped out the Nastrim so effectively! She banged the pommel of her saddle. How could she have been so stupid?

The warriors were very courteous, from the way they guided her away from the gorge and all that destruction, to the man who darted under her guard, grabbed her horse's bridle and brought her to a standstill before gesturing towards the tent: a hastily erected affair of lances and saddle blankets knotted together.

Reluctantly she dismounted and walked towards it while a warrior held the flap back. An officer followed her and bowed. 'You are indeed an honoured guest. Make yourself comfortable,' he indicated a pile of saddle blankets, 'and have some rest. As a gesture of goodwill you may retain your weapons. We offer you hospitality for your protection. Please do not try to wander off as you may become lost in this desert.' He bowed again and left, closing the tent flap behind him.

Lenyé stood up and poked her head out of the tent, taking in the scene of activity as the warriors corralled the horses and prepared to camp. The sun was going down but she could smell wood smoke and see the flicker of several fires. More importantly, she could smell cooking and realised how hungry she was. Her horse was picketed close by. Two warriors sat on the ground a few yards away guarding her tent.

She watched as a warrior replaced the bridle and reins on her horse with a rope halter, tied the end to the peg in the ground and removed her satchel. He jumped back as Ra-Na-Jiri raised his head out of a saddle bag. She'd forgotten about the cobra.

Lenyé laughed. 'Let me do it.'

As she strode across the ground both guards rose to their feet, but she waved them away. 'I'm not trying to escape.' She lifted the saddle bags off the horse's back and hung them over her arm. The warrior nodded his thanks, draped the harness and reins around his neck, unbuckled the saddle and slung it over his shoulder. He followed her into the tent and placed the saddle and harness on a saddle blanket and passed her the satchel.

'Thank you,' Lenyé closed the tent flap after he'd gone.

She placed the saddle bags on the ground and Ra-Na-Jiri slithered out. But instead of raising his hood and looking at her, he coiled up and laid his head on the ground.

'What's the matter, Ra-Na-Jiri?' Lenyé sat on her saddle blankets and reached out her hand towards him.

'Life's not worth living any more.'

Lenyé frowned at him. 'Why ever not?'

'I've lost all my worshippers.'

'Ra-Na-Jiri. There's more to life than being worshipped.'

'No there isn't. You don't know what it was like. They bowed down before me, and there was such a release of energy and good thoughts towards me. I can never be the same again.'

'Well, I still like you.'

'That's not the same as worship,' Ra-Na-Jiri hissed.

'You're the most beautiful creature I've ever met. When I first saw you, I couldn't take my eyes off you I was so fascinated.'

'You never told me that before.'

'No. Well. I'm telling you now,' Lenyé smiled at him.

'So, I've got one worshipper at least.'

'I'm not worshipping you. You're a special friend. That's all. I...' she was startled by a voice from the front of the tent.

Lenyé pulled back the flap. Two warriors brought her food and drink. She ate her meal after they had withdrawn, tossing titbits to the cobra as they talked.

She heard the familiar cry of the eagle outside the tent. 'Chuah-te-mok. Come in.'

The eagle settled outside, but refused to enter. 'I don't like being in a cage. Talk to me out here. We need to set you free.'

'What's the point? I've lost everything.'

'No you haven't,' Lenyé was startled by Ariella's low growl. 'Quick, let us in before your guards see us,' and the great cat crawled in, closely followed by Mamma Uza-Mâté. 'We scared the horse to distract them so we could slink past.'

As Lenyé hugged them both, she caught the rumble in the she-bear's throat, 'We've got to get you out of here.'

Chapter Thirty Five

That evening Rafé sat in a chair at the Henosite's cottage, laid the pigeon pouch on the floor so the birds wouldn't suffocate and studied Eawen's face. As Rafé sniffed at the infusion of herbs in his cup and felt the rising steam clear his mind and wipe away the fatigue of his journey, the old man leaned forwards.

'Rafé. What have we done? Morthrir is uncontrollable.'

'I agree. He's turned into a monster.'

Eawen nodded. 'I cannot accept the exposing of our identities has anything to do with the Lord Abbérron. Morthrir must respect our anonymity. We're all at risk if he dislikes anyone.'

'Like me, you mean.'

'Exactly. He should never have sent you away like that.'

'I'm glad I did go. The screams of that horse were awful.'

Eawen frowned. 'The Priests prepare themselves with fasting to clear the mind. You cannot break a fast on red meat and fire-juice. We protested, but he forced us to eat and drink with him, just to show off his power. The Summoners even had red wine in their packs for the chalice, but he wasn't interested.'

Rafé was pleased with Eawen's reaction, but wasn't sure how to sound him out. He glanced around the room and noticed the bust of a man's head on the mantelshelf and asked him about it.

'That's my Father,' Eawen settled back in his chair.

'It's incredible: the face is so strong and alive.'

'We were very close. He took me walking in the mountains as a boy until I knew every inch: he was my eyes. I helped him build the altar and receive the Summoners and call the other

Priests, till the image of Abbérron appeared and commanded us to do his will and seek the "Coming One". And so we laboured together until he died. I made that bust when I was fourteen.

'But surely you couldn't see?' Rafé tried to hide his surprise.

'I learned his features though my fingertips.'

'I'm astonished you created such an expressive face.'

'Do you know why they call me the Henosite?'

'No.'

'Because I believe in "The One", and all paths lead to "Him".'

'Who is that "One"?' Rafé was intrigued.

'The Lord Abbérron, of course.'

'What about the True King?'

'I think people get confused. The True King, if he exists, has been silent for centuries. At least Abbérron appears to us and has a strategy for ruling the entire Waking World. Out of the two of them, I know that Abbérron is Supreme. He must be "The One".'

'Tell me, my friend,' Rafé studied the man's face. 'Morthrir ordered the Sergeant to bring his horse back for him. Then he appeared at the castle not long after me. How is that possible?'

Eawen put his hands behind his head, but didn't reply.

'I was really suspicious,' Rafé carried on. 'So I checked all round the castle and into the woods and found a pile of stones in a clearing. It was the altar from Mount Malkamet.'

'That is serious, Rafé. Morthrir has desecrated the only place where the Lord Abbérron appears to his servants. If he has done that, then the Lord Abbérron may never appear there again.'

'But I thought Morthrir said, "*From now on Abbérron will no longer appear to you at any Convocation. For his power has been transferred to me. As far as you are concerned, I am Abbérron. And you will do exactly as I say, or face the consequences*".'

'Yes. I heard that too.'

'Perhaps Abbérron has taken complete control of Morthrir.'

'Possibly,' Eawen placed his hands on his knees and leaned forwards. 'But that wouldn't make Morthrir behave like he is.'

'So how does he move around and take things with him?'

'It's an ancient art,' Eawen leaned back. 'This is the first time I have heard of anyone actually performing it, and I suspect it has something to do with the Dé-monos arriving after you left.'

'Who are the Dé-monos?'

'Beings from another Realm. They were expelled from the Waking World in the Beginning, but Morthrir's words on the summit brought them back. They can walk through solid objects and move rapidly from one location to another without being seen by humans. Morthrir must have harnessed their power for transporting himself and anything else he wants to move.'

'What does all this mean?' Rafé sounded puzzled.

'We have established someone with so much spiritual power that he could wipe us all out whenever he wanted to. He will only keep us alive for as long as it suits his purpose. Like his shocking treatment of you. But what can we do about it?'

Rafé stared at Eawen for a few seconds before replying. 'Join me, my friend, in bringing Morthrir down.'

'I don't know,' Eawen hesitated. 'All my life I have wandered on the Grassy Plateau, scaling those heights, and always feel the Lord Abbérron's presence there. It's his Mountain. I cannot desert him, or the company of Priests, so easily. I can help you and let you stay for the night. But I have to trust the Hidden Power to make things right in the end. I cannot join you.'

'Then I need your advice. The cobra has shown me Lenyé is marching South to attack the palace with Nastrim archers.'

'Nastrim? They're the offspring of the Dé-monos.'

'It also revealed she has a sword. It's too small for a Nastrim weapon, and the scabbard is covered with gems, so it can't be a warrior blade either. It appears to have some kind of power.'

'That might be the Sword of Justice. Some say the Nastrim seized it from Zerigor when he lay dying.'

'What is the significance of such a sword?' Rafé asked.

'Only that Sword has any kind of power over the Dé-monos,

and it may affect Morthrir in the same way.'

'I see. The only difficulty is there are two of them. Identical.'

'Then you will have to work out which one is the real Sword.'

'One final thing,' Rafé lowered his voice. 'You remember the Convocation at Druis-cyf-rin?'

'The Great Oak Tree?'

'That night Beth went into a deep trance. We were travelling together with Quinn, and were camping not far away. I'm sure she was affected by the power we released.'

'Did she recover?'

'Yes, she did. I took her to Ishi-mi-réjá.'

'Why are you telling me this?' Eawen leaned forwards.

'After Morthrir dismissed me on Mount Malkamet, I found Beth and Quinn unconscious in the place above the ravine where all that resistance was coming from.'

'Hmm. Interesting. They are still young enough to be protected by the innocence of childhood,' Eawen paused. 'Don't under-estimate that. But I have never known the power of a Grand Convocation to be resisted for so long.'

As Eawen dozed off, Rafé wrote a note to Morthrir warning about Lenyé marching with the Nastrim to attack Terrazarema; but kept quiet about the swords. He wanted to understand them more. He would also keep his vision of the golden globe to himself. Rafé eased a pigeon from the pouch, attached the cylinder to its leg and released the bird though the window.

That should disturb Morthrir and make him take some action. As long as Rafé kept feeding him enough information about situations that would keep him guessing, he thought he could still push Morthrir far enough to bring about the man's downfall. Eawen hadn't exactly agreed to help, but at least he was sympathetic, which would make his task so much easier.

Chapter Thirty Six

Lenyé sat on the saddle blankets with Ra-Na-Jiri while Ariella, Mamma Uza-Mâté and Chuah-te-mok discussed escape plans. She hardly listened as inwardly she was grieving over her ruined hopes of Kyros, and the slaughter of the Nastrim and her heartache for Beth now she could no longer rescue her sister. She felt as if she was about to burst: like a vigorously shaken flask of sparkling wine but the stopper refused to come out. Suddenly all her pent up emotions erupted. With a cry she fell face down on the sand, agonising over the identity of that man in the forest.

'Lenyé,' she felt Ariella's whiskers brush against her cheek and heard the concern in the lioness' voice. 'What's the matter?'

Her chest heaved and her whole body was convulsed in agony as she blurted out her anguish: if the man really was Kyros, then their raging words against each other and the acrimony at their parting had completely destroyed their relationship. Nothing could ever undo that hurt now.

'Surely there's room for reconciliation?' Mamma Uza-Mâté's deep voice startled Lenyé as she tried to blink away her tears.

'No,' she sobbed, still prostrate on the ground. 'He made himself very clear. He said, *"If you are adamant in retaining these creatures as your allies, then I can have nothing more to do with you, whatever has been promised between us in the past".'*

'But you're free of the Nastrim,' Mamma Uza-Mâté was quick to point out.

'No I'm not,' Lenyé looked up through her tears. 'They've only been despatched to the *Death of the Undying*. I still have a duty to release them from that and I've no idea how to do it.'

'Let's focus on one thing at a time,' Ariella growled. 'If he referred to promises you made to each other in the past, that proves it was Kyros.'

'I agree,' Mamma Uza-Mâté put an arm around Lenyé.

'I told him now I knew where he stood,' Lenyé continued, 'I considered all ties between us to be sundered.'

'If…' Mamma Uza-Mâté began, but Lenyé cut her short.

'I said, "*We're through with each other!*".'

Lenyé shivered in the sudden silence as her words sank deep into her inner being: it didn't matter who the man in the woods was; something had died in her heart concerning Kyros and it really was all over between them.

'Do you want me to fly across and reason with him?' She heard the despair in Chuah-te-mok's voice.

'That won't work,' Lenyé raised her head to look at the eagle. 'He doesn't speak the language of all creatures. He won't understand you. It would have to be me in person or not at all.'

'We'll have to free you so you can talk to him,' Mamma Uza-Mâté's voice rumbled. 'We can't leave this unresolved.'

Lenyé rounded on the she-bear. 'If you think I'm escaping just to tell that man he was right and I was wrong: forget it. I will never do that!' She sat up. 'Even if he did know about our promises, I'm still not convinced it was Kyros in the forest.'

'What makes you say that?' Mamma Uza-Mâté cocked her head on one side.

'It sounded like his voice; and he knew a lot about me. But he could have heard all that from the real Kyros. And he didn't look right with that dark skin and long hair and beard. He talked about weird places and strange people. And he had one of my Uncle's warriors with him. It couldn't have been Kyros!'

'This isn't helping,' Ariella's growl changed to a note of anger. 'There's only one way to sort this out. Where is he?'

Lenyé glanced at the lioness. 'I left him in the forest at the

Pool of Alesco.' She shrank away as Ariella growled out: "*Kyros*"; the obvious anger changing to a terrifying snarl. Lenyé panicked at the lioness' growing rage. 'What are you going to do?'

'Sometimes your friends have to act on your behalf as they think fit.' The great cat sprang through the entrance.

Lenyé thrust her head out and saw Ariella bounding away towards the forest, still growling and snarling. She glanced at Mamma Uza-Mâté. 'Follow her. Don't let her do anything hasty.'

The eagle bobbed his head, 'Lenyé. We still need to get you out of here.'

'You're right. I can't just let these warriors escort me to my Uncle. I must rescue Beth and the others!' She wiped her eyes on her sleeve and shoved the remains of the supper into her satchel. 'Is there any dry grass near the horses that would burn easily?'

'Not near the big corrals. They're well away from the camp. But there are many horses picketed amongst the remains of all that tumbleweed and loose grass. What do you intend doing?'

'I need to create a diversion.' Lenyé lowered her voice and whispered to the eagle, 'Get Ra-Na-Jiri over to the biggest corral so he can panic those horses. Then you hover over the ones in the tumbleweed and act as my spotter. Leave the rest to me.'

'You want me to carry that snake? He nearly bit me last time.'

'Please, Chuah-te-mok. You want to help, don't you?'

The sun was descending into a great layer of cloud as the eagle flew off with Ra-Na-Jiri in his talons. Lenyé shouted to her guards, 'How about some light in here. I can hardly see.'

As one of them stood up, she called after him, 'Make sure it's a couple of lanterns. Flares will set fire to my tent.'

Once the lanterns arrived, she pulled the tent flap closed.

Then she cut some strips off a saddle blanket with her dagger, tied them onto several arrow heads, opened the doors of the lanterns and trailed the fabric in the oil reservoirs. She scrabbled in the coarse sand and pulled up three or four reasonable sized stones and laid the arrows on them so that the soaked fabric wouldn't stick to any sand. She crawled to the entrance of the tent and eased the flap aside. The two guards were huddled close together talking softly.

Lenyé pulled two more arrows out of her quiver, laid one on the ground and notched the other on her bowstring. She drew back the arrow, aimed at the nearest guard and brought him down. She had the second arrow notched and brought down the other guard as he moved. Lenyé dropped her longbow, slipped out of the tent, broke off the arrow shafts, and repositioned the bodies so that they looked as though they were still on guard from a distance. Then she was back in the tent, with the flap left open, notching one of the fire arrows and searching the night sky for any trace of Chuah-te-mok.

She saw the eagle dip to the left and then straighten, giving her an idea of the range. She opened the door of one of the lanterns, dipped the oil-soaked fabric in the flame, then drew back the bowstring to take aim. She loosed the arrow and ignited the next before loosing it. She did the same for the remaining fire arrows, then clipped the quiver to her belt, slung the longbow across her shoulder and waited.

Lenyé watched the tiny flames take hold and suddenly bloom into a running fire that ignited the tinder-dry tumbleweed and swept towards the camp in a raging fire-storm. She heard the terrified screams of horses as they broke their pickets and thundered away into the night, and more distant hooves as, presumably, Ra-Na-Jiri had stirred up other horses in the corral. There were shouts and men were running, trying to recapture the horses. The whole camp was astir.

She grabbed her satchel and crept out of the tent to her own horse, gentling its muzzle as it bucked and snorted at the mass fear of the other horses. She pulled the rope tether clear of the peg and leaped on its back, using the rope instead of reins and thrusting herself further forwards than usual to ride bareback, her heart hammering wildly in case she was caught. As the horse began to canter, she slid round to the blind side using its mane and the crook of her leg over its back to cling on so that her outline was hidden by its body and a warrior would think it was only one more crazed horse running off by itself.

When she was far enough from the camp and the glare of the fires, she swung herself back to an upright position, settling her legs into the natural crease between the barrel of the horse's body and its shoulder muscles, and flexed her toes up digging her heels in once to make him gallop towards the entrance of the gorge. That was the direction they would least expect her to take: her objective was to put as much distance between herself and the warriors and find somewhere to hide before dawn.

Once in the gorge, she slowed down, picking her way through the shattered remnants of the wagons and avoiding the discarded weapons, feeling suddenly sick at the sight of so many Nastrim corpses, with arrows sticking out of them. It took longer than she expected to pass them all. Dawn was already breaking and still she was hampered by the remains of the stampede.

She pulled the horse to a halt, dismounted and knelt down by a corpse, recognising Captain Turvil. She eased the helmet off so she could look at his face one last time. 'I have failed you and your trust in me,' there were tears in her eyes. 'I should have seen it and warned you earlier.' She stood up, placed one foot on his chest and eased the arrow out of him. 'Farewell, Captain Turvil.' She watched as his body sank into the ground and disappeared. 'May you come to your place of rest after all.'

She picked up his helmet and poured some of her precious water into it, drank a little herself and then held it for the horse. She ate a few pieces of dried meat from her satchel; but had nothing for the horse. Then she tethered it to a broken javelin head, and let it forage for any tufts of grass. Lenyé found a hollow in the side of the gorge, curled up with her cloak over her and fell asleep.

Chapter Thirty Seven

Morthrir entered *The Vault of Malrema* and locked the door.

The smell of fresh paint hung in the air, but he nodded with appreciation at the Head Crafter's attention to detail. The floor designs and the moon and stars on the ceiling and walls glinted in the moonlight under the air vents, and glowed brighter near him from the light of the time-candle he held. It was very nearly the hour to begin. He strode to the altar and placed the candle at one end before walking across to close the blinds over the air vents. He savoured the rich glow of the candle in the suddenly darkened room as he made his way back to the altar, noting the lines of the Hexacle and the other points marked on the circle.

He climbed onto the altar as the metal cross-piece of the time-candle fell away: midnight. Morthrir blew out the flame. The ensuing darkness was immense, like a hole into nothing. He fumbled his way to the centre of the altar, stood up and spread his arms wide.

'Let the Hidden Power of My Lord Abbérron be manifest in me,' he paused, waiting.

A light began to take root in him and spread outwards. The black walls, ceiling and blinds remained invisible, but the lines, stars and moon began to glow and he saw them quite clearly.

He faced the Eastern mark on the Hexacle, the most potent location as it pointed directly at Mount Malkamet. 'Spirit of Air, Fire, Rock and Water, attend to me and await my commands.'

Morthrir stepped down, walked over to the Eastern point, and paced down one line of the Hexagon, muttering, 'Air feed

Fire.' He missed out the next point of the Hexagon, walking across muttering, 'Let Fire melt Iron.' He carried on to the next point on the Hexagon muttering, 'Water temper steel.' He missed out the next point and paced across muttering, 'Steel cut Wood;' and carried on pacing to the respective points: 'Wood decay into Rock; let Rock be eroded by Water; let Water float Wood; let Wood be consumed by Fire; let Fire rise and renew Air.'

Then he paced from the Eastern point around the circle, pausing at all the marks and naming each occupant in turn: 'Priest, Priest, Summoner; Priest, Priest, Priest and Summoner; Priest, Priest, Summoner; Priest, Priest, Priest and Summoner.'

Once back at the Eastern point he turned and paced along the lines of the diamond in silence, linking up to the North, then West, South and, finally, East again. He carried on towards the North and stood on the image of the Sun, spinning once in a tiny circle over the Sun's face. He carried on to the Star at the West, Moon at the South and East for the second Star, doing the same motion at each. 'Let New Life arise from the Sun, Wisdom from the Stars, and Power to do great deeds from the Moon.'

Then he walked towards the altar, climbed up so that he was standing facing East, and raised his arms.

He spoke aloud, 'Let the Hexacle of Morthrir come to life. Let wisdom come to me and words of power go forth to accomplish my purposes. Let those who acknowledge my power and obey me attend this place. I name them as the Four Summoners; the Ten Priest; Vashtani, and the other five leaders of the Dé-monos. Let the inner Hexagon be reserved for those last named.'

He flexed his knees slightly and brought his hands together. But instead of using his palms as the Priest had instructed him at Druis-cyf-rin, he touched each opposing finger tip and thumb, and felt power flowing through him for his own use.

He spoke again, with a heightened sense of conviction in his voice, 'Let all events to establish my Kingdom and my rule throughout the Waking World be subject to this Hexacle in the

Vault of Malrema and no longer at Mount Malkamet.'

Morthrir smiled to himself over the matter closest to his heart: the army had just destroyed the Nastrim and taken Lenyé. He trembled in anticipation: she was within his grasp at last. He had ordered the Commander to treat her as an honoured guest.

Then he tried to picture Beth and Quinn's faces. If only he could see them, he could locate where they were and make himself appear in front of them. Youdlh had already captured two children to take their places at the funeral, but he couldn't afford to let Beth and Quinn be seen alive anywhere. Something was protecting them. 'What is it?' he yelled to the silent room.

He thought back over the other main event: Kyros' death was received with a wave of public sorrow. People laid flowers at the archway that led to the palace, and the Square remained heavy with the scent for two days. He announced the body had already been buried, as it was so badly deteriorated, rather than be in the procession. Only members of the Royal Family, senior officials and leading citizens attended a ceremony at the grave.

The crowd lining the streets had genuine tears in their eyes: Morthrir felt quite jealous at the man's popularity.

He paused, suddenly angry. 'Let the strength of my jealousy be changed into a greater emotion to draw all people to me and make them hold me in high esteem so that they bow the knee before me and acknowledge me as their rightful leader. Let affection for Kyros diminish and be replaced by a love for me and the power I hold.'

As he spoke, Morthrir felt the power begin to rise within him.

'Let the forthcoming funeral of Beth and Quinn be the turning point in the peoples' devotion to me!'

Morthrir smiled grimly to himself. With the power he now had at his disposal, this was just the beginning.

Chapter Thirty Eight

Kyros spent a fitful night in his room at Yanantha's house and awoke late. He found his clothes and boots cleaned and mended and left out for him; but once dressed and downstairs there was no sign of Yanantha: only his breakfast laid on the table.

He ate quickly and wiled away the morning pacing up and down and fretting at the outcome. Finally he strode out of the house and walked into the forest.

How could Lenyé have strayed so far from him in her plans? The more he thought of Yanantha, the prospect of a match between himself as the future King and the Prophetess became more obvious. Maybe the True King had allowed the break with Lenyé to make him see his error and give him the opportunity to find a better partner. Perhaps this was his sixth test: to free himself from Lenyé and take Yanantha as his wife.

He tried to quieten his swirling thoughts and focus on the name of the True King again. Maybe solitude away from Yanantha's house would help. But ever since he returned to the Waking World he felt there was a barrier in communication, as though the True King was unable to speak to him any longer.

He stopped and raised both hands above his head as if in surrender. He tried forming the name in his mind to speak it out, but couldn't; his breathing became laboured and he sensed a great weight pressing down on him and trying to grind him into the dust. 'Oh, My King,' he finally cried out. 'Do not desert me in my time of need. Come to my aid that I may throw off this oppressive feeling.'

As he spoke, fresh thoughts of Lenyé arose in his mind as if to taunt him. He didn't want to hear that name any more. He only wanted clarity about his relationship with Yanantha.

Before he could try again, he heard the soft moans of a lion in the distance ahead of him, and threw himself behind a tree as the animal broke into full-scale roaring. But the roars sounded like a human voice for he could hear his own name shouted, as if the creature was singling him out. He lifted his head as the roars changed to a series of grunts before dying away completely.

Kyros squatted behind the tree puzzling over the animal's behaviour. There were no answering roars, so it was alone. Perhaps a young male, banished from its pride: except the tone of the actual roars wasn't deep enough, so it had to be a female. But why in the forest? It wasn't a lioness' normal hunting ground. Out on the grassland plains, maybe; but not here. And females were seldom alone, unless there were cubs involved; and certainly not when hunting. But how could he hear his name in the roars? That was impossible. Maybe he was mistaken.

The soft moans started again, and when she broke into the full roar, Kyros realised the lioness was much nearer now. He thumped the trunk in frustration. He had no sword to defend himself with: only his dagger. He would be ripped to shreds before he was close enough to strike at her. Should he retreat to Yanantha's house while he still had time? He would have to be quick. He didn't fancy running with a lioness in pursuit!

He retraced his steps, quickening the pace as the sound of the lioness drew nearer. But he heard her overtake him on his left flank till she was in front of him. He veered away to the right and ran faster, trying to out distance her and cut across to regain the path to Yanantha's house. Either he had taken a wrong turn or it was further off than he thought, but he couldn't find the dense barrier of trees or the concealed entrance.

His mind was still in a whirl about Yanantha and his desire for her. Was he really mistaken as to the direction of her house, or was she deliberately not allowing him to find her before she had reached her decision? Surely she couldn't be that fickle: especially now in this crisis.

Then he heard an answering roar. But not the lion he was expecting: it sounded like a bear. A huge one. It wasn't roaring so much as using the huffing growl that indicated it was on the move. Again he could distinguish words: 'Ariella. Come back.'

The lioness roared in response: 'I'm going to kill him!'

'Ariella, wait. You don't understand.'

The sound of the lioness was fast approaching, but the huffing growl of the bear was closing in quickly.

Kyros raced to his right. How could he get away from these creatures? Branches might not support a lioness, but climbing wouldn't stop a bear. If he could circle round to the Pool of Alesco and lie hidden in the water with a reed in his mouth to breathe, he might fool them. The water would cover his scent.

The lioness' roar broke out on his left again, and he swerved right winding amongst the trees, desperate to get to the special beech tree and put his plan into action. The loud roars were following him in a tight curve. But he could still hear the huffing of the bear not far behind the lioness.

Kyros burst out of the trees and sprinted across a clearing. But before he reached the other side he was suddenly aware of a large creature leaping from a branch directly in front of him.

He struck out with his arm to ward it off, but the sheer weight and impetus bowled him over onto his back. He kept his head raised, but all the wind was knocked out of him. Kyros shook his head and found himself staring straight into the eyes of a man.

Chapter Thirty Nine

Morthrir sat back in the plush seats and heaved a sigh of relief as the funeral cortège pulled through the archway and his coach was momentarily hidden from the public eye. He found it a strain having to look so mournful and acknowledge the collected grief of the crowds, when all the time he wanted to laugh. The coach in front bore the Royal youngsters so at least he had the luxury of travelling alone in this one. He smiled at the welcomed privacy. When he re-emerged through that archway he would be one more step along the way to realising his goal.

The rest of the proceedings to commit the coffins of Beth and Quinn to their graves passed in a blur as Morthrir descended from his coach and listened to words that were supposed to send a person to some kind of resting place. It was all irrelevant to him: he was going to live for a thousand years. More if he gained enough power; and retained the favour of the Lord Abbérron. At this precise point, Morthrir was more concerned about building up the power structure that was going to survive with him for that length of time.

As a mark of respect he allowed the Royal youngsters to toss their flowers onto the coffins while he waited, as the senior member of the Royal Household, to cast the first soil to indicate that Beth and Quinn had officially passed from life to death.

Then the tediously slow procession back to the Central Square, and the minor key of the military band leading them.

He sat musing on the whispered words from the Priests and Summoners since he sent them out. Things were going well, except there was no news from Vashtani. He thought of Lenyé, and his words on Mount Malkamet: *"Let her fall in love with me and willingly become my bride"*. 'May this happen soon,' he whispered to himself, gripping the window ledge in anticipation.

Morthrir descended from his coach and made his way to the dais, erected for the occasion across the access arcade that led up to the palace. It was the focal point of the Central Square. The Royal youngsters sat with other military and civil dignitaries in the tiered seats behind him. He took in the mass of black flags in every window, the black arm bands of the Guard of Honour and bandsmen and the black covering of the dais itself. Only the enormous white drape emblazoned with the Krêonor flag and covering his sculpture was at odds with the solemn atmosphere. Somehow he had to move this crowd from their grief, however genuine, into a new optimism for the future; with himself as the centre of attention.

He mounted the dais and smiled at the sudden silence as everyone focused on him. Morthrir scanned the crowd to engage individuals; but they averted their eyes if he lingered too long.

'My friends,' he began. 'This is a solemn occasion. We have only just laid Prince Kyros to rest, and now the two youngest members of the Royal Families. We are uncertain how they met their end, but an attack by wild animals appears to be the most likely cause. We are therefore consumed with grief.'

He let the tremor in his voice connect with the mood of his listeners. 'Two such promising lives snatched from us... and we must bear the grief of that tragedy for many years to come... with fortitude and the strength that comes from each one of us.'

He paused to let his words sink in and waited for the almost audible sigh of grief welling up from the packed Square.

'I appeal to you at this time,' he continued, 'to remain calm and support those of us who are left. For the whereabouts of my brothers and their wives remains a mystery and Princess Lenyé is still missing. Therefore I have taken temporary measures to govern this nation wisely and in peace.'

He lifted his hand to his mouth to cough politely, but in reality he was gaining time, using the slight delay to allow his words to register with the crowd before continuing.

'But when Lenyé is found, maybe she will take an eligible Prince and consolidate her position here at Terrazarema.'

He glanced around, letting his eyes stare into the middle distance without focusing on anyone in particular, but conveying the sense of sincerity he wanted them to go away with.

'In the meantime I pledge to guard and protect the rest of the Royal Family, and look ahead to the day when the rulership of this once great nation is fully restored. It is my firm conviction that a man will arise from amongst us to control the destiny not only of the Krêonor Nation, but also the entire Waking World.'

Morthrir heard just the right gasp of surprise that he was aiming for and the subdued whisperings that confirmed he had moved them on from their grief and they were gripped by what he was beginning to expound to them.

'He will be so anointed with spiritual power,' the murmurings were rising in volume as his own voice increased and deepened in tone, 'that he will be able to set people free to connect with that power within themselves.'

Another pause to heighten the level of expectancy.

'That they might voluntarily come under his protection to be ruled by him, so that we all might live in peace and harmony.'

There. He'd done it. The absolute hush from everyone confirmed he had them dangling on his every word.

'He will be crowned King amongst us and wed his bride on the same day.'

Morthrir beamed as the applause broke out and held up his hands to indicate he hadn't finished.

'In anticipation, I have sent invitations to the Tsé-shâmé and the Harmoth begging them to put aside past grievances, and asking them to send emissaries of peace to our city that we may be reconciled with them. Please do not treat them as enemies but welcome them as friends and extend to them all the generosity of heart and hospitality of home that you can.'

The dying applause mirrored their puzzled expressions. He had to get them through this point and push them to one last ecstatic demonstration of approval for his policy.

'We are on the brink of a new day, a new understanding between the sundered Peoples and a new form of government that will draw all Peoples together and so benefit everyone. I believe this with all my heart. And I will be working hard to begin this reconciliation and may be away from the city quite frequently. Rest assured; I will always carry you in my thoughts.'

They were quiet now, watching his every move, waiting intently for what he would say next.

'In token of this unique bond we share, I have provided a monument in commemoration of this day, uniting us as we wait for the rightful heir to appear and assume complete rulership.'

He paused, focusing his mind and controlling his energy for the final thrust of his speech.

'I call upon you all to stand together. To stand united. And above all to stand supportive of those appointed at this time to rule over you and maintain peace and order.'

He smirked inwardly as he achieved the right inflection in his voice to end with. 'My friends. I give you a tangible reminder for you to honour in this Square. I beg you to think of me with all kindness and charity of heart as I labour on your behalf.'

Morthrir raised his hand as he stepped back, accompanied by a fanfare from the military band. He dropped his hand, and the cord securing the drape over the sculpture was severed. The covering fell away, and the sculpture of himself emerged, glinting in the afternoon sunshine.

The dignitaries behind him rose to their feet clapping loudly, and the applause was taken up by several in the crowd who had been primed by Morthrir's men. The Guard of Honour saluted and cried, 'We honour you, Lord Morthrir; we honour you, Lord Morthrir;' until the cry was taken up by the crowd and people everywhere were shouting and cheering.

Morthrir let the praise and adulation and general tumult wash over him. It was a moment to savour. He sensed that most in the crowd were genuinely enthusiastic towards him; but there was still a high number, generally the older or more well off, who seemed a bit surprised and reserved. Rafé was right. It was just as well he'd kept his options open concerning his brothers and their wives. The move to Fantrios was perfect. Now he could use the "wild lions" theory and dispose of them when the time was right. And the Tsé-shâmé were no longer implicated. That was important. When the foreign delegates started arriving, he wanted them to be welcomed with open arms, not hostility.

He stepped forwards again and motioned for silence. But the crowd took it as encouragement to increase the cheering. Three times he tried before they finally quietened down.

'My friends.'

The last of the clapping and cheering died away and he had to repeat himself.

'My friends. I feel honoured and privileged to represent a people who holds me in such obvious affection. For today will go down in our history as the day when we turned mourning into rejoicing, sorrow into joy, and despair into anticipation for a better future.' He bowed and stood up again. 'I thank you.'

The people burst out in wild applause, while the military band struck up a rousing popular melody, and the crowd swarmed around the dais breaking out in singing and dancing.

Morthrir looked on, leaning over and touching the eager hands that were raised towards him, fully satisfied with his spectacular success. He had achieved what he spoke through the Hexacle, and won the hearts of his people.

Chapter Forty

'Harbona,' Kyros cried out in relief. 'What are you doing here? Quick. There's a lioness on the loose!'

Harbona pushed himself onto his hands and knees, grabbed Kyros by the front of the jerkin and stood up, hauling Kyros to his feet at the same time. 'You're not going anywhere, My Lord. Not until you've heard what I have to say.'

Kyros stood dumbfounded as he listened for the lioness' roar; the creature must be nearly on them. Harbona's huge hands still grasped him tightly by the front of his jerkin and held him only inches away from the man's face. He felt threatened by the man's physical presence: not as tall as himself, but much broader in the shoulders with arms as thick as small tree trunks. Harbona started accusing him of deserting the love of his youth because of so-called higher principles, only to take up with another woman who appeared to be more desirable.

'I followed you, My Lord. That woman has bewitched you. You are not yourself any more. You have allowed yourself to be led astray by another. And I will not stand by and let you treat your real love so badly.'

'How do you know I was in love with Lenyé?'

'From that argument back at the pool.'

'It's over between us, Harbona. You saw that!'

'You have loved her for a lot longer than that. And she, you. It was there for everyone to see when you stayed at Onadestra. I know it was many years ago, but that kind of love never dies.'

'She has betrayed me.'

'No, My Lord. You have betrayed her.'

Kyros thrust his hands up between the man's arms and broke the grip on his jerkin. How dare Harbona try and determine whom he should marry. Yanantha hadn't bewitched him; rather she had shown love and hospitality in tending the wounds to his face. If anything, he had pursued her in his desire for her beauty and the giftings of a Prophetess that she would bring to their union. He pushed the man away, 'What are you going to do about it?'

Before he had even stopped speaking, Harbona darted in again, grabbed the jerkin and yanked Kyros close to his face.

'I'm going to beat some sense into you.'

'Harbona. I took you into my service on oath to be my bodyguard, not my adviser. Let go of me.'

'Sometimes, My Lord, a bodyguard has to do what is right for his master, even if his master doesn't understand at the time.'

'Let me go!'

'I will make it easier on you, My Lord.' Harbona pushed Kyros away, released his belt, letting it fall to the ground with his sword and dagger, and started stripping off his jacket and shirt.

'What are you doing?' Kyros looked askance at the massive muscles of the man's chest and arms and the steeply sloping dorsal muscles of the back as they narrowed to the man's waist.

'I challenge you to a wrestling match.' Harbona dropped the shirt on top of his jacket. 'To bring you to your senses.'

Instantly Kyros recalled part of his conversation with Hoffengrégor about this man, "I...*watched him wrestle a huge man to the ground and practically kill him. It took five strong men to break his grip and get him off his opponent. His comrades called him the Constrictor. Ironic that I should wrestle with some stranger back there and prevail, when close behind me was this formidable man. I'd stand no chance against him*". And Hoffengrégor's reply, "*Kyros, if you prevailed at the entrance to the spiral, then you have a strength that maybe you are unaware of*".

Hoffengrégor was talking about wrestling and prevailing against the True King. What use was that now if the True King was no longer speaking into his heart and guiding him?

He was distracted by the sound of the bear's huffing grunts breaking out afresh, not far away to his right, and growing to a mighty roar. But he didn't hear any words this time: just felt the enormous animosity between the two creatures.

'Well?' Harbona's voice jerked him back to the present. 'I'm going to count to ten, then the match begins whether you're ready or not. If you try and run away, I will hunt you down and make you face me again.'

Kyros sighed. Reluctantly he unbuckled his belt and dumped it on the ground with its impotent scabbard. Then he removed his jerkin, stripped off his shirt and adopted an attacking stance: slightly stooped with feet apart, legs braced and hands up ready to grapple his opponent.

Harbona finished counting and they touched hands before springing back and circling for an opportunity.

Kyros steeled himself, the reminder from Hoffengrégor of a strength he might be unaware of encouraging him into action. He feinted to the left, and as Harbona responded to block him, he caught Harbona's free wrist and began twisting the arm up behind the man's back. But Harbona was as quick as a snake, moving round on his feet and wrenching the arm back before the lock had any effect, and then flinging his arm up and throwing Kyros off balance. Before Kyros could counter, Harbona darted in under his guard and wrapped both arms around Kyros' chest, squeezing like a vice.

'I will crush the life out of you, My Lord, unless you agree to break off with this woman and seek Lenyé.'

'Who do you think you are to tell me what to do?' Kyros pummelled Harbona's face, trying to force the man back and break the formidable grip, but Harbona thrust his face down into Kyros' throat. Kyros grabbed the man's hair to pull him off.

'No man has ever broken my hold before,' Harbona's words were punctuated with short gasps as his grip tightened. 'You have two options, My Lord.' He panted for breath, grinding the next words out. 'Agree, or be crushed.'

'I am not giving in to you. You may be right,' Kyros gulped for air as the pressure on his rib cage began to affect his breathing. 'But you are taking a huge liberty with your rank!'

'As there is no one else present to render you this service, My Lord, then I see it as my necessary duty.'

Kyros heard Harbona's voice sounding harsh and strained in his ear as the man's muscles hardened against his skin.

With a shock of fear Kyros knew why Harbona was called the Constrictor. Every time he exhaled, and before he could gulp the next breath, Harbona's grip tightened, crushing Kyros' rib cage and preventing him from taking a full breath again.

'You must change your mind, My Lord.'

'Never!'

Vaguely Kyros was aware that the accompanying roars had ceased and the forest was strangely quiet, as if waiting expectantly for something.

He struggled for several minutes, then his legs went limp and he was hanging in Harbona's grip, his head slumped to one side. He couldn't focus any more and felt himself slipping away into oblivion. In desperation he mouthed the only words that came into his mind, 'Help me, My King. How can I serve you in the Waking World if my life is snuffed out so soon?'

His mind cleared and he heard the roar of the lioness on its own, only much louder. He must be dreaming for Harbona made no response. He felt the man's grip ever-tightening it's hold. He was drifting again, seeing flashes of light as darkness descended over him. He flinched at one mighty roar right behind him, then something massive hit him in the shoulder blades and he was falling forwards and Harbona was going down under him.

Chapter Forty One

Lenyé awoke well past noon the next day. She watered the horse before setting off, and left the helmet behind. Soon she was past the debris and cantering towards the end of the gorge, an idea forming in her mind. The warriors would take some time to round up their horses and get to Terrazarema. If she arrived first, she could catch Uncle Morthrir with only a few guards in the capital, confront him with the Sword of Justice and force him to release Beth and the others. She would have to ride hard and get there before the warrior army.

The horse burst out of the gorge and she glanced up, but saw no sign of the eagle and cobra. She alternated between cantering and walking across the plain for the rest of the day, approaching the head of Lake Sanchéso as the setting sun broke out below the clouds in a ball of fire. Lenyé dozed as the thudding hooves beat a rhythm in her mind. She was dog-tired and thirsty, and thinking of the streams flowing down through the forest and into the Lake. If only she could…

Lenyé snapped wide awake feeling the horse skid to a halt, its rear hooves slithering under its body as the front legs locked. She yanked the end of the halter rope up and slid her left hand down almost to the nose strap to pull the horse's head round; but it was too late. The horse reared up thrashing its forelegs in the air. Lenyé was thrown off and landed on her back completely winded by the fall. The last thing she remembered was the shrill neighing of the horse as it galloped away, and the disturbing thought in her mind: what had terrified it so much?

Chapter Forty Two

Morthrir walked briskly across the central courtyard of the palace towards the groom holding his horse. The sun was setting and the shadows were lengthening. He thrust his foot into the stirrup, swung himself into the saddle and ordered the groom to arrange his cloak so that it fell in a neat curve from his shoulders and held in place by the final folds over the horse's rump. Then he pulled his horse round before glancing down at Youdlh.

'I should be going, Sire. To congratulate my warriors.'

'Their victory over the Nastrim was certainly a triumph of tactics and skill,' Morthrir studied the man's face for any sign of resentment before continuing. 'But Lenyé is far more important. As a gesture of reconciliation, I must personally escort her to the palace, rather than let her feel she is being brought to me as a prisoner. The army can ride back separately. I need you here to oversee security. Do not fail me in my absence.'

'Very good, Sire.'

Morthrir kicked with his heels and the horse moved forwards in a quick trot. He had to time this so that no one could see what happened next. Under the archway leading to the boulevard heading West from Terrazarema towards Lake Sanchéso was the perfect place; otherwise he would have to trot for ages before being out of the city itself and away from prying eyes.

Morthrir was considering the right approach to take with Lenyé. He needed to convince her of the great delusion she must have been under all this time, mistaking his intentions towards her. Then he would have to wean her off any interest in Kyros:

that fool of an Apothecary had very nearly thwarted Morthrir's plans with his obstinacy, but had seen reason in the end. And he would also have to keep quiet about Beth for as long as possible: Lenyé was so close to the younger girl, it might turn her against him if she found out the truth. He knew he could play his part convincingly if he was able to pick the time and place to tell her.

But more importantly he wanted to win her. That was down to chance and circumstance and the manner of their meeting: especially her first impression of him. He glanced over his shoulder at the white cloak and smiled in appreciation. His chainmail and leg armour were freshly polished.

He projected his thoughts ahead of him, seeking out an opportunity to meet her in the most propitious circumstances to arouse her feelings for him. 'Let Lenyé, myself, and those one hundred warriors all be drawn together at the same time in the same place by the will of Abbérron.' Morthrir smiled to himself. Just enough warriors to make him look powerful, but not so many as to overwhelm her.

Morthrir heard the echo of his horse's hooves under the archway and focused his mind on Lenyé. Instantly he was in the middle of a desert, conscious of the company of warriors on horseback behind him. He raised his hand to acknowledge their salute.

Perfect. That was two out of the three things he'd envisaged. Where was Lenyé to complete his request? He cocked his head to one side, listening intently to voices ahead of him. Two voices, to be precise. And he recognised Vashtani straight away before he realised who the other one was.

He thumped his fist on the pommel of his saddle in sudden fury. 'What did Vashtani think he was playing at?'

Chapter Forty Three

Lenyé shook her head, sat up, and found herself engulfed by a dark cloud. She shivered. Almost immediately the cloud dissipated and she was surrounded by a ring of beings, the like of which she'd never seen before: of man-shape and as tall as the Nastrim, but utterly black, as if all light was consumed by them. Her eyes were riveted on them and she felt they were drawing something out of her. She shivered again as though the cold had nothing to do with the cloud: it was coming from these beings.

The ring of shapes parted in front of her, and another, slightly taller being approached, clothed in light. She blinked, momentarily dazzled.

'What have we here?' the being spoke.

The voice was deep and sent a chill shiver down her spine.

Lenyé scrambled to her feet but held her ground.

The being walked all the way round her. 'A lone Krêonor woman, bearing two swords,' he continued. 'I know them by their scabbards: my son, Acwellan, bore them.'

'You must be Vashtani. And these,' Lenyé swept her hand round in a great arc to indicate the ring of beings surrounding her, 'are all Dé-monos.'

'How do you know my name?'

'Acwellan talked about you and the expected Breaking-in.'

Vashtani stepped forwards. 'How did you get those swords?'

'I slew Acwellan in battle and took them from him and despatched him to the *Death of the Undying*.'

A gasp of dismay went up from the Dé-monos.

'You've done what?' there was a shocked note in Vashtani's voice. He took another step forwards.

Lenyé whipped the Sword of Justice out of its scabbard, held it in both hands and assumed an attacking stance. 'Don't come any nearer. She whirled round to threaten the Dé-monos behind her. 'Any of you.'

'No sword of this world can harm me,' Vashtani grinned.

Lenyé was at a loss. Then Mamma Uza-Mâté's words about the Sword of Justice flashed through her mind: "*It was given to the Krêonor by the True King…It's his Sword. Don't you understand? Justice is locked up in that Sword, not for this world only. The Waking World is the proving ground of Justice for the entire Universe*".

'This Sword belongs to the True King and it has power over every being in the known Universe. I am its new keeper.'

'Come now,' Vashtani's tone was more conciliatory, but the light emanating from him began to diminish.

Intuitively, Lenyé realised it started to flicker and dim as soon as she mentioned the True King.

'You cannot threaten all of us with one Sword, whatever its claim to fame,' Vashtani continued. 'We only have to wait till you faint from hunger or exhaustion and then you'll be ours.'

Lenyé lunged at Vashtani. 'Not if I can help it!'

Vashtani stepped back and Lenyé lunged again, forcing him further back. 'So this Sword does have power over you.' She stopped, feet apart, knees slightly flexed, still in an attacking stance. 'Order the Dé-monos to stand behind you so that I can see you all.' She raised the Sword to slice at Vashtani.

He held up his hand. 'Enough.' He glanced at the rest of the Dé-monos. 'Do as she says.'

Lenyé was relieved to see them comply and kept glancing over her shoulder till the last of them was standing behind Vashtani.

'Tell me,' he continued. 'What do you know of this True King of yours? Will he come to your aid, or will he send some dashing

Prince to ride up and rescue you instead?'

'I don't need rescuing. With this Sword in my hands, it's you that needs help.' She charged at Vashtani, sweeping the Blade back and forth through the air as she went. Vashtani backed off and collided with the Dé-monos behind him in confusion.

As Lenyé forced Vashtani back the last vestige of light that flickered about him went out, as though his shape had been cut out of the atmosphere and she was left staring into a world of utter darkness. She felt her energy drain away and her mind enveloped with her feelings towards Kyros and her despair over rescuing Beth to the exclusion of everything else.

She slumped to her knees, her head drooping forwards, but had the presence of mind to slice through the air in front of her eyes. Immediately she felt something snap, as if she had cut through an actual cord that held her in thrall to Vashtani. She reeled backwards crying out in her heart for help.

As her head cleared and she stood up, Lenyé was astonished to see a man on a horse appear from behind Vashtani and the cluster of Dé-monos. The man held out his right hand, palm forwards, as though swearing an oath. Power radiated from him and swept over the Dé-monos. Vashtani whipped his head round.

The mounted figure spoke, 'Vashtani. When I send you out on an errand I expect two things. Firstly, that you accomplish that errand as swiftly as possible. And secondly, that you display loyalty to me and me alone in all stages of your conduct.'

Vashtani turned round to look at the figure and the rest of the Dé-monos moved with him. 'But I am following your orders.'

Lenyé had a complete view of the rider. His fine chainmail corselet glowed pink in the rays of the setting sun and the polished greaves on his legs and the jointed sabatons on his feet sparkled despite the fading light. His head was bare and a silver circlet gleamed against his dark hair. From his shoulders a cloak fell in a graceful sag to cover the rump of his stallion; the fabric almost a pale cream against the whiter coat of the horse: the white plume of its tail hampered by the cloth, its white mane fluttering in the light breeze; only the tip of its muzzle and the nostrils and the eyes showed black against its white coat.

But it was the darker eyes of its master that drew her gaze away from the horse, and the deeper sense of mystery hidden in them as he glanced in her direction. She saw the glint of his signet ring as he pulled the reins and deliberately made the horse rear up, its front legs perfectly controlled, while he sat astride it with resplendent ease. He was not as tall and broad shouldered as Kyros but well built all the same: lithe rather than powerful. The cloak momentarily hung free; and the whole cameo of man and horse and cloak was imprinted on her memory, as though this man was showing off his prowess to her before letting the horse drop back to its standing position and the cloak settled again in its former luxuriant sag. Kyros had never appeared to her like that, to rescue her from danger.

Lenyé couldn't take her eyes off him. She thought she'd never seen such power and majesty in a man before, and her heart went out to him in love and admiration.

His eyes moved away from her and focused back on Vashtani. 'Then why are you interfering with Princess Lenyé?' the strength in his tone jerked her back to reality.

'A thousand pardons.' Lenyé was impressed to see Vashtani bowing his knee to this man. 'I had no idea who she was.'

'Well I'm telling you.' The man lifted his hand from the reins and pointed directly at Vashtani. 'Return to your business.'

Vashtani bowed low and began backing away from the man's presence, and the Dé-monos moved with him. 'Very good, My Lord Morthrir.'

Chapter Forty Four

Kyros felt he was awake in a vivid dream: it was the day Quinn, his two sisters and their courtiers rode to the Pavilion on the shores of Lake Sanchéso without him, while he took a detour and rode his horse through the wheat fields and bridal ways to reach Lord Alkram's Estates before sundown. Lenyé, Beth and their two brothers and attendants would have left at the same time. He deliberately avoided the road in case he ran into them. Kyros wanted to speak with Uncle Alkram alone, before he and Aunt Niamh left to meet up with his own parents at the Royal Hunting Lodge. If it went according to plan, he would catch up with Lenyé and the others sometime tomorrow.

He remembered his horse being led away to the stables while he was ushered into the hallway and escorted upstairs.

Kyros paced into the room as the courtier closed the doors. He ran his hand over the padded upholstery on the back of a settee, feeling awkward. He'd been in and out of this room all his life: the family salon on the first floor at the rear of the Royal Mansion, well away from the more formal rooms downstairs. So familiar; yet he felt like a stranger. He had to ask Lenyé's Father the question that would change their lives irrevocably.

He looked around as if seeing the room for the first time. The feminine touches from Aunt Niamh in the frieze around the top of the walls and the floral designs in the tapestries and drapes: a vivaciousness of character that set the room alight amidst the lofty proportions and masculine thrust of the fireplace.

He should have asked Lenyé, to make sure, but precedent

prevailed and he needed her Father's approval first.

What if his Uncle asked him outright: 'Does she love you?' He had to go with his instinct: the gestures, the glances, the fleeting moments recently with Lenyé on her own; but somehow...

He moved beyond the settee and lifted a blue cornflower from the vase on a low table and sniffed at it appreciatively; the soothing scent immediately calming him.

He smiled as he recalled that evening up the lane not far from here leading to the main farmhouse, when he tried to pick cornflowers for Lenyé and she refused to take them. Just a simple shared memory. This was her touch; it had to be. No one else would pick cornflowers for this room.

She inherited her Mother's liveliness and enthusiasm for colour and detail and beauty. But there was also her Father's quiet strength. The two strands forming a character in her that captivated him. That's what he loved the most about her.

He dropped the flower back into the vase and paced slowly between the settee and a chair, hands clasped behind his back, reliving every memory of her. He paused to gaze out of one huge window at the lengthening shadows in the garden below, fingering the rich brocade of the drape, and looking down into the grounds as if this vantage point gave a new perspective on his life. He saw again the boyhood memory of running across the lawn chasing Lenyé and the others around the flower beds and between the trees; and being chased back to the house in return, leaping at the wisteria and scrambling out of reach of their upflung hands. Happy times: carefree times.

Beth was little more than a toddler then; now she was ten. He knew Lenyé loved him as much as he loved her. More, probably. She had such a passion. And that look in her eyes when they last met.

He turned back into the room, recalling the mid-winter party when the room was ablaze from the chandeliers and sconces around the walls: they were playing reverse hide-and-seek. He found Lenyé first, squashed between the wall and the furthest settee where it had been pulled aside to make more room for the festivities. He squeezed in behind her and felt the quiver of her back and thighs pressing into him as she tried to suppress her convulsions of laughter. That was the first time he'd ever slipped his arms around her. She hadn't resisted either; rather she eased herself into him all the more, and ran her fingers along his arm, covering the back of his hand with her own. He held her tightly to himself, not wanting the moment to end. But then Beth padded into the room, located their hiding place from Lenyé's giggling, and wormed herself on top of them.

He wanted to ask her outright on holiday at the Pavilion; but he needed his Uncle's permission first.

There was a knock at the door.

He dropped his hands, and jerked his head up feeling guilty, as though caught in the act; like the time old Travers cornered him in the orchard as he was helping Lenyé down from the apple tree: *"No doubt you be King and Queen in the making, but that don't give you no right to be stealing my apples!"*. Travers may not be too bright, but he was as sharp as a piece of broken glass that day. How many others knew they were meant for each other, and were waiting for him to make the first move?

The courtier held the doors open as the private secretary entered. Kyros turned to him in surprise. He expected the courtier to return and usher him into the library to see his Uncle.

'Lord and Lady Alkram have already departed for the Royal Hunting Lodge, My Lord; not long after Princess Lenyé and the others left. We are not expecting them back for three weeks.' The secretary hesitated. 'Perhaps your business can wait till then?'

Kyros felt the dream change as a violent wind picked him up, carried him away from his Uncle's Mansion, swept him over a dark forest and deposited him on the edge of a cliff. He teetered on the brink, the precipice falling away to dark waters that crashed against rocks, and foamed white in the dim light. Either he let the gusts hurl him over with little or no resistance, or turned and thrust through the surging wind to safety.

Two people were caught up in the wind: one he could reach out with his hand and take; the other needed hard work to meet again. But he was unable to turn. Something was missing.

He felt a name rising up within him; of someone he held dear, a name he needed in his life: a name that required a great struggle, and would cost him everything.

He tried calling the name: her name. But he'd forgotten what it was, or how it was spelled, or what it sounded like. How can you know someone if her name kept eluding you?

The struggle increased in intensity and he was swaying around on the top of the cliff, one minute leaning dangerously far out over the brink, the next almost falling back onto the grass and heathers that grew on the edge.

Then he remembered what was missing: her Father was dead. How could any vow be binding without his consent? The only solution was for someone else to speak in her Father's place: but who? Apart from her two younger brothers, the only other male in the family was Uncle Morthrir: and that was unthinkable!

How could this be resolved so she could be released to him?

He looked up as the sound of the wind abated, and the force pushing against him died down.

Suddenly he remembered her name. He struggled, hardly able to mouth it, let alone say it aloud. But when it burst out of his mouth, he was shocked to hear himself shouting, 'Yanantha!'

PART IV

THE GREATER POWER

Chapter Forty Five

Lenyé felt a chill wind blow over her as Vashtani and the Dé-monos were swept away; and she was left alone with the mounted rider. No. Not quite alone, for she saw a hundred warriors behind him, but holding back several paces.

Suddenly she grasped the meaning of Vashtani's parting words, and recognised her Uncle. She'd never considered him handsome before, but something about his bearing and the tilt of his head and the sheer thrill of charisma that exuded from him held her spellbound.

'Lenyé,' Uncle Morthrir swung his leg over the back of his horse and dismounted. 'I am so relieved to have found you.'

He paced slowly towards her, reached out both hands to clasp hers and pulled her right hand off the Sword hilt. 'Come. You're safe now. Put up your weapon, for there is no need for anger or fear between us.'

Without thinking Lenyé lifted her left hand, removed the Sword from pointing at her Uncle, and slid it into its scabbard.

'That's better,' Uncle Morthrir smiled at her, bowed slightly, raised her hand to his lips and kissed the back. 'We have been absolutely devastated at your prolonged absence from the palace, fearing the worst for your safety.'

'My safety?'

'Yes. I'm afraid there has been a terrible misunderstanding, and you've been on the run from me fearing I would harm you; but in reality, I have been seeking you to protect you.'

'Protect me? I don't understand.'

'Please. This is no place to go into details.' He let go of her hand, swung round and barked out orders to his warriors, 'Pitch a tent for me with your javelins and saddle blankets. I need to talk to my niece in private. And have food prepared; she must be starving after being out on her own in the wilds for so long.'

Lenyé found herself caught up in a dream as the warriors obeyed her Uncle's instructions, setting up a tent and preparing food and drink; the sudden reek of wood smoke in her nostrils.

They sat on saddle blankets inside the tent with the flaps tied back. Lenyé watched the activity of the warriors and sipped a small tankard of wine while her Uncle talked. The last few weeks all seemed quite vague in the light of her Uncle's friendliness towards her and his obvious desire to make up for the ordeals she'd suffered and the misapprehension she'd been under concerning his intentions towards her.

'...so you see, we were trying to find you all to protect the Royal Family.' He turned towards her as he ended his summary of recent events and looked her in the eyes.

Again she saw those dark pupils and that intriguing sense of mystery they carried, intensified even more by his proximity. He was propped up on one elbow leaning towards her; and in the close confines of the tent his charisma, his muted voice and the heady effect of the wine were overwhelming; drawing her to him, so that she was leaning in his direction, their eyes locked together. How could she have been so blind to her Uncle in the past? She felt her heart beating faster...

A slight cough at the entrance of the tent made them both start. 'Dinner is served, Sire. Will you and the Princess eat here in private or join us round the campfire? It's considerably warmer there now that the chill of evening is upon us.'

Lenyé sat on a pile of saddle blankets in a ring of warriors around one of the camp fires. The night air was filled with the hubbub of voices and raucous laughter from the other fires; but initially, the talk around theirs was subdued and the warriors kept glancing at her and then turning away to their food and drink. Uncle Morthrir sat on her right and passed more food when her plate was empty and was very attentive to re-filling her tankard with wine. He became the life and soul of the small gathering, drawing some of the warriors into conversation and recounting stories and jests that had everyone laughing, including herself. But she noticed he deliberately kept the conversation away from recent battles and armies and anything that might include her activities.

When she was ready for sleep, her Uncle escorted her to the tent, and kissed the back of her hand in parting.

'Uncle Morthrir,' Lenyé hesitated, relieved she no longer had to fight him, but still feeling guilty over Captain Turvil. 'Please send an order to your army to remove any weapons from the dead Nastrim. That will release their bodies from this world.'

'Consider it done,' his eyes met hers. 'Sleep well, Lenyé.'

He smiled at her again, that sudden flash of white teeth against the rich fullness of his mouth and the swarthy skin of his face, so dark now in the light of the nearest camp fire. She'd seen him dressed in war armour before, but never such fine chainmail. The circlet on his head glinted slightly, and the cloak, almost pure white away from his horse, hung gracefully from his shoulders and wrapped him in an air of dusky mystery.

Lenyé thought he looked more like a King already than a mere Prince and she couldn't help the slight skip in her heartbeat as she gazed at him. He'd ridden up out of nowhere, in response to her silent cry, and rescued her from Vashtani when she wasn't expecting it. The thought flashed through her mind again: no one had ever done that before, not even Kyros.

'Remember,' he continued. 'You are safe now. Nothing will get past my warriors in the night. We keep a good watch.'

'Thank you, Uncle.'

Chapter Forty Six

Kyros awoke to find shafts of sunlight filtering through a leaf canopy above him. He raised his hand to shield his eyes from the light and found the movement of his arm dislodging twigs and dry leaves in every direction.

He thrust with his other arm and both legs only to find he was lying in a depression of leaf mould, with his shirt and jerkin spread over him, and covered in dry leaves.

He hauled himself out, dusted the dirt off his bare chest and arms, ran his fingers through his hair to dislodge a few fragments, and shivered slightly in a sudden breeze. He picked up his shirt and jerkin, put them on and then spun round at a sound from behind.

There, only a few feet away, the regal eyes surveying him and the forelegs braced on the ground before her, was a lioness. In that split second he knew it was the one that chased him.

Kyros saw the lioness' eyes change to narrow slits of yellow anger as she snarled. He was momentarily distracted by the muscles in her haunches bunching for the spring as the tail lashed from side to side, stirring up the dead leaves behind her.

He flung himself sideways; scrabbled in the leaf mould depression for the belt he'd felt digging into his back and whipped the dagger out of its sheath. Even as he turned to face his adversary, the lioness was on him, pinning him to the ground by the shoulders, her mouth open and the huge fangs only inches from his face, the over-powering smell of her breath filling his nostrils.

'Tell me what you said to Lenyé,' the lioness growled. 'She was in a terrible state when I left her. I want the truth.'

Kyros blinked, more astonished that she was speaking to him and he understood every word, than fearful for his life.

'That's enough, Ariella. Let him go.'

Kyros started at the new voice and craned his neck to see past the lioness' powerful foreleg. He gasped in surprise. It was a she-bear after all; and he was right: she was massive.

'Not until I get to the truth,' Ariella growled. 'Stay out of this, Mamma Uza-Mâté!'

Kyros saw the she-bear change into a blur of fury, her huffing grunts rising to a rasping growl and then into a full roar of rage as she hurtled into the attack. She caught the lioness in the flank and her momentum flung them both over Kyros. He whipped round into a crouching position, his knees flexed and holding the dagger poised to attack. The she-bear made a wide sweep with her forepaw and hit the lioness on the shoulder sending her sprawling. The lioness backed away snarling and then ran off as the she-bear lumbered towards her.

Kyros stood up, still holding his dagger at the ready as the she-bear turned back to face him. She stopped in front of him and rose up on her haunches, her ears twitching and her nose snuffling at him, the liquid brown eyes holding his gaze. He was astonished to hear her break the awkward silence.

'You must be Prince Kyros?'

'Correct. You're Mamma Uza-Mâté, if I heard the name right.'

'Yanantha must have conferred on you the gift of understanding and speaking to all creatures.'

'Yes. To communicate with each other by birds.' He frowned. 'I didn't expect to speak to animals. Why did you save me?'

'Because I believe in the Restoration, "*when all creatures are friends again, and we live in perfect harmony with the whole of mankind*". You're a Prince of the Krêonor and the rightful heir of the Restoration. I'm not sure Ariella sees it quite like that.'

'Ariella?' Kyros relaxed and sheathed his dagger, realising the she-bear intended him no harm. 'You mean the lioness.'

'That's right. She's too passionate about protecting Lenyé to understand fully what's going on.'

'Lenyé? How is she involved with Lenyé?'

'We both are. And Chuah-te-mok, the eagle. Yanantha sent us to help Lenyé find the Sword of Zerigor.'

'And how did she do that?'

'Lenyé infiltrated the Nastrim stronghold, killed Acwellan, the Executioner, and took the Sword. The Nastrim welcomed her as some divine being to help them in their hour of need and she led them to a great victory against your Uncle's warriors.'

'And now she's marching on Terrazarema with her army of Nastrim to finish off the rest of his troops and rescue Beth and the others.' He felt the bitterness in his voice and saw the she-bear jerk her head up in response.

'Not any more.' Mamma Uza-Mâté sighed. 'The Nastrim were defeated by your Uncle's warriors. The whole race has been destroyed.' Briefly she filled him in on the march from Mount Nastâri and the trap in the gorge. 'Only Lenyé survived and now she's held prisoner. You must rescue her.'

'Wait a minute. How did I get here? I remember being chased by Ariella and hearing your grunts, then Harbona wrestled with me and practically crushed the life out of me.'

'Ariella pounced on you, but I beat her off and carried you and your clothing and belt here and covered you up to keep warm. You slept most of yesterday and all last night. I couldn't take any chances with Ariella in such a mood, so I kept guard. But she must have been watching and slipped past when I went to have a drink just now.'

'Thank you.' Kyros was distracted by a low growl from behind the special beech tree and whipped round in time to see Ariella emerge.

Mamma Uza-Mâté began her huffing grunts and rose up on

her haunches. 'If you come any closer, Ariella, I'll carry out my threat and throw you into that pool.'

'You needn't bother. I'm sorry I behaved the way I did.' The lioness stalked up to Kyros and licked at his face. 'I was so angry for Lenyé's sake!'

Kyros recoiled from the rasp of her tongue on his skin, but recovered enough to slip his arm around Ariella's neck. 'I forgive you. Can we be friends?'

'Yes. But you need to know why I was so angry.'

'Go on then,' Kyros sat on a tree stump.

'When I first met Lenyé, she confided in me of her deep love for you. She thought you were lost to her in the Spiral on the island. And she was distressed you were unable to ask her Father for her hand in marriage.'

'That also bothered me.'

'But she said to me, "*I know one thing that won't change: Kyros will never break his word to me, or me to him*".'

Kyros jumped to his feet and kicked some of the leaf mould in the depression before rounding on her. 'Why are you telling me this?'

'Because I need to get to the truth about what has passed between you since.'

'She's allied herself with the Nastrim, our ancient enemies,' he gesticulated with his arms in anger.

'We tried to warn her about them,' Mamma Uza-Mâté broke in, 'but she ignored our pleas. Isn't that right, Ariella?'

'Much as I love her,' Ariella growled, 'I cannot understand why she has become so obstinate and only prepared to do what she thinks is right. She won't listen to anyone!'

'And she's using that Sword of hers as a weapon of war,' Kyros sat down next to Ariella and faced the she-bear. 'I had a serious warning for her as well: unless she learns to use the Sword properly she will end up like Zerigor. She refused to listen to me and that's why we parted.'

Mamma Uza-Mâté stared at him for a moment. 'But surely now that the Nastrim are dead, that's all irrelevant?'

Kyros sat silent for a while recalling Decatur's words in the ferryboat across the River Lammista-ké in the Realm of the Departed: *"All weapons forged in the Waking World do not have the power to fully kill us, but despatch us...to the Death of the Undying, where we descend into forgetfulness"*.

If all the Nastrim were killed by weapons of this world, then that's where they must be.

"Acwellan...is seeking to amass all the slain Nastârs here, in the Death of the Undying, and attempt a re-entry of our Fathers into the Waking World. That will raise us from our slumber and drag us back with them".

If their Fathers, the Dé-monos, were already in the Waking World; the Nastrim could return through the Spiral at any time.

"Acwellan's plan is to form an army for one final onslaught to avenge our ancient defeat and wipe the Krêonor from the face of the Waking World and rule in their place. He, of course, will make himself King".

That would be a formidable army. He hoped Uncle Morthrir had enough warriors left to defeat them. Then another thought struck him: what if his Uncle made peace with Acwellan and used the power of their army for his own benefit. The whole Waking World would become vulnerable then.

But Decatur also said: *"There is a Place of Rest where we are entitled to go, which we call Elasis; but we can only be sent there by someone wielding the Sword of Justice"*.

Kyros assumed that still applied even if the Nastrim returned from the *Death of the Undying*. Whoever wielded the Sword of Justice held the key to ridding the Waking World of the curse from the Nastrim for ever.

'Well?' Ariella growled with impatience.

Kyros jerked out of his reverie. 'No. I don't think their defeat affects the warning. We haven't seen the last of the Nastrim yet.'

'All the more reason to come with us and rescue Lenyé,' Mamma Uza-Mâté lurched to her feet. 'The sooner, the better.'

'Whatever has been agreed between Lenyé and myself in the past, I cannot be associated with her in any way as long as she refuses to deal with the Nastrim properly rather than using them for her own ends.'

'But she's so confused,' Mamma Uza-Mâté persisted. 'She's even persuaded herself that you're not the real Kyros. She thought your voice sounded familiar, but you don't look like the Kyros she remembers, and you had one of your Uncle's warriors with you. You must come and sort things out with her.'

Ariella cocked her head on one side. 'Was that the man wrestling with you? I couldn't work it out when I attacked you.'

'Yes, it was. He said he was going to bring me to my senses so that I would return to Lenyé.'

'Are you?' Mamma Uza-Mâté intervened.

'I don't know. I don't understand why he was doing that. He's supposed to be my bodyguard not my nursemaid. I treated him more like a friend than a servant.'

'Maybe he did it out of love for you,' the she-bear's voice was soft and gentle, 'and used his influence to help you come to your senses and change your mind. Did he succeed?'

'I cannot answer that question. There is too much at stake. And I am so torn inside.' Even now his love for Yanantha was uppermost in his mind. But he couldn't tell the lioness that. She would tear him to shreds if she knew he had cast his affections elsewhere. 'I need time to piece it all together.'

'Very well,' Ariella stood up and faced Kyros. 'I've left some dead rabbits by the pool; eat and regain your strength. You have until noon tomorrow to think things over.' She glanced at Mamma Uza-Mâté and gestured with her head slightly to one side before turning back to Kyros. 'We will meet you here.'

Chapter Forty Seven

Beth and Quinn waited at the very edge of the woods, studying the curve in the wall leading to the side of the castle where Beth thought the vents for the game larder must be. They'd spent the last three days, watching and waiting, but there was such a commotion of travellers going by and warrior divisions moving about, and guards pacing the length of the wall that there was no opportunity to cross the road, even at night.

They had headed back towards the castle from their original campsite and left the horse in a small clearing just below the line where the conifers started, with a stream flowing through it and plenty of lush grass growing on the banks. The horse was tethered on a long rope so that it could move about to eat and drink. They'd stashed the saddle and harness in the hollow of a tree trunk and left some food in the saddle bags, refilled the water skins, left one in the saddle bags and took the other with enough food in the leather satchel to last them a few days.

'If we don't get in today,' Beth thumped her fist on the ground in front of her. 'We might as well give up.'

'You're right,' muttered Quinn as he shoved his arm through the strap of the satchel and squatted on his haunches. 'We're going to have to take some risks. When those carts have reached the gates and the guards are distracted, we'll slip into the crowd and get across to the wall, before the guards turn round. Ready?'

There was a sudden commotion at the gates as the first cart was halted for inspection.

'Now!' Quinn was up and leading the way into the crowd.

They wormed their way through and onto the grass verge that ran along the base of the wall, and then walked to the corner as though trying to avoid the crush of the jostling crowd. Quinn checked no one was watching and slipped round pulling Beth after him. They found the vents easily enough and Quinn climbed down first, slithered to the floor and gave Beth a foothold on the palm of his hand to follow him.

'It's so cold in here,' Beth wrapped her cloak closer.

'I know,' Quinn scanned the whole room. 'Those big hooks on the racks must be for venison, and those smaller ones for game birds. No wonder it smells in here.'

'Never mind about that,' Beth crossed the room to the door and tried the handle. 'Paco left it unlocked after all. Come on.'

She eased the door open and they both slipped through taking care to shut it tightly after them.

Quinn led the way up the stone steps and tried the door at the top. 'This one isn't locked either.' He eased the door open a crack and looked out. 'Which way did he say to get upstairs?'

'Right,' she hesitated. 'Quinn. I'm so scared. We can't possibly get that far into the castle without being spotted.'

'I know. What do you suggest?'

'Paco said left takes you to the kitchens. Why don't we see if anyone's down there and we can listen out for any activity in the rest of the castle.'

'All right,' Quinn had the door open far enough for him to wriggle through. 'Follow me.'

They slipped into the kitchens only to hear voices and footsteps approaching down the corridor they'd just used.

'Quick,' Beth pulled open a door into one of the bread larders. 'In here.'

They crouched behind a large bread rack as the voices burst out loud on the other side of the door.

'All the way up those stairs and all the way back down again,' a rather motherly woman's voice was complaining. 'And none of the food eaten. They might've told us.'

'Waste of good food, if you ask me,' a light male voice responded.

'Don't worry,' the motherly voice was taking charge. 'I'll make sure some of us benefit.'

Beth glanced at Quinn and gripped his arm as she heard the staccato click of military boots coming along the corridor outside.

'Look out,' the male voice hissed softly. 'Sounds like someone important.'

There was the creak of a door.

'Captain,' the man's voice was back to normal volume. 'We are honoured to have you here in the kitchens, Sir.'

'I see my order didn't get to you in time.'

'What order, Sir?' the woman sounded flustered.

'Not to take any more food up to the top floor.'

'No, Sir.' There was a flat note of resignation in her tone.

'Does that mean our "special guests" have gone for good, Sir?' the man sounded slightly husky.

'What "special guests"? If anyone so much as breathes a word about what has been going on for the last few weeks, with extra meals upstairs, they will be in serious trouble.'

'Yes, Sir.' The man sounded eager to please.

Beth heaved a sigh of relief as she heard the Captain's footsteps receding down the corridor, and let go of Quinn's arm. 'We've got to get out of here,' she whispered.

Chapter Forty Eight

Lenyé rode a borrowed horse in the middle of the escort with Uncle Morthrir on her right as they set out soon after dawn. She was still in shock over his news confirming her parents' deaths; but her Uncle talked and joked as he'd done around the camp fire last night, and she was drawn away from her distressed thoughts into the warmth of his presence and began to laugh with him. The brittle wall that existed between them as niece and Uncle disintegrated and she felt that, now she knew her parents really were gone, they'd viewed him in an unnecessarily bad light; and he was a far more engaging person than she had ever known before.

They rode close enough for their knees occasionally to brush against each other, and were so deep in conversation that Lenyé had to lean over to catch his words as he lowered his voice.

Uncle Morthrir's talk was all about reassuring her and her siblings and cousins, and reinforcing that his intentions towards them had been entirely for their own good.

Lenyé glanced at the escort as they rode in a protective ring about the two of them. She was desperate to know about Beth, but decided to see for herself once they were in Terrazarema. She couldn't get the horror of that night when she fled from the burning hamlet, out of her mind. 'What happened to Kyros?'

'Alas.' Her Uncle glanced away and sat more upright in his saddle, seemingly caught off guard and at a loss for words. Then he turned back to her. 'He too must have been very confused, for he tried to swim out to the little islet on the Lake.'

'He was trying to escape from your warriors. They loosed arrows at him as he dived,' the sudden intensity of the memory filled Lenyé with renewed energy. 'I saw them!'

'Lenyé, you must understand. We thought your group was a raiding band of Tsé-shâmé. That's why the warriors flushed them out with fire arrows. When a powerfully built man, like Kyros, emerged with a sword in his hand, they naturally thought he was the leader and tried to stop him. Once they realised their error they sent a boat to rescue him.'

'Then why did they burn the island?'

'Is that what you think?'

'How else could it have been reduced to a charred ruin?'

'My warriors landed on the island and called him, but there was no response. They drew their swords to cut through the brambles. A sword must have struck a rock and the sparks started a fire. The undergrowth was tinder-dry and went up in a moment. My warriors escaped to the boat and kept calling for Kyros, but he didn't appear. They circled the island for hours in case he was alive. They went back even though the ground was still hot under their boots, and scrambled up to the top of the islet and found a badly burned corpse. All the warriors were accounted for, so they assumed it was Kyros. They brought him back to Terrazarema, but it was impossible to recognise him. Not even your brothers could help, and the girls were too distraught to say anything. The corpse was the right height and build, so we had to assume...' he broke off, a slight tremor in his voice. 'We buried him with full honours in the Royal Cemetery.'

Lenyé felt something cold steal over her heart that left her struggling: not so much with what her Uncle had said, but who she'd encountered at the Pool of Alesco. If Uncle Morthrir was right, then she really had met a madman and all her anguish of thinking it was Kyros who treated her so badly was completely unfounded. That must be right; the man was only after her Sword. Isn't that what he said, *"Give me the Sword. It's time for a man to use it again properly*". He was trying to trick her into relinquishing the Sword when she needed it. She might be grieving over the loss of Kyros, but she was also very relieved. She could let go of him now, knowing that she would always cherish his memory.

Her Uncle continued talking, but she wasn't listening any more; all she felt was a lightness in her heart. She knew she would grieve in earnest later, but now...

'I'm sorry to relate such horrific news,' her Uncle's words burst in on her conscious mind again. 'I can tell by your silence how shocked you are. You were close to him, were you not?'

'Close, yes,' she turned and flashed a quick smile at him. 'I'm grateful for your concern. Kyros will not be easy to forget.'

'Indeed not. And a tragic blow to our nation for he was destined to become King. What a catch for the right woman. But we used to hear rumours in far away Onadestra about how he cast his eye at pretty girls. Whoever married him would regret it though, worrying over whether he was being faithful to her.'

Lenyé suddenly realised what her Uncle was saying and listened more intently. 'I never heard anything like that.'

'Your parents probably kept that kind of news from you.'

Lenyé was confused: in an odd way she felt glad Kyros was dead, otherwise she had no option but to think the madman in the forest was him. Not only was she grieving over his awful death but now also struggling with his integrity towards her.

'In the meantime,' her Uncle continued. 'If there is anything I can do, or you wish to unburden yourself to me further, I am at your command. I...' He let his words tail off.

As she and her Uncle sat in the tent that evening, Lenyé asked a question that had been troubling her. 'If you were trying to protect me, why did you send an army to capture me?'

'They tried to rescue you from the Nastrim,' her Uncle replied. 'We thought the giants held you as a prisoner.'

'The Nastrim were defending me against your warriors.'

'These things always get a bit distorted in the heat of battle. We couldn't work out how the Nastrim had been so successful against us.'

'I showed them how to make longbows and led them in battle. Does that change your view of me?'

'Not if you were so deluded as to my intentions. Presumably you led them against my other army.'

'That's right. The Nastrim honoured me because I had become the new keeper of the Sword of Justice.'

'Ah. The swords you wear on your back. I've been intrigued by those ever since I rescued you. Why don't you show me?'

Lenyé drew the Sword of Justice, almost against her will. She could hardly bear to let her Uncle touch it, but she held it out towards him, and flicked her wrist to present the hilt first.

Uncle Morthrir took it and stood up, twirling the Blade about his head. 'It's beautifully made and the balance is perfect.' He pulled a silk handkerchief from his pocket. 'Hold this for me.'

Lenyé stood up and held it taut between her hands and as far in front of her as possible.

Uncle Morthrir backed off, and lightly touched the top of the handkerchief with the Sword. The Blade swung shimmering in the air and sheared through the fabric. She hardly felt any pulling of the silk, the Blade was so sharp.

'An impressive weapon,' her Uncle turned the hilt towards her and handed it back. 'How did you come by it?'

'The Nastrim had it, but they recognised I was the rightful keeper.'

'And the other sword?'

'An exact copy, to confuse anyone who cannot tell them apart.'

'Let me see if I can identify the real sword.'

Lenyé unstrapped both swords, turned her back on her Uncle and switched them round several times, before twisting round and proffering both hilts.

Uncle Morthrir took one of the swords by the scabbard, gripped the hilt and pulled. 'Is this some kind of joke? Why can't I draw it?' He tossed it back to her and beckoned for the other sword and drew it with ease. 'So I could attack you with this if I wanted to,' and he lunged at her, but Lenyé drew the other Blade and parried his thrust.

'So you can draw it, but I can't.' He paused and looked at her. Then he lowered his sword. 'Let us come to an agreement. We have both lost an army each, whatever the misunderstandings involved.'

'Yes.'

'You have a sword which appears to have certain powers that only you can wield.'

'Yes...' Lenyé wondered what was coming next.

'And I have one main army left. Not that I need it any more.'

'I don't understand.'

'Did you not see how Vashtani obeyed me? The Dé-monos give me a new kind of power that no one can oppose.'

Lenyé frowned. 'What are you suggesting?'

'Let us join our two powers together and create a strong basis to rule from.'

'I don't know how to answer that. I need time to think it over.'

'Of course. In the meantime, when we get to Terrazarema I suggest you have the Sword of Justice secured in the Royal Armoury. It wouldn't do for such a powerful weapon to fall into the wrong hands.'

Chapter Forty Nine

Once Mamma Uza-Mâté and Ariella were out of sight, Kyros climbed onto the branch of the special beech tree, settled his back into the familiar curve and felt the branch begin to sway. It was such a good place to think. He began going through the incidents that had happened since Stellatus left him.

Why did Abbérron have to use Uncle Morthrir to speak the words for the Breaking-in? Surely that wasn't so different to him speaking the name of the True King in the Realm of Travail.

So a human being had to be involved in both situations.

But why him, or his Uncle? What was so unique about either of them, that another human being couldn't do exactly the same?

Yanantha said, *"Your Uncle has met with that power and received his life back from the grave to do terrible deeds in the future"*.

But the same thing happened to him. He had met with the True King and passed through the River Lammista-ké, but not to do terrible deeds. Suddenly the True King's words flooded into his mind, *"I am Luchianó-bé, Lord of Light. I entrust you to carry my name with you. You have my authority to use my name in any Realm, but especially when you return to the Waking World"*.

So why did it all seem so vague now, and why wasn't the power of the True King's name working for him as it had done in the Realm of Travail?

Kyros snapped his fingers. 'Of course!' he muttered out loud. When he spoke on behalf of the True King, the En-luchés were released to do his bidding as though the True King himself was present and had commanded it. That must be the same for Uncle

Morthrir. When he spoke, the Dé-monos were enabled to do his bidding as though Abbérron had commanded them. So neither the En-luchés nor the Dé-monos had the ability to speak that word of power: they only carried out the instructions. It had to come from a human being so submitted to either the True King or Abbérron that only the human voice could release the spirit-beings to act accordingly.

When he spoke in the name of the True King, he was working directly with Luchianó-bé to accomplish his purposes. That must be the same for his Uncle to do those terrible deeds.

When Uncle Morthrir spoke he must have released some Dé-monos to attack the Guardians of the Spiral. Were they still grappling with them or had they entered the Waking World undetected? Maybe he would never know. Uncle Morthrir's main target, though, must have been to pull Vashtani and his cohort into the Waking World. Kyros chuckled; but unwittingly, his Uncle had brought Stellatus and a few En-luchés as well.

Why couldn't Kyros make contact with them though? It didn't seem to matter what he did, or thought any more, it was almost as if there was a stone wall in the way.

Then Kyros snapped his fingers again. Uncle Morthrir must have spoken another word of power against him before he could act on behalf of the True King. No wonder his own words had no effect. If that was the case, the only way to break that power was for him to reverse it and speak against his Uncle.

But whose word would be more powerful: Uncle Morthrir's, or his? And was it due to how tightly each of them could cling on to his utter trust in either Abbérron or the True King to back up the words either man spoke?

Which was the greater achievement: defeating the Guardians and opening up the Spiral, or destroying Malvi-Quîdda and binding the Dé-monos? If the latter, why had his Uncle's word prevailed and sucked the bound Dé-monos up into the Waking World? Maybe his Uncle was more powerful after all.

With a sudden clarity of insight Kyros realised it had nothing to do with either of them, but the power each man represented. Who was more powerful out of Abbérron or Luchianó-bé?

He racked his brains to recall anything that would help him. Suddenly he remembered Hoffengrégor's parchment. When the True King flung the Dangst Rock into place, *"there he commanded the spirit of air, fire, rock and water to appear and Abbérron came trembling before him. And he called for the Dé-monos and they cowered in his presence..."*.

So the True King was infinitely more powerful. He would have to rely on the integrity of the old Prophet's writings, plus, of course, his own impression of the True King at that first encounter in the cave mouth, leading to the Spiral, and his later experiences. He was certainly convinced in his own mind.

Where should he speak these words? By confronting his Uncle in person? Or could he do it anywhere?

Clearly Uncle Morthrir had spoken before Kyros was dragged back through the Spiral, so he wasn't limited by location. But the True King originally commanded the En-luchés to bind Abbérron and the Dé-monos to the Dangst Rock, which he called the *Place-of-Chaining*. Maybe he should do it there.

Kyros cried out to the True King hoping to hear that voice for confirmation. In the ensuing silence, he whispered: 'I will hide myself in the power of your name and wait for your timing, for now I understand why I feel so far from you.' As there was no one else to consult, he decided to set off for the Dangst Rock. The sooner this was done, the better.

Kyros shivered as the dusk deepened. He kindled a fire and sat turning the rabbits Ariella had caught for him so that they roasted evenly. The lioness was right, he needed to eat now and have food to take with him. The aroma of cooking meat made his stomach rumble in anticipation. He would sleep here and wait for Ariella and Mamma-Uza-Mâté before setting off tomorrow.

Chapter Fifty

Beth shifted her foot in the confined space of the bread larder to ease the feeling of cramp, but Quinn glared at her to keep silent. It was ages before the staff finished clattering around and finally banged out through the kitchen door. But they did learn something important. The motherly woman let on that she caught Paco in one of the larders stuffing a few extra provisions into his saddle bags for a night time escort he was involved in, heading for Fantrios. Beth recalled the woman's words: "*Begged me not to tell anyone or he'd be in trouble with the Captain, and kissed me on both cheeks. That man's got such charm*". Beth smiled at her memory of Paco. That must have been why he couldn't get back to unlock her door because he was assigned to other duties.

'Let's head for Fantrios,' Quinn hissed under his breath.

'Are you sure our parents were in that escort?'

'Who else would it be at night?' Quinn stood up, 'We must get out of here,' and led the way as they retraced their steps to the game larder. Beth climbed onto Quinn's shoulders and swung herself up through the vent, and then dropped down.

'Quinn,' she whispered. 'There are four guards at the corner of the wall. We'll never get out.' She tried several times, but the guards were still there. They decided to wait for nightfall, huddling together in their cloaks on the far side of the game larder, well away from the draft of the vents.

Quinn woke with a start. 'Beth. Wake up. We must have fallen asleep. It's dawn already.'

He gave her a leg up and she climbed through the vent.

'Those soldiers have gone.' She leaned down far enough for him to catch hold of her hand and scramble up the wall, using the rough stonework for finger- and toe-holds. But as they raced across the road, someone shouted. They dived into the cover of the trees and heard footsteps running towards them.

'Head for the stream that leads down to where the horse is,' Quinn's breath was coming in short gasps as he led the mad dash through the trees. 'You follow it and get saddled up, while I act as a decoy and draw them off.' As he finished speaking they both heard the sounds of men and the baying of dogs lower down in the woods.

'The whole garrison's out looking for us, even at this early hour,' Beth panted.

'Use the stream to hide your scent,' Quinn whispered. 'And be careful you don't scare the horse. Make sure you're really calm as you get to the clearing.'

When they reached the stream Quinn gave her a big hug and whispered in her ear, 'Stick to the lower half of the woods where there are more gaps between the trees for riding. Head for the path leading down to the ford. It's the only major landmark I can think of. I'll meet you there.'

Beth followed the stream, grateful for the rising sun to give her enough light as she scrambled across the rocks, taking every opportunity to get back onto the high bank and run alongside the water course, keeping it on her right. She was well down amongst the broadleaf trees and couldn't find anything like the clearing where they'd left the horse. Maybe Quinn had picked the wrong stream in their confusion back there, trying to keep ahead of their pursuers.

She stopped at the sound of dogs below her and further to the right. They weren't that far away.

This couldn't be the right stream. How many where there in these woods? She was pretty sure their stream was immediately below the castle. That's why they both thought this was it. The baying of dogs drew closer. Beth made the decision and darted away to her left racing through the trees and undergrowth and heading generally in the direction of the path leading down to the ford. As long as she kept roughly in a straight line, she was bound to strike the next stream. She'd been running and gasping for breath for what seemed like ages when she heard the sound of flowing water.

Beth stopped when she reached the stream and scooped water into her mouth while her breathing slowed. She glanced up. Which way? The clearing she wanted was just below the line where the conifers started, so she was too far down amongst the broadleaf trees. She crossed the stream, climbed the ridge of rock and began the steep trudge up through the woods.

At last she found the clearing and breathed a sigh of relief: the horse was still there. She gentled its muzzle but had to stop it jerking its head up and neighing and giving away her position. Once the horse had settled to her presence she hauled the saddle and harness out of the hollow, but she was so worried about how close the dogs were that her fingers wouldn't do what she wanted and it took forever to fasten the straps and get the saddle bags in place. Then she swapped the halter for the harness, stowed the halter in one of the saddle bags and mounted the horse, keeping her profile low on its neck and setting the horse at a light canter along the path through the trees. She glanced over her shoulder at the sound of dogs: they were behind and slightly below her, but gaining on her as she rode.

Chapter Fifty One

Morthrir's company set off early the following day, alternatively cantering and walking their horses. Morthrir was thinking and remained silent as he rode next to Lenyé. The handkerchief test proved her Sword was a formidable weapon. But he was angry about why he couldn't pull it out of its scabbard and she could. Did she have some kind virtue that he didn't? What was special about Lenyé? She was a young woman and part of the Royal Family, but nothing that set her apart any more than himself.

He smiled at her and made polite comments whenever she said anything, but she seemed content to take in the scenery, often pointing at something and asking his opinion.

'Why her and not me?' he fumed to himself.

Did the Sword have power to undo everything he'd worked for? Morthrir didn't know. What about his suggestion of joining their powers together: his authority over Vashtani; and her Sword? He would be invincible once they were married. But she had to accept willingly. Once the Sword was in the Armoury he would have control over it, and the En-luchés couldn't seize it. But Lenyé must never take it back or break free from him.

He glanced at her, 'Race you to those rocks.' He dug his heels in and began to canter, but let her pass him. They slowed from a full gallop, laughing together in the morning sunshine. Morthrir saw the innocent pleasure on her face and smiled to himself. She didn't suspect. She didn't suspect at all.

They arrived in Terrazarema at about midday to a rapturous

welcome in the Public Square. Lenyé couldn't believe it was all for her; a lot of the honour must go to her Uncle. Maybe it was in recognition of him saving them from a Tsé-shâmé invasion after all. She was intrigued by the sculpture and complimented her Uncle on how well it captured not just his physical appearance, but also the charismatic aura that he projected.

'Thank you,' he hid his smirk. 'It's kind of you to say so.'

As soon as they were in the palace she asked her Uncle to take her to the rest of the family.

'Wouldn't you rather wash and change first?'

'No. I have to see them now.'

'Very well.' Her Uncle led the way to a salon. The guard opened both doors and Uncle Morthrir ushered her inside.

Lenyé faltered in the doorway, remembering a mid summer party a few years ago. They were all bored during a gap between the afternoon activities and the evening feast, and were chasing each other in and out of the public rooms, and Beth disappeared. Eventually Lenyé burst into this room for the tenth time not expecting to find her, and there she was kneeling in front of the fireplace, coughing. Lenyé was about to laugh at the state of her, but realised Beth was really struggling: the girl had moved the summer fire screen and had been hiding up the chimney. She was covered in soot and her clothes were ruined, and, when Beth turned towards her, all Lenyé could see were the whites of her eyes and the flash of teeth from that impudent grin showing in her blackened face. Lenyé raced her upstairs, scrubbed her hands and face and borrowed some clothes from one of the cousins before anyone else noticed.

She shook her head, suddenly aware of the silence, and saw her two brothers and cousins rise and stand rooted to the spot, staring at her. Then she darted into the room and embraced them: she couldn't believe how much taller her brother Wilf appeared since she saw him last, his solemn eyes lighting up to match the grin on his face; and Festé, the family joker, chattering eagerly; and she hadn't seen Olathe and Nasima, since she pushed them out of the burning forester's cottage when they were so terrified. She hugged and kissed them in turn but the girls clung to her, refusing to let go, and sobbing uncontrollably.

Lenyé raised her head and glanced round the room. 'Where's Beth?' She turned to confront her Uncle. 'Where is she?'

'Come with me.' Morthrir knew he had to act swiftly to keep the developing relationship with her alive. He caught her by the hand, led her away from the others and out of the room.

'What's going on?' she tried to pull free from his grip.

'I've been shielding you from the terrible news.'

'What news?'

As they reached one of the smaller reception rooms she turned on her Uncle and thumped him on the chest. 'What's going on? Your Field Commander said you'd execute her if I didn't come voluntarily. It's true after all. I saw it in my cousins' eyes. You're nothing but a murderer!' She yanked her other hand free and pummelled him on the chest. 'Tell me. I have to know.'

Morthrir opened the doors for her. 'You might want to sit down.' When she didn't respond, he paced up and down in front of her explaining how Beth and Quinn had also misunderstood his intentions and managed to get out of the palace and run off, only to be found some days later so badly mauled by wild animals that they were hardly recognisable.

Lenyé felt tears pricking at the corners of her eyes. 'Wild animals?' Then she was sobbing, 'Not my Beth.' She collapsed into an armchair, drew her legs up to her chest and rocked backwards and forwards, making a moaning sound: 'Please, no.'

'I had to identify their bodies myself,' he knelt down in front of her, eased her hand onto an arm of the chair and placed his hand over the back of hers. 'After their reaction to Kyros' blackened corpse, it would have been too distressing for the others. Do you think I don't care? She was my favourite niece.'

Lenyé winced at the reminder: Beth was everyone's favourite.

Then she focused back on her Uncle. As he turned his head away, she saw tears brimming in his eyes as well.

'So I had them buried in the Royal Cemetery.'

Lenyé was silent for a while, grieving over the news. 'What about your Field Commander?' she finally blurted out.

'He was acting without orders, trying to win you for himself. If he'd survived that battle he would have been executed!'

'Take me to the Cemetery,' she wiped her eyes roughly with her sleeve. 'I need to see for myself.'

Morthrir tightened his grip over the back of her hand. 'I know what you're going through, for I have my own sorrows.'

'How do you mean?'

He stood up and walked away from the armchair. 'My beloved Faria.' He turned and spread his hands in front of him in a gesture of despair. 'Died in a hunting accident, a month ago.'

'Uncle. I had no idea.' She stood up, slipped her arms around his neck and held him as the sobs racked his slim body. 'So many deaths in our Families. Whatever's going on?'

Morthrir felt secretly elated over their shared grief: hers genuine; his feigned. It was binding Lenyé closer to him. 'I don't know,' he exaggerated his heaving chest as he tried to control his sobbing. 'These are difficult times. That's why I wanted you all safe here. I keep your brothers and cousins at the palace, and have their whereabouts checked every hour. If they go out into the gardens, soldiers are posted to keep watch over them.'

'Thank you. I'm sorry for the way I reacted over your Commander's threat. I realise now you would never have ordered that.' Lenyé paused, 'Is Beth's death why the others were so upset?'

'Probably. I don't know how to help them grieve, but I have to protect them. They are all that's left of the Royal Family, apart from you,' he wiped his eyes on his sleeve. 'And me. I've done the best I can for them. But they especially need you, Lenyé.'

Chapter Fifty Two

The following morning Kyros glanced up at the rustle of leaves and was startled to see Harbona.

The man was wearing his belt again with his sword and dagger in place; but his shirt was undone and not tucked in and his jacket was slung over his shoulder. He looked dishevelled and his eyes betrayed his exhaustion.

Kyros rose to his feet, his hand reaching for the hilt of his dagger. But Harbona forestalled him by kneeling on the ground.

'Forgive me, My Lord. I went too far in enforcing my views concerning Princess Lenyé.'

'I think I understand why you did it, for faithful are the wounds of a friend. The lesson has been well learned, and I am in the process of considering all you said. Let us put the incident behind us, for an urgent matter has come up that I must attend to, and I will need all your help and strength. Come and have breakfast with me.'

'Thank you, My Lord.'

Kyros' mind was in turmoil over Yanantha's answer: it was now three days since he'd asked her and no sign of a response. If he couldn't find her house before, what chance did he have of seeing her again, unless she sent word to him?

He checked the position of the sun and realised it was well past noon. Ariella and Mamma Uza-Mâté had not returned. But as he scanned the sky, the small black speck that attracted his attention became an eagle circling in rapid descent. It alighted on the ground in front of him and cocked it's head on one side.

'Prince Kyros, I have a message from Ariella and Mamma Uza-Mâté. They cannot come. Lenyé is on her way to challenge your Uncle in Terrazarema alone, so they are following her.'

'Chuah-te-mok, for I assume that is who you are. I do not have an answer for them yet.'

'But will you not come and aid her, or at least make for Terrazarema and rescue her?'

'I cannot say, for there is something else I need to do first.'

'Very well, I'll tell them. But I don't trust those two. If it wasn't for their concern over Lenyé, they'd tear each other apart. If only they would follow my example and obey Yanantha's instructions to watch over Lenyé, and leave their own squabbles out of it. They wouldn't even let Ra-Na-Jiri stay with them and help.'

'Who is Ra-Na-Jiri?'

'A cobra. One of Lenyé's travelling companions.'

'I see,' Kyros paused, thinking. 'Why don't you fly this cobra of yours to Terrazarema, leave him in the palace gardens, and he can watch out for Lenyé? Then you can fly back to me with any news of her once she's arrived.'

'Of course,' the eagle prepared to take off.

'Before you go, can you take a message to Yanantha for me?'

When the eagle agreed, Kyros lowered his voice. 'Please ask her to meet me at the Dangst Rock as soon as she can.'

Chuah-te-mok bobbed his head as he repeated the message, then raised his wings and was gone, his cry lost to the wind as he climbed the thermals to give him height.

Kyros led the way running South through the trees, with Harbona keeping pace behind, in order to strike the cliffs on the shore of Lake Sanchéso and approach the Dangst Rock. They camped for the night, set off again in the morning and reached the Rock itself by mid-afternoon. Kyros hoped Yanantha would be there with her answer, and they could discuss his plan; but there was no one in sight. He wanted to do this together with her: the future King of the Krêonor and his Prophetess. Surely that would increase the power released through both of them?

He was about to leap across the short gap to the top of the Dangst Rock when a bright light burst out around him and he fell to his knees blinded. Gradually the light lessened, or maybe his eyes had grown more accustomed to it, and he could make out the features of the one who stood before him.

'Stellatus,' he cried out in joy. 'Never have I been more relieved to see you. I thought I had been cut-off from all contact with the En-luchés for some reason.' He heard the shim of steel behind him and realised Harbona had drawn his sword. 'Put up your weapon, Harbona. This is Stellatus who was instrumental in rescuing you from the Dé-monos. Surely you recognise him?'

'No, My Lord. All I see is a blinding light and feel a powerful threat against you.'

'But he is my friend.' Kyros rose to his feet and made to embrace Stellatus in greeting, but something in the En-luché's manner made him hesitate.

'Kyros,' the voice was soft, but there was a questioning note in the tone. 'Be careful how you engage with Abbérron and the humans he tries to use in their moments of weakness. What you propose to do is not a light matter.'

'I'm seeking to reverse the word my Uncle spoke against me.'

'You did well to discern that. Indeed Morthrir has spoken a word to utterly destroy you. He has set a barrier between you and the En-luchés, so that your words are ineffectual. The True King himself has intervened and sent me to strengthen you. But Morthrir also spoke a word of power to start the Breaking-in, and that is far more serious. This is your fifth test: to break the word of Morthrir and destroy his works.'

'That's what I was planning to do. I had intended to speak from the top of the Dangst Rock, until you prevented me.'

'I stopped you because you are mixing your own desires with the True King's business. You are only acting for yourself. You do not know the full picture.'

'How do you mean?'

'Morthrir also spoke a word of confusion and conflict between you and Lenyé; a removal of all power and weapons she relied on and commanded that she come to him as his bride and fall in love with him. You cannot reverse any of these words singly as they are all bound up with each other.'

'What!' Kyros turned away in anger.

'You must want to be reconciled with Lenyé to proceed.'

'I'm not sure I like what I hear.'

'This is the sixth test, Kyros: the matter of your heart's affection. To cast aside Lenyé with no regrets proves Morthrir's words against you are having a disastrous effect, and will destroy you if you continue to pursue another as you are doing.'

'That's nonsense. Lenyé is no longer fit to be my bride, and I have chosen my course accordingly.'

'Kyros. You must return to your first love.'

'Why?'

'You do not realise how far you have fallen already as a result of Morthrir's words. The name of the True King is no longer effectual in your mouth. You must know that.'

'But surely the True King cannot condone her actions either. You are the one who warned me about the keeper of Zerigor's Sword. How can you be telling me anything different now?'

'Kyros. The True King can set a test before you. But only you can choose to face it or walk away.'

'I'm not walking away. I am trying to do it as best I can.'

'If you fail here, you cannot recover what you will lose. The True King puts a high price on fidelity, not only to him but also those you love and have made promises to. I will leave you to reconsider. If you try to scale the Dangst Rock before you are ready, then I will have to stand against you.'

Chapter Fifty Three

Lenyé knelt at Beth's grave and replaced the flowers. Her cousin, Nasima, said they forgot the water last time, so she poured some from the carafe she brought. She glanced at Quinn's grave, and then Kyros' a little further on. She would attend to them later: right now she only had thoughts for Beth. Lenyé whipped round at a sudden hiss. 'Ra-Na-Jiri. How did you get here?'

'Chuah-te-mok brought me, but I wish he hadn't. That eagle squeezes so tight I feel like a string of sausages!' The cobra hissed at her again. 'We're going to rescue you.'

'I don't think so, Ra-Na-Jiri. Since I lost my army, I'm not sure I want to escape. Please leave me. I need to be alone for a while.'

Lenyé saw him slither away and tried remembering the last time she saw her sister. Not in the forester's cottage, with their dirty clothes and Beth's tangled hair. She could only drag her fingers through and ease out the knots. Beth was patient, but whimpered from the pain. She had no comb or scissors to cut off the split ends. A knife would have been even worse. No. She wanted to hold on to the fun-side of her sister, and her laughter and music and the good times they'd had together.

She picked a seeding dandelion head, its overlong stalk unable to keep up with the wild grasses and meadow flowers of this oasis of peace on the fringe of the formal palace gardens.

She blew at the perfect white globe and watched the seeds drift away. With Kyros gone she had no man to say this about, so she changed the words slightly for Beth: 'I love you,' and blew again. 'I love you not.' She hesitated, tears welling up in her eyes.

'I love you, I love you not, I love you...' She blew once more, but the last seed wouldn't come away. She blew a little harder; still the seed remained. She blew as hard as she could, but the seed refused to budge. 'The dandelion tells me I love you,' she wiped her tears away. 'So it must be true!' She recalled the shock she felt after destroying the first warrior army when all her angry thoughts towards Beth had evaporated, and wished her sister was still alive so she could tell her.

Lenyé flung the remains of the dandelion away, but whipped round as a shadow moved over her: it was Uncle Morthrir.

'Who were you talking to?'

'Oh. I was just thinking about Beth and all the things I would like to have said to her.'

'Such as?'

'Uncle Morthrir. There are some things which pass between sisters that should remain private.'

'Of course.' He paused, smiling at her. 'Don't you think it's time to drop the "Uncle" bit?'

She looked up at him. 'But I've always called you "Uncle".'

He reached down and pulled her to her feet, his hand lingering on hers. 'That was as a child growing up. But you are not a child any more. You're a beautiful young woman.'

'What are you saying?'

'That it's time we treated each other as adults.'

Lenyé glanced at the swaying grass heads between them. She'd been sorrowing over Beth, but what of his sorrow? When she thought of Aunt Faria, there was always that warm smile. Especially when she and Kyros stayed for an extra week after the others went home. But behind the eyes there was a deep sense of loss: Aunt Faria must have secretly grieved over not having any children. Maybe her Uncle felt the same and she'd never noticed. With Aunt Faria gone, he had no one to remember her by.

'Unc...' she began. 'I mean, Morthrir,' the name without the title sounded so strange to her. She gripped his hand. 'Have you ever...' she hesitated. 'Did you ever want to have children?'

'My greatest wish is for a son to continue my family's name. But what's the use? Faria and I were unable to have a child.'

'But you're still young. Now that she's gone...' Lenyé left her words unfinished.

'You mean?' it was his turn to grip her hand tighter.

'I always thought you intended harm to my family. But now I see it was not so; that you really wanted the best for us.'

'And that means?'

'When you rescued me from Vashtani, something sparked in me towards you that I cannot explain.' She saw her Uncle's eyes narrow in surprise. 'That something has since fanned into flame.'

'Are you suggesting you are prepared to be mine?'

'I don't know. Maybe you need to ask me.'

'Very well.' Her Uncle knelt and raised the back of her hand to his lips before looking up. 'Lenyé. I have always thought you were beautiful. But your family was too far removed from me to ever express my feelings. Not just the physical distance, but... As if I never really belonged. I'm not sure I had the courage to voice those thoughts even to myself. I am the youngest brother, banished to a faraway castle. That's all I deserve in life.'

'But surely that has changed. If Kyros is dead and our parents as well, then you are next in line after my two brothers.'

'Thank you for stating the position so clearly. I will do what I can for your brothers. But since you have encouraged me, I will declare myself. I have been deeply in love with you for some time. I hid it for Faria's sake. But now that she's gone, I cannot remain silent. Will you take me as your own and be my bride?'

'This is all so sudden.' She thrust aside her feelings for Kyros: if only he was still alive! 'I have my own grief to bear.' Lenyé glanced at him. 'Morthrir, I cannot get you out of my mind...' she faltered. 'Or my heart. Grant me a few days to consider.'

'I would wait a thousand years for your answer.' He stood up and drew her towards him. 'Your *few days* is music to my ears.'

Chapter Fifty Four

Quinn stopped and listened to the din of pursuit in the woods: his chest heaving and his mouth parched. He sank onto a rock, pulled out his water-skin and gulped a mouthful. Then he was up, thrusting it back in the satchel and racing across the woods as the sounds closed in behind him.

He stumbled on another stream and followed it downwards till he was in amongst the broadleaf trees, but halted as he glimpsed movements below. He parted the leaves to see Beth fitting the harness to the horse before mounting and riding off. What was going on? Then he smacked himself on the forehead in frustration. He must have told her the wrong stream and now she had only just recovered the horse. Should he stay and help? No. He had to lead the pursuit away from her.

He raced off climbing up into the woods as far as the line of conifers before an awful thought struck him. There were warriors and dogs below her as well. He could tell by the sound of their approach that the dogs were still running to leash. Once they got a good scent, their handlers would let them loose and they would catch a horse in the woods quite easily.

Quinn veered round and down and made for where he thought Beth's trail would lead her. He caught a glimpse of the horse's rump and tail through the trees and realised she wasn't making as fast progress as he'd hoped. He crossed and re-crossed her tracks several times, before running alongside her trail. Then he turned off, almost at right angles, and headed down hill deeper amongst the broadleaf trees. He ran along hard-packed animal paths, skipping over exposed roots and avoiding every dead twig, the patches of sunlight filtering through the foliage alternately lighting the path and then throwing it into deep shade. He had to draw their pursuers away from Beth's tracks.

He went to ground, hiding amongst a tangle of shrubs. What was it Lenyé taught him? *"Cover your nose and mouth to break up the sound of your breathing"*. Where was Lenyé now? And how reliable was the news of her great company of soldiers? And Kyros? Had he escaped? Quinn had been so focused on finding their parents that he'd forgotten about his older brother. If only Kyros was here he'd know what to do. How he missed his brother's strength and leadership. Maybe Kyros would join Lenyé, march on Terrazarema and rescue them all. But where did Lenyé find these soldiers? It couldn't be the Royal Garrison: they would be no match for his Uncle's warriors.

Quinn was startled by the sound of pursuit from below. They hadn't found his false trail after all. He stumbled out of his hiding place making as much noise as possible to attract their attention. Then he raced off up the hill, crashing in amongst a thick, pathless section of conifers, thrusting aside the lower branches with his hands, his feet stumbling now and then on a sudden dip or a rotten stump hidden in the soft litter of dead pine needles, until he struck another stream. He jumped in the water and waded up hill before climbing out on the further side and started running straight across the woods before dropping down again.

That should give the dogs something to follow and confuse them far enough away from Beth to stop them finding her scent.

But all this running up hill had exhausted him. He squatted down and leaned forwards on his hands and knees gasping for breath and listening for the sound of pursuit. But the woods seemed strangely quiet. What was going on?

He carried on in a big arc up through the pine woods, but

already the day was wearing on and dusk was beginning to settle. He was in despair. Not another night in these woods! But he was some way from the path to the ford and he still had to find Beth. He headed down to the broadleaf woods and found a stream flowing past a huge tree. He back-tracked upstream and jumped in, wading down till he could scramble into the lower branches and find a nook to hide in for the night. At least the dogs wouldn't be able to trace his scent. He hoped Beth and the horse would be safe till morning. Water had soaked through his boots and his feet and lower legs were wet. He felt the cold creeping up his legs as he drifted off to sleep.

Quinn woke to a terrific baying of dogs above and behind him and knew they'd picked up his scent this side of the stream. He slithered down from his tree and started running. How far away was the path down to the ford? He had to put a serious stretch of water between himself and the pursuers. If only Beth had made it and was easy to find.

He broke out of cover to find he was on the right path; he recognised those twists leading up to the Grassy Plateau. But he was too high. He darted back in amongst the trees and half ran, half galloped down the slope, one foot landing in front of the other, gaining momentum till he was racing down hill.

Then he was in amongst the broadleaf trees, zigzagging in the welcome space and shallower slope, slowing himself down till he could grasp a slender trunk and stop completely.

Despite the running he was intensely aware of the coldness in his feet and ankles and found he was beginning to shiver.

He whipped round as he registered a sudden movement amongst the trees immediately to his right, and saw the outline of a horse's head. 'Beth,' he panted. 'Is that you?'

Chapter Fifty Five

Kyros sent Harbona to find a camp while he sat where Stellatus had stood and decided what to do.

He cried out again for help to throw off the oppressive feeling but had to accept the True King had spoken: firstly about Lenyé through Harbona, Ariella and Mamma Uza-Mâté, then that clarity of insight when he reasoned out what Uncle Morthrir had done, and finally through Stellatus putting it all together: once about the words of power, but three times about Lenyé.

What about Lenyé being allied to the Nastrim and using the Sword for the wrong reasons. Surely the True King would reject her for that? Maybe Stellatus was right: he had to do this in response to the True King, rather than use his own judgement.

'Very well. I will do it!' But he felt less than enthusiastic.

Kyros stood up and faced the Dangst Rock. He was about to leap across the gap but whirled round at footsteps behind him.

'Yanantha,' he gasped. Her beauty shone in the late afternoon sun like a veil around her, luring him away from the Rock.

'Chuah-te-mok, the eagle, brought your message, instead of a bird of Sorentina. I assumed it was urgent, so I came at once.'

'Yanantha,' Kyros walked towards her and took her in his arms. 'Tell me your answer? I cannot wait any longer!'

'My Lord,' she slid her hands up his chest and pushed herself slightly away from him. 'You gave me three days to consider,' she continued. 'They have been the worst days of my life.'

'How so?'

'My head says, "Yes", but...' she hesitated.

'…your heart says, "No"?' he finished the sentence for her.

'You don't understand. My Father was Hoffengrégor, and my Mother was Sorentina, daughter of Zerigor.'

Kyros was astonished. 'When you said you were of the line of those-who-see-the-end-from-the-beginning, I thought you meant you were one in a long line of Seers.' He passed his hand over his brow in distraction. 'That means you must have lived for…'

'…a thousand years.' Yanantha's laugh belied the anguish in her face. 'All that time I have watched over the Krêonor.'

'You must have desired a man in your life. Your Father may have been a Prophet, but your Mother was of the line of Kings.'

'I have dedicated myself to wait for the Final Restoration.'

'But that is coming to fulfilment. Surely you and I…'

'Kyros,' she interrupted. 'I have tried to explain. Do not tempt me beyond what I am able to bear.'

'Then your answer is, "No".'

She nodded.

'And there is nothing more I can say to persuade you?'

Yanantha didn't reply: the tears starting in her eyes.

Kyros spun away from her, his heart racked with anguish as he wrestled with his feelings. Slowly he turned, knelt on one knee and lifted her hand to his lips. 'I must beg your forgiveness, My Lady. I have done you a great wrong in asking; and an even greater wrong in pressing my case. Three times, now, the True King has spoken to me concerning Lenyé and I have been loath to heed his voice. But I cannot deny his counsel any longer. Please release me from my offer, for I must return to Lenyé.'

'Oh, Kyros.' Yanantha's eyes were brimming over, but she raised him to his feet and flung her arms around him, the tears hot on his neck. 'You are stronger than I. You have saved us both from a terrible match. It would have seemed right, but we would always live with that lurking sense of guilt that we had done wrong before the True King. With regret do I release you; but with joy I willingly forgive you!'

183

Chapter Fifty Six

Morthrir stood outside *The Vault of Malrema* gloating over the success of his words on Mount Malkamet: Kyros was dead and buried; the Nastrim Lenyé relied on had been utterly destroyed, she was very close to surrendering her Sword, and had clearly fallen in love with him.

He flung open the doors and saw everyone bow in the light that came from the time-candle held by a Priest. He strode to the altar and studied the prostrate figures: Jumar-jé and the other Summoners at the points of the compass; the Ten Priests around the circumference, and Vashtani and the five other Dé-monos leaders at the points of the inner Hexagon.

Morthrir listened as Jumar-jé, the Lead Summoner; Eawen, the Chief Priest; and Vashtani stood to report. The Summoners were well received by the Tsé-shâmé and Harmoth: delegates would be sent to Terrazarema shortly. The Priests' words of peace were eagerly received. The Dé-monos had overwhelmed the En-luchés. Only the rest of Vashtani's account surprised him.

'We were unable to contact the Nastrim army before they were destroyed at the gorge in the Plains of Lohr. All we found was the debris of war: not a Nastrim body anywhere.'

'Did you investigate any further?'

'Yes. We explored Mount Nastâri, but didn't find a single Nastâr. It seems the whole race marched on Terrazarema. They must have thought to destroy your remaining army fairly easily, capture Terrazarema and install their own King.'

'Hmph,' Morthrir grunted.

'We felt a power deep within the mountain itself, emanating a light that we dared not approach.' Vashtani continued. 'I suggest you send someone to find out what it is.'

Morthrir shrugged. 'This is no time to go chasing after vague feelings, even if the Nastrim race has been destroyed and anyone can now walk freely into their mountain.'

He glanced at the time-candle as the cross-piece fell away and climbed onto the altar. Tonight was the first opportunity to release the full power of his Hexacle. 'The rest of you may stand.'

There was a rustling of robes as they faced him. Morthrir nodded at the Priest to blow out the time-candle.

This was the moment he'd been waiting for as he savoured the plunging into utter darkness, heightened by the knowledge that six Dé-monos and fourteen men occupied the room with him. He placed his fingertips together, adopted his flexed-knee stance and began breathing deeply, his mind exploring each point of the Hexacle, testing every other mind for subservience. 'Let the Hidden Power be made manifest,' he cried, welcoming the light that began to radiate from him, reflecting on the white lines and stars and moon and illuminating the other figures.

He faced the Eastern point and raised his arms, 'We acknowledge all power comes from the East.' He turned round and faced the Western point, 'We speak against our enemies, for rebellion to our will comes from the West.' He turned to the Northern point, 'All our allies come from the North.' He turned to the Southern point, 'Let new alliances arise from the South.'

Finally he turned back to the Eastern point. 'Let the Hidden Power be released from here to accomplish all that I command.' Morthrir's voice was low and much deeper than normal; but he knew that every word filled the room.

In response to his pronouncements, the entire assembled company broke out into shouts of, 'We honour you, Lord Morthrir. May there be no end to your power and may your dominion extend throughout the Waking World!'

Chapter Fifty Seven

Beth rode the horse while Quinn ran alongside, holding the bridle to slow the pace and prevent any bolting downhill through the trees. They stayed well within the woods, keeping the main path to their left, and followed an animal trail that eventually brought them out by the river.

Beth gazed at the swollen torrent in dismay. 'Quinn. Look how deep it is. I can only just see the tops of the posts marking the ford on both banks. We're never going to get across here.'

'We have to. It's the last thing those soldiers expect. They'll keep hunting for us on this side.'

He motioned for Beth to dismount, and swung himself up in her place. Then he folded his cloak on the pommel of the saddle, and helped Beth to scramble up in front of him.

Quinn urged the horse forwards and guided him along the edge of the flooded river bank and kept walking him beyond the tops of the posts.

Beth whipped round in surprise. 'What are you doing?'

'I'm going to start well upstream and trust the current to carry us down as the horse swims. We have to get aground near the posts on the other side.' He pointed to the high bank beyond the ford leading downstream towards the bridge. 'We'll never get ashore if we miss them.'

He carried on for about a hundred yards upstream and then turned the horse into the river and kicked hard. The horse started walking forwards with the water swirling around his legs and gradually rising above his knees, then stopped and snorted.

'Here's where the deep water starts,' Quinn muttered in Beth's ear. 'Hold on tight,' and he kicked again.

The horse moved forwards and fell into the river, the water surging up over Beth's knees. Quinn clamped a hand over Beth's mouth to muffle her scream, as the horse panicked and thrashed his legs in confusion. 'It's all right. He's done it.'

Beth felt the horse relax and settle into an odd movement, half-bucking, half-plunging, as though galloping through the water. She leaned forwards almost against the horse's neck and held onto the mane. She was a bit alarmed at the noisy breathing, but soon realised the horse appeared to be enjoying himself.

Quinn was right, she thought. The current was pushing them downstream and the horse was cutting across the river in a long slow diagonal. She held her breath as they approached what looked like the line of the river bank leading swiftly to the two posts marking the ford.

The horse floundered as his hooves caught on the submerged bank and tried to rear up. Beth grabbed the horse's mane tighter and clung on, but Quinn was thrown off balance and lurched sideways: the reins torn from his hands.

'Quinn,' she screamed. 'Look out!'

The horse fell back into the river thrusting wildly against the strong current. Quinn obviously had one foot caught in the stirrup and was dragged along under water.

'Quinn!' Beth leaned over on one side and tried to grasp his flailing arm. 'Give me your hand.' She caught hold of Quinn's wrist and gripped tighter with her knees and feet around the horse's shoulders and the base of his neck. Quinn began hauling himself up her arm and flung himself over the saddle, choking and gasping for breath.

Beth snatched the trailing reins out of the water, eased the horse's head to the right and let him drift a bit further and then pulled his head to the left as they neared the posts. The horse swam in between them. His hooves were soon grinding on stones and his body came up with water streaming off, till he waded along the submerged path leading further up the bank away from the ford.

Once the horse was out of the shallows, Quinn slithered to the ground panting for breath.

Beth patted the horse on the shoulder. 'Good boy.' Then she dismounted, held the reins and hugged Quinn to her, trying to warm him up. 'Come on. We need to get you somewhere hidden to light a fire and dry you off. I don't want you catching your death of cold.'

She managed to coax Quinn to get one foot in the stirrup and swing himself up. Then she climbed up behind him and wrapped her arms around his chest.

Quinn took the reins and eased the horse into a walk, then turned the horse's head to the left and set off through the trees.

'Where are we going?' Beth sat more upright to wrap her cloak tightly around herself to stop her own clothes becoming sodden through contact with Quinn, and then settled into her position again with Quinn's back pressing into her.

'To Ishi-mi-réjá's cottage. We need more than a fire. It'll give us somewhere to rest and recover our strength and decide what to do. It can't be far. At least we're away from the sound of those dogs at last.'

'That's something to be grateful for,' Beth tried to sound cheerful. 'Let's hope we don't have any more mishaps on the way.' But already she could feel him shivering against her.

Chapter Fifty Eight

Lenyé heard the clunk of the lock and suddenly felt bereft of her weapons as she followed Morthrir and the Master of the Keys.

'Go to the Master of the Keys any time you like,' Morthrir spoke to her over his shoulder, 'and check them.' He caught her by the hand so she could walk with him. 'They're completely safe in the Royal Armoury. No one else will touch them.'

And check on them she did. Several times a day, at the outset, drawing the Sword of Justice and swinging it through the air, and swapping the two swords round in a corner of the room with her body shielding them in case someone had found a spy hole and was watching her. Then she would settle them back in the rack making sure she didn't overemphasise her contact with one sword over the other and perhaps give their identity away.

But her visits became less frequent as she spent more time with her brothers and cousins, finding solace in their company. The two girls, Olathe and Nasima, became less clinging and more adventurous. They accompanied her to the Cemetery without any bothersome warriors in attendance, once she made a case to Morthrir that if he really trusted her, the girls couldn't possibly come to any harm. They tidied up Kyros' and Quinn's graves and replenished the flowers on all three whenever possible. But it was Beth's grave where they lingered the most, talking about all the happy times they'd had with her.

Lenyé had been running and playing hide-and-seek with them earlier, but now she was kneeling by Kyros' grave and arranging the flowers. She wanted to be alone with him.

Her grief at his death had resolved itself at last: not just that he was gone, but the way it happened. To be trapped on that island and burned to death was unthinkable, but she had to let him go at last, whatever the circumstances of his passing.

Lenyé was relieved the madman who confronted her in the forest was not Kyros after all. He sounded so like Kyros: that's what confused her the most. But the skin was too dark: that wasn't sunburn; it had to be natural. And those cuts and bruises; where had they come from? She could accept the shaggy hair, but not the beard. Kyros let his beard grow when they went off camping for a few days in the summer and slept under the stars, but it was only thin and straggly. And he always shaved it off afterwards: he was very careful about his appearance. His beard had grown for a whole month when they were on the run from Morthrir's warriors; but it was still quite sparse. There was no way it would be that thick by now. It couldn't have been Kyros.

So why the doubts? Morthrir even showed her the death certificate that Doctor Nostrea had signed. If the Apothecary was convinced, it didn't really matter what anyone else tried to say. The man had known Kyros since he was a baby and kept a professional eye on him for the twenty years of his life.

She smiled ruefully: if Kyros was still alive, he would be twenty-one in a few weeks time. Lenyé adjusted a flower on the grave. 'I will always remember you, Kyros. For you were so special to me. Do not think ill of me if I take another in your place, for I cannot bear to live this life alone.'

Lenyé was unsure about what to do with her life. Yanantha sent her to recover the lost Blade of Zerigor, and now it was safe in the Royal Armoury. She also warned about the Power that sat behind her Uncle. But all Lenyé had seen of it was benign and made Morthrir into a more attractive and accessible man. Her Father and Kyros' Father must have been mistaken: she didn't think Morthrir had ruled the household for ill from the nursery upwards after all. Maybe he was sent to give a warning cry to awaken the Krêonor from a slumber they'd fallen into; and they didn't like it and the implications it had for them.

Now Morthrir was their protector and had power over Vashtani and the Dé-monos to do his bidding. And she had brought the Sword of Justice home at the same time. Surely the coming together of his power and her Sword could only mean good for the Krêonor people.

But still nagging at the back of her mind was the question: how was she supposed to use the Sword? Apart from cutting through a metal hasp when she was chained to the Execution Rock by Acwellan, and holding Vashtani at bay, she hadn't really made much progress in answering that question.

Had she missed something between the warning of Yanantha about Morthrir, and the changing circumstances of her life?

No. She had to hold on to the present. Her brothers and cousins were all that were left to her out of the two families. And Morthrir. The name had become so familiar to her that she no longer stumbled over missing out the "Uncle" bit. She felt herself drawn to him in a way she couldn't explain, unless…

Lenyé was surprised by Morthrir approaching from the gate at the side of the formal gardens. She saw him glance at the girls playing so carefree, and heard the genuine appreciation in his voice: 'They're so much happier now that you're here.'

He bowed before her and extended his hand to lift her up. 'And I'm pleased to see you've adjusted so well to Kyros no longer being with us. Such a tragic episode,' he paused and let the silence grow before clearing his throat. 'I wonder if you have found time to think about our future together; and whether you are any closer to an answer?'

Chapter Fifty Nine

Kyros watched Yanantha walk away into the forest with her head bowed. He felt a part of him had died, as if something that had created the deepest yearning in his heart was gone for ever. Strangely he felt at peace. Glorious though the outcome of his desire could have been, it only ranked as second best. The True King was wiser, and knew the right path for him to follow in life.

He thought back to when the True King revealed his full name to him as Luchianó-bé, Lord of Light, and his own reflections at the time. In response to that revelation, Kyros remembered that he only wanted to be continually in his presence, and to love and serve him in return, whatever the cost.

If he'd known then the pain involved, maybe he would have thought differently. But he had come too far and learned too much about the True King to turn back now. He had to remain faithful to that original call: for the name of the True King had protected him against the folly of his own desires.

But it was Lenyé who troubled him the most now and his reaction to her plans and her lack of concern over his warning.

He had a sudden vision of Osâcah labouring under the blazing sun, a trowel in one hand and a basket of seed in the other. He heard the man speak. 'Kyros, we have pierced the darkness that weighed down on us and the light of the True King shines through. He has promised to push back the Dé-monos.'

The vision enlarged and he watched Osâcah drop the trowel and basket and stand with his right hand raised towards him. 'I speak the power of the True King over you, my friend. Be set free from your confusion to do his bidding.' Then the vision faded.

Kyros felt a new strength within himself. 'Oh, My King,' he cried aloud. 'The dark night is over and I surrender my thoughts of Lenyé to you. I choose to trust you for the outcome.'

He turned and sprang onto the top of the Dangst Rock. The sun was setting, but he faced East and focused on the flattened summit of a distant mountain. That must be Mount Malkamet, he thought, where the True King challenged Abbérron and commanded the chaining of the Dé-monos to this very rock.

He raised his right hand and felt a presence around him far brighter than the setting sun. New energy coursed through him.

'In the name of Luchianó-bé, Lord of Light, I reverse all words of power spoken by my Uncle Morthrir. Let the point of entry be sealed; let the Guardians of the Spiral be restored; let the power of Abbérron in the Waking World be broken; and let the Dé-monos be judged according to my word already spoken against them!'

The light around him grew brighter.

'Let the confusion and conflict between Lenyé and myself be reversed; let us come together in love and be reunited. Let the power of the name of Luchianó-bé, Lord of Light, be restored to me and any weapons the True King chooses to give her be restored to Lenyé. Let all power that Uncle Morthrir relies on be stripped away,' he continued. 'And let Lenyé be released from any words of binding, so she is free to marry whomsoever she will without any coercion. Let the evil which he intended return to him; and let it be as a curse falling upon his own head!'

Kyros raised his other hand as well and turned towards the West. 'Let the name of the True King, Luchianó-bé, Lord of Light, be lifted up again in the Waking World; to honour, praise and magnify him throughout the lands. And may all Peoples come before him in peace and harmony. So let it be!'

He lowered his hands and waited expectantly, wondering what would happen next.

Chapter Sixty

Morthrir sat at his desk exulting in his success with Lenyé. Her weapons were in the Royal Armoury and she was never going to get them back. But she didn't seem too bothered. Maybe she didn't know what the Sword was capable of.

And his superb timing, catching her by Kyros' grave on her own. She hadn't actually answered his question, but she wasn't hostile either. The signs were there in her face. Morthrir was certain she would say, "Yes" to him. Such a sweet, innocent...

Morthrir heard a noise, like a great avalanche pouring down a mountainside. Then it hit him, deep in his belly.

He staggered up from his desk and lurched towards the door but his legs buckled and he collapsed in a heap.

What was happening? He felt so weak. Maybe he released too much power in the Hexacle and his body couldn't take it. He needed to get away and hide from prying eyes and think.

Morthrir crawled to the door and banged on it with his fist.

One of the guards opened it and cried out, 'Sire! Are you all right? Whatever's the matter? Shall I call for help?'

'Get me upstairs, both of you.'

They walked him up the stairs and put him to bed. Morthrir shook uncontrollably and beads of sweat poured off his brow.

'Let me call your servants, Sire. Or the Apothecary.'

'No. I'm all right.'

'Princess Lenyé, then. She'll know what to do.'

'Don't you dare. If either of you tells anyone, I'll have your heads off. Now get back to your posts!'

Chapter Sixty One

Kyros blinked as a dazzling light engulfed him. Gradually he was able to make out a face in the blaze and recognised the features. He fell face down, too awed to even raise his head.

'Kyros. What are you doing down there?'

The voice was instantly recognisable, and the very one he'd been yearning to hear ever since returning to the Waking World.

'You set me seven tests, My King. And I have only accomplished the first four. I have attempted the next two….'

'You did well in the fifth and sixth tests; for you chose fidelity above the desire of your eyes, and have recovered your authority to use my name. But I have not come about your tests. Life in the Waking World is very different from what you experienced in the Realm of Travail: like interacting with other people. Already your most significant relationship is sundered…'

'But she's planning to disobey your…' Kyros hesitated, realising too late that he'd interrupted the True King.

'And your Uncle has spoken words of power against you,' the True King carried on. 'You may have reversed these things in my name, but unless you face up to those two issues and put them right, you are unable to do anything else.'

Kyros raised his head, 'But what about the Breaking-in?'

'What does the Rancher do when his buffalo thrust through a fence into a neighbour's farm and damage the crops?'

'Send in his herders to round them up and mend the fence.'

'Precisely,' the True King chuckled. 'The Rancher needs a foreman who obeys his instructions to put the damage right.'

'But the Dé-monos are a bit more of a handful than buffalo. Last time it happened, you had to expel them yourself.'

'That's why I've been training you,' the True King pointed at Kyros. 'Ever since Zerigor's defeat, I have looked for a man to stand in the gap between the Realm of the Blessèd Throne and the Waking World as my representative. The Dé-monos are now subject to you through your use of my name.'

'But what about my Uncle?'

'The fate of the Dé-monos is closely bound up with his. It is one thing to speak a word of reversal against him and the power he uses, but quite another for it to come to pass. You have to act.'

'How?'

'Did I not say, "*You must gather my people and speak my name to them, for they have largely forgotten it or scoff at it*". The best way to accomplish this is to head for your capital city and begin.'

'You mean, go to Terrazarema?' Kyros frowned. 'What shall I say to them?'

'Tell them it is time to undo the effect of the curse that entered the Waking World at the Beginning. For the evil released then has tainted everyone since, and turned them away from the knowledge of my name. As a result they have chosen to go their own way in life and ultimately follow another.'

'You mean my Uncle?'

'That's right. And the Hidden Power operating through him.'

Kyros felt puzzled, 'Why have you waited till now?'

'Evil takes a long time to grow to its fullest extent, when all its poisons are drawn together and can be lanced in one go: like an angry boil on a person's skin. I am using you to do that.'

'But how do I speak your name to them?'

'As the people gather to my name they are freed from the curse and protected in the conflict to destroy its evil.'

'But if my Uncle catches me this time, then…'

'Kyros,' the True King cut him short. 'You are the man!'

Chapter Sixty Two

Lenyé was finishing breakfast in the dining room next to the private council chamber when a courtier burst in, bowed and asked her to come quickly.

'What is it?' she demanded as she followed him upstairs.

'The Lord Morthrir has taken to his rooms and won't let anyone near him. He hasn't eaten anything since early evening yesterday.'

'Is he ill?'

'We don't know. He won't let anyone enter. Maybe you could…'

They arrived outside Morthrir's suite and Lenyé banged on the door with her fist. 'Morthrir. Are you all right?'

'Go away.'

'But it's me. Lenyé.' She tried the handle but the door was locked from the inside. 'I must see you.'

When there was no answer she sent the courtier to summon the Master of the Keys and waited in the corridor.

'What's going on,' she heard Morthrir's voice through the door, but he sounded quite feeble compared with his normal confident tones.

She knelt down and put her mouth to the keyhole. 'You sound ill, Morthrir,' she rattled the door handle. 'Shall I ask Doctor Nostrea to come and see you?'

At last the Master of the Keys arrived, unlocked the door and Lenyé pushed past him.

'I'm not having that Apothecary anywhere near me,' Morthrir

shouted from his bed. 'He's absolutely useless.'

'You didn't think that when you had him sign Kyros' death certificate.'

Morthrir was silent for a minute. 'He does have his uses, I suppose.'

'What's the matter?' Lenyé sat on the edge of the bed. 'You don't seem yourself at all today. Tell me what's happened.'

'About sunset yesterday I was sitting at my desk in the private council chamber, and felt a sudden shock, deep inside. It was as if all my power was draining away from me. I felt sick and dizzy and just managed to get myself up here before collapsing on the bed.'

'Why didn't you send for me at once?'

'I didn't want you to see me like this. I thought you might despise me for being so weak and reject me. I couldn't bear that.'

'Then you don't know me at all. I wouldn't do that to anyone. I'll call Doctor Nostrea to check you over and make sure?'

'No. Being singled out to receive such power as I have been given is bound to take its toll eventually. I would prefer to see Eawen the Henosite.'

'That old man with the strange eyes you pointed out to me the other day? How can I find him for you?'

'I don't know. Last time I needed help, I called out and he came.'

'Then hadn't you better call for him now?'

'I've been doing that ever since I climbed into bed.'

PART V

THE GATHERING

Chapter Sixty Three

Rafé checked the weapons in the Royal Armoury against his list, keeping up the pretence for as long as possible, while edging round to the corner of the room he needed to inspect the most.

When he arrived at the palace a few days ago Rafé saw Morthrir ride in with Lenyé at his side, and she had two swords strapped across her back. They had to be the swords he mentioned to Eawen. He asked Morthrir about them and was told they were secured in the Royal Armoury.

He was desperate to examine them for himself. Rafé fooled the Master of the Keys to allow him access as part of his routine duties, but was only interested in Lenyé's swords. He paused at the rack and studied the gems embedded in the scabbards as they flashed in the light from the flare the Master of the Keys held. His eyes flicked to the longbow above and then back to the swords. If Eawen was right, one of these must be the Sword of Justice. But which one?

'Where did these come from?' Rafé glanced at the Master of the Keys. 'I don't have them on my list.'

'They belong to Princess Lenyé. Morthrir had them placed in here for security reasons.'

Rafé laid his scroll and quill pen aside, selected one of the swords and pulled it out of the scabbard.

'Wait a minute,' the Master of the Keys sounded alarmed. 'No one is allowed to touch them except the Princess.'

'I'm only examining them to complete my itinerary.'

Rafé swept the blade around his head two or three times

before sheathing it and returning it to the rack. Then he lifted up the other sword and tried to draw it, but it was stuck fast in the scabbard. 'That's odd,' and he tried again. He examined the hilt and scabbard to see if there was a latch or a hidden button that would release the blade. This must be the Sword of Justice.

He tried pulling again, but as he did so he had the same picture in his mind of the cobra slithering towards the lone mountain, and coiling itself around the globe. He recalled Vashtani's words at the start of the meeting in *The Vault of Malrema* when he reported his findings at Mount Nastâri: "*We felt a power deep within the mountain itself and emanating a light that we dared not approach. I suggest you send someone to find out what it is and report back*". So the globe was at Mount Nastâri. Somehow the globe was connected to the Sword he held in his hands.

Immediately he was in control of the snake. He forced it to look more closely at the globe and saw a tiny sword extending from the top; with most of the blade buried in the globe and its hilt guard making it look like a small cross. Maybe he should persuade Morthrir to take Vashtani's advice and let him go and recover this globe and find out what it was and the power that came from it.

Rafé was startled by a voice from behind him: 'What exactly is going on in here?'

He whipped round to see Lenyé staring at him.

'Oh,' he hesitated. 'Just a routine check on the stock of weapons held in the Armoury,' Rafé glanced away from her penetrating stare as he tried to gather his thoughts. 'To ensure no registered weapons have gone missing.'

'And why do you have my Sword in your hand?'

'I was examining them both so I could write up a proper description in my itinerary of new weapons.'

'Well, don't. They are not available to the Royal Guard.'

'I understand one of these blades has special properties that makes it a powerful weapon in a particular person's hands.'

Lenyé felt shocked that Rafé knew. 'Why do you say that?'

'It's my duty to be aware of what is stored in the Armoury.'

Lenyé sensed her rising anger. 'They are here as a security measure in case someone tries to steal them. Only I am permitted to touch them. Make sure you record that as well.'

Rafé shifted awkwardly. 'If I am right, then it could be considered a national heirloom and should pass to the Crown and no longer be the prerogative of any one individual.'

'Don't be absurd,' she fumed. 'Morthrir placed them both in here at my request. I will make sure he confirms this with you. No one is allowed to touch them. Including you!'

'Yes, Your Highness.'

'Rafé,' Lenyé's anger was getting the better of her. 'This is the first time we've met since escaping from that foresters' hamlet. I saw you pointing out Kyros to Youdlh's warriors so they could loose their arrows at him. Kyros might still be alive if you hadn't done that. Who knows how badly wounded he was when he swam out to the island. When his body was eventually found and brought back, it was too badly disfigured by fire to be recognisable. You have a lot to answer for.'

'But...'

'And I find you here,' Lenyé registered the look of surprise on the man's face, 'in Terrazarema, serving Morthrir as you once served King Dareth as though nothing had happened.'

'There is an explanation,' Rafé handed her the Sword. 'You...'

'I'm sure there is,' she cut in, 'but not now. I will order the Master of the Keys to lock this room after you've gone.'

'Very good,' Rafé gathered up his writing things and began backing towards the door.

'And if I ever find you in here again,' Lenyé's voice was cold and steady. 'I will have you arrested. Do you understand?'

'Yes, Your Highness.'

Chapter Sixty Four

At dawn the next day Kyros led the way as he and Harbona ran through the forest and out onto the open heath lands that led to Terrazarema. He anticipated several days journeying, but by sundown, as if they'd been lifted up by unseen hands and carried in the faint melody of song that he heard every now and then, they were within a mile of the city walls. Even as they came to a halt, a brightness blazed around them and the familiar form of Stellatus approached him out of the blinding light.

'Well met, Kyros. Your words on the Dangst Rock allowed the True King to send aid so the En-luchés could force through the barrier of darkness that was present when we entered the Waking World. Now we can accompany you to do your bidding, and guard you with the light of life.'

'Thank you, my friend.'

'Do not fear what opposes you: the name of the True King is not just a place of refuge for you in the Waking World, but a weapon of power in your mouth. He will do great things through you, which have never been witnessed before.'

Once Stellatus had left, Kyros and Harbona made camp, but were surprised by the arrival of Chuah-te-mok, who told Kyros that Ariella and Mamma Uza-Mâté failed to catch up with Lenyé.

'I left Ra-Na-Jiri in the palace gardens as you asked, but she refused to talk to him,' the eagle bobbed his head.

Kyros frowned, 'I'll have to try and find her.' He pulled the metal cylinder in its cloth wrapping from his pocket. 'Please take this to Yanantha for me. Tell her, "*it contains a scroll from the Book of Beginnings, which can only be opened by the right person at the appointed hour"*. Ask her to keep it safe with the parchment I left with her. If I am captured, I don't want this cylinder to fall into the wrong hands.'

After the eagle had gone, the two men discussed their strategy. Harbona was to remain here: his swarthy skin had hardly been changed by the sun in the Realm of Travail, so he would be recognised by Morthrir's soldiers. Kyros would walk into Terrazarema, relying on his long hair and beard and darkened skin to act as a disguise. If Lenyé was confused, he felt confident everyone else would be fooled. He would return at nightfall. Kyros sighed: the command of the True King to gather the people was still ringing in his ears. Trying to find Lenyé as well would make his task that much harder.

The following morning Kyros entered the city gates glancing around to see if anyone recognised him. He was coming to his own capital city, but felt an utter stranger. Whether his disguise was that convincing or Stellatus was blinding people's eyes to his real identity, he couldn't tell. What he did know was that his own eyes were opened in a way he'd never known before. As he studied people's faces he could see beneath the surface and tell what they were thinking. Uppermost in their minds was the immediate effect of Uncle Morthrir and his troops and what was going to happen next. Some were clearly fearful of the worst; but others were expecting a better kind of rule from him. Any attempt by Kyros to call them back to a knowledge of the True King would be seen as a direct challenge against his Uncle.

He tried engaging a few passersby in conversation, but they were too busy about their own affairs to stop for long. How do you gather a people who don't want to be gathered; and how do you proclaim a name to them that they had largely forgotten or didn't care about any more?

He reached the Central Square noting the bustling activity

around the covered stalls and booths of the market on the left, and the arcades of shops around the other three sides: familiar, yet different. The sculpture said it all. Clearly his Uncle was imposing himself whether the people liked it or not.

He could detect a sense of fear pervading most of the crowd and followed people's nervous glances to the soldiers grouped in strategic positions around the edge of the Square; a far cry from the two sentries who used to stand on duty at the head of the archway leading to the palace under his Father's rule. Although they wore the uniform of the Royal Garrison, he guessed by their swarthy features that these must be his Uncle Morthrir's troops. He walked towards the middle of the Square, sat on the edge of the fountain and watched the crowd milling around. How was he going to engage their attention? Stand up and shout for silence in the midst of this throng!

Then he spotted the boy, the son of a warrior if his brown face and dark hair were anything to go by. Or rather, the boy spotted Kyros; gazing at him with a puzzled expression. The lad was sitting on the hard paving slabs while a woman, obviously his Mother, was standing slightly behind him haggling with a stallholder over the price of some meat. The boy was lame, judging by the two wooden crutches lying on the ground next to him. Kyros only realised how lame the boy must be when his eyes eventually took in the legs: they were so crooked and misshapen and thin, like mere sticks, and unlikely to be capable of even bearing the lad's weight.

Suddenly Kyros saw beyond the outer infirmity right into the boy's heart: all the anguish of not being able to walk or run and play with his friends; of always being left out. But he saw something else. Despite the frustration and loneliness, the boy never gave up hope of walking. Instantly Kyros knew why the boy was looking at him like that: there was such a sense of expectancy in the lad's face.

A great feeling of compassion welled up within Kyros. If ever the power of the name of the True King was needed, it was here. Why shouldn't the lad walk? The boy was only a few yards away. Kyros looked him straight in the eyes and called out, 'Stand up and come to me.'

The boy grabbed his crutches and tried to raise himself; then looked up despairingly at Kyros.

Kyros felt his hands begin to tingle. 'Put your crutches down.'

The boy threw them aside and began crawling on his upper arms and elbows, his useless legs trailing behind him.

Kyros rose to his feet and took a pace away from the fountain towards the lad. 'I said, "*Stand up and come to me*".'

The boy stopped and struggled into a sitting position. He was too far from his crutches to reach them. He glanced up at Kyros.

Even though the lad was still some way from him, Kyros stretched out his hand. 'Reach out your hand to me.'

The boy did as he was told.

'Now. In the name of Luchianó-bé, Lord of Light, stand up and walk!'

The boy kept his hand stretched out, but used the other to haul one leg under him so he was partly squatting on his haunches. He pulled his other leg up under him. Then he leaned forwards and took his weight on his hand while he eased himself into a kneeling position, dropped his other hand to the ground to steady himself, and managed to move forwards on his hands and knees. He jerked his head up and looked at Kyros, his eyes ablaze with astonishment. Then he reached back with his hand and pulled one knee up to his stomach. His foot dragged along the paving stones till it was underneath him.

Kyros stood there, arm still outstretched, looking the lad directly in the eyes. He was aware of a movement behind the boy, but his eyes didn't flicker from the lad's face. Something was going on in the boy, and it needed all Kyros' concentration to keep him moving. Kyros began to feel a tingling sensation in the atmosphere around him till the very air itself was throbbing, and felt a great love for the boy welling up within him like a huge reservoir, the intensity so great that he thought he was going to explode. Suddenly the dam burst and a wave of love gushed out of him and overwhelmed the lad.

A voice shouted, 'Ramâno. Stop! What do you think you're doing?'

But it was too late. At that precise moment the boy pushed down; there was a sharp clicking sound as his leg straightened and took the strain and he was rising to a standing position. His other leg swung free and, as he put his weight on it, there was a further series of clicks. Then the boy was staggering forwards, walking forwards, running forwards, his face flushed with excitement. He covered the few feet that separated them and flung himself at Kyros.

Kyros felt a surge of joy sweep through him, like he experienced when he surrendered his dream to Luchianó-bé in the River Lammista-ké. Instinctively he raised his other arm, caught the boy in mid air and swung him round several times, holding the lad tightly against his chest and letting the lad's legs swing free in concentric circles.

In the giddiness of the moment Kyros staggered backwards and sat down awkwardly on the edge of the fountain, but managed to set the boy across his knees before the lad fell and hurt himself.

'I knew,' the boy was ecstatic. 'I saw a light around the top of your head like a big serving plate. I knew you could heal me.'

Kyros shook his head. 'I didn't heal you; but the True King who sent me...' Suddenly he was aware of the lad's Mother standing in front of him, arms akimbo, and scowling with anger.

'Who do you think you are, taking my boy away from me?' She lunged forwards to grab him by the shoulder, but the lad ducked and she missed. 'Ramâno, get off that stranger's knees. You don't even know who he is.'

'But Mamma. This man healed my legs.'

'Don't talk such rubbish. I won't have it. Do you hear me?' She rounded on Kyros. 'How dare you build up my sons hopes like that? Vagabond! Look at you. How could anyone like you heal my son? You don't know how much I've longed for him to walk, and wept in agony over him in the darkness of sleepless nights. A couple of yards doesn't prove he can walk. It was a cheap trick. And I've got to live with this and help him again after you've gone. You...'

But the boy cut her short. 'It's true, Mamma. Look!' Ramâno slipped down off Kyros' knees and started running in a great ring around the fountain.

The Mother's shout of astonishment made several people jerk their heads up and look in their direction.

'Ramâno. Don't you dare run away like that. You've never been so far from me in your life. Look out!'

People started gathering round to see what was going on.

'That man healed the boy!' Kyros recognised the stallholder the Mother had been bargaining with. 'I saw it happen with my own eyes. He hobbled up to my stall with his Mother. One minute the boy was sitting on the ground, the next he was up and running to this stranger. I was so shocked that I dropped the piece of meat I was holding.'

'I don't believe you,' a voice called out from the crowd. 'How could anyone learn to walk properly that quickly?'

'If you don't believe me,' the stallholder pointed to where the boy had been sitting. 'There are his crutches. He won't be needing them now. Look at him go.'

All eyes riveted on Ramâno as he continued to run round the fountain with his Mother chasing after him.

'I don't believe it either,' another voice called out. 'Those are the legs of a normal, healthy boy. He couldn't possibly have been badly crippled a few minutes ago!'

But a few people, who had seen the whole spectacle, shouted out in support of the stallholder.

The stallholder approached Kyros. 'You may have done an incredible deed, but you owe me for a piece of prime buffalo steak. It fell, cut-side down, when I dropped it, and the dust's stuck to it. I can't sell that now!'

Other voices started calling out, 'Who are you?' and 'How did you do it?'

Kyros stood on the edge of the fountain and held up his hands for silence. 'I didn't heal that boy. I come to you in the name of the True King to call you back to a knowledge of him and his ways. It's his power working through me.'

'What True King?' a voice shouted out.

'That's all about Zerigor,' an old man said. 'Why has he waited until now before taking any interest in us?'

And so the argument raged around him. Kyros saw others join the knot of people as it rapidly grew into a large throng.

Some soldiers made their way over. 'Break it up, break it up,' one of them shouted.

'Get back to your business, before I call out the whole Guard!' his comrade drew his sword and threatened those on the edge of the gathering.

People started breaking away and disappearing into the larger crowd still milling around.

'You. On the fountain. Get down, or I'll arrest you for causing a disturbance.'

Kyros sighed and climbed down. The soldiers strolled back to their place on guard duty. Finally, only Ramâno and his Mother and the stallholder were left. Ramâno ran over and flung his arms about Kyros' waist. Kyros eased himself free of the boy's grip, knelt down in front of him, turned him around and presented him to his Mother. 'Dear lady, it was important for you to let your grief and anger over the years of his life come out like that. Thank you for being so honest.' Gently he pushed the boy forwards. 'Receive your son again.'

The Mother also knelt. Ramâno raced across and flung his

arms around her neck. Kyros saw the tears streaming down her face as she looked up at him.

'Not only can Ramâno walk,' her voice was thick with emotion. 'But also a great weight of anger and guilt has disappeared from my heart. I will never forget what you have done for me and my boy.' She paused to kiss Ramâno on the forehead before looking up again. 'Thank you, good Sir.'

The stallholder started protesting again about the useless piece of steak.

Ramâno's Mother wiped her eyes with the back of her hand and turned to him. 'Do not bother this man any more with such trivial matters. Please wrap it up, put it in my basket and charge it to my normal account for the Royal provisioning.'

That evening Kyros retraced his steps to the campsite. He had a few conversations with small groups who re-gathered after the soldiers moved on. Some still clung to their assertion of witnessing the little boy being healed, but most were sceptical and called him a travelling conjuror, who fooled people with his tricks. Kyros realised this was one way to gather people to talk about the True King, but he didn't know how to overcome their scepticism. He put it out of his mind as he walked, and let his thoughts dwell on the True King instead. 'Who am I that My King should work so mightily through me? Let the people come in greater numbers,' he muttered to himself. 'And may they begin to receive your name more favourably.'

As he sat round the camp fire with Harbona, he was startled by a dark shape falling out of the sky towards him, the great wings folding as the eagle settled on the ground in front of him. Chuah-te-mok had a message from Yanantha, and Kyros was shocked at what he heard: "*A few days ago I saw Lenyé ride quite willingly with her Uncle to Terrazarema. Worse, from the way she was behaving, she had obviously fallen in love with him*".

Chapter Sixty Five

The following day Morthrir was no better, so after the midday meal, Lenyé took her brothers and cousins to the Cemetery. She watched them chase each other through the grasses and into the shrubbery at one side. She wasn't too bothered about letting the girls out of her sight with Wilf and Festé around. She wanted to change the flowers on Kyros' grave by herself.

The shock of finding Rafé in the Armoury and the flood of memories, especially Rafé pointing out Kyros to Youdlh's warriors, was fresh in her mind. But she realised now that she was in love with an ideal, not a man. Kyros could never be all the things she dreamed he would. It was impossible. Now she was not only saying goodbye to Kyros himself, but those dreams as well. Slowly she was awakening to the growing sense of reality in her life: that all this was in the past, and her future lay with Morthrir. His recent illness showed he was human after all, yet he carried a far greater aura of power than Kyros had ever done.

A sudden movement amongst the tall grasses in front of her made her jerk her head up in time to see Ra-Na-Jiri approaching.

'Have you finished your thinking,' he hissed at her.

'I wish you wouldn't keep doing this, Ra-Na-Jiri.'

'Ariella's frantic with worry. She's desperate to see you.'

'I can't let her come into the city. The guards would kill her before I could do anything. And I daren't tell Morthrir I want to bring my lioness to the palace. Give me more time.'

'By the way,' Ra-Na-Jiri continued. 'Ariella and Mamma Uza-Mâté said they met Kyros in the forest. They pleaded with him to rescue you, but he refused because of the Nastrim.'

'They've never met Kyros before, so how do they know what he looks like. That man in the forest is definitely not Kyros.'

'How can you be so sure?'

'Because Kyros is dead. This is his grave. And I'm mourning the memory of the Kyros I once knew. The real Kyros. Will you stop trying to interfere and leave me alone!'

Lenyé watched the movement of grasses as the cobra slithered away. She finished pouring water into the vase and was straightening one of the flowers when a shrill scream from the shrubbery had her up and racing for her two cousins, her heart pounding in alarm. She would never forgive herself if anything happened to them.

When she found them, her brothers were nowhere in sight.

'Who are you?' Lenyé glared at the boy sitting with his back to a tree while she comforted her cousins. 'It's all right, Nasima,' she whispered in the girl's ear. 'He's not going to hurt you.'

'I'm Ramâno.'

Lenyé's brothers came crashing through the bushes in front of her. 'Where have you two been?'

'We came as soon as we heard Nasima scream.'

Lenyé turned back to the boy. 'What are you doing here?'

'I often slip out of the kitchens when Mamma doesn't need me, or to get away from the other lads when they laugh at me. This is my favourite place. No one ever comes here, until now.'

'Why would they laugh at you?'

'My legs were completely crippled and I couldn't do the things they did. But not any more,' the boy jumped to his feet and started climbing the tree he'd been leaning against. 'Two days ago, I couldn't do this. Look how strong my legs are now.'

Lenyé gasped in amazement. 'You must be the boy everyone's talking about.'

'That's right. The Healer in the Central Square did it.'

'Wait a minute,' Lenyé frowned. 'Not everyone thinks he is a healer.'

'I know. I help him as much as I can to convince people, but they think I've been all right all the time and I'm making it up to trick them into thinking he actually is a healer.'

'That's what I heard.' She glanced at the others. 'Why don't you go and chase each other out in the open again? I'll help Ramâno find his way back to the kitchens. And don't go running off anywhere before I get back.'

Once they'd gone, Lenyé sat on a tree stump and beckoned to the lad to come down from his tree. When he refused, saying he preferred to sit on a branch, she stared hard at his legs. It couldn't possibly have happened. He looked like any other boy.

'Did he really heal you?'

'Of course. Ask my Mamma. She didn't throw away my crutches because people kept on questioning her about it. And she's so happy. She's always singing about the True King and how he did such a great deed for us.'

'The True King?' Lenyé was startled. 'Where does he fit in?'

'The Healer says he can only do his work because the True King sent him and gives him healing power for other people. You should see how amazed they are when he cures them.'

'Does this Healer have a name?'

'He won't tell anyone. He's as tall as one of you Krêonor, but dark skinned like a Tsé-shâmé, with a great mop of hair and a beard. I've never seen anyone like him before.'

'I have. I saw a man in the forest a while ago who looked just like that. I thought he was a madman from the way he was talking. So he's the one pretending to be the Healer.'

'He does heal people. He healed my legs. I swear it. And I've seen him heal lots of others.'

'I think it's time you went back to the kitchens, Ramâno. Your Mother might be getting anxious.'

'We'll have to be careful,' Ramâno grinned at her. 'I saw a big snake in here yesterday. I think it was a cobra. I'll protect you.'

'That cobra doesn't worry me,' Lenyé stood up and held out her hand to the boy. 'He's a friend of mine.'

'Really,' Ramâno slithered to the ground. 'Can I meet him?'

'Not now, Ramâno. I think it's more important to get you back to your Mother.'

'Princess-Lady,' Ramâno stopped scampering ahead and came and held her hand as she walked him back through the shrubbery. They had almost reached the path that led round the back of the palace, past the stables and up to the kitchens. He looked up at her with a solemn expression in his eyes.

'What's the matter, Ramâno?'

'Why were you kneeling by that grave? I saw you from the edge of the shrubbery before your cousins found me.'

'I was mourning the loss of someone very dear to me.'

'Do you know who's buried there?'

'Of course I do. Morthrir told me.'

'I saw it happen. I couldn't sleep one night so I crept out of doors and came to my hiding place in the shrubbery. This was before my legs were healed, so it took a long time.'

'Why are you telling me this?'

'Because someone needs to know.'

'Know what?'

'I saw them.'

'Who?'

'I'd been sitting there some time when three men arrived, two of them carrying a coffin. They put it down and the other man made them dig a grave. It took them quite a while. When they finished, they put two ropes under the coffin and lowered it in.'

'Why were they doing it in the dark?'

'Because of the next bit.'

Suddenly Ramâno was clinging to her, his face ashen and he was sobbing.

'What is it, Ramâno?' she felt the boy start to shake violently.

'The other man, who'd been watching and telling them what to do, pulled out a dagger, stabbed them both, shoved their bodies in the grave and covered them up with soil.'

Lenyé knelt down and held the boy to her, his racking sobs preventing him from continuing. 'Take your time, Ramâno.'

'I haven't slept properly since. I keep seeing pictures in my head,' he paused and gulped. 'There are three bodies in that grave,' he blurted out almost in her ear. 'And only one of them's in a coffin.'

She wrapped her arms around him and continued soothing him with her hands until the shaking gradually subsided.

'I waited ages after he'd gone, in case he was watching to see if anyone was around. I was terrified I'd fall asleep and someone would find me in the morning and report me.'

She stroked the back of his head and pressed his face into her shoulder until the sobs began to die down. Then she held him at arms length, so she could look him in the face. She no longer doubted his tale. No one could have made that up and reacted so strongly in the telling.

'Do you know who those men were?'

'One of them was the big Commander.'

'Youdlh?' Lenyé started in surprise as Ramâno nodded.

The boy wiped his sleeve across his eyes. 'And I can guess who the other two were.'

When he didn't say anything straight away she prompted him, 'Go on.'

'A few weeks back, when the warriors were out trying to find you and the others, we had news that a badly burned body was found on that island on the lake. Two of our warriors brought it back to the mainland and buried it in the forest. All the warrior women here were petrified in case it was their husband. But the body couldn't be properly identified. Then Youdlh and those two warriors and some Doctor-man were sent to dig it up and the Doctor-man reckoned it was Prince Kyros. So, of course, all the warrior women were happy. The men brought the body back in a coffin on a cart. The Doctor-man took charge of it. Next morning there was a big procession through the Central Square and everyone mourned the loss of Prince Kyros.'

'How does this affect what you saw?'

'The night I hid in the shrubbery was the night they brought the cart back. It was that coffin they were burying.'

'And the men who were killed?'

'They were the two warriors who found the body in the first place and were sent to bring it back with the Doctor-man.'

'What are you saying?'

'There's something very odd about the body that was buried. Maybe the Doctor-man was wrong and it wasn't Prince Kyros, and so Youdlh had to silence those two warriors.'

Lenyé stiffened as the implication dawned on her. 'But why?'

'Because they're the only ones who ever saw the body except Youdlh and the Doctor-man.'

'How do you know it was those two warriors?'

'Because they've disappeared. No one's seen them since.'

As she cradled Ramâno in her lap and tried to comfort the boy, her own thoughts were racing. Quite apart from the horror of what Ramâno had witnessed, who ordered such a terrible deed? Was Youdlh acting on his own initiative, or was it Morthrir? And if so, why? To make her think Kyros was dead, and there was no alternative for her but to marry Morthrir instead? Surely Doctor Nostrea would never have signed the certificate if he wasn't convinced the corpse was Kyros. What if he was wrong as Ramâno thought? Then Kyros was still alive. If that was the case, then perhaps the madman in the forest wasn't so mad after all. It could have been Kyros.

The only way to settle this was to go and see Ramâno's Healer for herself.

Chapter Sixty Six

The next day Kyros returned to the Central Square and was astonished at the size of the crowd, especially as the market stalls were closed. Many had brought their sick and infirm relatives and begged him to heal them like the little boy.

For three days, Kyros laboured amongst them speaking healing and wholeness in the name of Luchianó-bé. He felt the power of the True King present with him, like a great throbbing of the atmosphere around him. He was as amazed as the people at the healings that occurred. Many cripples walked, those with skin diseases saw the debilitating sores drop off, and the blind and deaf were cured.

Each day Ramâno joined him for some of the time and would strut up and down and shout, 'If he can do it for me, he can heal you as well!' Many came forwards as a result of his urgings.

Kyros was so encouraged by Ramâno. 'You need to become like this little boy,' he would cry out. 'Receive this gift of healing as a child would, without questioning or thinking it's impossible. Trust completely in the name of the True King!'

'Call that a lame leg,' Ramâno yelled at a man hobbling towards them, his stick tapping loudly on the paving slabs. 'I couldn't even stand up without help, and he healed me. Get in line and wait your turn. An hour's not going to make that much difference to you.'

Despite Ramâno's shouting and prompting to form an orderly line, Kyros didn't work like that. He would wait some moments listening to that reassuring voice in his heart, and go to

218

speak over someone way down Ramâno's queue; then he'd come back and find someone else, as though sensing the most needy. Quite often when those people were healed it would generate a greater release of power around him and others were healed immediately without him having to touch them.

But not everyone was healed, and his heart bled for them. In the midst of his labours he cried out silently to the True King for an answer. He heard the whispered response to his heart: *'Everyone is on their own journey. If they aren't healed immediately, it doesn't mean they won't receive from me at another time in their lives. I am only asking you to gather my people and speak my name to them.'*

That name was now on everyone's lips and a great excitement and sense of expectancy swept through the city. But Kyros was in despair. Whenever he started to speak more fully about the True King, the crowd began arguing with him and dispersed quite quickly.

Ramâno was great fun to have around and Kyros picked up a lot about him from the boy's constant talk: his Mother's name was Marie-anna and they came to the capital with the warriors some weeks ago and his Mother had a job in the Royal kitchens. 'She's the best cook they've got,' Ramâno boasted, 'and now she's singing all the time she's so happy for me: she's a different person! And she's making up new songs about what the True King's done. The palace kitchens are full of her songs.' Then there would be a gap while Ramâno shouted to people in the crowd to come forwards for their healing. Then it was back to his quick smile and incessant chatter. 'I'm going to be a warrior when I grow up. Papa was a warrior. I want to be like him. He's dead now. Killed in a battle two years ago, just before my fifth Birthday. Now that I can run and jump, I'm going to learn how to ride like the other boys. But I need someone to teach me.'

Each night Kyros went back to camp exhausted but elated in heart for he knew the people were gathering in response to the calling of the True King. He just needed to hold their attention when he began to explain about the True King more fully.

One day Ramâno came to him looking very downcast.

'What's the matter, Ramâno?'

'I don't want to be a warrior any more. I don't want to take life in anger, even if it's honourable like the warriors in battle.'

'What's brought all this on?'

Ramâno was silent for a while; then blurted out his story about the burial and the murders. 'I told the Princess-Lady, and she helped me. But I still feel sick about it, deep down inside.'

Kyros was caught off guard by the obvious reference to Lenyé, but wrapped his arms around the boy, and held him close. 'Sometimes healing of our bodies is not enough.'

'How do you mean?' the boy looked up at him with an expectant gleam in his eye.

'The True King is more concerned with what goes on in our hearts and what we think about, and the things that trouble us.'

'You mean he can heal this sick feeling as well?'

'If you really want him to.'

'How's he going to do it,' the boy sounded so excited.

Kyros was quiet for a while, studying the boy's face, chest and stomach, and then raised his right hand. 'Let the shock and fear that has taken root in you be wiped away in the name of Luchianó-bé, Lord of Light; and let his peace fill your mind.'

Ramâno stared at him with eyes wide in amazement.

Kyros sighed. The trauma Ramâno experienced when he witnessed those murders had affected the boy quite badly. How many more were there like him? Kyros' eyes were opened to see darkness over many people; but he also saw the crowd teeming with En-luchés: the light from them almost blinded him. The effect of his words over the crowd was like a pitched battle, enabling the En-luchés to release people from the hidden things that troubled their lives.

He was startled by Ramâno's exuberant shout.

'I feel so different. All that fear has gone. I want to be like you and heal people on the inside as well as the outside.'

'I'm pleased for you, Ramâno. Be careful. The True King doesn't heal like that for you to do great deeds, but so you can know and love him and walk in peace with him. He's far more interested in a relationship with you than what you do for him.'

'I don't understand. I don't know your True King, yet I see you. But I don't know who you are or where you live. How can I be like you if I don't know these things?'

Kyros was taken aback. He didn't want to upset the boy, but those two things had to remain hidden for a little longer. When he explained this to Ramâno, he saw tears welling up in the boy's eyes.

'You don't want me to follow you any more do you?'

'It's not that,' Kyros tried to comfort the lad. 'But you need to be with your Mother. I have no proper place to lay my head at night. I can't let you live like that.'

'All right, then,' the boy brightened. 'I will call you Mister Healer until I know your real name.'

As he walked back to camp that night Kyros pondered the words from Yanantha. If only that bit about Lenyé falling in love with his Uncle wasn't true. He could bear anything except that. He hoped Lenyé was being coerced against her will; and that she loved him still. When would his words on the Dangst Rock begin to have an effect? Maybe he should start acting now to make it happen as the True King said. But how could he speak to her?

Suddenly he remembered the occasion before they set out on holiday when he chased Quinn from the kitchens in the palace, and they discovered the secret passageway that led from the stables to the throne room. He could get into the palace undetected, but how was he to find her before he was seen?

He approached the camp at dusk, and was startled by a low growl as a huge black shape reared up out of the darkness.

'Mamma Uza-Mâté. Ariella. What are you doing here?'

'We followed Lenyé to the city, but were chased away by the guards,' Ariella rubbed herself against him in greeting.

'We hung around outside the main gates for a few days, but couldn't work out how to get in to see her,' Mamma Uza-Mâté growled. 'Then Chuah-te-mok told us where to find you.'

Kyros stroked Ariella and gave Mamma Uza-Mâté a hug.

'Chuah-te-mok brought us a message saying Ra-Na-Jiri saw Lenyé with a richly dressed man who he assumed was your Uncle,' Mamma Uza-Mâté continued. 'He tried to have a word with her after the man had gone, but she was reluctant to talk.'

'I know,' Kyros sighed. 'Chuah-te-mok told me.'

'We came to see if you had any ideas,' Ariella sat back on her haunches.

'I can get into the city unrecognised, at the moment,' Kyros hesitated, not wanting to mention about the secret passageway. 'I suggest you stay here till we can work out a plan to rescue her.'

'Lenyé's changed, Kyros,' Mamma Uza-Mâté's deep growl made Kyros feel uncomfortable. 'I could hardly believe the rest of Ra-Na-Jiri's message. Apparently she wasn't in any hurry to escape from the palace at all.'

As he lay wrapped in his jerkin, Kyros was still troubled by Mamma Uza-Mâté's final words. He found himself repeating Lenyé's name to himself as he dropped off to sleep: 'Oh, that you would shake yourself free of Uncle Morthrir's influence,' he murmured; 'and choose the man you really want. If only I could come to you and persuade you to return to me.'

Chapter Sixty Seven

Morthrir heard a knock at the door, rolled over in bed and thrust himself up on one elbow, 'Who is it?'

'Eawen the Henosite. You called to me in your mind, Sire.'

Morthrir sat up eagerly, 'Come in, my friend.' He watched the Henosite close the door and approach the bed before whispering, 'Something's happened to my spiritual power.'

'When you say "*happened*", what exactly do you mean?'

'Three days ago at sunset, I felt a deep shock inside and all my power drained away from me. I still feel sick and dizzy.'

'I see. Have you displeased the Lord Abbérron in some way?'

'No.' Morthrir frowned. 'As far as I'm concerned, Kyros and his brother are dead. I have the last two boys here at the palace, and Lenyé is about to accept me as her husband. I am very close to being crowned King and seizing all power.'

'If that's true, you have accomplished much very quickly. The only conclusion I can come to is there is another power at work.'

'Abbérron's power is supreme. You told me so yourself.'

'I know. But I feel troubled in my mind. What do you make of this Healer in the Central Square?'

'He's a fake,' Morthrir smacked his hand on the bed. 'No one can do the things people say he does.'

'Have you seen him for yourself?'

'No. I don't go gawping at wandering conjurors like that.'

'The whole city has gone out to him and hangs on his every word. They say he does miracles in the name of the True King.'

'So?' Morthrir glared at the Henosite. 'Abbérron is more

powerful. You're not having second thoughts are you?'

'No. Of course not. Do you know who he is? The crowds keep asking for his name, but he refuses to identify himself.'

'What are you suggesting?'

'I have some skill as a sculptor of faces. I will make a likeness for you to see. That means persuading him to let me feel his facial features, but I'm sure that won't be a problem.'

After Eawen had gone, Morthrir summoned Youdlh and told him the Henosite had free access to him even in his private suite.

'Very good, Sire.'

'I want extra guards posted in the Central Square to watch that so-called Healer. Do you know what he looks like?'

'Tall. Dark skinned. Great mop of hair and a beard. I'd say he was a Krêonor, but not looking like that. Maybe he's come from the Tsé-shâmé.'

'You mean a spy?'

'Doubt it. A spy wouldn't parade himself in public like that.'

'Double the guards. I don't want him causing any problems.'

'Problems?' Youdlh sounded puzzled. 'He's not causing any problems. He's solving them. My warriors have seen him heal so many people they're absolutely astonished.'

'I don't want to hear this.'

'You may have to reconsider your view, Sire. There's a boy in the palace who was completely crippled in both legs until he met the Healer. Now he's running round faster than any of the other lads, and he's impossible to catch.'

'Really. What's his name?'

'Ramâno. His Mother works in the kitchens as one of the cooks. Now she's always singing about the great miracle the True King has done for her and her boy.'

'In that case, have her arrested and locked in one of the downstairs salons till I have decided what to do with her.'

'On what charge, Sire?'

'Trying to poison my food. That's why I've been so ill!'

Chapter Sixty Eight

On the third day Kyros looked up into the crowd from the person he was speaking over and saw in the distance a beautiful young woman watching him, an amused smile playing at the corners of her mouth. He took in the light cream of her dress that set off her tan, and the matching parasol, and her hair plaited in braids from her temples and gathered to a clasp at the back, the rest cascading loosely over her shoulders and tumbling down her back like liquid gold. She caught his eye and turned away, twirling the parasol in front of her as though she was hiding from him.

He gasped with shock as he recognised Lenyé. He'd forgotten how captivating she was to look at. Even in the midst of his labours he had never stopped thinking about her, and he knew he loved her more now than he ever did. A pang of anguish seared his heart: Lenyé wouldn't be dressed like that if his Uncle didn't think very highly of her. And she wouldn't be allowed out on her own if he wasn't confident she would return to the palace. So it must be true: Lenyé had fallen in love with his Uncle.

Did she recognise him? And if so, would she betray him?

He wanted to go and talk to her, but caught a glimpse of soldiers behind her. Then he noticed the slight frown of uncertainty on her brow and read the confusion in her heart, and a ray of hope flashed through his mind. She…

Kyros felt a sharp elbow in the ribs and glanced down to see Ramâno grinning at him, the boy's eyes darting away in Lenyé's direction before focusing back on him.

'Mister Healer. That's the Princess-Lady I spoke to in the Royal Cemetery. She thinks Prince Kyros is buried there, but I told her it wasn't true. So the Prince must be alive somewhere and they still haven't found him.'

Kyros shook his head, wondering if Lenyé would realise now who he really was. 'What's that got to do with me?'

'We're good friends. I can take messages to her if you like.'

'Thank you. I'll bear that in mind.'

'She's got a pet cobra called Ra-Na-Jiri. He's massive, at least eight feet long and as thick as my leg; and she talks to him. I wish I could talk to a snake. I wonder what he'd say to me?'

Kyros smiled: he couldn't risk the lad being involved. The cobra was still the best way to persuade Lenyé to escape.

Lenyé watched the Healer being jostled in the Central Square. For three days she'd heard about the amazing healings, and then Ramâno's boast; so she was using Morthrir's illness as an opportunity to slip out to see for herself. It was the man from the forest: she recognised the darkened skin and full beard and long, unkempt hair. But she couldn't decide from this distance whether it was Kyros or not.

The Healer climbed onto the edge of the fountain and waited for silence. But before he could say anything a voice shouted, 'Who are you? You talk about the True King, but what is your name?'

'Why do you seek my name?' the Healer called back. 'For it is hidden from you for a while. I am here to declare the name of the True King to you and perform his deeds amongst you.'

'How can we accept that if we do not know who you are?'

'That's right,' someone else called out. 'You look like a wandering vagabond. How can we trust you?'

'Do not judge by my looks, but by what I do. The knowledge of the True King must increase while I remain unknown.'

But the crowd demanded all the more to know who he was.

Lenyé was amazed at what the Healer said. If this really was Kyros, then what a change in him: where was the opinionated, self-confident young man she once knew? It couldn't be him.

'Do not be so concerned about me,' the Healer continued. 'It is more important for you to know the purposes of the True King and be gathered to his name.'

Lenyé felt a stab of guilt go through her heart at the mention of the True King's purposes. She was reminded of her thoughts when she had defeated the first warrior army and why the Sword of Justice stuck in its scabbard when she needed it. She only *"knew of the True king as some distant figurehead presiding over the affairs of the Waking World. If it was his Sword, then she would have to know him for herself"*. But what had she done about it? Maybe the Healer's words would help, and she began listening to him again.

'…for he is seeking to rid the Waking World of the curse that entered at the Beginning,' the voice of the Healer jerked her back to the present.

'Why has he taken so long?' an old man called out.

'Because his people need to prepare themselves. That curse has tainted everyone born into the Waking World and we need to be free of it. The only way is to return to a knowledge of the True King.'

'Are you saying we should reject Morthrir?' another shouted. 'Only a few days ago he talked of *"a man who will arise from amongst us to control the destiny of the entire Waking World"*.'

'That's right,' a woman at the front spoke up. 'This man will be *"so anointed with spiritual power that he will be able to set people free to connect with that power within themselves, that they might voluntarily come under the man's protection to be ruled by him so that we all might live in peace and harmony"*.'

'I didn't know about this speech,' the Healer replied.

'Morthrir also said, *"the man…will be crowned King amongst us and wed his bride on the same day"*,' the woman continued. 'So we thought it was going to be Morthrir.'

'Then you come along,' the old man shouted, 'and do all these healings and we begin to think you might be the one.'

Lenyé watched the Healer intently as he spread out his arms in his appeal to the crowd.

'All I can do is to tell you there is a day approaching when those who choose to follow the True King now, and walk in his ways, will be called upon to stand fast in the final onslaught to rid the Waking World of the evil caused by that curse.'

Lenyé heard a buzz of conversation in the crowd as they discussed this, and caught various individual comments, but no one spoke out in challenge.

'If you call on the name of the True King,' the Healer continued, 'it's as though he is right there with you to protect you. Those who remain faithful to the end will enter into his rest. Those who ignore his call, and prefer to be masters of their own destinies, will be overcome by that evil and caught up in a bitter conflict on the wrong side. Then it will be too late to change their minds.'

'How do we know what you're saying is the truth?' someone shouted from the crowd.

'I could not do these works if I wasn't speaking on the True King's behalf. You are seeing a release of his power through me. These healings are the beginning of the Restoration.'

He pointed at the crowd. 'Even if you knew I had come back to you from the Realm of the Departed, you would still struggle to accept my words. I am only with you for a short time to warn you of what is about to happen. I beg you to think carefully about what I am saying. All you need is…'

There was a commotion where the Healer was pointing, as a blind man pushed his way forwards, tapping on the ground with a cane. 'Please help me,' he called out. 'I must meet the Healer.'

Lenyé gasped. It was Eawen the Henosite. What was he doing here? Morthrir obviously trusted this strange man, and she felt a

228

chill of fear as if the Henosite was here for no good; that if the Healer really was Kyros, the man might betray him to Morthrir.

Someone in the crowd called out, 'It's the Henosite. If you can heal him, we will accept what you're talking about.' Willing hands helped the Henosite on his way.

'What can I do for you, my friend?' the Healer asked.

'I feel honoured to be in your presence, good Sir. I cannot see you. Please allow me to shake your hand and run my fingers over your face that I may know you better.'

'Why not let the True King heal you? Then you can see for yourself.'

'No. I am not worthy to ask that. Please grant me my request.'

'Very well. Go ahead. But I will also do what I can for you.'

As the Henosite ran his fingers skilfully over the Healers face, Lenyé saw him pause with one hand at the top of the Healer's head and heard the catch in his voice. 'What is this? It feels like a disk around your head. I can put my fingers through it.'

The Healer shrugged and Lenyé watched in awe as he placed one hand on the back of the Henosite's head, and covered the old man's eyes with the other. Then she heard for the first time words of healing spoken over someone: 'Receive your sight, in the name of the True King.'

Nothing happened. 'He couldn't heal him,' someone shouted. 'Why should we accept what you say?'

The Healer knelt down and shovelled dust into the palm of one hand and spat on it, rubbing his hands together as he stood up. 'This is not a question of healing your sight, but rebuilding your eyeballs.' He smeared some paste over both of the closed eyelids, and replaced his hands on the Henosite's head and eyes.

But before the Healer could say anything, the Henosite spoke in a low voice, and Lenyé had to strain forwards to catch his words. 'I felt a circle of energy about your head. Tell me your secret and let me do the things you do.'

The Healer laughed. 'I have only one thing to say to you, my friend. For a long time you have struggled between two masters without knowing it. You have submitted to Abbérron assuming he is either greater than the True King or they are both the same. But they are not. You can no longer continue like this, for either you will love the one and hate the other, or despise the one and secretly serve the other.'

'How can you say that to me? Abbérron is all I know!'

'Your eyes will not be healed immediately, but only after your inner eyes have been opened to see the truth in what I say.'

The Henosite wrenched himself away with a terrible cry and stumbled into the crowd, frantically tapping ahead of himself with his cane. 'Out of my way. Out of my way. I must get away from him. Don't listen to him. The man speaks nothing but lies!'

The Healer called after him, 'May you meet the one I serve.'

Lenyé watched for a while longer as the Healer spoke words over many others. She felt power emanating from him and touching people with a simple love that not only healed the infirm but brightened the lives of everyone else around him. Then she realised with a shock that Morthrir was the exact opposite. His power drew attention to himself and made him appear vastly superior to all others.

What was it about the Healer? She felt torn between the desire to go as close as possible, and a sudden fear of him: if he could say and do things like that, what kind of power was he using?

How could it be Kyros? Maybe the death certificate was correct and Ramâno's corpse in the Royal Cemetery was Kyros after all. But even if the Healer wasn't Kyros, she felt drawn to him in a way she couldn't explain... She was distracted by some guards walking purposefully in her direction. Immediately she broke away from the crowd and wended her way back towards the palace thinking over all that she'd seen and heard.

She had to find out whose body was in the grave. And there was only one way to prove that to her satisfaction.

Chapter Sixty Nine

The next day Morthrir was up and found Eawen in the playroom on the third floor. The bust of the Healer on the table was nearly finished but the old man sat on a chair rubbing his eyes.

'What's the matter with your eyes?' Morthrir wasn't too concerned. 'Got some clay in them?'

'No. They're itching and hot. I can't work like this.'

'Well, rub it away. I must have this job finished urgently.' He examined the bust. 'What a peculiar man. He has the features of a Krêonor. In fact, he looks familiar. What sort of height was he?'

'Tall, Sire. I had to reach up to him.'

'You're sure about all that hair and beard. It confirms what Youdlh told me. He can't be a Krêonor looking like that.'

'Ahhh!'

Eawen's yell made Morthrir whip round in alarm. 'What is it, man? I don't want anyone else to know you're working up here.'

'They're burning,' the Henosite clawed at his eyes as if trying to scratch them out. 'They're burning. I can't stand it.'

'What are you on about?'

'My eyes. The Healer touched my eyes.'

'Why did you let him do that?'

'I couldn't stop him. He smeared something on them.'

'Well, wash it off.'

'I can't. The paste he used has soaked into my eyelids, and now I know the truth.'

'What truth?'

'The True King is greater, the True King is greater, the True

King is greater!' The Henosite danced around the room, and punched the air as he hopped and cavorted. 'He is the True King over all, and even Abbérron must bow the knee before him.'

'What are you saying?' Morthrir caught the Henosite by the shirt and yanked him close. 'Are you betraying me?' Then he noticed the Henosite's eyelids. Ordinarily they were closed and sunk into their sockets, but now the eyes began to swell under the lids and fill out. The eyelids flickered and finally opened.

Morthrir screamed, let go and backed away in horror. 'This is a trick of that conjuror. Get away from me!' He couldn't bear that incredible grey of the Henosite's irises: not a bland, uniform colour like a stone; but a living grey, flecked and facetted with a myriad of textures that sparkled like diamonds.

'I can see!' the Henosite shouted. 'I can see you. I no longer have to feel anyone's face to know them.'

'That Healer did this, didn't he?'

'Of course he did. Never in the history of the Waking World has a man born blind had his sight healed. It took place right in front of you. You have to admit he's done an incredible miracle.'

'It's some kind of trick.'

'He said my eyes would only be healed when my inner eyes were opened to see the truth.'

'I don't care what you say. The True King is not greater than Abbérron. I know because Abbérron is with me, all the time...' he glanced at the Henosite but the man wasn't looking at him.

'What's that?' the Henosite pointed with his finger.

'A window.'

'No. What's that coming through it?'

'Daylight, of course. What do you expect? That's what a window's for. To let the light in.'

The Henosite walked to the window. 'I never imagined anything like this.' He ran his hand over the glass in a large circular movement. 'But it's not the right kind of light.'

'What do you mean?'

Eawen turned to Morthrir. 'He's a window onto another world, letting the light through. There was something around the Healer's head, like a big dinner plate. But it wasn't hard; almost as if it had no substance. I could push my hand right through. It felt like energy to my finger-tips. Now I think it was light.' He glanced at the window. 'But not that kind of light. The Healer is a two-way window. What power is filling this man to radiate such intense light and yet draw me in towards another being?'

'Rubbish, man.'

'That's what's missing.' Eawen swung round to his sculpture. 'There's too much hair.' He grabbed a sculpting knife and sliced through the clay, removing a mass of hair and laying it gently on the table. 'It would have been about here. If I can construct...'

'Wait a minute,' Morthrir strode forwards, seized the knife from the old man's hand and cut more clay away from where the hair was and scraped clay off the jaw where the beard had been.

'What are you doing?' Eawen tried pulling Mothrir's hand away. 'You have destroyed the man's image.'

'No I haven't. This is the real image, but all that hair and beard was masking it. And right under my nose, too. I thought it was a much older man. How dare he!' He grabbed Eawen by the shirt again and dragged him close up to his face. 'Get your things out of here. I'm taking charge of that bust. I don't want anyone else to see it or know you've been working on it.'

'Why ever not?'

'And don't you dare breathe a word of this to anyone. On pain of death.'

'Why? What have I done?'

'I must have that Healer arrested immediately.'

'I don't understand.'

'That man,' Morthrir released the Henosite's shirt and raised his hand to point at the bust, his whole arm trembling. 'That man,' his voice reached a high-pitched crescendo till he was screaming, 'That man is my enemy, Kyros!'

Chapter Seventy

In the early afternoon, Lenyé sat at the desk in the private council chamber. There was no news of Morthrir's condition so she intended to use her freedom to full advantage before visiting his bedroom to check on him.

She was trembling like a leaf, knowing that she shouldn't be in here. But it was the only safe place away from prying eyes to have this meeting.

There was a knock on the door in the wall behind her, leading to the spiral staircase and down into the gardens below.

She gripped the edges of the desk to stop herself shaking, and glanced round. 'Come.'

The door opened and Doctor Nostrea entered. He closed the door gently behind him and crossed the floor to the desk.

Lenyé didn't trust herself to stand properly, so held out her hand instead. 'Thank you for coming, Doctor.'

The Apothecary raised her hand and kissed the back. 'I am honoured to be invited here for this meeting, My Lady.'

He released her hand and she indicated a chair for him.

Lenyé leaned forwards slightly over the desk and lowered her voice. 'Did you bring the document?'

'Yes. Here it is.' Doctor Nostrea took a scroll from the folds of his cloak, removed the ribbon and unrolled the parchment.'

'Thank you, Doctor. I couldn't find the palace copy, and didn't want to disturb my Uncle as he is unwell.'

The Apothecary gestured towards the document, 'I think you will find everything is in order. It's a standard format. Only the insertion of names and description of the deceased and circumstances of death differ from any other certificate.'

Lenyé studied the parchment. 'The reason I asked to see you is to check you were certain it was Kyros.'

'What makes you think it wasn't?'

'I understand the body was badly burned.' Lenyé watched the Apothecary closely and noticed a slight narrowing of his eyes. 'Surely that would make identification somewhat difficult.'

'Difficult. But not impossible.'

'So how did you convince yourself it was Kyros?'

'He was a tall man, and well-built, like Kyros.'

'Some of my Uncle's warriors are of similar stature.'

'True. But Kyros was seen swimming out to the island. So we would expect him to be there.'

'Then there was a fire,' she continued. 'Why would Kyros let himself be burned to death rather than finding a way of escape?'

'The corpse was dressed in warriors' attire.'

'Oh. So maybe he'd overpowered one of his attackers and was preparing to slip down through the rest of them in disguise, steal the boat and row away.'

'That was a very real possibility and one of the determining factors that finally convinced me.'

'Was there no ring on his finger that might identify him?'

'I'm sorry to say there was not much left of his hands. Any ring might have slipped off or been pilfered by one of the warriors who brought him back to the mainland.'

'Did you question them?' Lenyé raised an eyebrow.

'I must admit I only thought of that afterwards, by which time they had rejoined their unit and were presumably posted out with their whole company. I couldn't find them again.'

'So what you're really saying is that there is only circumstantial evidence that it was Kyros. Surely it would have been safer to record this as the death of an unknown person?'

'But then there's the whole family situation to consider. How

235

would you have felt coming back to the palace, not knowing he was dead and therefore unable to grieve for him properly?'

'What happens if he's still alive and walks back into the palace to challenge your assertion?'

Doctor Nostrea sighed and placed both hands palm down on the desk in front of him. 'I had a rather intense interview with your Uncle, outlining the very points you have been making. But he has powerful means of persuasion at his disposal.'

'Are you saying you signed this under duress?'

'Let's just say I wasn't completely convinced.'

'I see. What about Beth and Quinn then?'

Doctor Nostrea retrieved his copy of the certificate, rolled it up, retied the ribbon and returned it to a fold in his cloak. 'There was no shadow of doubt in my mind in their case. The two bodies were very badly mauled, but were the right size, colour of hair and any intact features bore a strong resemblance to both of them. I only wish, for your sake, it was not so.'

'In that case…' Lenyé was about to rise and close the meeting, confident that her nervousness was over, but jerked her head up at the sound of the door opening. 'Morthrir!'

Doctor Nostrea whipped his head round. When he turned back to Lenyé his face was ashen and his eyes were full of fear.

'What is the meaning of this?' Morthrir closed the door with a deliberate click and strode into the room. 'What are you doing in here without my leave?' he eyed the Apothecary. 'Get out.'

Doctor Nostrea fairly raced across the floor as Morthrir turned to face Lenyé.

'Not that door.'

Lenyé saw the man pause with his hand on the door handle.

'You can go out this way,' Morthrir pointed to the door leading to the spiral staircase. 'And make sure no one sees you in the gardens. I don't want the whole palace to know you were having a clandestine meeting with my niece.'

After the Apothecary had gone, Morthrir stood looking down

at her. 'Well? What has that idiot been telling you?'

Initially Lenyé felt shocked at Morthrir bursting in like that, but now she was able to control her shaking and use the energy. She stood up so abruptly that the chair crashed to the floor behind her, and walked round the edge of the desk to confront him. 'How dare you make accusations about that man or draw wrong assumptions from my meeting with him. I asked him here to confirm the bodies in those three graves were recorded correctly.'

'And were you satisfied with his answers?'

'Completely. Beth and Quinn were relatively easy to identify, but for Kyros he had to use his best professional judgement.'

Morthrir stared at her, the expression of anger evaporating from his face. Then he burst out laughing. 'I like that. I'm impressed by what you've done.'

'How do you mean?'

'You didn't just accept my word, when you obviously had doubts, and were prepared to follow it up. I have a great deal of respect for you. You have traits that I would find admirable in a wife. I will await your decision concerning us in due course.'

'If you want a favourable decision from me, Morthrir, then please leave me alone for a little longer. I came in here for some peace and quiet to think things through, and I haven't quite finished yet.'

'Of course.' Morthrir turned on his heel, walked across to the door and let himself out.

As soon as he was gone Lenyé collapsed to her knees on the floor, her face in her hands, sobbing as the reined-in emotions finally overcame her. She'd faced down Morthrir, protected Doctor Nostrea and found out the truth. Clearly the Apothecary was not convinced. So Ramâno was right. The body in the Cemetery wasn't Kyros after all.

Chapter Seventy One

Kyros was disturbed about the points in his Uncle's speech that people in the crowd had mentioned. If this was the Hidden Power using him then it was very subtle, mixing a bit of truth with enough clever words to disguise Abbérron's counterfeit and keep people from acknowledging the True King.

As he made his way out of the city that night, he was startled by a cloaked figure that exited a dark alley and collided with him. He stopped but the figure darted away, the hood slipped from the face and he recognised her instantly.

'Lenyé. What are you doing here?'

She disappeared up the alleyway. Kyros gave chase but lost her in the gloom. He carried on down the alley, then stopped. As he retraced his steps, the figure ran back up the alley.

Kyros caught her by the arm. 'Lenyé. We need to talk.'

'No we don't. I see someone with long hair and a full beard and darkened skin, who does incredible deeds and speaks of things I do not understand. How can I know if you are Kyros?'

'I picked cornflowers for you when we were younger. The day I proposed, you wore a cornflower-blue dress. Remember?'

Lenyé started back in surprise. She couldn't deny those things had happened, but they seemed so long ago. Did she say "Yes" to Kyros? It was as if her memory of that day was blanked out and she had another man in her life. She broke the silence that had settled between them. 'No. I haven't forgotten. By these memories alone I have to accept you are the real Kyros. But you spoke terrible things to me that day in the forest.'

'Let me explain.'

'There's nothing more I want to hear from you or say to you.'

'Then why are you on your own in an alleyway that cuts across my route out of the city? You followed me, didn't you?'

'No, I…'

'Even if you won't talk to me, I must talk to you.'

'Not here. We might be seen together.'

'Lenyé. I need to ask: do you love Uncle Morthrir, or me?'

'I don't know. I'm so confused!'

'We parted with harsh words and a sundered relationship. I don't know what came over me. But I am ashamed of my words, and have found out why we both treated each other so badly.'

'How do you mean?'

'Uncle Morthrir has immense spiritual power because he is in league with Abbérron, and has spoken a word of confusion against us, a word of power for my destruction and a word of power to make you fall in love with him against your will.'

'But Kyros. He needs me.'

'Like a trinket to parade on state occasions. He doesn't love you at all. What kind of a marriage is that?'

'He's very considerate towards me…'

'And that's enough for you?'

'What am I supposed to think? You disappear, then return and tell me what to do with that Sword. You despise me for being allied to the Nastrim, but they're dead now.'

'I know. Mamma Uza-Mâté told me.'

'I had to escape from Morthrir's warriors.'

'So how did you end up here?'

'Vashtani claimed me for his bride. I held him at bay with the Sword of Justice, but was surrounded by Dé-monos. Then Morthrir rode up and ordered Vashtani to let me go. I was astonished. Vashtani obeyed him. Morthrir gave me a warrior's horse to ride to the palace with him and his escort.'

'Why is it Morthrir this and Morthrir that, and you no longer call him Uncle? Does that mean you've fallen in love with him?'

'What else was I supposed to do? We'd broken apart.'

'Lenyé, I'm pleading with you to come back to me.'

'Kyros don't. I can't bear it. Your sisters and my brothers are prisoners in the palace. Beth and Quinn are dead...'

'What?'

'Originally I thought he ordered me to come to the palace or he would start executing them one a day, starting with Beth, then Quinn, then the others. I still had the Nastrim army to fight my cause, so I refused, intending to come and rescue them by force. Then I find out the order never came from Morthrir and he was trying to protect us all. Beth and Quinn didn't understand and escaped, but were killed by wild animals. The rest are safe, but kept virtually as prisoners in the palace for their own protection.'

'I can't believe this is true. Are you sure?'

'Of course I'm sure. I saw their graves, Kyros. It must be true!'

'All the more reason to come away with me.'

'But not now. I can't leave the others. They need me as well.'

'Then I'll have to find a way to get you all out.'

'Kyros. That's impossible.'

'No it isn't. I need to know whether you will part from Uncle Morthrir's hold over you and come back to me.'

'Give me a day to decide and I will let you know.'

'Very well. Tomorrow evening I will send Chuah-te-mok to the palace gardens for your answer.'

'Morthrir is watching your actions. He doesn't know who you are but is intrigued by your power to heal people and welcomes it because it means more people who are fit enough to work and pay taxes. But your talk about the True King is threatening him. He wants you arrested. While you're in a crowd he daren't in case there's a riot. But he'll find a way to get you on your own. His men might even be watching us now. Be careful. You're safe in a crowd.'

She leaned over, kissed him on the forehead, and was gone.

Chapter Seventy Two

Beth awoke with the sun streaming in through the windows of the cottage. She wriggled into a more comfortable position on the rug on the floor and pulled up her cloak. She couldn't get the nightmare of the last few days out of her mind: hiding that night in the woods with the horse and hearing the men and dogs not far off; Quinn falling into the river the following morning and getting soaked; and, despite his constant shivering, he insisted on doubling back and watching their trail, but there was no sign of any pursuit. They travelled for the rest of the day and night and most of the next day before they found the cottage. By then, Quinn was shaking so badly he could hardly stay on the horse. She managed to haul him into the cottage, remove his wet boots, strip off most of his sodden clothing and bundle him into bed with all the blankets she could find to keep him warm. She lit the kitchen stove and the living room fire and kept them stoked up all the time, but for the next four days Quinn had gone through alternating periods of chills, high fever and sweating.

But it was more than a physical ailment. He kept calling out Ishi-mi-réjá's name over and over again, telling her to hold on and not let go. Once when he was sweating and thrashing his head and arms from side to side, he suddenly shouted out, 'Ishi-mi-réjá. We need you!' Then he slumped back in the bed and was shivering again, his eyelids partly open and his eyeballs rolled upwards so she could only see the whites of his eyes.

She hardly dared to leave him, but needed to draw water from the well, heat it on the stove and make hot cloths to wipe

241

his face with. She'd been out to lay traps and then retrieve the rabbits to replenish their dwindling stock of food.

All the time there was this strange feeling of being here when the old woman was… Dead? If she wasn't, it would be hard to explain Ishi-mi-réjá's actions. She wouldn't have deserted them on the mountain.

Beth stretched, threw off her cloak and stood up, before wandering around the familiar room touching various things and trying to imagine the old woman being there. Maybe the power on the mountain was too much for her. Even now Beth felt the shock of that stone disintegrating in her hands again, and the awful power released against her through the thunder storm.

She slipped into the kitchen, her mind in a whirl. Then she thrust open the back door and walked round to check the horse was still securely tied to a picket peg in the middle of the only patch of grass near the cottage. The horse nuzzled her hand and she patted his cheek.

Beth sighed. It was some time since they were on Mount Malkamet: Ishi-mi-réjá was not coming back. Something terrible must have happened to her, and it confirmed how delirious Quinn was if he kept calling for her like that. Beth went back into the cottage and found Quinn beginning to stir.

She sat on the edge of the bed and felt his forehead. 'Quinn. It's gone. The fever's gone. Can you hear me?'

Quinn's eyelids flickered and he tried to prop himself up on an elbow. 'Where am I?'

'We're in Ishi-mi-réjá's cottage.'

'Why…?'

Quickly she explained what had happened, and helped Quinn to sit up.

'I'm starving. Is there anything to eat?'

Beth left him wrapped in blankets while she went to prepare breakfast and brought it in on a tray for them to share at the bed.

Quinn concentrated on eating while Beth talked about her

sense of loss at Ishi-mi-réjá's disappearance.

'She's not gone,' Quinn bit into a piece of bread.

Beth looked up at him, startled. 'What makes you say that?'

'I saw her. She was falling down into a great dark pit, and it was getting hotter and hotter towards the bottom.' He paused in his eating to wipe a hand across his forehead. 'That's all I can remember. It was terrible. I thought I was going to die.'

'It was only a dream, Quinn. You were calling out her name in your sleep. She's gone, and she's not coming back.'

'I felt so certain when I woke up, but maybe you're right.' He took a swig of water. 'Let's finish breakfast. Then I want to get up and have a good look round. There must be something to show us what's happened to her.'

'Before we do anything,' Beth rose from the bed and flung open the windows. 'We need to get rid of this stuffy atmosphere.' She took a deep breath of fresh air as a light breeze stirred the curtains at one of the windows. 'I've had the fire and the stove stoked up all this time to keep you warm!'

Beth brought him his clean clothes and left him to dress while she cleared away the remains of the food.

Quinn felt very weak when he stood up, but forced himself to move about and examine the mantelshelf. Something wasn't quite right. 'Hey, Beth. What do you make of this?'

Beth ran in from the kitchen at the sharp note in his voice and stood next to him. 'What?'

'There,' and he pointed with his finger.

'I don't see anything.'

'Exactly. Take a look at the rest of the mantelshelf.'

'Nothing's changed since we were last here.'

'Yes it has.' He pointed along the mantelshelf. 'It's covered in dust. But not there,' he pointed back to the original spot. 'That's where Ishi-mi-réjá kept her stone. Why is there no dust there?'

'I don't know. Maybe she hadn't done any dusting for a while, and it's thicker everywhere else.'

'No. The cottage was immaculate when we last stayed. There has to be another explanation. Let's cup our hands around this bit and see if anything happens.'

Beth followed his example and filled in the gaps between Quinn's hands where he curved his fingers. 'Do we need to say anything?'

'Shh. I can feel something.'

'So can I,' Beth gasped. 'My fingers are trembling.'

'What do you think's happening?'

'I don't know. It feels like when I held up the stone on the mountain before everything went wrong. Oh, Quinn. Let's stop. I don't like this.'

'Carry on for a bit longer. I can't believe anything to do with Ishi-mi-réjá is wrong.'

'Quinn, my arms are shaking. I want to stop.'

'Look,' Quinn indicated with a jerk of his chin. 'What's all that grey stuff?' As he spoke, a stream of fine grey dust began pouring in through a window onto the mantelshelf between their hands, and formed itself into a familiar shape, like a grey bread roll with spines protruding out of it down one side.

'It's her stone,' Beth gasped in amazement.

The stone filled out to its full size with yellow and white swirls and veins appearing in the smooth greyness.

Beth felt her hands stop shaking, broke the circle with Quinn, picked up the stone and turned it over. 'Look, there are those funny little dimples. It's exactly the same as the stone that cured me, and I held above my head on the mountain.' She glanced at Quinn. 'What does it mean?'

Chapter Seventy Three

The following morning Kyros was astonished to find the narrow street he used to enter the city thronged with people. When they spotted him, a loud cheer went up and many men came forwards, lifted him onto their shoulders and bore him down the street and into the Central Square.

Immediately he knew this was a significant day. There were far more soldiers on guard than previously and he saw archers posted at some of the third storey windows in the buildings surrounding the Square.

Kyros should have demanded an answer from Lenyé sooner but knew he had to respect what they agreed. Besides, he'd already primed Chuah-te-mok to fly to the palace gardens for Lenyé's answer at dusk; and Harbona had slipped into the city last night, under cover of darkness, to arrange enough horses. It was too late to change all that now.

If she said, "No", all his hopes would be dashed. But if she said, "Yes", Chuah-te-mok had an escape plan to pass on to her for later that night. He thought about Lenyé's warning to stay in a crowd. That was all very well during the day, but by evening he had to get to the back of the palace without being arrested.

He knew this would be the last day to speak to the people for some time. He lifted up his voice in a great plea for them to put aside their reservations about the True King, but was distracted by someone pulling the bottom of his jerkin from behind.

'Hey, Mister Healer. Did you like my welcome this morning?'

Kyros whirled round at the sound of Ramâno's voice. 'What

do you mean, "*your welcome*"?'

'I followed you last night, so I know which route out of the city leads to your camp.'

'You shouldn't have done that.'

'Oh yes I should. The soldiers are going to arrest you today because that Morthrir-man is worried about what you're doing. I hear news when I go to the palace with my Mamma. So I thought you must have crowds of people around you all day. Then they can't arrest you because they're afraid the people will cause a riot. So I spread a rumour of where you come from each day.'

'That was very thoughtful of you.'

'And I saw you talking to the Princess-Lady. You know. The one that the Morthrir-man wants to marry.'

'Yes...'

'And she called you Kyros. You're the missing Prince that the warriors are trying to find. Aren't you? So you're a Prince and a Healer. That's amazing. You'd make a much better King than the Morthrir-man. Now I know roughly where you live, and I know your name. So can I follow you?'

'Keep your voice down.'

'Only if you say, "Yes"!'

'Listen, Ramâno. I am here at the command of the True King. But other things are going on which make it more complicated. If you breathe a word to anyone about who I am or where I'm staying, I'll be in a lot of trouble.'

'Don't worry. I can keep a secret. I'll still call you, "Mister Healer".'

'Good. Carry on today as you've been doing and no one will suspect anything different.'

'Does that mean I'm following you?'

'If you like.'

'And will I get a light around my head like you have?'

'You mentioned that before,' Kyros sounded genuinely puzzled. He wondered if it could have anything to do with the light around Zerigor's head that he read about in Yanantha's parchment, but dismissed it from his mind. It couldn't be.

'It's really bright,' Ramâno grinned.

'But I can't see it.'

'Never mind. I must go back to Mamma first and take her some fish from the market. She's preparing pike to her own recipe for a special meal tonight. She thinks that Morthrir-man is going to ask the Princess-Lady for her answer.'

'Her answer?' Kyros felt the Square begin to spin and heard a roaring sound in his ears.

'Whether she's going to say "Yes" to marrying him or not. The whole city's waiting. Then he can set the date for the coronation and have the wedding on the same day.'

Kyros staggered as if he'd been struck a heavy blow and managed to sink down onto the edge of the fountain.

'What's the matter?' Ramâno's shrill voice startled him. 'Are you all right?'

'Nothing…'

'You're in love with the Princess-Lady, aren't you?'

Kyros glared at the boy.

'And you're going to rescues her, aren't you?'

'Shh. Keep your voice down.'

'Can I help?'

'No.' Kyros frowned. 'It's far too dangerous.'

'I'm big and brave and strong. I can be a warrior one more time. Then I'll be like you again!'

Once the boy had departed on his errand, Kyros tried to concentrate on the needs of the people around him as he spoke words of healing and release over them and proclaimed the message of reconciling everyone to the True King. But he was in anguish of heart over Lenyé. What if she said "Yes" to Uncle Morthrir? 'Oh, My King,' he whispered in his heart. 'No one can force another against their own will. If only she would make the right choice.'

The day wore on and he was constantly glancing up at the sun, keeping a check on the time and trying to work out how he was to get to the back of the palace later. He was so concerned about Lenyé.

He was interrupted in his musings by Ramâno darting through the crowd and diving straight at him. Kyros just had time to open his arms and catch the lad before Ramâno was clinging to him and sobbing in his ear.

'Ramâno. Whatever's the matter?'

'It's my Mamma. That Morthrir-man is ill and said she poisoned his food. They've locked her in one of the rooms in the palace till they can move her to the dungeons. It's all your fault!'

Kyros staggered to the fountain with the lad in his arms and sat on the edge. 'What makes them think she did it?' His mind was racing: was this the result of his words on the Dangst Rock?

'You know that piece of buffalo steak that got dropped when you healed me. They found it in the bin next to the table where she was preparing his food. So it is your fault.'

'And what did they do with the steak?'

'Threw it to the dogs.'

'Did any of the dogs die?'

'No.'

'That proves she didn't poison his food.'

'The Morthrir-man said she was a spy because she was singing so much about your True King,' Ramâno pummelled Kyros on the chest with his fists. 'I heard the other cooks whispering about it. So it's still your fault!'

'Let me see if I've got this straight.' Kyros held the boy tighter to stop the pummelling. 'Are you denying that the True King healed your legs so you could walk?'

Ramâno continued sobbing in his arms.

'Well. I'm waiting for your answer.'

Ramâno pulled away slightly and shook his head.

'And are you denying that your Mother was changed so much that she couldn't stop herself rejoicing?'

Again the lad shook his head.

'Sometimes people invent lies to hide what is really going on. And they don't always understand how important the True King is to us, and want to silence what we say about him; so they start doing things to us which may not be very pleasant.'

'But why have they taken Mamma away from me? She hasn't done anything wrong. You must come and rescue her!'

Kyros sighed. This was making things even more complicated.

'You can do it when you rescue your Princess-Lady. I know which room Mamma's locked up in.'

'Very well, I'll try. But I need you to help me.'

'How?' the boy looked up, his eyes suddenly bright with anticipation.

'You must trust me and do exactly as I say.'

'What do you want me to do?'

'Go back into the palace. Can you do that?'

'Of course. They may have locked Mamma away, but the other cooks are still very friendly towards me. They think I'm a walking miracle.'

'Good. Find the Princess you mentioned. Tell her to get your Mother moved to the same room where her brothers and cousins will be waiting. It's the downstairs salon with the chainmail corselet on a pedestal outside.'

'You mean the one with the big helmet above it?'

'That's right. Wait with her in the passageway for my signal.'

'What passageway?'

'The one that comes up from the kitchens. She'll know. Stay close to her. And tell her to bring her weapons with her, that's very important. Have you got that?'

'Weapons. Weapons. Yes I understand.'

'Make sure she brings all of them.'

Chapter Seventy Four

Morthrir stared out of a window in the private council chamber, clasping his hands behind his back, and heard the door open and the sound of footsteps. He had ordered Rafé and Youdlh to meet with him. He was still incensed over the Healer being Kyros!

He turned as Youdlh snapped to attention.

'You sent for us, Sire?'

'I did, and...'

Rafé coughed, 'You're looking better this morning, Sire.'

Morthrir bit back his annoyance at the interruption. 'Thank you, Rafé. It was only a matter of time for that poison to work its way through my system. Fortunately it wasn't a lethal dose.'

'You still think it was the boy's Mother?' Youdlh relaxed and stood at ease.

Morthrir scowled at him. 'What other explanation is there?'

'I thought...' Youdlh faltered as Morthrir glared at him.

'Go on, man. Spit it out. You thought...?'

'I thought you might have seen the Healer, privately. You've recovered so quickly, and...'

'Healer. What do you know about that Healer?'

'I've posted extra guards as you commanded, Sire. And doubled them on the key strategic points that lead up to the palace and out to the other important parts of the city. We've questioned people in the Square to see if they know anything about him or where he's staying. I've even spoken to a few of my warriors who have benefitted from his healing touch over old wounds. Everyone speaks so highly of him, he's...'

'So you've done what you've been ordered to?'

'Yes, Sire.'

'And yet you've failed to spot the obvious.'

'I don't understand, Sire.'

'Rafé,' Morthrir deliberately ignored Youdlh's comment. 'What do you think?'

'I agree with Youdlh. I've heard nothing but praise. Everyone speaks very highly of him. The whole city's gone after him.'

'Exactly. It's happened so soon after my speech at the funeral that the crowd must think he is the man I was talking about. The man that was to be raised up amongst us, so filled with spiritual power that he would draw all people to him.' Morthrir paced up and down smacking his fist into his open palm as he spoke. 'That speech was meant for me. I am the one to arise. I am the one to be crowned. I am the one to take a new bride. And this upstart slips in through the back door and steals all my thunder. Do you know who he is?'

'No, Sire,' Rafé glanced away from Morthrir's dark stare.

'No, Sire,' Youdlh shuffled his feet, but remained looking at Morthrir's face.

'I had Eawen make a bust of the man's features. Take away that shock of hair and the beard, and he's none other than my nephew, Kyros. The man you've been searching for,' Morthrir turned his burning eyes on Youdlh. 'The man you should have arrested weeks ago on a charge of treason against me!'

'That's impossible, Sire.' Rafé burst out. 'I've seen him for myself. His skin is far too dark for any Krêonor. And Kyros is too young to grow a beard like that.'

'I'm surprised at you, Rafé. You've known Kyros for long enough. Do you think I don't recognise my own nephew?'

'I can't simply march out into the Square and demand the man has a shave and a haircut, Sire. I would need to see Eawen's bust for myself.'

'It is hidden securely. If that crowd gets wind of the Healer's identity, I am ruined; and everything I've said to the people will be totally undermined. We have to act quickly and seize him.'

'That would only stir up a riot, Sire,' Youdlh was quick to point out. 'My soldiers feel it in the very atmosphere of the Square. The crowd loves the Healer. If anything was done against him; they would rise up and tear us to pieces, weapons or no weapons.'

'What am I supposed to do,' Mothrir's eyes shifted back to Rafé. 'He's building up his reputation and biding his time till all the people are on his side. I can't just let this man draw their hearts away from me with some nonsense about returning to a knowledge of the True King.'

'But many are beginning to talk about the Restoration,' Rafé sounded thoughtful. 'That's what's drawing the people to him. And the healings, of course.'

'Rubbish!' Morthrir smacked his palm against the wall. 'It's part of his conjuring act. When he's got enough people on his side, he's going to demand I release Lenyé. If she sees him steal my power she's likely to go over to him. She still hasn't given me her decision.'

'Why is he keeping his identity a secret, Sire? If we've been fooled, no one else is likely to recognise him. We just wait.'

'It only takes one idiot to blurt out his name,' Morthrir started pacing up and down again.

'We go on watching his movements, Sire,' Rafé continued, 'and find out where he's staying. Someone must be sheltering him. Once we've found that out we can capture him at night when he least expects it.'

'Very well. Youdlh. See to it,' Morthrir reached a decision at last. 'And when you have the right security measures in place, I want you to ride out in person and recall your last remaining army to the city. I'm going to need every man we have to contain this threat. I'm surprised they haven't returned already. What's keeping them?'

PART VI

THE UNVEILING

Chapter Seventy Five

Lenyé sat in an armchair in the salon that had been appointed for her use. Her brothers and cousins were playing cards and making quite a noise, but she was happy to be a little away from them on her own. She needed to think over recent events.

She was shocked to learn that Kyros was alive as the Healer and hear his talk of Morthrir's words of power spoken against them both. She had to get this clear in her own mind. Morthrir's remarks in the private council chamber, praising her for her courage to find out the truth, were very precious: no other man had ever shown her that amount of respect, not even Kyros.

She'd almost forgotten about her parchment with Yanantha's sayings, and brought it to read to make sure she hadn't missed anything. It suddenly seemed urgent and she had to do it today.

Thinking about her friends who brought those words made her realise how much she missed them. Her mind went back to Ra-Na-Jiri's comments about how the others treated him and were jealous because he was riding with her. But the cobra argued with Ariella when he first arrived. And Chuah-te-mok seemed fairly antagonistic towards Ra-Na-Jiri. Would they ever settle their differences and be reconciled?

As she read, it was the second part of the words Yanantha had sung over her that particularly caught her attention:

Not by might or human strength
shall the final victory be won...

What final victory? Yanantha had never really explained it. Or had she? She recalled Yanantha's words again: *"For behind your Uncle Morthrir there sits a far greater power than any mortal can ever challenge unaided. That power is what you have to bring down and vanquish. But it is beyond mere human wisdom and strength to ever master. Without the lost Blade, even Kyros' return will avail little".*

But the power Morthrir drew on appeared to be good. Why should she have to bring it down?

The destruction of the Nastrim left her troubled over their fate: they were locked in the *Death of the Undying*. How could she possibly fulfil her promise to despatch them to Elasis?

She thought of her conversation with Acwellan at Mount Nastâri concerning the Nastrim: *"Not until the secret way is opened up...and the Dé-monos re-enter our world, can they return here".* But if Vashtani was here, then all the Nastrim, including her army, were free to return to the Waking World. What was it he said: *"They can never be killed again in this world by ordinary weapons. Only the Sword of Justice would have any power over them".* So the Nastrim could be gathering out there somewhere.

She was struggling with Kyros urging her to return to him, and Morthrir pressing for her answer; but wasn't ready to decide on either. Suddenly she knew what she had to do: find the Nastrim and despatch them to Elasis with the Sword of Justice.

The quatrain Ra-Na-Jiri brought her about the swords, ended:

The haft of one is secret marked
And only one of twain is sacred true

She'd removed the secret mark so no one, other than herself, could tell the swords apart: not even Acwellan. What about the Sword being sacred? That must refer to the True King and how the Sword was to be used. If Kyros was right, then despatching the Nastrim was the most important thing she could do.

Lenyé realised she hadn't checked on the Sword for some days. She glanced at the others, but they were too absorbed in their game to notice what she was doing. She rolled up her parchment, tied the cord, and left to find the Master of the Keys.

Chapter Seventy Six

Rafé sat in his room at the palace in Terrazarema and listened to Eawen's story of his meeting with the Healer.

'I still have difficulty with doorways,' the Henosite laughed.

'Why's that?'

'Because there's nothing there. When I relied on touch, I could feel round the wall and onto the door frame. Or tap on the floor with my cane. I can't distinguish between solid wall and nothing in the gap by looking. I'll just have to get used to it.'

Rafé couldn't take his eyes of the Henosite's face; the man was absolutely radiant. And the eyes: that incredible living grey. He was amazed. He never thought such a thing could happen.

'... but here is the dilemma, my friend,' the Henosite paused and looked at Rafé for some time before continuing. 'I can no longer openly support Morthrir and what he is doing. When we last met, you voiced similar concerns and I refused to listen to you, except to hide you and speed you on your way. But you're right. Morthrir has become a monster. I was shocked at what happened on Mount Malkamet, but I was prepared to carry on supporting the cause to usher in a better world for everyone.'

'So what's made you change your mind?'

'I've seen him.'

'Who?'

'The True King. Rafé, there is a difference. The Healer said I had to decide between the two.'

'How did that happen?'

'After Morthrir left me to clear up my tools, I saw the True

King come to me in that room. He had a gift in his hands which he passed to me. I was astonished, but he said, "*Go ahead. Open it*". I did as I was told and untied the ribbon and opened the lid of the box. But there was nothing in it. I looked up in surprise, but the True King smiled and asked me what I most wanted to put in the box. I knelt down before him and said, 'I have nothing to put in it. I only want to love and serve you as my Master.' But he lifted me up by the hand and told me to speak those words into the box. I did so, and found myself replacing the lid and re-tying the ribbon. Then I gave the gift back to him.

Rafé moved slightly, but didn't interrupt.

'And he said,' Eawen continued, '"*That is the most precious gift anyone from the Waking World can ever give me. I will keep this gift till we meet again. Then we can open the box together and see what your promise has turned into*".'

Rafé was utterly spellbound by Eawen's tale. 'Has he given the box back at all?'

'Not yet. The Healer was right: I have to choose between the True King and Abbérron. If I want to see that box filled, I can only serve the True King. Rafé, I cannot jeopardise that by any involvement with Morthrir whatsoever. I want you to witness my renunciation of the Priesthood.'

'Certainly, my friend. What do I have to do?'

'I will say the words, and you confirm you have heard and accepted them on behalf of the Priesthood.'

As Rafé completed the simple ceremony he felt suddenly troubled. He'd infiltrated the Priesthood to keep watch over Morthrir. But now he was caught up in a spiritual battle and was uncomfortable about the outcome for himself.

Chapter Seventy Seven

'I think it's been sent to us as a sign,' Quinn took the stone from Beth and turned it over in his hands. 'When you were still in that trance, I asked Ishi-mi-réjá if she carved it.'

'What did she say?'

Quinn glanced up at Beth. 'She said, "*Not likely. That thing is so ancient there wasn't anybody around to carve it when it was formed. That's my miraculous stone. That's my ishi-mi-réjá. That's me*".'

'So what does it mean?' Beth persisted.

'Somehow the life of Ishi-mi-réjá and this stone are linked. Now that it's returned, I think we have to call her back.'

'How?'

'Maybe we should put it on the pillow and imagine she's lying there; like you were in that trance.' Quinn went to the bed, placed the stone on the pillow and arranged the bedclothes as if Ishi-mi-réjá was really there. He sat on the edge, leaned right over, placed one hand on each side, and glanced at Beth.

'And then?' Beth frowned.

'Sing over her; like she did for you.' Quinn smiled. 'You've got the better voice. You sing.'

'Sing what?'

'Something simple. Try repeating, "*Come home*".'

As Beth began singing, Quinn felt a tingling sensation down his spine: the simplicity of the melody touching a nerve in him. When she hit the first note of the descant the bed opened up into a deep pit. 'I can see her.' He leaned down into the gaping hole.

'Quinn!' Beth stopped singing. 'What are you doing?'

Chapter Seventy Eight

Morthrir was writing at his desk in the private council chamber when he became aware of a presence in the room, and looked up.

'Vashtani. What are you doing here?'

'It's time you and I had a little talk.'

'When I think that is necessary, I will send for you.' Morthrir dipped his quill in the ink pot and continued writing.

'Listen to me,' Vashtani approached the desk. 'Abbérron's power in you has diminished. That means another power is contesting you. I think it's the Healer in the Central Square. And you've sat here, behind closed doors, and done nothing about it.'

'If Abbérron's power in me has diminished,' Morthrir laid his quill down on the porcelain drip-dish, and looked at Vashtani. 'Are you implying your power has increased?'

'Naturally. I'm not prepared to take orders from you forever. My agreement with Abbérron means a time will come when...'

'Excuse me,' Morthrir held up his hand. 'This is a temporary decrease in my power. One of the cooks tried to poison me. The guards found a piece of buffalo steak covered in grit in the bin next to her preparation table. But I am fully recovered now.'

'I'm pleased to hear it.'

Morthrir ignored the interruption. 'The Krêonor Throne is one step to ruling the Waking World. Only a man can sit in that throne with the backing of the Hidden Power.' Morthrir glared at Vashtani. 'Let us paint the scenario. If that power is Abbérron, and the man is me, where do you fit in?'

Vashtani didn't respond.

'As a loyal and devoted servant, you may well rise to a significant position with considerable influence, could you not?'

Still Vashtani was silent.

'As a rebellious self-seeker...' Morthrir's voice tailed off.

'We're not there yet,' Vashtani muttered. 'I am the only one who can do anything about this Healer. You must act at once.'

Morthrir eyed him coldly. 'Of course it would depend on how well you served this man during his ascent to the Throne.'

'Will you stop going on about possibilities in the future and concentrate on what is at hand. I know who the Healer is.'

'So do I; and I shall have him seized shortly.'

'That's still not quick enough. You do not know the full extent of his powers. I met him in the Realm of Travail.'

'Really?' Morthrir tried to keep the distain out of his voice.

'He overcame us with the word of his mouth. That's how I was chained when I first came to you on Mount Malkamet.'

'And how do you propose to overcome him now?'

'I am only subject to him because of the Sword of Justice.'

'You said so before; but what exactly would that Sword do?'

'It has power to release the judgements of the True King against us. At the Beginning the True King presented the Sword to Zerigor and banished us from the Waking World. My son, Acwellan, snatched it from Zerigor and has been the keeper ever since. He was slain by your Princess Lenyé, and I was about to recover it from her in the desert when you intervened. I do not know where the Sword is any more, or who has access to it.'

Morthrir kept the smirk off his face. 'And you say I have sat behind closed doors and done nothing about this?'

'Correct.'

'I have it safe in the Royal Armoury.'

'Here?'

Morthrir smiled. 'Yes.'

'Can you use it?'

'Not yet.'

'What do you mean, "*Not yet*"?'

'I cannot draw the Sword, but Lenyé can. I am awaiting her decision to marry me. Once she agrees and is joined to me, I can encourage her to use it for whatever I desire.'

'You're forgetting the old writings,' Vashtani glared at Morthrir. 'Hoffengrégor, said: "*...not by the hand of any man shall the Ancient Blade be regained...*".' He looked up. 'No wonder you can't draw it. That's probably why Lenyé can: because she's a woman. What if she refuses to marry you?'

'She won't. I am confident her answer will be "Yes".'

'There must be a quicker way to solve this. My son, Acwellan, could draw the Blade. Therefore, as his Father, I can too. I will prove it to you. Take me to the Royal Armoury.'

'There are two identical swords to confuse anyone trying to steal the Sword of Justice.'

'So?'

'If you can draw the Sword of Justice,' Morthrir eyed Vashtani closely, 'how will you know which is which?'

Vashtani was silent for a moment. 'If I am able to draw both, and you cannot draw the real Blade; then you can try first and indicate the Sword of Justice to me by your failure.'

Morthrir drummed his fingers on the desk. As long as Vashtani was unable to identify the Sword, Morthrir controlled him. But once Vashtani discovered a means of telling them apart, Morthrir would begin to lose his mastery over the Dé-monos.

'What are you waiting for? With that Sword in my hands, I can destroy the Healer. Surely that's in both our interests?'

Morthrir thrust himself up from the desk. 'Very well,' he scowled at Vashtani. 'Let us put this to the test. Come with me.'

Chapter Seventy Nine

'Please hurry,' Lenyé followed the Master of the Keys to the Royal Armoury. She was worried about who else might have access to her swords since the incident with Rafé. Suddenly she heard voices from the end of the corridor, thrust past the Master of the Keys and pushed open the unlocked door. Morthrir held one of her sheathed swords, while Vashtani stood opposite him beside the sword rack with the other. 'What's going on?'

'Lenyé,' Morthrir whirled round in surprise. 'This is an unexpected pleasure.'

Lenyé frowned. 'I thought only the Master of the Keys could unlock this door. You said so yourself.'

'I have a key for emergencies. To arm the reserve guard if the Master is unobtainable.'

'Why is Vashtani here?'

'He was interested in seeing your swords for himself.'

Lenyé watched as Morthrir tried to draw the sword. Vashtani distracted her by pulling his sword partly out, but she was convinced the sword in Morthrir's hand moved slightly in the scabbard. So Vashtani had the Sword of Justice. She felt a sudden fear creep up her spine: how was she going to get it from him? She glanced at Morthrir, willing him not to draw it any further.

'I can't move it,' Morthrir shrugged. 'Let me try yours.' He threw it to Vashtani and caught the one from the Dé-monos.

Vashtani whipped his new sword out of its scabbard. 'Now I have the Sword of Justice.'

'Morthrir,' Lenyé shouted at him. 'Throw me your sword.'

Vashtani rounded on Morthrir. 'With this sword in my hand, not even you have any power over me.'

Morthrir stepped back tugging at his sword in vain.

'Your sword,' Lenyé repeated, thrusting out her hand. 'Throw it to me.' She saw him hesitate. 'Just do it!'

'No you don't,' Vashtani advanced with his sword extended, but he was too late. Morthrir tossed her the sword.

Lenyé drew it and sighed with relief. She was right: Morthrir had the wrong sword and tricked Vashtani into swapping.

Vashtani was on her, sword raised for the stroke, but she parried the blow, twisted her wrist and flicked his sword away.

'You think you can save yourself with that imitation,' he shouted. 'But only the sword I hold has any power over me.'

'That's what you think,' Lenyé adopted an attacking stance and hacked at Vashtani's sword, driving him back to the wall.

'No sword in the Waking World can have that affect on me.'

Lenyé flicked her wrist again, parried one of his blows and sent his sword flying out of his hand to clatter on the floor.

'I think you had the wrong blade all the time.' She advanced until Vashtani was trapped against the wall with her Sword at his throat.

Vashtani raised his hand and pointed at Morthrir. 'You tricked me into giving you the Sword of Justice. What are you playing at? You may have had a submissive servant before, but not any more. I'll find a way of triumphing over you, Morthrir. I'll find a way!'

With that, Vashtani disappeared through the wall.

Lenyé glared at Morthrir. 'I'm taking my weapons back as I can no longer trust the security of this place!'

But more than that, she thought: if what Captain Turvil had said was true when they talked before the Nastrim army originally marched out, she would need the Sword of Justice to despatch them to Elasis. Lenyé was desperate to get away from the palace, find the Nastrim and fulfil her oath to him.

Chapter Eighty

Kyros glanced up into the sky and shaded his eyes against the sun as it sank below the treetops in the gardens behind the palace. He thought his eyes were playing tricks on him and tried to refocus. But the black dot grew and came rapidly towards him, high up in the evening air.

It was Chuah-te-mok with Lenyé's answer. The eagle dipped his right wing twice. Kyros was annoyed: the signal meant she hadn't given their Uncle her decision after all. Why was she taking so long? He must find her and help her.

The hard part was getting to the stables unobserved. He'd racked his brains all day, but hadn't worked out how to do it. There were still plenty of people around, but the guards remained at their posts as well. He couldn't walk towards the palace and expect to pass through unchallenged.

He cried out in his heart to the True King for wisdom, but all he heard were the faint words, "*Just try*".

Kyros began moving deeper into the crowd, stopping now and then to speak words of healing and release over various needy people, but all the while edging towards the avenue that led up to the palace. The nearer he got to the market stalls, the more the crowd thinned and opened up to let him through, but many closed in behind and followed him.

'Where are you going?' someone shouted from the crowd.

Another responded, 'That way leads to the palace. Are you going to challenge Morthrir?'

Kyros didn't say a word, and kept on walking. He entered the great pillared and arched portico that separated the booths from the market stalls, and saw a number of soldiers move across to bar the way.

'You cannot approach the palace,' the officer barked.

Kyros kept on walking towards the man.

The two columns of soldiers behind leaned their lances towards each other, forming a triangle to block the entrance.

Kyros sensed the crowd behind jostling to see what would happen. He raised his right hand and spoke quietly, 'Open up in the name of Luchianó-bé, Lord of Light.' He felt the same throb of power in the atmosphere around him and the soldiers fell back, bowing to the ground and snatching their lances aside.

Kyros walked between them, passed through the portico and turned left at the end of the street to take the lane that led to the stables at the back of the palace. He heard a disturbance behind him as the crowd surged forwards but were halted by the guards springing to their feet.

As soon as he was out of sight he felt himself lifted up and moving faster than he could run; the soft melody of song he'd heard before playing in his ears and the air stirred around him as if fanned by huge wings.

He blinked, and found himself at the back of the stables. He was vaguely aware of Harbona falling to his knees before him, and a number of tethered horses rearing up and neighing in a wild frenzy.

But Kyros only had eyes for the figure before him and the blazing light around him. The figure appeared to be veiled in light, and Kyros could see no features or make out any form clearly except for a drawn sword in the figure's hand, so he cried out in a loud voice, 'Are you for me or for my enemies?'

'Neither,' the voice was soft, but so full of power that the ground beneath Kyros' feet shook. 'As Commander of the Hosts of the True King have I come. The place on which you tread is too pure for any footwear of the Waking World. Remove your boots and put them to one side.'

Kyros took them off and bowed with his face to the ground.

'Stand up, Kyros. For the favour of the True King rests upon you. You are to enter the stronghold of your Uncle and pluck the captives from under his very nose. He is holding them to bargain with against your legitimate claim to the throne. By so doing, he is directly challenging the True King. Let the anointing and power of Luchianó-bé himself rest upon you.'

In that brief moment Kyros' eyes cleared and he saw the figure before him in breath-taking clarity. So like Stellatus was he that Kyros gasped in amazement; but different: bigger, much bigger, his stature reflecting his power. As the vision began to fade, Kyros saw the wings lift up behind his back and sweep down, raising a gale that surged around Kyros and blinded him with dust. He rubbed his eyes; but the figure was gone.

Kyros was startled by Harbona grabbing his arm.

'My Lord, I cannot control the horses. They're likely to break their tethers!'

'Let me try.' Kyros moved amongst the horses, gentling their muzzles and quieting them. Then he turned and embraced Harbona.

'What was the light that so disturbed them, My Lord?'

'A Great Messenger from the True King, who has come to command us,' Kyros smiled at him. 'Is everything ready?'

'Yes, My Lord. Seven horses as you ordered. I have muffled their hooves with hay shoes used by the warriors, so we may ride along the streets without too much noise.'

'That was a good thought. But we need two more horses.'

'What for?'

'Ramâno and his Mother are coming with us.' Briefly Kyros explained what had happened to Marie-anna.

'You will only need one horse, My Lord. Ramâno may be healed, but he still doesn't know how to ride and would slow us down if he has a horse of his own. I suggest he rides behind you.

Are you sure you can get so many people out?'

'I promised Ramâno; and I will not go back on my word.'

'Very well, My Lord. I will acquire one more horse while you are in the palace. Here is a coil of rope, which may be useful. Also, don't forget to put your boots on.'

Kyros looked at Harbona with a puzzled expression on his face. Then he glanced down at his feet and laughed. 'You're right. I was forgetting the command of our recent visitor.'

He hauled on his boots, left Harbona to find another horse, dragged aside a mass of creepers to uncover the trap door into the secret passageway and pulled it open. He slipped his legs over the edge and stood on one of the iron rungs of the ladder to close the trap door above his head. Then he climbed down and set off under the stables, feeling the passageway begin to rise as it approached the rear of the palace.

Soon he noticed a flicker of light on his left and almost at ground level. As he came up to it he realised it was an iron grill, and by the aroma knew he was close to the kitchens.

'Good,' he thought to himself. 'At least I'm in the palace.' He carried on for several paces and started feeling the wall on his right where he thought the small doorway into the passage of the palace must be. At last his fingers felt a thin crack in the wall running horizontal, and then turning at right angles. He felt the crack down to the floor, found the corresponding one on the other side and traced the extent of the doorway.

Kyros moved further on, tapped three times on the wall and listened intently, but there was no answering signal. Where was Lenyé? Had she changed her mind?

He was about to tap again when he heard a commotion from back down the passageway. It must be coming from the vent by the kitchens. Voices were raised, and he heard Ramâno's high-pitched yell cut short.

Chapter Eighty One

Morthrir strode down the steps with Rafé trying to keep up. He was desperate to renew his spiritual power since his illness and only Rafé was available to accompany him. He paused outside *The Vault of Malrema*, fumbling for the key. 'Where's Youdlh?'

'You sent him to recall the army. Remember?'

'I need him here now.' Morthrir unlocked the door and thrust Rafé in. 'Get over there and take your place on the East mark.'

'But Sire, that's not my normal position.'

'Just do it!' Morthrir sliced through the air with his hand in frustration. 'That Healer walked towards the soldiers at the approach to the palace a while ago, and then disappeared.'

'He usually leaves the Square about this time each night.'

'But he never walks towards the palace. He might be breaking in as we speak.'

'I doubt it, Sire. There are too many guards about.'

'Most of them are still in the Square. That's why I need Youdlh! I ordered the Commander to withdraw to the palace, but it may be too late. Your wait-and-see tactics have failed.'

Morthrir climbed onto the altar and pointed at Rafé to take up his position.

'This isn't going to work, Sire.'

'Why not?'

'We need the rest of the Priests at least.'

'There isn't time to contact them all.'

'What about the Summoners?'

'I don't need them.'

'What about drawing the blinds, Sire?'

'This Hexacle is not dependent on darkness, but on the willing co-operation of the participants.'

'But we have no robes, Sire. This doesn't feel right.'

'Just stand where I order you to.'

'But Sire. It won't work while you are consumed by anger.'

'It has to. I must find that man before he finds me.'

Morthrir took up his stance, knees slightly flexed and finger and thumb tips together, slowed his breathing and focused his attention on the image he had last seen at Mount Malkamet. 'I call upon the Hidden Power to let me see where Kyros is, what he is doing, and what his intentions towards me are.'

He waited, his breath catching in anticipation of the answer.

'If I don't know,' Morthrir's voice quavered with a rising note of despair, 'I cannot act, and all that I have laboured for will come crashing down. I cry out to the Lord Abbérron to come to my aid and answer me!'

Nothing happened.

Morthrir made a third appeal, but still nothing. 'It's no good,' he broke his stance and stood up straight. 'I thought all power now came from the *Vault of Malrema* and this Hexacle. What's gone wrong?' He glared at Rafé, 'Well?'

'I've already told you, Sire. I think the biggest factor is your agitated state of mind.'

'What about the army?' Morthrir fumed. 'Where is it?'

'There's been no news from Youdlh, Sire.'

'What's delaying him?' Morthrir sat on the edge of the altar, his legs dangling down, and slumped forwards with his head in his hands and his elbows digging into his thighs.

'What do you propose now, Sire.'

Morthrir sighed. 'I have to get ready for dinner with Lenyé. I'm expecting her answer tonight. If she says, "No", at this stage, the people will never accept me.'

Chapter Eighty Two

Kyros crept back along the passageway, crouched down and put his eye to the grill into the kitchens. He saw the cooks bustling about preparing food and sending up trays and plates with the footmen.

He heard a raised voice directed at a small figure with his back to Kyros. 'If you want to stay in here, go over by the wall and keep out of the way. Can't you see we're busy?'

The figure shuffled towards Kyros and sat down, blocking out most of the light.

'Ramâno,' Kyros whispered and saw the head jerk sideways. 'It's me. Kyros.'

'Mister Healer. I knew you would come. Where are you?'

'Shh. I'm right behind you, in a secret passageway.'

'Is that how we're going to get out?'

'Yes. Why aren't you with Lenyé in the passage further up?'

'Your Princess-Lady had to go for that special meal I told you about. She didn't seem too interested in escaping with you. I waited where she showed me. Then I was chased away by the Captain. Said I wasn't allowed up there any more.'

'Where's this meal happening? In the main dining hall?'

'No. Some small dining room near the private council chamber. She has to let him know before they finish.'

'Listen, Ramâno. Tell me when no one is looking in your direction. I'm going to open a door and let you into this secret passageway. But I don't want anyone to see.'

'The cooks are going back into the main kitchen and the

footmen are taking the trays upstairs,' Ramâno whispered.

Kyros eased the latch up and felt the block of stone move slightly. 'Slide your hand along the wall to your right. You should feel the edge of the opening.'

'Found it,' Ramâno whispered back. 'They've all gone!'

'Now,' Kyros eased the block open.

Immediately Ramâno's arm and shoulder were through the gap, and he squeezed the rest of his little body in while Kyros held the top of the block and prevented it from swinging right open. As soon as Ramâno was in the passageway Kyros pulled the block to and heard the snick as it closed. He put his eye to the grill again to check no one had entered the kitchen.

He ushered Ramâno ahead of him till they came to the opening for the passage in the main part of the palace.

Kyros slipped the coil of rope off his shoulder, dumped it in the passageway, tapped on the wall and waited. But there was no voice raised to question the knocking. 'I'll open this block to let you out. Make sure no one's around and I'll follow you.'

'Why do I have to go first?'

'Because you're big and brave and strong,' Kyros whispered fiercely. 'And if you're seen, they're used to you in the palace.'

'But if that Captain catches me again, I'm in deep trouble.'

'If they see me, we've had it.' Kyros pulled the catch back and eased the block outwards. 'Now go!'

Kyros saw Ramâno push the block further open and stick his head out. Then the boy wriggled his small body through the gap and pushed the block back into place.

'Hey!' Kyros heard a shout of surprise and the tread of heavy boots breaking into a run. 'How did you get back in here?'

'Help,' Kyros heard Ramâno's shrill cry and the patter of his feet as he ran off towards the main part of the palace. When the sound of heavy boots had passed him and faded away, Kyros eased the block of stone open. There was no one about as he slipped out of the opening, eased the stone into place and heard the reassuring click of the latch.

He headed towards the front of the palace and reached the main salon. He tried the double doors but they were locked, and rattled the handles in despair. He'd forgotten to ask Ramâno for the key.

'Who's that?'

Kyros was startled by his cousin's voice on the other side of the doors. He crouched down and whispered through the keyhole, 'Wilf. It's me. Kyros. I've come to get you out.'

'Kyros!' his cousin sounded ecstatic.

'Shh,' he whispered back. 'Not so loud.' He whipped his head round at the sound of approaching feet. 'Someone's coming.'

He slipped into an alcove next to the doorway that contained a pedestal supporting the fine chainmail corselet and helmet of a senior officer. Kyros squatted behind the pedestal and waited, his heart beating fast. He saw Ramâno pause in front of the alcove and look down the corridor he'd come from and then turn to run on straight ahead.

'Ramâno,' Kyros whispered, as he reached out a hand, grabbed the boy and drew him into the alcove. 'I need the key to the salon. Have you got it?'

'Of course.' The lad fished in his pocket, 'Here it is.'

Kyros closed his hand around the key, but jerked his head up at the sound of heavy boots. He pushed Ramâno out of the alcove. 'You'd better get going and lead them away from here.'

Ramâno sped off and Kyros caught a glimpse of three armed men as they swept past pursuing the lad.

Kyros waited till the sounds died away before emerging and fitting the key. But try as he might it wouldn't turn. 'Ramâno must have taken the wrong key from the cupboard,' he fumed to himself. 'Now what do I do?' He paused and cried out in his heart, 'Help me in my time of need, My King.'

He ducked into the alcove as he heard the patter of Ramâno's footsteps approaching again, then reached out and pulled the boy in with him. 'You gave me the wrong key.'

The boy pulled another key out of his pocket. 'Try this one.'

Kyros took the key. 'You're staying with me this time.'

They were out of the alcove. Kyros fitted the key to the lock and it turned. He opened one of the doors and pushed Ramâno in ahead of him as heavy footsteps echoed in the corridor outside. Kyros eased the door to behind him, refitted the key and locked it from the inside.

'Kyros!' the voices of his sisters and cousins exploded around him, and he had to ward them off.

'Lenyé told us you would be coming,' his cousin, Wilf, was obviously struggling to keep the surprise out of his voice. 'But I hardly recognise you.'

'Shh. No time now. Quick, Ramâno.' He grabbed the boy by the hand, dragged him across the room to a settee, bundled him over the back and leaped after him, pulling Ramâno down and covering the lad with his arm and shoulder.

There was a rattle at the doors; then a harsh voice sounded. 'Why are these doors locked? Who's in there?'

There was a bang against the woodwork of the doors as everyone remained silent.

'Answer him,' Kyros hissed as he peered round the end of the settee. He glared at Wilf.

'It's me, Wilf, and my brother and our two cousins.' Kyros watched as Wilf stepped up to the doors, carefully slid the key out of the lock, thrust it into his pocket and then moved back from the doors again. 'We were escorted here and locked in to await my Uncle's instructions.'

'Hmm.' The voice came again, followed by a clink of keys. Kyros heard the lock turn and ducked down as one door opened.

'Did you hear anyone running past outside a moment ago?'

'No.'

'That's odd.'

Kyros gripped Ramâno's shoulder to stop him sniggering.

'There's a boy called Ramâno on the loose,' Kyros detected the annoyance in the Captain's voice. 'Son of one of the cooks. He's been hanging around this part of the palace with a guilty look on his face, even though I told him to get back to the kitchens. He's given everyone the slip. Have you seen him?'

'No, Sir.'

'And both doors have been locked all the time?'

'We were locked in by one of the guards. So, no. We haven't touched them.'

Kyros grinned to himself at Wilf's honesty, even if it wasn't quite the whole truth, realising that his cousin had artfully defused a very real problem. If the Captain searched the salon...

'Very well. I'll leave you alone.'

Kyros heard the Captain mutter under his breath about the odd way the boy had disappeared, before the reassuring bang of the doors and the rattle of the key in the lock.

They waited several seconds as the sound of footsteps retreated down the corridor. Then Kyros was out from behind the settee and hugging his sisters, Olathe and Nasima, and embracing his two cousins, Wilf and Festé. He introduced Ramâno to them and they all hugged him as well.

'I'm going to be a healer. Like your brother.'

'Healer?' Olathe frowned at him.

'Not now,' Kyros intervened. 'We have to get you out of here.' He spun round and looked at Ramâno. 'Why did you have two keys? I nearly died when I couldn't open the door, and heard the clatter of your footsteps being chased by the Captain.'

'The other one's for Mamma.'

'Your Mother. Where is she?' He glanced around the salon. 'It never occurred to me she wasn't here.'

'She's still in the blue room where they first took her.'

'The other side of the throne room. That's miles away. Why is she still there?'

'The Princess-Lady grabbed the key when we raided the key

275

safe. But I couldn't get near the room to let her out and bring her here because of the guards. That's when the Captain caught me.'

'Never mind. We have to get the others safe first.'

Kyros took the key from Wilf, unlocked one door and peered out. There was no one about and no sound of any footsteps. The others filed out and he locked the door behind them. Then he pulled the mail corselet off the pedestal and put it on. 'There. No one's going to question me wearing this.' He grabbed the helmet and crammed it on his head. 'And that completes the disguise. If anyone stops us I can say I'm moving the Royal Youngsters to another room.'

'What about me?' Ramâno's high-pitched voice startled him.

'You have a very important role. I need you to help me get your Mother out.'

Kyros led the way to the corridor with the entrance to the secret passageway, checked there was no one approaching, pulled the latch and helped his sisters and cousins through the opening. 'Head that way,' he pointed past them in the gloom, 'and you'll come out by the stables. My comrade, Harbona, has horses ready. Wait for me and I'll join you as soon as I can.'

He pushed the stone block to, grabbed Ramâno by the hand and led him off towards the blue room.

'Did you say Harbona?' the boy twisted his head up to look at Kyros. 'He's a very valiant warrior. Why is he helping you?'

'Shh! If we're stopped, I'm escorting you to the Captain,' Kyros whispered. 'But if you must know, I rescued Harbona from some very evil enemies and he has sworn to serve me.'

'Instead of the Morthrir-man?'

'That's right.'

Kyros stopped at the blue room, fitted the key in the lock and opened one of the doors.

'Mamma,' Ramâno raced across the room and flung his arms around her neck as she stood up from her armchair.

Kyros was vaguely aware that her wrists were manacled in

front of her and she wasn't able to catch the boy. She fell backwards into the armchair with Ramâno on top of her.

Kyros strode across the room and heaved the boy off. 'Get up, Ramâno, we have to be quick.'

'Ramâno,' his Mother's voice quavered slightly. 'Who is this man?'

'He's the Healer. Don't you recognise him?'

'No. Not in that helmet. I thought he was an officer.'

'We've come to rescue you,' Ramâno's high-pitched voice shrilled loudly in the room. 'Hurry,' and he tugged at her hands.

'Keep you voice down,' Kyros hissed. He turned to Marie-anna. 'Walk ahead of me, My Lady, and pretend to be my prisoner. Ramâno. Hold my hand again.'

Kyros guided her from behind, then told her to stop before they reached the kitchens. He released the block of stone and helped her into the secret passageway.

'When I shut you in,' Kyros whispered to Ramâno. 'Grab that coil of rope; turn to your right and head towards the top. At the end you'll find a grill that looks down into the Throne Room. It's heavy, but you can lift it out. Once you've done that, get ready to lower the rope onto the balcony. If I rescue Lenyé, we'll head for the balcony and climb up your rope.'

'You mean the Princess-Lady,' Ramâno looked up at him with expectant eyes. 'So we're all going to escape together?'

'That's right.'

'What if you don't make it?'

'Put the grill back; get down to Harbona and escape. I'll have to think of another way out for Lenyé and myself.'

With that, he bundled Ramâno into the secret passageway and closed the stone block on them.

Chapter Eighty Three

'Lenyé,' Morthrir was taken aback as she entered the private dining room. 'Surely the new clothes were for tonight?'

Lenyé raised an enquiring eyebrow. She'd already dismissed Kyros' escape plan: he couldn't possibly rescue her from the palace, despite Ramâno's excited pleas. So instead she would have to persuade Morthrir to let her go and find the Nastrim.

Morthrir stared at the faded blue cloak and cut-down dress; his eyes tracing the long boots as they disappeared under the short hem; the two sword handles protruding above her shoulders; and the longbow and quiver: exactly as he'd seen her in the desert. 'This must be in honour of our first meeting,' he smiled at her. 'You come to me as a Huntress whose arrows have pierced me deeply.'

'I am dressed like this,' she stared back at him, steeling herself against the charisma of the man, 'because I need to seek out the Nastrim and release them from this world for ever.'

'Lenyé,' Morthrir's mind was racing: he couldn't allow her to go running off on some obscure errand. 'Let's talk about it over dinner.' He walked round and shut the door behind her before taking her hand in his. 'I dismissed the two guards outside the private council chamber, and placed more at the far end of all the corridors, so no one can hear us. There are no footmen to serve us, for I am your host tonight. We are entirely alone in here.'

Morthrir kissed her hand and drew her to the table, trusting the intimacy of the setting would soften the atmosphere between them. 'Let us drink,' and he lifted the clay vessel by its handles from the cooling basin and poured the sparkling wine into two goblets on the table. He replaced the wine vessel, passed a goblet to Lenyé and held out his own for a toast. 'To a favourable outcome,' and he touched his goblet against hers.

Lenyé's heart sank; she was wavering in her resolve already. 'A favourable outcome,' she faltered as she tried to smile at him.

He helped her to be seated, placed platters of cold meats and chopped vegetables and bowls of dips on the table between them and sat down on the other side. He passed various dishes and listened as she spoke of her distress at not fulfilling her promise to Captain Turvil.

'But Lenyé, the Nastrim were destroyed. There's no way they can return. You need to let go of all this and be free to live your own life.' He refilled her goblet and changed the conversation.

Lenyé was silent, thinking over what he'd just said.

'Now for the appetizer,' Morthrir cleared away the platters and served her from the side table. 'Fillets of pike, using a recipe by one of my cooks from Onadestra,' he served the fish onto her plate until she gestured with her hand, and then scooped some of the sauce over the top. He replenished her goblet, laughing and drawing her out into another topic of conversation.

The scent from the candles and the strong wine were making her light headed. Lenyé felt her last resistance over the Nastrim evaporate and she only had eyes for Morthrir. He was right. Why should she care about them? After all: Acwellan was dead; the whole race had been destroyed; and they were never coming back. She was free to lavish her attention on Morthrir.

'Tell me if you are in love,' Morthrir smiled, 'for I am eager to know.' He sat in rapt attention as Lenyé recounted her first impression of him rescuing her from Vashtani: his power and majesty; that tilt of the head; his dark eyes; the tone of his voice and sense of mystery and his sheer charisma. He counted off the points as she spoke; smiling to himself at his preparation, and attention to detail, and the way he had carried things off.

Then she was highlighting her gratitude for being rescued: no one had ever done that for her. And how she felt drawn into the warmth of his presence and how blind she must have been to his graces, and found him to be so much more engaging as a person than she'd ever known before.

When she paused, Morthrir cleared the dishes and placed a bigger platter in front of her, and helped her to the main course.

'Prime buffalo steak rather than venison, but then it is a little early in the year for the best stags.' He poured red wine into two larger goblets. 'Ten year-old special reserve,' he assured her, 'slightly on the young-side, but an excellent vintage.'

'You helped me to grow up,' Lenyé continued.

'Really?'

'I was but a girl till I met you. Now I am a woman, with a woman's heart and a woman's love to bestow.'

'So, what is your decision?' Morthrir leaned back with the goblet in his hand, but his heart was pounding. 'You wore your old clothes to defy me. But that's not what you really feel, is it?'

Lenyé had a stab of guilt over Kyros; but she was desperate to hear those special words again. 'Morthrir. You said you were in love with me, and had to declare yourself and not remain silent.'

'That's right. I…'

'Say it to me.'

'You mean?' Morthrir felt time slowing as he leaned forwards and very carefully placed his goblet on the table. He eased his chair back, walked round to her side of the table and dropped to one knee. As she swivelled in her chair to face him, he took her hand in his, feeling a strong rise of emotion: the cut-down dress and long boots making his heart race. 'I said I would wait a thousand years for your answer, yet you have come to me tonight of your own free will. Lenyé, you are so beautiful. I never thought I would ever have the right to say this to you, but I…'

'Say it again,' and she leaned forwards as he held her hand.

'Lenyé. I…'

Chapter Eighty Four

Kyros strode to the small dining room next to the private council chamber, and flung open the doors. His eyes swept the room taking in every detail from the intimate lighting of a few candles, the part-finished meal on the table laid for two, the vase of flowers, and especially the two participants.

The heavy scent of musk from the candles hung in the room and Kyros felt a rising anger at all the subtle tricks his Uncle was using to win over the girl he loved. But it was Lenyé herself who caught his attention. She was dressed as he had seen her in the forest near the Pool of Alesco: that cut-down blue dress, the matching cloak and thigh-length boots; her longbow propped against the table with the quiver lying on the floor and the two swords strapped to her back with the hafts proud of her shoulders. But it was her hair that took his breath away. The golden strands were gathered into a single plait starting at the centre of her crown and running down the back before coiling round her head from the left and pinned along the right hand side; a few wayward strands accentuated the soft nape of her neck, while several tightly-curled tendrils hung down from her temples almost to her chin. She was more beautiful than ever.

Lenyé sat on a chair with its back to Kyros, but had swivelled to her right with her arm extended. Uncle Morthrir was kneeling on the floor, about to kiss her hand. They both jerked round in his direction, a look of shock etched on their faces.

'Who do you think you are, bursting in like this?' Uncle Morthrir was up on his feet with shoulders leading and head thrust forwards as though about to break into a full-scale charge.

Kyros closed the door behind him, removed his helmet and let it drop to the floor.

'Kyros!' He heard the venom in his Uncle's voice. 'So the Henosite was right after all. Guards. In here!'

'There are no guards: they're too far away to hear you,' Kyros kept his voice low. 'It's just you and me and Lenyé.' He raised his right hand. 'You have spoken words against both Lenyé and myself and have sought to usurp the Kingdom for your own purposes. Those words have been reversed, and the evil you intended will now fall on you.'

Uncle Morthrir staggered back, his face ashen with sudden shock, and he clutched at his chest. 'That's not possible. The words of my Lord Abbérron can never be overturned.'

'They can if one greater than Abbérron is present.'

'There is none greater than Abbérron,' his Uncle took a pace towards him, the colour returning to his face.

'We are about to put it to the test.' Kyros stared hard into his Uncle's eyes. 'Lenyé,' he glanced at her. 'I presume you were about to give Uncle Morthrir your answer. As this concerns me closely, I suggest you say it now for both of us to hear.'

'Kyros,' Lenyé startled him with the sharpness of her tone. 'How dare you interrupt us like this!'

'What were you about to say to him?'

'I...' she hesitated before standing and facing Kyros, her eyes straying to their Uncle. 'I don't know what to say now. I've never seen you like this before. My heart fails me, for now I am terrified of you.'

'You are sensing the presence of the True King, who is with me and goes before me. And that is no bad thing; for fear of the True King is the beginning of all wisdom. You must choose today between walking with me and obeying the True King, whom I serve, or uniting yourself with this usurper.' He gesticulated towards his Uncle in disgust. 'Which is it to be?'

'I need more time...'

'I gave you the day you requested, I cannot wait any longer. I'm entitled to your answer.'

Uncle Morthrir cleared his throat, 'You cannot go with this man, Lenyé. For the power of Abbérron has been released against him. If you join with Kyros, that power will be against you as well. And he is far greater than this so-called True King.'

'That's wrong,' Kyros cut across his Uncle. 'Lenyé, you're free of all words of binding spoken over you. Only you can choose.'

Lenyé glanced at Kyros, 'There is only one way for me to find out who is telling the truth.'

Kyros saw Lenyé grab the handles of the two swords on her back, but only one sword came away as she jerked her arms upwards. Her look of shock as she wrenched at the unmoving sword changed to astonishment as she swept the free sword aloft, the blade whistling back and forth through the air. She released the other sword, transferred her hand to the haft of the free one, and held it two-handed in an attacking stance, the point hovering between himself and Uncle Morthrir.

'Lenyé,' Kyros heard the uncertainty in his Uncle's voice. 'It is so unseemly of you to threaten either of us with that sword.'

'Stand back. Both of you.' Lenyé darted at Kyros, scythed at the air above his head, rounded on Uncle Morthrir and did the same, before sweeping the blade above her own head. As she did so, she lurched to one side as though she'd been dangling from a rope that had now been severed.

Lenyé thrust the blade straight at Uncle Morthrir's neck. He stepped backwards, but she kept threatening him till he was pinned against the wall. Kyros heard the razor-sharp blade rasp on the stubble under his Uncle's chin.

'You know what this is, don't you?' her voice was ice cold.

Uncle Morthrir tried to shake his head but stopped as the point of the sword probed against his throat.

'It's the Sword of Justice. It wouldn't come out of its scabbard when I was in battle to take life so I had to use the other instead. Now the other won't pull out but this one will. This Sword is not for taking life, but judging a person's inner motives. Kyros was right. You've been trying to manipulate me against my will.'

Uncle Morthrir put his hand up to the blade and attempted to pull it away. 'If it's not for taking life, then spare me the discomfort of holding it against my throat. I haven't been trying to manipulate you but save you from an unwise match with this vagabond. I will make you Queen of the Krêonor with the power of Abbérron to back me up. What more could you want?'

'I don't think you understand the power of this Sword,' Lenyé continued. 'I have cut myself free from both of you and now I can choose either of you or none at all.'

'But surely you need one of us, at least?' Kyros heard the slight whine of self-pity in his Uncle's voice.

'For the moment it's neither of you; for I still need to find the Nastrim and release them. But I will go with Kyros.' Lenyé held out her hand to him. 'If you won't help me, maybe Kyros will!'

'No,' their Uncle collapsed to the ground.

The cry startled Kyros as he stepped past his Uncle, caught hold of Lenyé's hand and drew her towards him. 'If you really want to release the Nastrim, I will help you all I can.'

Uncle Morthrir struggled to stand, but fell back clutching at his heart and panting with exertion: his eyes wild with fear.

Kyros opened the door while Lenyé sheathed the Sword, grabbed her longbow and quiver and followed him.

'This way,' Kyros raced into the private council chamber, threw open the door at the back to the spiral staircase and the garden below, and then dragged her across to the map stand.

'Aren't we escaping through the garden?' Lenyé whispered.

'No. That's to fool any pursuers,' and he eased open the door behind the map stand onto the balcony in the Throne Room and began hauling her after him.

'But Ra-Na-Jiri's out there somewhere. We must take him

with us.'

'There's no time,' Kyros felt her trying to drag him back through the door. 'Chuah-te-mok can get him and join us later.'

Kyros almost fell as her resistance ended and she followed him. He was relieved to see the grill already removed from its place and Ramâno faintly discernable in the dark gap. He gave a soft whistle. Ramâno poked his head out and dropped a length of rope down to the balcony.

He could hear his Uncle's shouts and heavy footsteps running along a corridor.

'I don't believe this,' Lenyé glared at Kyros. 'You orchestrate a grand escape but have no weapons to accomplish it. Here. Take my longbow and quiver of arrows. At least you can trust me to organise our defence!'

Kyros fumbled the weapons from her and helped Lenyé get a firm grip. He watched her climb up the rope, keeping her legs straight and leaning backwards as she walked up the wall. There was a bang on the door in the private council chamber and shouts. Lenyé had to make several attempts to get her head and the protruding sword hilts into the gap. As soon as she had wriggled through, Kyros swarmed up the rope behind her. There were more shouts outside the throne room. He thrust the longbow and quiver into Ramâno's hands and squeezed through the gap. He turned, pulled up the rope and slotted the grill back into place, just as the guards burst into the throne room itself.

'Mister Healer,' Ramâno's shrill voice made Kyros whip round in alarm. 'What about the manacles on Mamma's wrists. She can't move very easily like that.'

'Shh, Ramâno,' Kyros whispered. 'They'll hear you.' He peered through the grill and saw figures running up the steps to the balcony.

Lenyé crawled forwards, 'Let me see.' She examined the manacles in the dim light, then drew the Sword of Justice and held the blade against one. 'If it worked for me, it must surely work again.' She sliced downwards and cut clean through the metal. Then she cut the other manacle away.

'Thank you,' Marie-anna whispered. 'What an incredible sword.'

'You go first, Mister Healer,' Ramâno's high-pitched voice echoed in the passageway. 'Then we can see where we're going from the light about your head.'

'What light?' Lenyé sounded puzzled.

'Ramâno's convinced there's a light around my head the size of a serving plate. But I can't see it.'

'Neither can I.'

'Nor me,' Marie-anna's voice startled Kyros. 'You must be making it up, Ramâno.'

'No I'm not, Mamma. It was because I saw the light that I was healed. What's the matter with everyone? I see it around his head all the time!'

'Light or no light,' Lenyé muttered in the darkness of the passageway. 'You'd better lead on, Kyros.'

'Follow me,' Kyros wormed his way past the lad and his Mother. 'Ramâno. Keep your voice down. It carries too easily in the confines of these walls.'

Chapter Eighty Five

'Keep singing,' Quinn shouted at Beth. 'I nearly lost her then.'

He heard Beth pick up the descant and continue the refrain over and over and over again, the sweetness of her voice and clarity of the notes setting up a vibration in the room that surged down through the hole in the bed and swirled about Ishi-mi-réjá. He felt his head and shoulders pulled in with a great blast of heat, and lost his grip with his right hand.

'Quinn,' Beth's scream shattered the beauty of her singing, and he nearly fell right in, but felt her grab his left hand as he began to slip.

'Don't stop,' Quinn yelled. 'It's incredibly hot down here and dark and stinks of rotten eggs. There she is. She's being gored by monsters like great bulls and savaged by others like enormous dogs. Hold on tight. I'm going to reach down to her.'

Quinn hung over the edge of the hole, his knees on the floor and the tops of his thighs pressing against the side of the bed. He could hardly breathe it was so hot, and found himself taking short gasps that didn't satisfy his need and left his lungs seared with pain. He adjusted his grip on Beth's hand and leaned in reaching down with his other hand. 'Further, Beth,' he shouted. 'I'm nearly touching her fingers. Sing louder. That might help.'

Beth was dragged against the edge of the bed, and thrust with her knees to stop herself falling on top of Quinn. She forced herself to carry on singing, but needed something to hold onto. She lunged for the stone on the pillow, grabbed it and held the stone aloft, much as she had done on Mount Malkamet. Instantly she felt power flooding into her voice and she sang at a volume and intensity she had never known before. Beth felt the pressure against her knees lessen and she was able to stand upright and hold Quinn's hand with a strength greater than her own.

Quinn felt rather than heard the change in Beth's voice and was able to lean much further in and make another grab at Ishi-mi-réjá. For a split second their hands were gripping each other, but then hers slipped away through his fingers. He lunged again and missed her, then again and this time he thrust down far enough to grip her by the wrist, and felt her grip his. He pulled hard against Beth's hand, but she was like a rock, totally immovable, and he was able to haul Ishi-mi-réjá up. He saw the bulls and dogs falling away from her, but she was streaming blood from the terrible wounds.

He raised his head and Ishi-mi-réjá burst out of the hole after him and lay across the top of the bed, with her arms and legs spread out. She was covered in blood and her clothing was rent and tattered in many places.

But there was nothing underneath to support her. Quinn could still see down into the darkness and feel the heat on his face and smell the stench. 'Quick, Beth. Place the stone on her forehead and change your song to, "Be healed".'

Beth did as she was told, stifling her desire to shriek at what she saw. But as she sang, the gaping wounds on the old woman began to knit together before her very eyes, and the flows of blood from the various gashes ceased and the skin became completely sound. Beth kept on singing, marvelling at what she had seen and aware of the bed itself reforming, till it was solid under the old woman, and the bedclothes were now visible and crumpled around her.

The old woman slumped back on the bed and lay sleeping deeply with such an expression of peace on her face.

Chapter Eighty Six

Kyros groped forwards a few paces in the dim light of the secret passageway and then stopped to remove his mail corselet.

'Why are you doing that?' Lenyé's voice startled him. 'If you won't bear any weapons, then at least chainmail will turn an enemy's blade and you can escape unharmed.'

'The True King is my shield and defender,' Kyros whispered. 'He will guard me and bring me through to a place of safety.'

'And what about the rest of us?' Lenyé wasn't giving up. 'I can only understand fighting off an enemy with weapons.'

'My greatest desire for you Lenyé is that you may come to know the True King for yourself.'

'It's all very well for you to say that, but I intend to look to my longbow and swords. At least I know how to use them!'

Kyros sighed and led them down the passageway, feeling the wall with his hand as they descended by a series of steps. When they came to the end he climbed up the rungs of a metal ladder set into the wall and pushed at the roof. A crack of light appeared and he heaved till a hinged trap door opened. He thrust his head out and looked round. Then he pushed till the trap door fell away from him and banged on the ground.

Harbona's face appeared in the opening. Kyros backed down and helped the others up while Harbona pulled them out. Kyros came last, closed the trap door and dragged the creepers back into place to hide any traces of their escape.

His sisters and cousins were already mounted and Lenyé swung herself into the saddle of a waiting horse. Harbona darted over to an eighth horse and fumbled with the hay shoes, but the horse kept stamping its hooves and not co-operating.

'There was a lot of activity the other side of the stables for most of the time you were away,' Kyros heard the exasperation in Harbona's voice, 'so I had to remain hidden. I only found this one twenty minutes ago, and I still haven't got the hay shoes on.'

'Here,' Marie-anna was on her knees beside him and holding the hoof. 'Let me help.' She gentled its muzzle.

Harbona tied the hay shoe and finished the other front hoof. Then they did the back ones as well and the horse was ready.

Kyros swung himself into the saddle and Harbona heaved Ramâno up behind. Harbona and Marie-anna mounted and they set off. Kyros and Ramâno led, with Harbona in the rear, as they headed past the clump of trees leading to the lane that would take them out West towards Lake Sanchéso.

They reached the end of the lane, turned left on a cobbled road and wound their way amongst the outlying houses and taverns towards the edge of the city. Night had fallen and people were indoors. Kyros was grateful for the hay shoes deadening their sound. Suddenly a door banged and a few warriors rushed out of a tavern and stared open-mouthed. One of them pointed at Lenyé. There was a shout. Several men ran into the road and tried to grab their bridles as their horses swept past.

But already they were beyond the tavern and the cobbles changed to coarse sand as they emerged onto the plain. The shouting didn't die down though, and presently Kyros heard the sound of hooves behind them. He yelled at Lenyé to take the lead, while he fell back to join Harbona.

'Not good news, My Lord. That must have been one of the warriors favourite drinking houses judging by their numbers.'

'How many?'

'I counted eight. They'll catch up with us easily. These hay shoes slow us down. There's no time to stop and take them off.'

'You ride on with the others, Harbona. I'll hold them back.'

'What about the boy. He's in danger with you.'

'Everyone's in danger as long as Lenyé is with us. Now go!'

Kyros slowed right down watching Harbona catch up with the others. He smiled at the dark shapes of Ariella and Mamma Uza-Mâté as they bounded out of the shadows and joined Lenyé; while the eagle, with a large snake dangling from its talons, swooped overhead. At least Lenyé had her friends with her.

He saw Lenyé turn and shout, but couldn't hear the words. She made a gesture of drawing a sword, but he waved her on.

Kyros muttered to himself, 'Oh, My King. If ever there was a time I need your help, it is now. Come to my aid.'

'Who are you talking to?' Ramâno's high-pitched voice jolted him out of his reverie.

'I speak to the True King himself who is always with me.'

'And does he talk back to you?'

'Of course.'

'Is your True King going to open the warrior's eyes to see that disk of light over your head? It's really bright now that we're out of the city.'

'Can you still see it?'

'I don't know why you keep asking. I see it all the time.'

'Shall I stop and let you get down to run off and hide?'

'Certainly not. I may want to be a healer like you, but I have a warrior's heart. I want to see what happens.'

Kyros slowed his horse, pulled its head round and started cantering back towards the approaching horsemen. When they were within a hundred yards, he slowed right down and halted.

There was a shout from in front and Kyros saw the lead warrior pull up and stop.

'Why are you pursuing me?' Kyros released the reins and lifted his right leg over the neck of the horse, swivelled round and slid to the ground so he wouldn't knock Ramâno with his leg in a normal dismount. He thrust the reins into Ramâno's hands and took a pace forwards.

The warrior slackened his reins to let his horse shake its head. 'I'm arresting you for abducting Princess Lenyé. One of my men recognised her as you galloped past.'

'She is leaving the palace of her own free will, and I am escorting her for protection.'

'You're that Healer, aren't you? I recognise you from the Central Square. And that's the little boy you healed sitting on your horse. There's an arrest warrant out for you for trying to stir up an insurrection.'

'You had plenty of opportunities to arrest me in the Square in broad daylight. Why are you resorting to the cover of darkness?'

'I have my orders. Two of my men have ridden back to the garrison to get re-enforcements. Are you going to come quietly?' The man drew his sword and urged his horse forwards.

'Now, Mister Healer,' Ramâno's shrill voice broke in. 'Do your True King stuff!'

As Kyros raised his right hand, there was the whizz of an arrow and the leader tumbled from his horse. He heard the lioness' roar and the screams of terrified horses as they threw their riders. Kyros whipped round to grab his reins and caught Ramâno as the boy flung himself off their own horse straight at him. He turned back to see Ariella burst in amongst the other warriors closely followed by Mamma Uza-Mâté. Lenyé hacked at a warrior with her sword, then ran him through while the lioness and she-bear finished off the others.

Lenyé wiped her sword clean with a handful of sand. 'What kind of a Prince do you call yourself?' She glared at Kyros. 'No weapons whatsoever. How did you think you could hold up six armed and mounted warriors when you were on foot?'

'The True King...' Kyros hesitated at the fury in Lenyé's eyes.

'You were the youngest Commander in the Royal Garrison, not because you were the King's son but for your prowess in arms and ability to lead and inspire. Why do you refuse to wear a sword now?'

'But Princess-Lady,' Ramâno wriggled out of Kyros' arms and jumped to the ground. 'You've ruined everything. He was about to do his True King bit.'

'And what exactly does that mean?'

'The True King was going to make those warriors bow the knee before him and recognise him for who he is.'

'I don't think so, Ramâno. Kyros may have been doing a very brave thing. But those warriors would have cut him to pieces.'

'She's wrong, Mister Healer,' Ramâno whipped round to look at Kyros. 'You tell her!'

'Maybe your precious "True King" only turned out to be me in the end.' There was a distinct sneer in Lenyé's tone. 'Someone with a bit of clear thinking and strategy in battle, instead of all this nonsense you keep giving me!'

Kyros ignored Lenyé and stared into Ramâno's eyes. 'Sometimes serving the True King means laying down your life in this world, rather than taking other lives.'

'And what good would that do?' Ramâno sounded shocked. 'All that healing. All those words of wisdom about the True King, and you'd let a warrior run his sword through you rather than resist. I thought you had some sort of power over these people!'

'Ramâno,' Kyros knelt down and wrapped his arms around the boy. 'Sometimes you have to make a sacrifice to save those you love the most.'

'And that's what you were prepared to do?'

Kyros nodded, but was startled by a snort from Lenyé.

'Not much point in rescuing us and escaping, only to throw your life away recklessly. Why don't you get yourself a sword?'

PART VII

THE ENCOUNTER

Chapter Eighty Seven

Morthrir heard the racing of feet in the corridor outside the private council chamber where he was talking to Vashtani about how to capture Kyros and Lenyé. He looked up as Youdlh burst through the door and dropped to one knee in front of the desk.

'Strike off my head, Sire.'

'Why?' Morthrir rose from his desk, walked round and stood looking down intently at the top of Youdlh's bowed head.

'I hardly dare speak the news, Sire.'

'Spit it out, man,' Morthrir's impatience was clearly audible in his voice.

'The army, Sire. It's gone!'

'What do you mean, "*Gone*"?' Morthrir glanced at Vashtani and then refocused on Youdlh.

'Completely wiped out, Sire.'

'What?' Vashtani sounded incredulous. 'There's nothing left out there to contest an army that size.'

'You mean...?' There was a catch in Morthrir's voice as the implications hit home. '...I have no more warriors left?'

'What happened?' Vashtani stood behind Youdlh.

'We were attacked by the Nastrim.'

'That's impossible,' Morthrir began striding up and down. 'According to Lenyé they were all wiped out at the gorge.'

'All I know, Sire, is that thousands of Nastrim surrounded us, with Acwellan, their Executioner, leading them. I recognised him from my Field Commander's description when we originally negotiated to have Lenyé released to us.'

'I don't understand,' Morthrir paused in mid-stride. 'Lenyé told me she killed him in the first battle up at Mount Nastâri and took the swords from him.'

'I'm certain it was him,' Youdlh continued. 'They must have taken the longbows from the aftermath of the battle at the gorge and used them to decimate our ranks with long-range volleys. When we closed in for hand-to-hand combat, our weapons made no impression on them at all. They were indestructible.'

'Wait a minute,' Vashtani interjected. 'You saw thousands of them?'

'Yes. Far more than at the previous two battles put together.'

'Led by my son, Acwellan?'

'That's right.'

'And they were indestructible?' Vashtani queried.

'We didn't kill one of them.'

Morthrir winced. 'How many of you escaped?'

'Thirty-three, Sire.'

Morthrir smacked his hand against the wall in fury.

Vashtani cleared his throat in the sudden silence. 'I know what's happened.'

'What?' Morthrir spun round and stared at him.

'The battle at the gorge must have despatched the last of the Nastrim to the *Death of the Undying*. That means the remainder of the race was wiped out.'

Morthrir frowned at him.

'When the Spiral opened up at your word of command, not only did we come through, but all the Nastrim from the *Death of the Undying* were permitted to return. That's why there were so many of them. The entire Nastrim race is here.'

'Is that why Acwellan was leading them,' Morthrir glanced at Youdlh and then back to Vashtani.

'Correct. And they are immune now to any weapon forged in the Waking World,' Vashtani continued. 'That's why they appear to be indestructible.' He paused. 'And that's why I couldn't find them earlier. They were all still in the *Death of the Undying*.'

'So Lenyé was right,' Morthrir began his pacing again. 'There really are Nastrim out there to be dealt with.'

'There is one problem though,' Vashtani continued. 'Acwellan has sworn vengeance against the Krêonor for their victories over him at the Beginning. Now that he has returned from the *Death of the Undying* and is no longer harmed by weapons of this World, his next move will be to march on Terrazarema. I'm not sure even I can stop him.'

Youdlh raised his head. 'But we have nothing left to defend the city with, Sire. Except the Guard of Honour.'

'I need those Guards to catch Kyros and Lenyé.'

'Only the Sword of Justice can despatch the Nastrim to their place of rest,' Vashtani glared at Morthrir. 'But because of your stupidity, Lenyé has it!'

Morthrir recoiled at the venom in Vashtani's voice. He felt suddenly vulnerable: there wasn't time to call all the participants together and use the *Vault of Malrema*, so he would have to rely on his current level of power. He knew he was taking a huge risk. He stared into Vashtani's eyes. 'Go and persuade Acwellan to accept my authority and join our cause.'

'Not after the way you treated me in the Royal Armoury,' Vashtani's voice was as cold as ice. 'I consider myself free from you to gather all the other Dé-monos, join with Acwellan and march on Terrazarema. I will also seize Lenyé for myself. You're on your own, Morthrir!'

With that, he was gone.

Chapter Eighty Eight

Kyros re-mounted and Lenyé helped Ramâno up. They set off in pursuit of the others followed by Ariella and Mamma-Uza-Mâté; Chuah-te-mok flew overhead with Ra-Na-Jiri. But they hadn't gone far before they heard the thudding of hooves behind them.

Ramâno glanced over his shoulder, 'Mister Healer. There are many warriors following us.'

'That must be the re-enforcements from the Royal Garrison the lead warrior was talking about,' Kyros turned his head to see.

'They're gaining on us!' he heard a tremor in the boy's voice.

'Do not be afraid. The True King will come to my aid.'

Lenyé skewed round and grunted, 'Not enough weapons between us to take them on. What do you intend doing?'

'Hush,' Kyros caught the faint refrain of singing around him, and sensed a surge of power in the very atmosphere. 'Listen.'

'What is it? I can only hear the thudding of hooves.'

Kyros felt the movement of Ramâno's small body against his back as the boy looked round.

'Why are the warriors going backwards?' Ramâno shrilled in his ear. 'Is your True King holding them back?'

'No,' Kyros chuckled. 'They're not really going backwards. It's just that we are going much faster. Do you not hear that singing? We are being lifted up on the song of the En-luchés.'

'Who are the En-luchés?'

'Beings from another world who are obedient to the True King and placed at my disposal.'

'Kyros.' Lenyé's voice cut through their conversation. 'What's happening? We're out-distancing those warriors. Surely the hay shoes would slow us down.'

'Princess-Lady,' Ramâno shouted back. 'The Healer is doing his True King stuff.'

'Don't be ridiculous, Ramâno,' Lenyé snorted with contempt.

'That's why the Healer doesn't carry any weapons,' Ramâno's voice quavered with emotion. 'You have to believe in him now.'

'I don't know about believing in things; I'm relieved to see we're escaping. But even if we outrun them for a while, they will catch up with us eventually.'

'Quiet, both of you.' Kyros glanced at Lenyé. 'I feel the wings of his presence. The Great Messenger from the True King is here. Nothing can stand against us now.'

'Mister Healer,' Ramâno interrupted. 'What's that behind us?'

Kyros whipped round and saw a dark cloud overtake the warriors and come speeding after them. 'Dé-monos. Lenyé, take the boy and ride ahead to the others. I will hold them back.'

'No,' Ramâno wrapped his arms tighter around Kyros and clung to him. 'Don't send me away, or I will always despise myself as a coward. Where you go, I will go. The enemies you face, I will face. Where you die, I will die. I want the power that is in you to be in me. How am I supposed to become a healer if I can't see what you do? I'm not leaving you.'

'You have asked a hard thing, Ramâno. But if you see what I see, then the True King will grant all that you ask and more.'

'I'm staying too,' Lenyé pulled on her reins to slow her horse. 'I do not fear the Dé-monos with the Sword of Justice in my hands. I have already proved it against Vashtani.'

'No. You must go. The others will need you and your Sword before I've finished here. Besides, if you really mean to deal with the Nastrim, they must be somewhere ahead of us.' Kyros raised his right hand and spoke with a tone of command, 'Oh, Winged Messenger of the True King, lift up this lady on her horse and bring her swiftly to her brothers. Let the lioness and the she-bear go with her.' He slowed his horse, but Lenyé and her friends sped away and were soon out of sight.

Lenyé caught up with the others. They were crouching behind a ridge on the plain that swept up to the forest above Lake Sanchéso, and holding their horses' reins. Harbona was already climbing the ridge.

She dismounted and joined them. 'What's the problem?'

'There,' her brother, Wilf, pointed. 'We don't know what they are.'

She turned to follow his finger and saw a mass of Nastrim pour out of the forest and race towards them. She was right: they had come back. Then she recognised the lead figure: 'Acwellan!' she gasped. It never occurred to her that he would be leading them. How could she fulfil her oath to Captain Turvil now?

'What shall we do?' there was a note of fear in Wilf's voice.

'Stay here,' Lenyé remounted and cantered round the end of the ridge and rode up the sloping plain, overtaking Harbona. 'Go back and protect the others,' Lenyé yelled at him. 'I have the only weapon that can challenge this threat.'

She pulled her horse to a halt and waited for Acwellan to reach her. 'What are you doing here?'

'It's my pretty little maiden.' Acwellan held up his hand and the others halted behind him. 'I said we would meet again? The great Breaking-in has happened, and we have been released from the *Death of the Undying* and sucked up the Spiral. A great influx of newly dead joined us from a recent battle and we have armed ourselves from the scattered swords and javelins of their defeat. The entire Nastrim race is with me. Vashtani and the Dé-monos are already here. We were hurrying to join them and form an invincible alliance that will have all the Waking World in our grip. We destroyed a whole warrior army on the other side of that forest,' he jerked his thumb over his shoulder. 'Now we march on the capital city. There is no force left to stop us!'

'Except me,' Lenyé's voice was soft, but steady.

Acwellan roared with laughter. 'You?' he was still chuckling. 'Don't you understand? No weapon can stop us now.'

Lenyé swung her leg over the horse's shoulder and slipped to the ground. 'Except the Sword of Justice.'

'You're not thinking of challenging me are you? I still intend to present you to my Father, Vashtani.'

'Not if I can help it.'

'Wait,' a voice cried out, and Lenyé recognised Captain Turvil as he stepped forwards. 'This is Princess Lenyé, and we were marching on Terrazarema to rescue her siblings when we were wiped out by those warriors.'

'What?' Acwellan roared. 'So she is a Krêonor after all. And you were using a Nastrim army to fight for her?'

'She saved us from the first army that camped outside Mount Nastâri, and has commanded us ever since.'

'When have the Nastrim ever been led by a human, let alone a Krêonor?' Acwellan glared at Captain Turvil. 'What's the matter with you? I'm your leader again and you'll do as I say.'

'You don't understand,' Captain Turvil held his ground. 'We promised Lenyé that we would fulfil our oath and serve her.'

'Nonsense. Those already in the *Death of the Undying* from the wars at the Beginning seek vengeance on the Krêonor.' Acwellan raised his voice, 'Is that not so?'

He was greeted with a thunderous response.

'What about the rest of you?'

There was some murmuring and jostling, but no one spoke.

'Do I take that as "Yes"?' Acwellan roared.

Still there was no answer.

Another Nastâr stepped forwards from behind Captain Turvil. 'I think you misjudge the mood of the Nastrim.'

Lenyé recognised Decatur by his missing hand.

'You are dragging us back to the Waking World,' Decatur continued, 'to renew old hatreds because of a war a thousand years ago. 'But many of us have resisted your leadership and desired to be despatched to Elasis, our place of rest.'

'That's right,' Captain Turvil agreed. 'Only Lenyé has the power to do that for us with the Sword of Justice.'

'I see,' Acwellan frowned. 'So we have a leadership contest: the Krêonor woman or myself.' Acwellan turned to Lenyé. 'Why don't we settle it by single combat?' He raised an eyebrow as he studied her. 'If I disarm you, then I hand you over to my Father.'

'And if I kill you?' Lenyé stared him in the eyes.

'You won't. But if you do, the rest of the Nastrim are yours to command.' He raised his voice again. 'Do you all agree?'

There was a shout of "Yes" from those Decatur and Captain Turvil represented, but only a muted response from the others.

'Very well,' Lenyé sighed. 'What weapon will you use?'

'One of those swords you bear, and you can use the other. As you currently hold the swords, I insist on having first choice.'

Lenyé unbuckled the swords and swapped them round several times, before presenting the hilts to Acwellan.

He reached out, hesitating over one hilt, and then grasped the other. Lenyé watched him run his thumb round the hilt guard, that long, cruel smile playing across his lips. With one swift movement the blade was shimmering in his hand.

'You have just made a terrible mistake,' Acwellan adopted an attacking stance with the sword in his right hand. 'In a few minutes you will be mine to present to my Father!'

Lenyé drew the remaining sword and threw the scabbards to one side. She knew by the weight it was the Sword of Justice, and was thankful for her foresight in having the nick in the other one removed. She had tricked Acwellan into thinking he was holding the Sword of Justice. No wonder he was smiling like that.

She glanced round and realised that Harbona and the others had caught up with her and formed a horseshoe shape around her, while the Nastrim fanned out behind Acwellan.

So far the Sword of Justice had refused to let her use it to take life in battle. But as the Sword slid out so easily it must be all right. Why this time? She recalled Kyros' words as they argued at the Pool of Alesco, *"The first task the new keeper of the Sword must do is despatch the Nastrim to their place of rest"*. If that's what she had to do, she would start with Acwellan.

She noted the missing helmet and the rent in the chest of his chainmail where she had previously rammed her sword right though him.

Acwellan flicked his sword forwards.

A shout from the Nastrim drowned out her cousins.

She touched blades with him and they both stood off, circling for an opening. He lunged at her, but she turned his blade and forced him back with a hacking stroke. Lenyé saw his eyes narrow.

'The maiden has grown in expertise,' Acwellan muttered.

Then he moved in with a series of blows and counter blows that left her reeling.

A cry of expectation went up from the crowd.

Lenyé knew of his speed and prowess from when he fought Decatur. There had to be a way to outwit him. But all she could do was parry his blows as she backed away.

Last time they met, she flung hot embers in his face, swarmed up a rock for the height advantage and launched herself at him like a human javelin with the sword held out in front of her, and the impetus drove it through his chainmail. But there was only an expanse of coarse sand here: nothing to give any advantage.

Because of his great height she couldn't reach for his throat or face, it might throw her off balance. Somehow she had to thrust her sword into that rent in his chainmail. But all she could think of was "javelin". Wait a minute. An idea was forming in her mind. She needed to use his strength and speed against him; that meant provoking him into a temper so that he would lose control, and make him try to kill her rather than just disarm her.

'When we last fought at Mount Nastâri,' Lenyé knew she had

to spur him into action straight away, 'and you were about to pass to the *Death of the Undying*, you said you would have your *"revenge"*. I assumed you meant to kill me.'

Acwellan grunted, turned her sword away and struck hard at her, but didn't reply.

'What about Vashtani?' her breath rasped in her throat from exertion as she parried his blow. 'Have you told him about me?'

'Only in thought,' Acwellan raised his sword for another stroke. 'But he'll know all right.'

'So if you kill me,' Lenyé ducked and hacked at his back as her opponent swept past, 'you'll have your Father to face.'

'Who says I'm going to kill you?'

'You'll have to, because you're too clumsy to disarm me!'

'Don't be ridiculous,' he stepped back watching for another opening in her guard. 'You're no match for me and you know it!'

'What's Vashtani going to say when he comes to claim his new bride and finds out you killed me?'

'I'm not going to kill you, but I don't care how badly I wound you to disarm you. I agree; I said, *"I shall have my revenge"*. That means handing you, alive, to my Father.' His eyes blazed with sudden rage. 'And that's all I'm interested in!'

Lenyé smiled to herself. Her plan was working. Now that she'd incited him, she needed to use that blind fury to her advantage.

Acwellan hurled himself forwards to attack and the crowd roared in response. As he lifted his sword, she feigned being struck on the jaw by the hilt and flung herself as far away as possible to get some distance between them. She landed on her back, with her arms on the ground above her head, momentarily winded. Lenyé eased the Sword over to grasp the handle with both hands, the coarse sand grinding against her thighs above the tops of her boots. She let her head droop to one side and partially closed her eyes as if stunned, hearing the venom in his voice: 'You were right. I'm going to kill you after all!'

Chapter Eighty Nine

Beth watched as Ishi-mi-réjá opened her eyes.

'Thank you, Beth,' the old woman's voice was very weak. 'I only sang one song over you, but you sang two over me. You reconnected me to my stone and healed me.' Ishi-mi-réjá glanced at Quinn and smiled, 'Thank you, as well; you never gave up, did you. You snatched me out of that terrible pit and delivered me from those dogs, and saved my life.'

Beth drew a blanket over her tattered clothing. 'You look exhausted. I think you need to sleep for the remainder of today and tonight. And Quinn still needs to recover his strength.'

Quinn stepped outside the front door for some fresh air while Beth brought a basin of water for Ishi-mi-réjá to wash and change. Beth took the bedding into the kitchen, soaked it in cold water and then scrubbed the blood stains with some wood ash that had fallen through the grate of the stove. She could still smell the stale sweat on the blankets from when Quinn was wrapped up in them during his fever.

'I'll get the worst of it off and hang the bedding up to dry,' she called to Ishi-mi-réjá. 'I can sort it out properly another time.'

When Beth came back into the living room, the old woman was sitting up on the bed with a cloak over her and chatting to Quinn. Ishi-mi-réjá smiled. 'Why don't you both go and pick mushrooms in the woods today. If I'm strong enough tomorrow, we'll have a long talk.'

Chapter Ninety

Kyros reined in his horse, turned its head to face the approaching dark cloud, and waited.

'What are the Dé-monos like?' Ramâno gripped tighter.

'Do not look into their eyes,' Kyros felt the boy shiver, 'or they will suck the life out of you.'

'What are you going to do, Mister Healer?' there was a note of panic in the boy's voice.

'Oh, My King,' Kyros spoke out with authority. 'Open the eyes of this young lad that he may see what I see.'

He felt Ramâno lean to one side and peer round him.

'What are those?' Ramâno's voice was filled with awe. 'I see many beings of light, taller than men, surrounding you.'

'You have seen the En-luchés as they serve those who walk with the True King? Our warfare is not against humans, as my Uncle so foolishly supposes, but against dark powers that have come down to us from their own high Realms.'

'Do you see them all the time?' Ramâno whispered.

'Not in the Waking World. And certainly not until I obeyed the True King's command to go to Terrazarema and call his People back to a knowledge of his name.'

Kyros broke off as a figure approached. 'Stellatus, my friend. It's good to see you.'

'Come, Kyros,' Stellatus looked serious. 'We must fall back, for we are seriously outnumbered; but re-enforcements should arrive soon.'

Kyros heard the song of the En-luchés as they were lifted up and sped across the plain, followed by shouts of triumph and screams of victory as the Dé-monos poured after them.

As they touched down on the plain, Kyros took in the tableau: Harbona, Marie-anna, the lioness, she-bear, eagle and cobra, his sisters and two cousins in a horseshoe shape; while facing them he recognised Decatur at the front of a great crowd of Nastrim. The open space in the middle was dominated by a huge Nastâr, brandishing a sword and charging at a human figure lying on its back on the ground. Whoever it was appeared to be unconscious, judging by the splayed out limbs and lolling head. As his eyes focused on the face he realised it was…

'Lenyé!' he shouted and urged his horse forwards, but was hindered by the Dé-monos.

'Harbona, Stellatus!' he cried; could neither of them come to her aid?

The Dé-monos pressed through the En-luchés: blood-lust in their eyes; and their derisive yells rang with mockery in his ears.

'Oh, My King, though I cry to you last when I should have appealed to you first, I call upon you now to help her.'

Lenyé heard a gasp from the spectators, and her cousins' shrill cries of, 'Look out, Lenyé,' were drowned by the greater shout of, 'Now, Acwellan. We will have you as our leader.'

Lenyé saw Acwellan back off, then race towards her: sword raised for the death-stroke. She had to judge his speed precisely if this was going to work. She whipped her knees up to her chest, snapped her eyes open and thrust her feet away, jack-knifing her body, and jerking her arms forwards over her chest before releasing the Sword. She heard it whistle through the air, saw the point disappear into the rent of his chainmail and the whole Blade penetrate right up to the hilt guard. She thrust her elbow against the sand and rolled to her right to avoid his toppling body. With a cry, Acwellan dropped his sword, clutched at his chest and collapsed to the ground where she had lain.

A yell went up from the crowd, followed by utter silence.

Lenyé stood up, retrieved Acwellan's sword, snatched the scabbard from the ground and slotted in the blade. She walked to Acwellan, stooped down and heaved the huge body onto its side to withdraw her Sword. She grabbed a handful of sand to wipe the Blade clean, but realised there was no blood on it.

An anguished cry arose from the Dé-monos.

One of the Nastrim called out, 'What's happened? Why hasn't his body sunk into the ground like it does when a Nastâr is despatched to the *Death of the Undying*?'

Suddenly Kyros saw Osâcah and the Pilgrims emerge from the forest, sprint towards him and form a ring around the Nastrim, with Lenyé and the others in the middle. He urged his horse forwards and the Pilgrims let him into their circle.

'Acwellan!' Vashtani wailed. 'Let me come to you,' and he thrust against the En-luchés. 'We are robbed of your revenge.'

'What's happening?' Ramâno wriggled to get a better view.

'Shh, Ramâno. Listen.' Kyros heard the urgent pleas of the Pilgrims to the True King to intervene, and raised his right hand. 'Vashtani. I have already spoken words of judgement against you in the Realm of Travail. Now the En-luchés will be strengthened against you!'

Immediately Stellatus and his followers rallied and were able to drive the Dé-monos back, forming a protective ring outside the circle of Pilgrims.

Kyros turned to face Lenyé to see the outcome of Acwellan's death. 'Watch and wait,' he whispered to Ramâno. 'Do not be afraid. The True King will come to our aid at the right time.'

Chapter Ninety One

Rafé stood outside the door to the private council chamber considering the possible link between Lenyé's Sword and the vision of the golden globe. The Sword obviously had some kind of power but he wanted to test Morthrir on how much he knew. The golden globe was an unknown quantity. If Morthrir could be convinced that finding the globe was important, it might help to confuse him and divert his attention from more immediate issues. Rafé would have to pick his moment carefully.

At the answer to his second knock, Rafé pushed open the door, noting Morthrir's curt 'Yes,' as the man glanced up from the desk.

'I wanted to talk to you, Sire, about Vashtani's comment in *The Vault of Malrema*.'

'Really? The whole thing was absurd. I don't have time to go off on a wild goose chase. My entire destiny hangs in the balance.'

'Not if we seek out this power he mentioned. Remember you wondered yourself if Lenyé had received any special powers from the Nastrim. I think the power resides at their mountain, not in that sword. '

'Then why does Vashtani fear it so much?'

'I'm not convinced he does. He's trying to fool you for his own purposes.'

'So why could Lenyé draw the Sword and I couldn't? It must have some kind of power.'

'There has to be a simple explanation, Sire. Probably a secret catch in the scabbard. Who tried first, you or her?'

'She did. When we were at camp out in the plains. No. Wait a minute,' Morthrir drummed his fingers on the desk. 'I did.'

'And was there any opportunity for her to do something to the sword when you weren't looking?'

'She turned her back to me and swapped the swords around so I couldn't tell them apart. Then she offered both and asked me to choose.'

'So she could have set a secret catch without you knowing? Was there any other opportunity?'

'Yes. When I was with Vashtani in the Royal Armoury. He drew one, but there was no opportunity to try the other before I threw it to her to defend herself. Then she forced Vashtani to leave, so I assumed she had the Sword of Justice. It must have power of its own to do that.'

'Not necessarily, Sire. Vashtani may have had his own reasons for disappearing at that point.'

'What exactly are you driving at?'

'Vashtani said, "*We felt a power deep within the mountain itself and emanating a light that we dared not approach*". I think that is the power you need to counter what has being going on recently with the Healer.'

'But I can't spare any warriors to send them all the way to Mount Nastâri at this time.'

'You don't need to. I wanted to ask leave of absence to go myself, Sire. Alone.'

'I see.' Morthrir sat drumming his fingers on the desk. 'How long will you need?'

'Not more than two weeks, Sire.'

'Very well. But don't let anyone else know what you're doing.'

'Thank you, Sire. I'll make preparations to leave in a few days so that no one can link my actions to this meeting.'

Chapter Ninety Two

Lenyé glimpsed the darkness of many Dé-monos, held in check by a few dazzling figures and a ring of humans dressed in white. She was aware of Kyros on his horse, but reeled as a great noise erupted from the Nastrim and she heard them arguing over what was going to happen to them now that Acwellan was dead. Already they were forming into two distinct companies.

With a bellow of rage many of them ran at Lenyé with drawn swords. At Decatur's shout, other Nastrim rushed to defend her and she was aware of Captain Turvil yelling commands till she was surrounded by supportive Nastrim. Some of the attackers broke through and she had to fight them off, her mind not only grappling with every thrust and parry, but also her astonishment at the Sword of Justice allowing her to use it in battle.

Kyros saw Vashtani lead his Dé-monos to break through the ring of En-luchés and attack the Pilgrims, causing some of them to collapse. Vashtani reached the Nastrim facing Lenyé. 'Grab her Sword, like Acwellan did to Zerigor!' he roared. 'With that Sword in my hands, we will be invincible and can conquer the Waking World.' Many Nastrim surged forwards and turned to oppose Lenyé; but a number of En-luchés forced Vashtani back.

'Hold fast,' Kyros galloped round the circle of Pilgrims urging them to close rank. 'Trust in the True King.' He saw Osâcah and his companions fall to their knees, hands lifted in supplication, as their cries to the True King for help intensified. He was startled by Ramâno's high-pitched voice.

'Come on, Mister Healer. These people might be holding back the Dé-monos, but it's time you did your True King stuff. If we're fighting *"against dark powers that have come down to us from their own high Realms"* as you say, it's his battle not Lenyé's.'

'You learn quickly, Ramâno.' For the lad's benefit Kyros cried aloud rather than whispering to himself, 'Oh, My King. Come to her aid.' Instantly he heard the response in his heart, *'Do not ask me to fight your battles. You speak the word of victory over her!'*

Kyros stood in his stirrups and felt Ramâno scramble up to stand on the horse's back with his hands on Kyros' shoulders.

'I want to see what happens,' the boy whispered in his ear.

Kyros raised his right hand, 'In the name of Luchianó-bé, Lord of Light, let the power of the True King be released in the Waking World to bring victory.'

Kyros heard a tearing sound above him as though someone had ripped a heavy linen veil in half, and glanced up to see a rent appear in the sky. Brilliant light poured through as a figure came flying straight towards him. Kyros couldn't take his eyes off the being, so beautiful were the wings clothed in white like the feathers of a swan; and the light about the head was utterly dazzling. He felt himself mesmerised by the steady beat of those wings, and the speed at which the being flew; his heartbeat slowing to mirror the wing beats of the Great En-luchés: for this, surely, was the full revealing of what he only glimpsed at the stables and felt as they journeyed by horse. The downdraft of the Great En-luchés' wings raised a tempest in the Waking World that swept over the Nastrim as they battled.

He felt Ramâno lean round him and point to the sky. 'I see him, Mister Healer. Is this the *"more"* you promised me?'

Kyros nodded.

As the being swooped down and settled in the midst of the defending ring of Nastrim, Kyros felt Ramâno's arms slip around his neck, the boy's whole body trembling against his back. The lad pointed again and whispered, 'I see Lenyé wrapped up in him as if she's hidden in a bright cloud!'

The boy was right: Lenyé appeared to be clothed in the Great En-luchés' presence.

'What's going on?' there was a tremor in Ramâno's voice as the lad pointed at the sky. 'I see horses and chariots of fire and thousands of En-luchés holding drawn swords and lances with pennants fluttering from the tips, like an enormous army.'

Kyros glanced up to see the En-luchés sweep down with a thunder of hooves and the grinding of many wheels. 'You're seeing them revealed in all their glory.'

The En-luchés burst upon the ranks of Dé-monos outside the ring of Pilgrims, and attacked the few which had managed to penetrate the protective circle.

'Look, Ramâno. The Dé-monos are falling back in confusion.'

'What about Lenyé?' Ramâno's high-pitched yell made him whip round in alarm.

Kyros saw the Great En-luchés reach up to the handle of his sword protruding between the double arches of his folded wings; the blade sparkling brighter than the noon-day sun as he drew it. The Great En-luchés reversed it in his hands and held it before him, with the blade pointing downwards.

But Lenyé appeared to be oblivious of his presence as she cried out in a loud voice, 'Enough!'

Both companies of the Nastrim stepped back in amazement as she plunged her Sword into the ground at the exact moment that the Great En-luchés did the same.

Kyros watched while the Great En-luchés paced with her between the two Nastrim companies, as she measured out a line to the left of the Sword; turned with her as she turned, and paced back, passing the Sword and measuring out a line to the right; turned again, walked back with her and finally turned with her to face the opposing Nastrim.

Lenyé held up her arms, and the Great En-luchés followed

315

her movement. 'The Sword of Justice stands between us,' she cried. 'Those of you, who seek to defend me, fall back behind this Blade and the line I have just walked along. Those who follow the counsel of Acwellan, stand on the other side.'

So commanding was her presence that the Nastrim obeyed without a murmur: many retreated behind her; but quite a few rushed through their ranks and turned to oppose her.

'As I understand it,' her voice rang out. 'You can never be at peace in the Waking World, for you are consumed by a bitter conflict within: either driven by a lust for war and conquest; or a yearning to bear offspring, which you can never fulfil. And so you are ever torn in two.' She paused as her eyes swept the Nastrim in front of her. 'How much longer will you wrestle with this affliction? You have just seen Acwellan despatched to Elasis. That is why his body did not sink into the ground; and clear proof of the power of the Sword of Justice over you.

There was a shout of agreement from those behind Lenyé led by Decatur; but those in front only muttered inaudible words.

'I am a Princess in the Royal House of the Krêonor and the Sword of Justice has rightfully come to me. Only I can deliver you with this Sword. Will you agree to let me do this for you?'

There was complete silence from the Nastrim.

'Both companies of Nastrim must now pass under this Blade.' Lenyé addressed the Nastrim in front of her. 'Then your lust for bloodshed will go down into death.' She turned to those behind her. 'What benefit is there if you desire to bring forth life but do not have the power to do so? That too, must go down into death.'

She turned to the front again and addressed them all. 'And so you will find release from the constant striving between your two natures. The manner of your choice will determine how this is to be accomplished: either willingly for your benefit, or your destruction if you refuse.'

'We don't care about this sword of yours,' a voice rang out from in front of her. 'We want revenge against the Krêonor!'

316

'There are enough of us to grab that sword,' another voice cried out. 'Like we did to Zerigor of old.'

'She might get a few of us first,' another agreed. 'But not all. Why give up the chance to rule in the Waking World?'

'What do you gain,' Lenyé shouted down the voices, 'if you conquer this world and remain forever tormented within? That is not a victory worth having!'

But the opposing Nastrim rushed forwards, weapons poised for the kill, their bellows of rage drowning out all other sounds.

Kyros kept his hand raised and felt a deluge of power rushing through the rent in the sky, pouring through him and flooding out over Lenyé. His heart was lifted up to the True King; and Osâcah's words, by the special beech tree, rang in his ears: "*You must recover your position of authority with the True King in order to fulfil his purposes in the Waking World*". 'Oh, My King,' he whispered. 'You have restored all that I ever had from you and far more. Let one stroke be enough to despatch the Nastrim.'

He watched Lenyé reach for the handle of her Sword.

The energy for the stroke began as she pulled the Sword out of the ground with both hands, her right arm looping over her head, the Blade swinging round over her left shoulder and trailing behind her as her left arm completed a second loop over her head, leaving the Blade momentarily cocked, parallel to the line of her right shoulder, and poised for the blow. As she sank onto her left knee her right arm straightened, accelerating the Sword into a great arc, cleaving the air in front of her, the flat of the Blade turning over as her right arm began to flex for the follow-through, and the hilt passed over her left shoulder and the Sword finished up behind her back and pointing downwards.

Even in the blur of the whole stroke, Kyros saw the Great En-luchés mirror her every move: sinew for sinew, muscle for muscle, limb for limb. Or did she follow him? Kyros couldn't tell;

their movements were so co-ordinated it looked like one final, deadly stroke.

Where Lenyé's Blade merely cut through the air immediately in front of her; his Awful Blade, glittering with unbearable light, scythed through the Nastrim like some Mighty Reaper harvesting a field of corn. The onrushing columns went down from right to left before them as if the Nastrim were an undercut chalk cliff finally collapsing into the raging fury of the sea.

Kyros heard a sigh of relief from the remaining Nastrim; a shout of victory from the Sacred Pilgrims as they erupted to their feet, arms held high and fists pounding the air; and a cry of despair from the Dé-monos as they shrank back in horror.

'She's done it, she's done it, she's done it!' Ramâno danced up and down on the horse's back and pummelled Kyros' shoulder blades with his fists, while the horse snorted and reared.

Kyros glanced round, 'I thought you said this battle belonged to the True King?'

'But if she hadn't done her part, none of it would have happened!'

Kyros sank into the saddle to control the horse and felt the boy slip down behind him to sit on the horse's back.

Lenyé saw dark images arise from each dead body and gather together as one condemned company before being blown away by a sudden breeze. She stood up as the remaining Nastrim approached her, the Sword still in her hands.

'What about rescuing your sister?' Captain Turvil stepped forwards. 'We swore to aid you in that. Should we not complete the task before we go?'

Lenyé studied his face before replying. 'Thank you for thinking of my own trials.' She paused, feeling tears pricking at the corners of her eyes with the sudden reminder of Beth. 'My sister is dead. And I have the rest of my family here with me; so I release you from that oath.'

'Then please despatch us to Elasis.'

As Lenyé held the Sword in both hands and the remaining Nastrim voluntarily lined up in front of her, Kyros saw the engulfing figure of the Great En-luchés mirror her every movement. He glanced round at Ramâno and grinned at him as their eyes met: the boy obviously saw it as well.

Decatur hoisted Acwellan's body onto his shoulder and addressed Lenyé. 'Though we were enemies in life, I will take his body out of respect, not only for him, but you as well. We will not leave any trace of the Nastrim in the Waking World. I will go first.' The others pressed forwards, hoisted the remaining dead bodies onto their shoulders, and formed a single line.

As they walked beneath her Blade, each Nastrim vanished in turn. The column of Nastrim was so long that Kyros could see Lenyé's arms beginning to shake with fatigue; but he also saw the Majestic Figure and the Stronger Arms and the Greater Sword blazing with light around her and steady as a rock.

Lenyé looked up as the last one approached, 'Captain Turvil. When those warriors defeated your army in the gorge I despaired because I had failed you. Now I am overjoyed to be able to do this for you. When I first came amongst the Nastrim I feared the evil I had heard of by report. But in you, I have found only good. I will always treasure your friendship.'

As he came alongside, he smiled at her, 'You have done us a great service. We were in danger of being poisoned by Acwellan's hatred. Farewell. For now we go to our rest.'

Kyros walked his horse forwards and dismounted, but was startled by Lenyé's tone as she spoke.

'Satisfied?' She sheathed her Sword. 'I've done as you asked!'

Lenyé stared at the battle still raging between the En-luchés and the Dé-monos beyond the ring of Pilgrims, and then glared at Kyros. 'Why haven't you dealt with the Dé-monos yet?'

'The Healer-man is holding them back by the word of his power,' Ramâno's shrill voice made them both turn. Ramâno swung his leg over the horse's back and slithered to the ground. 'I am going to have that power some day because I saw…'

'Shh, Ramâno.' Kyros drew the lad to him and rested his hand on the boy's shoulder. 'It is not always a good idea to blurt out what the True King has shown you if others cannot see it.'

With a shout the Pilgrims closed in around Kyros, and he introduced Osâcah to Lenyé.

'So these are your farmers,' she glared at Kyros. 'They don't bear any weapons either!'

'The True King has answered our pleas against those who took our lives,' Osâcah gazed at Kyros. 'And we have finished our replanting: the Plains of Lohr will once again be fruitful. This is a picture of what is happening in the spirit-realm of the Waking World: bringing forth life where once there was only desert. Our task here is complete. Please release us.'

Kyros ignored Lenyé's hostility and embraced Osâcah, 'You are a faithful friend to me. Go now, with my blessing upon you.'

Stellatus and a number of En-luchés gathered round and broke into song, lifting up the Sacred Pilgrims and escorting them back to their place of rest before the True King.

Kyros glanced at Lenyé, and then turned to address the Dé-monos. 'Vashtani,' he shouted, 'you may have been freed from your bonds, but I have not released you and your followers from my words over you. Go. And if I ever see you again, the judgement of Luchianó-bé will fall upon you.'

The remaining En-luchés, with their horses and chariots, surged forwards at his words and the Dé-monos turned and fled.

Kyros glanced up in awe, for the Great En-luchés had spread his wings and lifted from the ground. As quickly as he came, he sped away, and only the pure melody of his flight was left imprinted in Kyros' mind.

Chapter Ninety Three

'Well,' Morthrir paced up and down past Rafé in the private council chamber, and then turned to glare at Vashtani. 'You come whining back to me with some pathetic tale of defeat!'

'We ran into Kyros,' Vashtani quailed before Morthrir's eyes. 'But he hindered us. I saw my son, Acwellan, poised to strike Lenyé the death blow.'

'What? You stood by and watched and didn't try to stop him!'

'I couldn't do anything. We'd pushed Kyros back as far as possible, but his resistance strengthened.'

'So what happened?'

'I thought she was unconscious, but she suddenly came to life and threw her Sword at Acwellan as though it was a sawn-off javelin. The Blade went straight through a rent in his chainmail, and he fell to the ground.'

'At least that's stopped the threat of him attacking us here in Terrazarema.'

'You don't understand. She used the Sword of Justice and pierced him through the heart. My son is dead. Acwellan has passed from this world and will never come back. This is a terrible day and I have sworn vengeance against her!'

'You will do no such thing. If you lay one finger on her, I will destroy you.' Morthrir glared at Vashtani. 'Is that understood?'

The two of them remained with eyes locked until Vashtani dropped his gaze.

'Yes, My Lord.'

'What about the rest of the Nastrim?'

'Some of them tried to seize the Sword from her and we broke through the En-luchés to help them. But then Kyros called up one of the Great Ones whom we dare not name. He swept the attacking Nastrim away. And she forced all the others to walk under her Blade. They have all gone too.'

'Did you bring Lenyé back with you?'

'No.'

'I see. So are you saying you have failed me?'

'No. Of course not.'

'Good. Then I will overlook your words at our last meeting. You, and the rest of the Dé-monos, can accompany me when I go to reclaim my bride.'

'I dare not, My Lord. Thousands more En-luchés have entered the Waking World and surrounded Kyros. He was terrifying; like the Captain of a mighty army: I could barely look at him. This is just a foretaste of what is to come. He will execute the pending judgement he has outstanding over us and we will be dragged away by the En-luchés.'

'Then you'd better withdraw till I call for your services again.'

'If you want my advice, seek out this power at Mount Nastâri, My Lord.' Vashtani stared at him. 'You will need it to succeed.'

'I never leave anything to chance and have already made preparations to recover it,' Morthrir glanced at Rafé and back to Vashtani. 'I will send someone a bit more reliable than you!'

Chapter Ninety Four

Rafé waited in the ensuing silence as Vashtani disappeared through the wall. His mind was in a whirl debating how to push Morthrir to over reach himself. This was the opportunity he wanted, and re-focused on Morthrir's face as the man spoke.

'What do you suggest, Rafé?' Morthrir glared at him.

'In the light of what has happened, I think you need to use your powers of travel to follow hard after Kyros and Lenyé.'

'What makes you say that?'

'You arrived at Onadestra as quickly as I did, and I had a horse. Then you were here in Terrazarema far quicker than me, and I left only a day after you. I assumed you received some kind of power from the Convocation to enable you to do that.'

'An intelligent guess, Rafé. Who else knows?'

'Possibly some who were with you on Mount Malkamet.'

'What about this power you say is at Mount Nastâri. Should I not wait till you've found out what it is?'

'No, Sire. You go in person, and confront Kyros and Lenyé before they disappear again. You could be there immediately.'

'So this new power you're talking about, isn't going to help at all?'

'Not straight away, Sire. I think it will aid you in your overall objective some time in the future.'

'I see. So it's down to the power I currently have through the Lord Abbérron himself, to stop those two escaping my net.' He stared at Rafé. 'You're right. Everyone else has utterly failed me.' Morthrir smacked his fist into the palm of his hand. 'I will go.'

Chapter Ninety Five

Morthrir placed the marred bust of Kyros on the Western point of the Hexacle. He stood on the altar facing East and slowed his breathing, visualising Mount Malkamet. He let the rhythm carry his thoughts till he saw himself on the flattened summit and heard afresh that awe-inspiring voice: *"Turn and face West towards Lake Sanchéso, and the Eye of Hoffengrégor, and the cursèd spot on the Dangst Rock where the Seer stood and prophesied the Restoration of the Krêonor. Speak my words against him"*. The weight of those words and the power contained in them sank deep into his being as though he was drinking a great draft of fresh mountain water that renewed and revived him.

But it wasn't the Eye of Hoffengrégor he was seeking, or the Seer he was speaking against. He wanted to locate and destroy his nephew once and for all. He couldn't let the man slip out of his clutches now that he was so close to achieving his purposes.

'Why is it always out the West our troubles come,' he muttered to himself as he turned and faced in the other direction.

Morthrir concentrated on the bust. He closed his eyes and focused beyond the sliced away hair and scraped off beard until he saw the living face of Kyros; then spoke a word of command.

Immediately he was standing on the ground leading towards the forest above Lake Sanchéso. In front of him were Kyros and Lenyé and the rest of their families and some others preparing to mount. He heard thudding hooves and turned to see a company of his reserve warriors gather in formation behind him.

'Kyros,' he shouted. 'Release Lenyé to me.'

Kyros trotted forwards. 'Uncle Morthrir. Lenyé has chosen to come with me. If you try to take her, you will be brought down and your words come to nothing and you will be destroyed.'

Morthrir staggered back at the potency of Kyros' words, yelling to his warriors. As they picked up the pace, he saw Kyros and the group around Lenyé gallop away at an extraordinary rate, while his own warriors were left trailing in their wake.

He fell forwards on the ground in despair, sensing his dream of ruling with Lenyé slipping from his grasp.

But then he scooped up a handful of coarse sand, clenched his fist and let the sand trickle out between his fingers, recalling afresh his thoughts as he signed the contract with Abbérron: "*I've stretched out my hand and will not pull it back, or let Lenyé and Kyros hinder my plans. I need a greater power than armies of the Waking World. I must have absolute power: the power of the Lord Abbérr…*".

He knew that he would triumph, for then he couldn't fully say that awe-inspiring name; but now Abbérron had taken root within him. He was Abbérron, and no one could resist him.

Morthrir stood up and flung the rest of the sand away. He needed more power now, not when Rafé returned from his trip.

'My Lord, Abbérron,' his cry echoed off the cliffs at the head of Lake Sanchéso. 'If I am denied the Sword of Justice and the power of the Dé-monos, release to me something else to confound my enemies.'

'Faster, faster,' Lenyé glanced over her shoulder and shouted at the younger ones to keep up. 'We must get away while the moonlight holds.' She glared at Kyros as he drew alongside. 'We can't rely on this way of travelling. We'll have to stop and water the horses and eat and sleep. We only have my longbow and swords to fight them off. And Harbona's sword. Why didn't you bring some weapons? This is madness!'

Kyros rounded on her. 'Why are you so antagonistic? You chose to come with me rather than stay with our Uncle.'

'But only to despatch the Nastrim. Do not think I look any more favourably on you. You've changed, Kyros. You're not the man I knew and loved. How can you be a King if you refuse to take up arms? And I'm scared of this power from the True King that you carry. I'm not sure now that I made the right choice.'

Kyros was silent, inwardly grieving, as his eyes took in the moonlight glimmering on Lake Sanchéso to their left as it rushed towards them before they hurtled into the darkness of the forest, their horses avoiding the trees. Then the company halted and they dismounted and hugged each other in sheer joy at being free of their Uncle. They removed the saddles and bits, tethered the horses for the remainder of the night and found places to sleep around their special beech tree at the Pool of Alesco.

Kyros watched in surprise as the four animals gathered round Lenyé and heard the sharpness in her voice: 'I don't even want to talk about it!' He couldn't hear their replies, but she cut them dead and deliberately broke away from the little group.

He followed her with his eyes as she remained aloof; refusing to rejoice with the rest of them, seemingly distant and on edge as though she wanted to re-saddle the horses and continue riding.

'Those warriors might catch us off-guard if we're not careful,' she shouted over her shoulder as she stormed off to the edge of the pool and sat on a rock. 'What will you do about escaping then, Kyros. We're not that far ahead of them!'

As the rest of them moved about the campsite preparing for sleep, Kyros sensed the awkwardness between himself and Lenyé. It was more than the lack of weapons and the uncertainty of their escape. He sighed. How could he bring about a full reconciliation between them? He'd rescued her, and brought her to a place of safety beyond the reach of their Uncle. But he couldn't force her to return to him in her heart. He checked the horses and fondled their muzzles, making sure their pickets wouldn't pull free. 'Oh, My King,' he whispered to himself in the darkness. 'What must I do to win her again?'

Chapter Ninety Six

Lenyé couldn't sleep. They had covered each other with dry leaves to keep warm in the night. She helped the others, but was the last to lie down, and only partially covered herself, refusing offers of help from the lioness and the she-bear.

As she stirred, the sparse leaves rustled and fell away. She raised her head to see if she'd disturbed any of the others, but no one moved, not even the four animal-friends. Lenyé stood up, buckled both swords across her back, left her longbow and quiver where she had lain, and stole away from the camp.

She shouldn't have treated her friends like that. They had followed her to Terrazarema, and waited for an opportunity to free her, but she'd resisted. Then that outburst when everyone else was rejoicing at being free and Mamma Uza-Mâté asked her about her feelings for Kyros. And that expression in Ariella's eyes at her response. It was almost as if she'd run her Sword through the lioness' heart. She didn't deserve such faithful companions. For their sakes alone she had to sort herself out.

Despite releasing the Nastrim, she wasn't sure if she'd done the right thing: leaving Morthrir for Kyros. Morthrir rescued her from Vashtani immediately after her silent cry for help. And he'd looked the part: riding up on his horse and commanding Vashtani. He seemed to have limitless power at his disposal. Kyros appeared as a wandering vagabond, with no weapons and talking to the people about the True King and healing in his name. It was a different kind of power. She felt it especially when they were in the private dining room. But it wasn't the sort of power a King needed for ruling.

Kyros' reluctance to bear any weapons nearly cost him his life. If she hadn't doubled back, he would be dead. And it was her Sword that destroyed those attacking Nastrim. Kyros just sat on his horse and watched. When they faced Morthrir, he unleashed his warriors against them. You must have military power to be a King and hold onto your throne. Kyros could never make a King. At least Morthrir chased after her: that proved he loved her. But did she love him? And there was an invisible barrier between herself and Kyros. How was she to decide between the two of them? Something wasn't right. With her head she still said "Yes" to Morthrir, but her heart said…

Suddenly she recalled Yanantha's words again from before she found the Sword: Kyros had returned *"much changed"*, *"in a way unlooked for"*, and his *"destiny"* was still unclear. But she was struggling with more than her feelings or expectations for Kyros. It was something far deeper she needed to resolve for herself.

She wandered away to the head of the pool where the little spring bubbled out of a crack in the rock and ran down a short gully before pouring into the pool itself. She knelt down, cupped her hands at the source of the spring and drank appreciatively. It was always such a delicious shock: ice cold water, and yet so fresh and vibrant. You couldn't drink too much in one go.

Lenyé stood up and walked further round the edge of the pool, heading for the break in the rock where the water overflowed. Here it cascaded away into the lower levels of the forest in a series of falls and rapids festooned with rocks and boulders that had been dislodged by the force of the water.

She loved this place where the water flowed down into secret rocky grottos; over arched by great ferns that danced and shimmered with droplets of water in the day time, but now looked like huge grey hands waving in the dimness of night. The stream had a never-ending voice, sometimes quiet as the small volume of water tinkled its way artfully around boulders and into pools before moving on; or, when the heavy rains over-filled the pool above, it came gushing down in vast cataracts that made your ears deaf to all other sounds. Now its voice was muted as if it wanted her to drink in its unwavering song.

Then she heard a voice calling her name: 'Lenyé'. She whipped round, startled, to check if anyone at the camp had missed her, but she could vaguely make out the heaps of dead leaves: no one had moved.

There it was again: 'Lenyé'. She didn't recognise the voice; but didn't feel any fear either: it wasn't that sort of voice.

When she heard her name for the third time, she whispered in response, 'Who are you?'

'I know your lying down and your rising up.'

Lenyé glanced at the branches overhead as they moved in the slight breeze, and then back to the ferns. Surely her mind was playing tricks with her. It was only the wind.

'I understand your thoughts from afar and am acquainted with all your ways.'

'I beg your pardon?' She couldn't help herself. Wind didn't sound so clear and distinct. Maybe it was only the water after all.

'There's not a word on your tongue I do not know.'

Lenyé clapped a hand over her mouth.

'Do not fear. For I have known you before you were born and my thoughts are always with you.'

'How…?'

'I have called you by name and appointed you for great deeds.'

'But I…'

'Why is it, then, that when you stretch forth your hand, your heart holds back?'

'I don't understand.'

'Come to me and find rest, for you have laboured long in your own strength and according to your own wisdom.'

Lenyé saw a soft light through the ferns below her, throwing their feathered fingers into stark silhouette. Without thinking she stumbled down into the rocky grotto, thrusting the ferns aside, stooping low, even squatting so the handles of her swords wouldn't snag in the fronds and over-hanging branches, her boots slipping now and then on the wet boulders. As she climbed further down, the light whitened and intensified till she had to shield her eyes with her hand. But still she scrambled down the rocks; she had to: she was being drawn to the light whether she wanted to or not.

She pushed through the last of the ferns and gasped. The light was so intense she had no option but to bow down to shield her eyes from the brilliance, one knee on a rocky outcrop, the other slithering into a pool till the water was over the top of her boot and ice-cold against the exposed skin of her thigh. But she hardly noticed, for the voice was filling her mind again.

'Well met, Lenyé. You have come in response to my call.'

She felt a hand grip her own, and a wave of peace washed through her. The hand began to lift hers, and she raised her head. Either the light was less intense now, or her eyes were more accustomed to it, for she could discern the face of a man: the most beautiful man she had ever seen. He was smiling at her: a smile that went right through her and drew out everything she had ever said or thought or done; sifting through her whole life as though he had been with her, holding her hand all the time.

'It is enough that only one knee entered the water, for it is too cold for you to be plunged in. Therefore let my love cleanse you from all the taint and confusion and weariness of your journey.'

Suddenly she was weeping over her obstinacy in using the Nastrim army, and her stupidity at letting her Uncle lock away her Sword and nearly losing it to Vashtani. As her anguish died down, she felt a thrill rush through her as if all the things in her life that he examined had been plunged into the stream below and brought out again like wet and glistening stones. She felt clean and whole and new, and could look at him without fear.

There was his wonderful smile that would stay with her for ever, and always make her come back to him for more: the man was pleased with her. Lenyé sighed in delight. Before she could even ask about the man's identity, the answer arose in her heart: '*I am the True King.*' All the antagonism she felt at Kyros following the True King's ways and refusing to bear arms melted away.

'Why do you think I sent you to recover the Blade of Zerigor?'

Lenyé started in surprise, 'I thought Yanantha sent me.'

'Yanantha is very wise, but she does not know everything.'

'She said, "*If you are truly the one, then once you find the Blade, it is down to you and you alone to use it for its rightful purpose*".'

'That is correct. You are the one.'

'But I don't know how to use it.'

'You are already learning; for have you not despatched the Nastrim to their Place of Rest?'

'Yes. I decided to obey Kyros' warning for the new keeper.'

'You did well, for he was only passing on my command.'

'Please will you tell me how to use the Sword from now on?'

'I will be with you, to guide you, but cannot force you. Your relationship with Kyros and the secret of your heart's affection and the struggle you are going through can only be resolved when you decide what to do with the Sword. Your choice will determine who else can draw it and affect the destiny not only of the Waking World, but all the other Realms you do not yet see.'

Lenyé reached up to her shoulder with her left hand and drew the Blade of Zerigor. It slipped from its scabbard so easily, and felt even lighter than usual. Still kneeling, she held the blade horizontal in front of her but it felt awkward, so she lifted her other hand to stop the tip from wobbling, and presented it to the True King, bowing her head. 'I surrender it to you.'

He smiled, 'I gave it to Zerigor and his heirs. You take it.'

Then he was gone and she was left alone, kneeling on a rock, with only the drawn Sword of Justice in her hands to confirm what had transpired.

Chapter Ninety Seven

Rafé finished packing his saddle bags, slung them over his shoulder and walked briskly down towards the stables. He was travelling light with two horses, one to ride and one to lead, and then swap over when the first tired. He anticipated a quick journey to and from Mount Nastâri.

He was still intrigued by Vashtani's words about "*a light that we dared not approach*". But the Nastrim had lived in that mountain for centuries and hadn't been affected by it. Possibly they had discovered it and used it themselves. So why was Vashtani so scared by it?

The globe in the vision was definitely linked to Lenyé's Sword; and in a flash of inspiration he knew that the sword on the globe was a replica of the Sword of Justice. No wonder he felt the connection so strongly in the Armoury before Lenyé surprised him. And possibly that was why Vashtani feared it so much.

So why was the vision given to him by the cobra?

If he ever did find this globe, and Lenyé really had escaped from Morthrir with the Sword, then the globe was likely to be of more value to Lenyé, than Morthrir. After his last conversation with the Princess, he wasn't at all sure how he was going to present it to her. But it might improve his standing in her eyes.

Chapter Ninety Eight

'Kyros,' the dead leaves rustled as Lenyé brushed them off him. 'Wake up,' she whispered and shook him by the shoulder.

'What is it?' he grabbed her by the wrist.

'Shh. Don't disturb the others. We need to talk.'

'Can't it wait till morning?'

'It is morning. Come on. The dawn's just breaking.'

She led him by the hand and they crept away from the camp, skirted the special beech tree and walked away into the forest.

Kyros frowned, 'Where are we going on? The last time we were at the Pool of Alesco, we argued and broke apart.'

'I know. We need to be out of earshot of the others. You were right, and I was wrong. I've seen the True King.'

'Are you sure? What happened?'

'Everything I trusted in had to be stripped away: the loss of the Nastrim army and the hope of rescuing Beth was utterly devastating. But they had to go. And I foolishly surrendered to my enemy the very weapon entrusted to me. Yanantha's words over me were: *"not by might or human strength shall the final victory be won"*. Now I know the True King's strength and I am so grateful to him for delivering me and restoring the Sword of Justice into my hands. But I can no longer claim it as my own.'

'Why not?'

'It was originally presented to Zerigor by the True King.'

'But it was taken from him because he didn't use it properly.'

'I know. Hoffengrégor decreed no man could draw it again, so a woman had to recover it. But this Sword is too great for me to use. Therefore I'm returning it to Zerigor's heir. You must have it.' She unbuckled the Sword, knelt in front of Kyros and presented it to him. 'Receive what is yours by right.'

'As a man, how can I draw it against Hoffengrégor's words?'

'Because I trust the True King to answer my request.'

'Then I receive it with a grateful heart, for you did this willing.' As he took the Sword, he held her hand and raised her to her feet, gesturing to her left shoulder. 'And the other sword?'

'That's a copy to deceive others. Acwellan would always switch the swords around so none of the Nastrim ever knew which one he would use for execution.'

'But he must have had some means of telling them apart.'

'There was a nick on the hilt guard of this sword which he could feel with his thumb. I had it filled in and smoothed over which completely fooled him when I faced him again in battle.'

'So how do I know you have given me the right blade?'

'I can tell them apart by weight alone. Clearly he couldn't. Neither could Uncle Morthrir.'

'I see. So I am always going to be dependent on you to tell me which sword is which?' Kyros held the scabbard in his left hand and pulled on the handle of the Sword. It slid out easily.

Lenyé gasped. 'So you can draw it as well. The True King has overruled Hoffengrégor's words according to my request!'

Kyros swung it to and fro listening intently to the sound as it sliced through the air. 'It's beautifully balanced.' He dropped the scabbard and held out his left hand. 'Pass me the other blade.'

Lenyé drew it and handed it over.

Kyros took it and repeated the movements. 'Same point of balance.' He looked her in the eyes, 'But the first Sword is much lighter. So it must be the Sword of Justice.'

'Then I'm not the only one to know the difference by weight!'

'It would appear so,' Kyros chuckled.

'But just the two of us,' Lenyé smiled at him. 'That's what I asked for.'

'You say this Sword is too great for you to wield. But it is also too great for me. Let us maintain Acwellan's deception and alternate the swords between us, for there was some wisdom in what he did. As a woman, are you not also Zerigor's heir?'

'You mean,' she faltered.

'...both of us.' Kyros thrust the sword tips into the ground, turned and held out his arms to Lenyé.

'Oh, Kyros,' she sobbed and flung herself at him. 'I'm so sorry for the things I said, and the thoughts I had about you since. Especially that time when we were reconciled in the past. It wasn't true at all, what I said. You did change. So much. And now I've gone and spoiled it all. Please will you forgive me?'

'Most willing. For you have pulled a deadly arrow from my heart. And I must ask the same, for I turned away from you in anger. Will you forgive me as well?'

'Of course,' Lenyé stepped back and smiled at him. 'I had a living dream flash before my eyes and saw you as I was fighting the Nastrim,' she hesitated. 'I thought I stood alone, but you were there with me and I saw a great light coming from you and surrounding me, and a Greater Sword around my Sword. Now my eyes are opened and I see that we really are one.'

Kyros held her close and felt her melting into him as her arms entwined about his neck in return and her tears were hot on his skin. He moved his head back slightly, his eyes locked on hers: and the look of love that flowed from her took his breath away.

'Oh, Kyros,' her voice was husky with emotion. 'The True King said to me, *"Your relationship with Kyros and the secret of your heart's affection and the struggle you are going through can only be resolved when you decide what to do with the Sword"*. I have chosen and bestowed the Sword, and you have confirmed that choice. Now the struggle is over. You are the one I love and always will.'

Kyros nodded in understanding. 'The True King commanded me to return to my first love, for I too have gone away from you in my heart and desired another.' Then he clasped her to him and whispered in her ear, 'Let us re-confirm our words to each other on the Dangst Rock. For you and I are pledged to each other and will become one in marriage.'

She didn't say anything at first, but he felt her nod her head as she stood muffled in his arms. Then she blurted out between her sobs, 'Oh, Kyros. I strayed so far from you and thought I'd never hear you say that to me again. Of course I will.'

They held each other a while longer, till the tears were spent.

Kyros whispered, 'Let us now take these swords together and learn how to use the Sword of Justice to good effect.'

Lenyé let go of Kyros, took a pace towards the swords, and pulled them out of the ground. She turned to him, 'Which sword will you bear? You chose.'

'No. Not yet. For the Sword of Justice, in your hands, is a powerful weapon. Bear them a little longer on behalf of us both? For you will have need of them.'

'But what about you?'

'I am destined to walk armoured only with the power contained in the name of the True King.'

Lenyé paused, recalling Yanantha's words about Kyros: *"If he does return, he will be much changed"*. There was such an inner joy and peace about him from his confidence in the True King. Rather than despising his unwillingness to bear arms as a sign of weakness, as she had done before, she loved him all the more for it, because now she understood and had entered in for herself.

Then words began forming in her mind for Kyros from the True King. But as soon as the words began, they petered out and left her grasping for the remainder. Then she heard the voice from her encounter, and sensed that precious smile. *"Go ahead. Speak. And the words will come to you"*. She opened her mouth, obedient to the voice despite her confusion, and spoke directly to Kyros. 'A day will come, My Lord...' she hesitated wondering what else to say. Suddenly words came tumbling out of her mouth as though another was speaking through her, even though she remained in full control of her faculties, '…when you will ride forth with the Sword of Justice at your side and the very words of your mouth will be like a sharp, two-edged Sword. None shall withstand you and all the enemies of the True king will be brought low and vanquished before you!'

Kyros stared at Lenyé in astonishment, for no one else had ever spoken to him before with such authority and he received her words into his heart as though they were a fire, burning into his bones. 'And you, My Lady,' he eventually managed to respond, 'will be drawn to my side that we may walk together and our union will unlock the Restoration, and our wedding feast shall be a time of reconciliation for the Ancient Peoples.'

Lenyé smiled at him. 'Our marriage will be not only for us, but as a sign of hope to all who come after us. One thing I will say to you from my encounter with the True King. When he issues a command, it is not possible to move on in his purposes until those who follow him have completed it.'

'I don't understand.'

'His command to Zerigor was to rid the Waking World of the Nastrim. That has remained unfulfilled for a thousand years. My regret is that I delayed and did not complete the task sooner.'

'So you're saying, "*Now is the time for the next stage in the completion of the True King's purposes*"?'

'Exactly.'

He held out his left hand to her. 'Now that you have surrendered to the True King, we need to say this in unity.'

Lenyé took his hand and stood next to him as they faced East.

Kyros raised his right hand and spoke while Lenyé repeated each line after him, 'In the name of Luchianó-bé, Lord of Light, let the Waking World be cleansed of the curse originally brought by the Dé-monos and left to pollute the Waking World by the presence of the Nastrim. Let the Hidden Power of Abbérron be broken and the Dé-monos finally driven from the Waking World. And let the reign of the True King be released amongst us.'

Chapter Ninety Nine

The following day Quinn felt much stronger: the walk in the woods for mushrooms the previous afternoon helped him get over his giddiness. He and Beth sat at the table and filled Ishi-mi-réjá in on the events since that night on the mountain.

Ishi-mi-réjá shrugged her shoulders. 'It wasn't me who took you to that shepherd's cot. Whoever it was saved you from being linked to that point of resistance by your Uncle.'

'It must have been Rafé, then,' Quinn glanced at Beth. 'There was only one horse left, so he must have taken the other. Why didn't he mention it to me?'

'Never mind that now,' Ishi-mi-réjá continued. 'We have to stop your Uncle.'

'But Lenyé can do that.' Briefly Beth talked about her sister's great army and their own attempt to get into the castle. 'We must free our parents from the Royal Hunting Lodge at Fantrios.'

The old woman frowned. 'I need to decide how best to help you before trekking all the way up there.'

'But what about you?' Quinn shuddered. 'What was that awful pit I dragged you out of?'

Ishi-mi-réjá closed her eyes, a look of horror etched on her face. 'I encountered a greater power on Mount Malkamet than I've ever know before. And it was totally evil. There were four men, called the Summoners, surrounding the altar your Uncle lay on. They are the prime movers in everything to do with your Uncle. They seized me and cast me down to the pit, leading to the Realm of Consumption.'

'Is that where the heat and flames and stench came from?'

'That's right. And those bulls and dogs were trying to destroy me. But I was able to see into the minds of the Summoners and read their collective memory concerning your Uncle, some years ago. I cannot tell you now. If you were caught and they found out you knew what I have seen, you would be killed instantly.'

'And your stone?' Quinn pressed her for an answer.

'That's not the first time the stone has been damaged. Twice the spines were broken off, and once it was split in two; yet it has always recovered to its rightful state. But it hasn't disintegrated before. And I have never been so close to death. It felt like many days I laboured with those creatures goring me with their horns and tearing me with their teeth, scarcely able to breathe it was so hot: like being inside a furnace. Then a greater power broke something over me and I began to rise up in the pit away from the heat, and I saw your hand reaching down to me. It was the innocence of you two children that overcame the evil, enabling the dust of *ishi-mi-réjá* to gather together and reconstitute the stone to its proper shape and so draw me out of their grasp.'

'What about uncovering the secret behind Uncle Morthrir's rise to power you told us about,' Beth cut in. 'Is that what we did on the mountain?'

'No,' Ishi-mi-réjá chuckled. 'Too many people were present or knew about it for that to be a secret. You still have a vital part to play,' she glanced from Beth to Quinn and back again. 'Both of you. I know a lot more about that secret now. But before you try again, there's something else you need to do first.'

The old woman asked Quinn to take the saddle and the rest of their belongings outside and wait while she changed her clothes.

Quinn walked round to the back of the cottage, down past the well to where the horse was tethered, and saddled up, swapping the halter for the reins. He secured the saddle bags in place, and walked the horse back up towards the cottage.

He watched as Ishi-mi-réjá darted out of the back door, opened the door in a small lean-to shed against the wall and selected two odd-looking tools, with a long tapering spade-blade at one end, and a cross-piece for the grip at the top of the handle.

She held them aloft and grinned at him, 'One each for both of you.' Then she raced back inside the cottage and he heard the two of them banging about, pulling windows closed and securing the back door before emerging at the front.

Quinn led the horse down the path and Ishi-mi-réjá waited as Beth mounted and sat in the saddle. Quinn swung himself up onto the horse's back behind her. He felt the easy walk of the horse as they followed Ishi-mi-réjá onto a track running nearly due South through the woods.

They hadn't gone far when Quinn leaned forwards, 'If I'm not mistaken,' he murmured in Beth's ear. 'The road must be a little way off to our right. If we carry on as we are, we're going to end up at Druis-cyf-rin.'

'The Great Oak Tree,' Beth whipped round in alarm to study Quinn's face. 'I don't want to go there again.' She turned round to face forwards. 'Ishi-mi-réjá. Where are we heading?'

But the old woman didn't answer.

'If this is going to affect Beth badly, like last time,' Quinn called over Beth's shoulder as his cousin reined in the horse to a halt. 'I don't think we should go any further.'

The old woman turned and looked at them. 'We will only approach the Great Oak Tree in broad daylight. And you didn't have me with you before.'

'But why are we going there?' Quinn persisted. 'Fantrios is in the other direction.'

'We can attend to your parents later,' the old woman smiled. 'There's something you need to find first, that no Krêonor has seen for a thousand years. Something that will finally replace your Uncle's authority in the Waking World.'

Chapter One Hundred

Lenyé strapped both swords across her back, and then whipped round at a sound from behind. 'Ariella, Mamma Uza-Mâté, Chua...,' she broke off. 'All of you. What are you doing here?'

'Forgive us, Lenyé, if we overheard words between you and Kyros,' Ariella's growl was so low, Lenyé had to strain to catch the lioness' words. 'But we couldn't help following when we heard you waking Kyros.'

'I should be the one asking you to forgive me,' Lenyé went down on her knees and held out her arms to the lioness.

Ariella was on her, bowling her over. Mamma Uza-Mâté waded in, hauled her to her feet and hugged her. Chuah-te-mok bobbed his head and Ra-Na-Jiri raised himself up, playfully flaring his hood. Lenyé lifted her arms and they all fell silent. 'I don't deserve such good friends. Thank you for sticking by me, even when I treated you so badly.'

'Never mind that,' Mamma Uza-Mâté burst out. 'We're so delighted for you both.' There was an awkward silence as the animals glanced at each other. Then Mamma Uza-Mâté turned to Ariella and apologised for her behaviour. Chuah-te-mok joined in apologising for being aloof, and they all apologised to the cobra for their attitude towards him.

Suddenly Lenyé looked up in alarm and reached out to grasp Kyros. 'Who's that?' she pointed through the trees.

Kyros felt the tremor in Lenyé's hand as she gripped his arm. 'And I've come without my longbow. How stupid of me!'

Kyros followed her pointing finger. 'Judging by the light that comes from him, I think we have nothing to fear.'

As the figure emerged from the trees, Kyros recognised him immediately. 'Hoffengrégor!' He darted forwards to embrace his friend; then turned to present Lenyé.

'How my heart is gladdened,' Hoffengrégor smiled at them both, 'for now I know the Restoration is soon to be fulfilled. But, My Lady,' he glanced at Lenyé. 'Something troubles your heart.'

'I didn't believe Kyros when he said he'd met you,' Lenyé hesitated. 'We've cleared the air between us, but I still wasn't sure about some of the things he said till I met the True King.'

Hoffengrégor smiled, 'You and Kyros have come through tough trials, yet remain faithful to each other. You asked the True King to overrule my words so that Kyros could draw the Sword of Justice, and you spoke powerful words for each other. Hold out your hands and I will endorse those words over you.'

The old Prophet placed his hand over Kyros' with Lenyé's underneath. 'In the name of the True King, I confirm two things: firstly, the reversing of all words spoken against you; and secondly, allowing you both to wield the Sword of Justice. I also release the words you have spoken over each other. May the gift of prophecy grow in you to discern the True King's heart and speak his words of release and guiding and power over others.'

He removed his hand and pulled theirs apart. 'In union and as individuals, may you be strengthened and blessed.'

'Thank you,' Kyros bowed his head to the old Prophet and then embraced Lenyé.

Hoffengrégor turned to Ariella and the others, 'My friends. Because you have served Lenyé and Kyros well and have resolved your differences, you will be amongst those who take the good news of peace to every creature in the Waking World.'

Mamma Uza-Mâté threw back her head and laughed in delight. 'Now I know the Restoration has begun, *"when all creatures are friends again, and we live in perfect harmony with the whole of mankind"*.' They all joined in laughing with her.

Then Lenyé gripped Kyros' hand. 'One thing I don't understand. Will you always be able to heal people?'

'I don't know. It brought hope to many and focused their attention on the True King for a season. But those healings have little value unless the people enter into a vital relationship with the True King for themselves, like you have done. For he calls each one of us by name, but the choice to respond is theirs alone.'

Lenyé was silent, pondering his words in her heart, but was startled by Hoffengrégor.

'This scroll is for you, Lenyé, for you were always eager to find records of the Ancient Wisdom. I saw this vision in the Waking World but could only record it after I descended to the Realm of Travail. It remained hidden in my dwelling so I was unable to give it to Kyros when I first met him. I consider you are now worthy to break the seals and read its contents.'

Lenyé was so overcome; yet raised her head to ask a question. 'Why did all this distress happen between Kyros and myself?'

Hoffengrégor was suddenly serious, 'It was important for you, Lenyé, to lose everything in this world that you relied on, so that you could learn to fully trust in the strength of the True King. For he tests those he loves to prove what is really in their hearts. You both had to come before the True King in order to break the power of your Uncle's words over you.' He turned to Kyros. 'Your fifth and sixth tests are now completed.'

'Thank you, my friend,' Kyros smiled at the old Prophet. 'But how did you get here? Is the Spiral still open for anyone to come and go as they please?'

'No. You spoke words of power from the Dangst Rock. Do not be surprised when they are fulfilled; for the point of entry to the Spiral in the Realm of Travail has been re-sealed and the Guardians of the Spiral restored. I have been sent to you by the True King to open the way before you.'

'Back to the Realm of Travail?' Kyros sounded puzzled.

'No. To help you fulfil your heart's desire.'

'I don't understand.'

'Did you not tell me of your dream to find the Krêon of Tulá-kâhju?'

'The Crown of Life?' Lenyé glared at Kyros, 'You never told me you'd brought that up again.'

'I haven't talked about everything I did in the Realm of Travail.' He glanced at Hoffengrégor. 'What about my dream?'

'As Zerigor lay dying, he confided in me. The night before the people were forced to flee from the inundation on their island, he had a premonition of disaster. So he hid the Crown of Life in a strong-room at the top of the Royal Ziggurat, the great building that reached to the skies and reminded them of the True King's presence high above.'

'How does that affect my dream?'

'The Ziggurat was built to withstand any heavy flooding from the sea.'

'Then the Crown wasn't swept away by the inundation?'

'No. And he also told me he placed a certain key in a sealed urn next to the Crown.'

'Key,' Lenyé stared at Hoffengrégor. 'What key?'

'To unlock the cylinder containing the scroll I gave Kyros.'

'Another scroll?' Lenyé frowned. 'Kyros, you never told me.'

'Why is that significant?' Kyros ignored the interruption.

'Zerigor gave me the empty cylinder to secure my writings. Once closed, only that key will open it. He said the Ziggurat was designed to be accessed from the top; so if the island was ever overwhelmed by the sea, it would still be possible to re-enter their ancient stronghold.'

'Why are you saying all this?' Kyros persisted.

'Because now is the time for both of you to seek the sunken island and recover those two items: the Crown for Kyros to release his Kingship and the key for Lenyé to unlock the knowledge you will need to overcome your enemies. Kyros, this is your seventh and final test and it will usher in the Restoration.'

END

OF

BOOK II

IN

THE RESTORATION

OF

THE CROWN OF LIFE

A COLLECTION OF WRITINGS

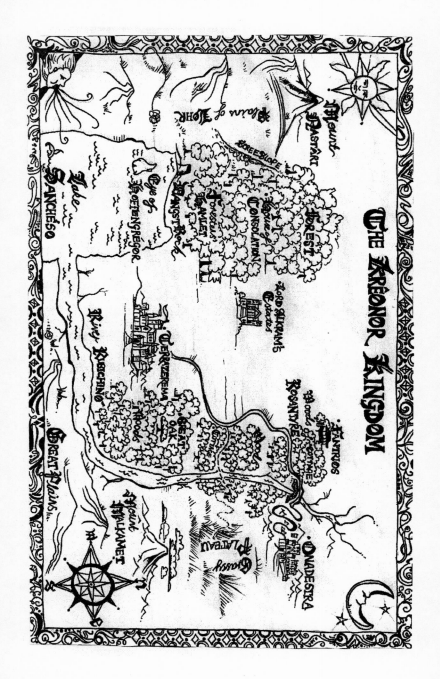

THE HEXACLE OF MORTHRIR

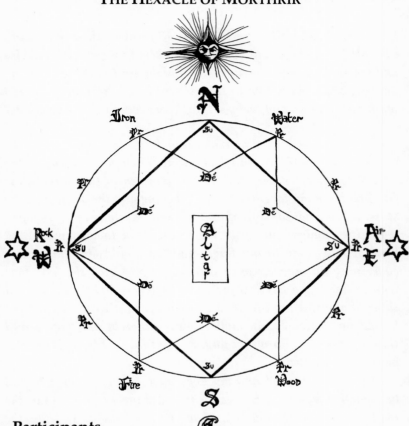

Participants
Pr = Priest (10)
Su = Summoner (4)
Dé = Dé-monos Leader (6)

Location
N = North = Allies
E = East = Power
S = South = Alliances
W = West = Enemies

Elements
Air = Life
Fire = Consumes
Iron = Cuts
Water = Floats
Wood = Decays
Rock = Erodes

THE COMINGS (FIRST PART KEPT AT YANANTHA'S HOUSE)

I, Hoffengrégor, called by the True King himself, who is Lord over all the Realms, and appointed by him to receive the Peoples and instruct them in the way they should go; to all the sons and daughters who ever live to hear the voice of the True King and walk in his ways; do hereby set forth an account of the Comings.

For I observed all that was around me: the grandeur of the mountains and the crashing of the waves upon the shore, the beauty of the trees and flowers, the warmth of the sun and the soft breeze on my face, the chill of evening and the wonder of the stars, the companionship of animals and the song of birds. For I was given understanding of their voice and they of mine, and birds would come to my finger and we would sing harmonies concerning the marvels of the Waking World. And the food that was to hand and easy to pick and tasted so delicious, and all things bountiful for life. And I delighted in all that I saw and beheld and entered into understanding thereof and I perceived that wisdom was born that day. But one thing it lacked for utter perfection: the Peoples.

And then I looked and my eyes were lifted up and I beheld beyond the Westering waves an island more fair even than the land in which I walked. And in its midst I saw the Bara-mâla-ké, the blessèd Peoples, dwelling in perfect harmony. Then I perceived Zerigor, wearing the Krêon of Tulá-kâhju, the Crown of Life, that blazed around his head, and all the Peoples radiated light from their heads, like a circlet of fire around their brow when seen from one angle, or a flat disc of light above their heads from another: and I saw from afar the Perfection of the Peoples. For the island had no need of light by night, or even on a dull day, for the Light of Life shone about them. And I thought, surely when they have multiplied and filled their island, some brave seafarers would seek other places to live and raise their

i

offspring and so venture to my shore that I might welcome them in the name of the True King, for it was not permitted that I should take the wings of the seas and go to them.

But alas, as I looked and beheld I observed over a period of some time that the light about their heads flickered and went out, one by one, and the blaze from the Krêon of Tulá-kâhju was diminished and there arose a terrible conflict between the Peoples. As I cried out to the True King for understanding it was revealed to me that the Tsé-shâmé had sought after a secret knowledge to give them power to overcome Zerigor and place their own ruler in his stead. Many were cast down and breathed no more. And there was a dividing between those who remained in the Waking World and those who perished and went down to the Sleeping World, and I perceived that the span of life for those left in the Waking World was reduced to no more than one hundred and twenty years before they, too, went down to the Realm of the Departed. And it grieved my heart that this should be, and I sought in my reason what manner of Peoples are these who paid such a terrible price for not persevering in seeking to live together in harmony and resolving their differences without recourse to bloodshed. And I knew not.

So I walked some time, bowed in grief. For surely these Peoples tarried overlong in their blessèd isle and failed to go forth and make landfall with the rest of the Waking World, and so at an early stage may have come under the wisdom and teaching of the True King, and thereby preclude this disaster. It is one thing to encounter the True King for a brief moment as they did on their island; it is quite another to embrace his teachings and sustain the reality of that encounter over an entire lifetime. For I perceived that these Peoples had given heed to the Voices that whisper in all men's hearts and breed thoughts of dissatisfaction and overlay the foundations of a harmonious disposition with the desire to put down others and be first in all things. And so, as I mused, it seemed clear to me that by provision of the True King himself, the seeds already sown in their hearts were come to fruition and we might behold what manner of Peoples these are: whether they regard each other more highly than themselves and treat each other as they would have others treat them and so fulfil the earnest desire of the True King, or become selfish in their ways and want the best for themselves to the exclusion of others. For which is more precious in the eyes of the True King: another person in all their beauty or the accumulation of wealth at the expense of others. And so their deepest intent was no longer hidden and the taint of the Voices they harkened to was finally exposed.

So I considered how best to greet such Peoples should they venture to my shore. For it appeared to me, even from such a distance, according to the eyes of discernment given to me by the True King, that they had descended into the arrogance of ruling without mercy, the idleness of wanting without working and the resentment of serving without appropriate reward. And it seemed a great folly to me that these Peoples could not excel in their separate giftings for the common good. But no counsel arose in my heart to instruct me, and I deemed that matter to be beyond the extent of my wit.

Who, then, would arise to heal the rift that came about in the Beginning?

Then I looked and beheld, and lo a mighty ring of waves surrounded the island and rushed inwards and crashed upon its shores in a vast inundation that carried away all things and hid the island in a great mist. And out of the deluge came fleeing, boats and crafts of all kinds and people clinging to whatever floated, and they were borne upon a great wave that swept them to my hither shore. So I hastened to come down to them and make what provision of food and clean water to drink and shelter that I could contrive, for they were exhausted; and I thought surely they will put away all animosity from amongst themselves and fall in with a considered plan to fortify their spirits and rebuild some semblance of a settlement for themselves where they could gather sufficient food for many hungry mouths and so prosper together in spirit and in health.

For out of the flood came three Peoples: firstly, the Krêonor, tall and long-limbed and pale to golden skinned, with striking features and brightness of eye, and hair ranging in colour from fair to dark; secondly, the Tsé-shâmé, who were shorter and broader and of a swarthy countenance and darkness of eye and hair, except for some dark-haired Krêonor who stayed close by them and refused to look me in the eye and seemed at variance with their own brethren; and thirdly, the Harmoth, of much darker skin than the others and a blackness of hair and a stature in height and girth somewhat between the other two.

The Krêonor accepted my help and counsel gratefully; but the Tsé-shâmé refused, saying they would never serve another again, and took themselves off in their war boats some way down the coast and were lost to sight; while the Harmoth, full of anger at the Krêonor for failing to protect them against the onslaught of the Shâmé army, spurned my aid and wandered away inland.

A cloud of anxiety covered my meditations for I had forebodings of evil yet to come. Through the vision and discernment given to me I was able to see from afar and discover the intent of the Tsé-shâmé, and it was after this fashion.

Four of the rebel Krêonor in particular had not been idle, but had delved deeper into the subtle arts of the Tsé-shâmé learned in Bara-mâla, fearing their brethren, who had remained faithful, would arm again and crush them completely. They were drawn to Mount Malkamet where they put their arts to the test, and invoked the supreme spirit of air, fire, rock and water. And so Abbérron appeared to them and they willingly bowed down before him and worshipped him to receive power to act against the faithful Krêonor and were rewarded with unending days.

Then Abbérron commanded them to speak with one voice and release the Breaking-in. As they did so a huge fissure burst open at the peak of the mountain and Dé-monos from another Realm poured through, taller than any man and radiating a bright light. The rebel Krêonor swore on oath before Abbérron to be allies with the Dé-monos through all subsequent generations; then set off to seek out the Tsé-shâmé to join in this alliance.

But the Dé-monos lifted up their eyes and beheld the Krêonor women from afar and saw that they were beautiful, and ran swiftly to the heart of the Krêonor encampment, broke through the defences and carried off many thousands of the fairest women and took them as wives. Their offspring were named the Nastrim, after one of the leading Dé-monos, and were as tall and quick and strong as their Fathers, as fair in form and feature as their mothers, and, once grown to full stature, formed a formidable army.

Meanwhile, the rebel Krêonor had gathered the Tsé-shâmé and spoken words of counsel in their ear concerning the Hidden Power of the Lord Abbérron and stirred up the Tsé-shâmé to join forces with the Nastrim.

But Zerigor, King of the faithful Krêonor, appealed to me for help and I cried out to the True King over all Realms, to aid them, reminding him of their calling and how he had set them apart by decree to rule in Bara-mâla. The True King came in the fire of the rising sun, with a numberless host of En-luchés, beings filled with the light of life, so dazzling were they to behold.

In his wrath the True King sliced off the peak of Mount Malkamet with his sword, crying out, 'Never again shall any creature enter the Waking World by this route!' He cast it far away where it lodged on the brink of the cliffs overshadowing the Plain of Sanchéso, and called it the Dangst Rock, or Place-of-Chaining. For there he commanded the spirit of air, fire, rock and water to appear and Abbérron came trembling before him. And he called for the Dé-monos and they cowered in his presence and the light they radiated when they first appeared vanished completely, and they were cloaked in darkness. The True King ordered his En-luchés to round them up and bind them to the Dangst Rock.

Then he pronounced his verdict upon them: Abbérron and the Dé-monos were forbidden to ever again re-appear in the Waking World. If, by any chance, they did, the final judgement would befall them. The True King's eyes flashed like fire and at the word of his command the ground shook once more, and Abbérron and the Dé-monos were blown back through the fissure in Mount Malkamet, and the jaws of the opening snapped to with a bang that reverberated around the mountain range and the entry point was sealed. All that was left was a great gash below the summit where the fissure had split the rock.

Then the True King himself knelt before Zerigor and presented the man with his sword. 'Guard it well, for this is the Sword of Justice. By it, you must rid the Waking World of the Nastrim. For their Fathers, the Dé-monos, brought with them a curse of evil, which even now pervades the very atmosphere of the Waking World and touches all things with its taint. Not till the Nastrim are fully purged from your world can this evil be lifted and joy and laughter and unity between all Peoples and creatures be restored.' With that, he and the En-luchés were caught up in the air and disappeared from sight.

Then I observed that even though I could still commune with all birds and creatures of the Waking World, the Krêonor, whom I had taught and bequeathed the gift of speaking and understanding the language of all creatures were now no longer able to converse with them any more. And even the creatures themselves were at variance with each other, and forsook the former cordiality that existed between them and enmity sprang up and set one species against another, some killing for food: and they remained slaves to a compulsion that rises up and takes over and drives them remorselessly, so that all creatures now live in fear for their lives.

This also occurred amongst the Krêonor themselves, who no longer gladly obeyed their King and gave him joy in his pronouncements, but wanted recompense and reward for all the things they formerly gave themselves to with gladness of heart and satisfaction in performing for the common good. And amongst the lush flora I found that no longer did the plants for food spring up wherever there was need, but rather their growth slowed and the trees took time to mature and other plants of baser nature and unyielding in fruit for food or crops to eat, sprang up and stifled the growth of the more desirable plants. And I deemed the Waking World was departing from its former glory into chaos.

Forthwith, I counselled the Krêonor to stand firm and arm themselves and go out and meet with the Nastrim in open battle and so purge the Waking World of this evil as the True King decreed. But even as they did so the Nastrim and their Tsé-shâmé allies came upon the Krêonor, routing them and chasing them through the Plains of Lohr. Only by the intervention of the Pilgrims who dwelt there were the Nastrim halted and the Krêonor were able to escape and regroup.

The Nastrim were so enraged that they butchered the Pilgrims while their rebel Krêonor and Tsé-shâmé allies looked on and applauded the deed. For the Pilgrims raised no weapons of defence, save that they trusted only in the name of the True King to preserve their lives beyond the grave.

Then the Nastrim and the rebel Krêonor marched through the night and came suddenly upon the faithful Krêonor at daybreak. Even though Zerigor resorted to using the Sword of Justice as a weapon of war, his last resistance was beaten down and it was snatched from his hand. Then I cast the Sceptre of Authority to the East and the golden Orb of Universal Rule to the North lest they also should fall into the hands of the Nastrim. As these emblems fell away, the ground quaked, and the Plain of Sanchéso began to fill with water and form a vast lake, broken only by a single mountain top that became a tiny island.

Even as I pen these last words, I, Hoffengrégor, command whomsoever shall open this remnant of parchment and read these words, to not only recover the Sword of Justice but also despatch the Nastrim from the Waking World, otherwise all is lost and the Krêonor will be no more.

LENYÉ'S SCROLL

Sung: *...not by the hand of any man*
shall the Ancient Blade be regained.
Not by might or human strength
shall the final victory be won...

Birds: *If for vision, be an eagle*
Soar beneath the heavens above
Looking down, discerning all things
Maid of honour, bring new life.

Chuah-te-mok: *If for ruling, be a lioness*
Bright the huntress, crowned in splendour
Let your courage match your virtue
With great strength now be endowed

Ariella: *If for waiting, be a she-bear*
Incubate from death to life
Guard your offspring, guard them fiercely
Use your power, rich in mercy

Mamma Uza-Mâté: *Beware the Executioner*
Sword of Justice is his prize
You must pierce his last defences
Seize the Sword as you arise

Ra-Na-Jiri: *Two Swords in splendid jewels bound*
Reflecting moonlight on their shimmering blades
The haft of one is secret marked
And only one of twain is sacred true

LIST OF CHARACTERS

Name	Description
Abbérron	The Hidden Power
Acwellan	The Nastrim Lord High Executioner
Alkram	Lenyé's Father
Ariella	The lioness who rescues Lenyé
Beth	Lenyé's younger sister
Chuah-te-mok	The eagle sent to Lenyé by Yanantha
Dareth	King of the Krêonor and Father of Kyros
Decatur	Self-appointed liberator of the Nastrim
Eawen	Chief Priest of the Hidden Power
Faria	Morthrir's wife
Festé	One of Lenyé's brothers
Harbona	A Captain in Morthrir's army
Hoffengrégor	The Ancient Prophet
Jumar-jé	Leader of the Summoners
Ishi-mi-réjá	Lady of miraculous powers
Kyros	A Prince of the Royal Krêonor Family
Lenyé	A Princess of the Royal Krêonor Family
Luchianó-bé	The True King
Mamma-Uza-Mâté	The She-bear who comforts Lenyé
Marie-anna	Ramâno's Mother
Morthrir	Uncle of Kyros and Lenyé
Nasima	One of Kyros' sisters
Nostrea	Apothecary
Ogandés	King of the Nastrim
Olathe	One of Kyros' sisters
Osâcah	Leader of the Sacred Pilgrims of Lohr
Quinn	Younger brother of Kyros
Rafé	Royal counsellor
Ramâno	Warrior boy
Ra-Na-Jiri	Cobra who comes to Lenyé's aid
Sorentina	Daughter of Zerigor

Name	Description
Stellatus	A Leader of the En-luchés
The Henosite	Spiritual designation of Eawen
True King	Lord over all Realms
Turvil	A captain in the Nastrim army
Vashtani	Dé-monos Leader and Acwellan's Father
Yanantha	Prophetess who sings over Lenyé
Youdlh	Commander of Morthrir's army
Wilf	One of Lenyé's brothers
Zerigor	First King of the Krêonor

PLACES

Bara-mâla	Island of the first civilisation
Dangst Rock	Place-of-Chaining
Druis-cyf-rin	The Great Oak Tree
Eye of Hoffengrégor	Islet on Lake Sanchéso
Lammista-ké	The River guarding the Realm of the Departed
Malkamet	Mountain used by Abbérron
Malvi-Quîdda	Fortress of the Dé-monos in the Realm of Travail
Nastâri	Mountain of the Nastrim
Onadestra	Morthrir's Castle & City
Rubichinó	River leading to Onadestra
Sanchéso	Lake, but formerly a Plain
Terrazarema	Capital of the Krêonor

THE THREE ANCIENT PEOPLES

Bara-mâla-ké Krêonor, Tsé-shâmé, and Harmoth	Collective name of the: